MW01167308

BOOTH

A NOVEL

JASON PELLEGRINI

BOOTH

This book is a work of fiction. Names, characters, places, and incidents are either products of the author's imagination or used fictitiously. Any references to historical events, real people, or real places are used fictitiously. Any resemblance to actual events, places, or persons, living or dead, is entirely coincidental.

First Edition November 2016
Printed in the United States of America.

Story by Jason Pellegrini
www.jasonpellegrinibooks.com

Edited by Jessica DeLuca

Cover Design by John Caruso
www.johncarusodesigns.com

Author Photograph by Erik H. Lee
EHLPhotography@me.com

ISBN-13: 978-1537480961
ISBN-10: 1537480960

To my grandfather, Patrick French, who passed away while this story was being written.

"Now he belongs to the ages…"
-Edwin Stanton

PART I

REFLECTION

April 26, 1995

The Last Hour Begins

One hour was all that remained in the life of Joseph William Bateman. Sixty short minutes—thirty-six hundred seconds—counting down until his heart beat no longer.

Joseph, age twenty-six, was scheduled to be executed at dawn by the state of Florida for murder in the first degree. Until then, he sat on his small bed, leaned against the wall of his cell, and ate jellybeans.

When asked what he wanted for his last meal, he could've chosen anything. There were plenty of dishes he would've loved to have had one last time. In the end, Joseph chose jellybeans.

"And don't be cheap about it," he told his corrections officer. "I want one of those big ass bags."

He hadn't had a single craving for jellybeans—or any sort of sweets, for that matter—in almost nineteen years. Not since his seventh birthday. On the eve of his execution, however, he had a sudden hankering for the explosion of

1

sugary goodness one experiences from crushing those tiny balls between their teeth.

He shoved his hand into the bag, which had lasted him the night, and was now three-quarters empty. He popped a jellybean into his mouth and ran his tongue against the candy's sugary coating. This was crucial, as he needed to detect which flavor he was about to bite down into. His taste buds picked up the faint hint of liquorish, and he immediately spat it out onto the floor. There, it joined the rest of the black jellybeans from the bag.

He had always hated the black ones. Liquorish was disgusting, and he wasn't about to let the vile taste of it ruin his last meal. Plus, he was leaving a fantastic little mess for the guards or custodial staff to clean up once he was no longer an occupant of the cell. The thought of someone cleaning up after him was pleasing. It was his last little way of sticking it to The Man. In the final minutes before death, every little victory counted.

He dove back into the party-sized bag. This time around, the end result was far more satisfying. Joseph bit down into the candy, and an explosion of orange flavoring erupted in his mouth.

Joey Beans, he thought as he chewed on and swallowed the artificially flavored delight.

It had been a long time since he had thought about that nickname. It was one his mother had given him when he was little.

Joey Beans.

He didn't actually remember getting the nickname. He was too young when his mother first gave it to him. When he was older, however, she told him stories about how he was an absolute nightmare to bring to the movies because he would fidget in his seat and talk nonstop while the film was playing. He was constantly getting on the nerves of his mother, not to mention everyone else in the theater. No matter what methods she tried, his mother could not get her son to just sit still and be quiet.

That was until she discovered his love for jellybeans.

All she had to do was put a bag in his hands, and Joseph would sit still, and remain silent until the end credits rolled. It wasn't long before Joseph earned his cute nickname.

Joey Beans.

Looking back on it now, as his life wound down to its abrupt yet well-deserved ending, it amazed Joseph how his mother was capable of finding a single happy memory in the entire mess that was her adult life. He had always wondered how she was able to endure all that she had. Even if it hadn't been for their children, most would reach an inevitable breaking point. Not his mother, though. She may have been bent, twisted, and mangled, but she never broke. It must have been those small moments she held onto that kept her sane and strong enough for as long as she needed.

Joseph hadn't inherited that trait. When he thought back on his life, all he could remember was the hatred and suffering that made him the man he was today.

As dawn approached, and he continued his quest to polish off the industrial sized bag, Joseph reflected on the night he'd just had. It had been his last night on Earth, and even though his options were limited, he had been determined to make it a good one. The end result was a feeling of accomplishment.

He had requested a priest. He wasn't a religious man, by any means, and had zero interest in the Lord's forgiveness, but it was one of the few rights Joseph had left, and he planned on taking full advantage of it. He felt he deserved to have a little fun before his death.

Joseph had been throwing down jellybeans—black ones to the floor, all others into his mouth—one after the other when the priest arrived.

"Hello, Joseph," the priest said. He was a frail looking man, who was probably nearing the end of days himself. "How are you tonight?"

"Oh, you know…" Joseph responded. He put the bag of jellybeans down beside him, and looked the priest in the eyes with a false mask of solemnness on his face. "Could be better, Father."

As their conversation began, the thought entered Joseph's mind that, if he wanted to, he could kill the old man right where he stood. Before anyone could react, the priest's pencil neck would be broken, and he'd be finding out firsthand if there actually was a Kingdom waiting on the other side, or if he had spent his life serving some grand fabrication. It would also earn Joseph a stay of execution, which would prolong the days he had left on Earth.

Joseph had no interest in that, though.

Besides, he wasn't going to kill someone just because he could. He wasn't some heartless monster, after all. Still, the knowledge that he had that sort of power was intoxicating. Especially when the judicial system had stripped away every right he had, including his right to live.

"You must be scared," the priest said.

"I am, Father. I'm afraid of what waits for me on the other side."

"Well, that's natural. The possibility of eternal damnation can be overwhelmingly frightening."

"It is, Father…It is."

Externally, Joseph had added fearfulness to the mask he wore. Inside, however, he laughed hysterically at this man of the cloth's expense.

Joseph didn't fear the unknown. He could not care less whether he burned in eternity for his sins, or if there was absolutely nothing once his heart stopped pumping life through his body.

"Shall we pray, then?" the priest asked. "Shall we ask God for his forgiveness?"

"Do you think he'll forgive me?"

"The Lord is forgiving of all his children if they are truly willing to repent for their sins."

"Okay, I'm willing to give it a try. I mean... If God is willing to forgive me for what I've done, then there's no reason I should be afraid to ask Him for that forgiveness."

"Exactly," the priest said. "Now, let us pray."

Joseph had started to get down on his knees to begin his prayer when he burst out laughing.

"I'm sorry... I'm sorry..." he said, as he pantomimed wiping tears away from his face. "You just sound so goddamn ridiculous."

"Son, it is a sin to use the Lord's name in vain," the priest shot back. There was no longer compassion in his voice. The con was up.

"Well I'll be God-damned!" Joseph responded. He was still fully embracing his fit of hilarity. "I didn't even know that."

"I see now that this has been a waste of both of our time," the priest said, and made a movement to leave.

"No, no, no..." Joseph said, attempting to suppress his obnoxious laughter. "I'm sorry, Father. I really am. It's just that you sound so damn hilarious." He burst out laughing again. "Do you actually believe what's coming out of your mouth?"

"I do. The Lord has been very good to me."

"Well, he hasn't been very kind to me."

Joseph flipped a switch, and all the humor drained from his face. He got up from the bed, and walked towards the priest. The old man shrank away as Joseph approached. Undoubtedly, he realized, as Joseph had only moments before, that this young man, who had killed before, could snap his neck like a decayed twig.

"Let down your guard, Father," Joseph said. "I have no interest in hurting you, but I also have no interest in your campfire stories. I don't believe in your almighty God sitting on a throne up in the clouds."

"Then why did you ask for a priest?"

"Boredom, really. I think I deserve to have a little fun before they send me off and bury me in the ground."

"Your fun should not be at the expense of our good Lord. Despite what you believe, He is very much real, and He is with you in your darkest hour. I pray that in the end you realize that, and ask for His forgiveness."

"I don't need your prayers, Father. Tell you what, though... I don't exactly remember how all this works, whether it's you or the nuns who speak to the Lord..."

"The Lord speaks to us... not the other way around," the holy man corrected.

"Well, if He's around to talk, then He's around to listen. You let Him know that if He has forgiveness for me, I'm not interested in it. He can choke on it, for all I care."

Satisfied that he had said all he needed to say, Joseph returned to his cot and his jellybeans.

"May God have mercy on your soul," was all the priest had to say before leaving.

"I told you," Joseph yelled as the door to his cell slammed shut, "I'm not interested. Tell Him to take His holiness somewhere else!"

Lights out had come a few hours after his visit with the priest had abruptly ended. Joseph lay there in the dark, unable to find sleep. He didn't have long to live, and desired to hold on to every last moment he had while he was still alive. He did not consider sleep to be a smart use of his time.

Boredom arrived quickly, and Joseph decided he needed to keep himself entertained. He had yet to discover his technique for identifying jellybean flavors in the dark, so

BOOTH

continuing his quest to finish the bag before dawn was out of the question. If he accidently bit into one of the black ones, the taste of liquorish would surely cause him to heave, and despite the satisfaction of making a bigger, nastier mess all over his cell, vomiting was not something Joseph felt like doing on the last night of his life.

Instead, what he did was think of Jennifer Aniston. In the fall of that previous year, a new television show debuted called *Friends*, a comedy about six friends living in Manhattan. However, that wasn't the appeal of the show for a prison full of men. What made the sitcom so desirable to inmates in Joseph's cell block were the three beautiful young women who starred in it. Come Thursday nights before lights out, there was only one thing that every man in the prison wanted to do, and that was watch *Friends*.

Now, as he lay there in the dark, Joseph's mind drifted to one specific moment during an episode that aired earlier that year.

Jennifer Aniston's character, Rachel—the stuck up, prissy bitch, who had that fucking loser, Ross, harping over her constantly—had just come out of the shower. She was using the towel that had been covering the upper half of her body to dry her hair. What she failed to notice was that Chandler, her likely-gay friend who lived across the hall, was in the kitchen getting a beverage from the fridge. When he finally lifted his head, he saw Rachel in all her glory. They both screamed, and she quickly grabbed an afghan to cover herself up.

The exact shot that Joseph was envisioning was Aniston in the foreground facing away from the camera towards Chandler, who was standing in the background. Her tan bare back was completely exposed for the audience to see. This garnered quite the positive reaction from all of the inmates watching that night. So much so that the guards had to threaten to turn off the show if they didn't quiet down.

As he thought about her sexy back, he also tried to imagine how nice her ass, which was out of the frame, might be. He felt his penis begin to harden, and figured since this was going to be his last opportunity to do so, he might as well take advantage of it.

He reached down, gripped his penis, and began to rub it. It wouldn't be long before his thoughts shifted away from the actress who played Rachel Green to someone else entirely.

Fitting, Joseph thought as Aniston's replacement took form. *She was the person I fantasized about the first time I jerked off. She might as well be the person I think about the last time, too.*

Alexandra Casings.

He thought about her touch. The feel of her lips against his. He imagined what it would be like to be inside her one last time. Climbing on top of her, getting between her smooth legs, and sliding into her, like he had so many times before.

As he relived those moments with her, he could feel his orgasm drawing nearer. Then his thoughts began to shift, yet again. Joseph went from thinking about the woman she had once been, to envisioning the woman she had become. He hated that woman. She was nothing but a selfish whore.

He imagined his hands slipping around her neck as he was inside her. Of course, she'd just think he was being playful at first, but as his grip began to tighten, she'd become alarmed.

Orgasm drew even nearer as he imagined her neck in his grasp as he applied pressure to her windpipe. She'd try to tell him to stop, but there'd be no air passing through to produce the words. Still, he'd know what she was trying to say, and it would only make him squeeze harder. She'd become frantic at the realization that her life was in peril. The mental image of the all-encompassing terror plaguing her eyes almost made him come right there and then. He managed to calm himself down, and prolong his orgasm... for now.

He wasn't ready for his fun to be over just yet.

She'd grab at his wrist, and attempt to pull his hands free from her neck. She'd fight to get the air she desperately needed back into her lungs. Her struggles would prove useless, though. He was far too determined, and his grip was far too powerful. She'd scratch and claw. She'd even manage to draw blood, but her fighting would prove futile. He'd squeeze harder, and then harder. He'd watch her eyes as he did so. He'd stare deeply into them, as he did so long ago when they were lovers. They were so full of life back then, but now he planned on watching them go blank.

The strong sensation of his impending orgasm returned, and Joseph knew there'd be no stopping it this time. He began to masturbate faster and, as he did, he imagined seeing the life drain from those eyes. Like sand slowly passed through a sieve, so would her existence from this world.

In her final moment, he'd see one last look of desperate hope, a hope that maybe he'd have a sudden change of heart, and release her from his grip right in the nick of time. There would be no change of heart, though, and she would realize that as she died.

As he saw the blank stare of her dead eyes, Joseph let out a pleasurable moan. This was followed by the feel of warm semen on his penis and pooling between his thumb and pointer finger.

Alexandra Casings.

The only woman he had ever loved.

Joseph removed his hand from his penis, and let his ejaculate collect in his palm. He then took the bodily fluid he had collected, and smeared it across the wall next to him. Yet another delightful surprise for whomever was put in charge of cleaning his cell.

As he lay there, recovering from what might have been the single greatest orgasm he had ever experienced, Joseph felt euphoric. Despite his current set of circumstances, he was content. He wasn't thinking of his impending death. Instead, he decided to savor the small things that would give him one last feeling of satisfaction before his life ended, like jellybeans, or masturbating while fantasizing about fucking and killing the woman you had murdered for.

One of those small things that made Joseph especially happy was the fact that he'd be sharing his death day with John Wilkes Booth—Joseph was also the same age as America's most infamous presidential assassin had been when he died outside of a farmhouse in 1865, but he wouldn't realize that until later on... After the walls came crumbling down.

Joseph wasn't exactly a model student, but one thing he loved was history. The one event he knew more about than any other was the assassination of President Abraham Lincoln at Ford's Theatre on April 14, 1865. However, it wasn't Lincoln who drew Joseph's attention to this specific event in American history.

It was Booth.

John Wilkes Booth, one of history's greatest villains, was Joseph Bateman's hero. He had unlimited respect for the man, because he had stood up for what he believed in, and did what no other dared to do.

He took down a tyrant and killed a nigger-lover.

Lincoln's love for a race that was meant to serve the white man would cause an entire nation to nearly crumble, and would lead to a civil war that resulted in the loss of a million American lives. Still, somehow he was praised as a hero, and history remembered him as just that.

Joseph knew the truth, though, and he knew who the real hero had been. It was the man who put a bullet in the back of the nigger-loving tyrant's head.

It was a true honor to die on the same date as your hero. Not many people got to experience that proud feeling, but Joseph Bateman did.

Eventually, like waves on a beach during high tide, sleep crept up on Joseph. He had thought the sandman would not be visiting him on his last night on Earth, but he was wrong. Apparently, all it took was a mind-blowing orgasm to open the gates and let sleep in.

As he lay there in the dark, slumber slowly taking him, Joseph ran his fingers carefully over his chest. He was tracing the outline of the letters that made up his tattoo. However, it wasn't the words inked onto his chest, an infamous historical quote, that he was thinking about.

His mind fixated on his hands.

As the moments passed and his eyelids grew heavier, he thought about his hands. A single word passed through his mind, over and over. The word repeated like a compact-disc with a scratch in it, causing it to skip. That word was *useless*. He brought his hands up to his face, and although his cell was dark, Joseph could vaguely make out their outline.

Useless... he thought as he stared at them. *Useless...*

Joseph couldn't figure out why in that exact moment he thought his hands were useless. That wasn't what bothered him, though. What had him entranced was the unsettling feeling of déjà vu that swept over him as he stared at his extremities. It was so vivid that Joseph was convinced he had gone through the exact experience once before. However, before Joseph could pinpoint the significance of that single word in relevance to his hands, his eyes closed, and he drifted towards sleep.

Useless... he repeated in his mind as his eyes closed and he faded away. *Useless...*

He had only slept for two hours. His cell was as dark as it had been when he fell asleep. For all he knew, he could've been asleep for minutes or hours. It didn't matter, though, because come dawn he'd be dead, and the amount of sleep he had gotten the night before would be a moot point.

The things that had been on his mind before his descent into sleep were no longer prominent. Neither his hands, nor the word *useless* (*useless*) were any concern. Instead, what Joseph felt was the strong urge to satisfy his sweet tooth. He picked up his bag of jellybeans, and it was there that he discovered he could test the flavor of the treat by running his tongue over it.

Joseph decided to spend the final hour of his life reminiscing. Although reminiscing wouldn't have been the word he would have used to describe what he was doing. Reminiscing sounded like you were fondly reliving all the joyous memories of your life. That was not what he was doing. There were no fond memories of Joseph Bateman's life. Even the ones that should have been happy memories, like his mother's adorable nickname for him or memories of Alexandra Casings, were all tainted, and now spoiled.

No, Joseph was not reminiscing.

He was reflecting.

Murdering one man did not get him to where he was in life (although he'd soon learn he was actually very wrong about that). A long series of unfortunate events had landed him on Death Row.

So Joseph Bateman, in the closing hour of his life, chose to reflect.

June 22, 1974

Joey Bean's Escape

Some monsters are born evil while others are created. Many people would believe, given the life he had lived, that Joseph Bateman was a victim of circumstance and environment. Joseph would learn later on, once the walls came down, that he was destined from the day he was born to walk a path that would lead him right into the electric chair.

For the average person, their first memory may involve being tucked tightly into bed while having a bedtime story read to them by a parent. They might remember visits to their grandparents' house for Sunday dinner, or perhaps they'd recall playing tag with their first childhood friend. While most people got to enjoy fond memories of their childhoods, Joseph's earliest memory was of lying awake in bed at night, terrified at the sounds of his father's pickup truck making its way up the dirt driveway.

For any young child, the sound of their father returning home from a long day would be enough to send them from their beds, running full speed towards the door so that they could greet their dad with a warm hug. This was not the case for Joseph. Instead, the sound of tires rolling over loose dirt and rocks detonated an explosion of fear throughout his little body.

Hank Bateman, the father of Joseph William Bateman, did not know his own biological father, and the man who had sired him wasn't even aware of his son's existence. Truth be told, Hank's mother wasn't sure if her son's father was even alive. Shortly after their one night together, her suitor was shipped overseas to fight the Nazis on behalf of Uncle Sam. All she knew of him was his name, and she wasn't entirely sure she had correctly remembered it. Regardless, it was the name she gave her son, so that he did not have to have his mother's, and be labeled a bastard by society.

Despite not ever having known his biological father, Hank Bateman had a stepfather who he knew well. Isaiah Matthews was the pastor in a small town in Connecticut, and even though he delivered sermons every Sunday on behalf of God, Isaiah Matthews was not a good man.

He never failed to remind Hank's mother exactly what she had been before she met him, a sinning whore. He had saved her from a filthy life of carrying the children of men with whom she had sinned, and had given her a purpose: to carry the pastor's own children. He had reproduced six times with Hank's mother, and all six of his children were female.

As Hank grew up, he learned very quickly that the girls wanted nothing to do with their half-brother, a title they refused to acknowledge. To them, he was just a product of their mother's sins, and not worthy of their love or attention. More importantly, Hank Bateman avoided interactions with his half-sisters at all costs, because he knew what would happen if his stepfather caught him so much as glancing in their direction.

Growing up, Hank Bateman constantly found himself on the receiving end of a thrashing via Isaiah Matthew's belt. The majority of the whippings were because Isaiah had caught his stepson staring at his daughters with eyes he had considered to be full of sinful desire. Other times, Isaiah Matthews would find whatever excuse he could to whip the tar out of Hank. His justification was that he was beating the sin out of his stepson. Unfortunately, being a product of sin, at least in Isaiah's mind, Hank could never fully be ridded of the dirtiness that plagued him, which gave Isaiah Matthews a constant excuse to whip his stepson until the boy's back was welted and bloodied.

His mother did nothing.

Hank Bateman received his last thrashing at the age of thirteen. This was because it would be the last time he ever saw Isaiah Matthews, or anyone else he was supposed to call his family, ever again.

One spring day, while the girls were playing outside on their bikes, one of Hank's half-sisters took a pretty bad spill. While she lay there on the concrete, scraped up and hysterical, Hank decided to be a good big brother and save the day.

He helped his injured sister up, and told her he would help her back inside the house. He wouldn't get very far, though, because the moment Hank walked through the front door, he felt the familiar explosion of pain as leather met flesh. He had been accustomed to that dreadful sensation across his back, but this time Isaiah Matthew's belt had connected with his face, and with this brand new point of impact came a whole new kind of pain.

Hank collapsed to the ground and tears spilled from his eyes. He instinctively covered his face, which still stinging and already throbbing. This would prove to be a terrible mistake.

Over the years, Hank had learned that the key to surviving an Isaiah Matthews beating was to just take it. The moment he resisted, or tried to cower and cover up, was the moment the beating intensified. He therefore received a hard boot to the gut for attempting to protect himself. Hank's hands went from his face to his stomach. With his stepson's face exposed, Isaiah Matthews brought the belt down once again. This time it wasn't the hard leather that made contact.

The metal belt buckle smashed Hank in the dead center of his face. He felt another explosion of excruciating pain, and an instant buildup of pressure in his nose. Within seconds, he could feel and taste the blood that was pouring from his nostrils. His nose was broken; any doctor would've told him that had Hank ever decided to seek medical attention for his injuries.

Hank had been too distracted by the awful pain that he didn't notice his stepfather walk away from him. One moment Isaiah Matthews was standing over his stepson with a leather belt in his hands and, the next, he had returned with a double-barrel shotgun which he pointed right at Hank's face.

Hank felt the warmth seep down his legs as his bladder failed him, and he began to cry as he looked into the black eyes of the shotgun.

"You keep your filthy sinning hands off of my daughter, you hear?" Isaiah Matthews told Hank. "I won't let you dirty her or any of my girls. Murder is a sin, and I am a man of the Lord, but if I ever see you near this house again, I will kill you. I have no doubt the Lord will forgive me, because He will know I did what I had to do to protect my family from those who desire to lead them towards a life of sin and filth."

He gave Hank one more hard kick to the gut for good measure, and a warning.

"You have five minutes, boy," Isaiah Matthews said as he left the room. "Otherwise, you'll be meeting your Maker, and there's no room in Heaven for bastard products of sinning whores."

Hank Bateman didn't need five minutes. He fought to get to his feet, and stumbled towards the front door. He took one last look at the house he had grown up in. In the corner he saw his mother. The woman who had carried him for nine months and birthed him had been attempting to remain hidden out of sight during her righteous husband's violent fit. The two—mother and son—stared at each other across the distance of the small living room. Hank saw sadness in her eyes, but it meant nothing to him. He hated her for bringing this life upon him, and doing nothing to stop it. He wished she had drowned him or left him in the frigid winter cold to die after he had been born. Even that would have been more humane than what she allowed him to be put through his entire life.

Hank stared at his mother for a few moments, and hoped his hatred was getting through to her. He spat a mixture of phlegm and blood in her direction, and left the home of Isaiah Matthews forever.

In the years that followed, Hank Bateman would find himself living on the streets when he wasn't in and out of shelters. It was during those years that Hank found his most loyal friend.

The bottle.

Unable to cope with his present or find closure for his past, Hank found solace in alcohol. Like so many without a place to call home, he chose to drown his sorrows.

He spent years as a vagabond. He traveled up and down the road and from town to town. He'd usually have to leave a town after an alcohol-fueled violent altercation in which he was lucky if he didn't find himself in jail, the hospital, or worse.

After five years on the road, Hank found himself back in that small Connecticut town where he had grown up, and had been treated less than human.

Looking back, Hank could not recall the circumstances which brought him back to the one place he considered the closest thing to Hell. What he did remember was the feeling of dread which consumed him at the possibility of coming face-to-face with Isaiah Matthews. The last thing on Earth he had wanted was to see the man who had ruined his life. However, Hank's fears would be put to rest not long after his arrival in town as he learned his stepfather, mother, and half-sisters were no longer members of the small community.

They were all dead.

Even though it had been over a year since the tragedy when Hank arrived in town, the death of Pastor Isaiah Matthews and his family was still a hot topic amongst the small Connecticut community. As the story went, one of Pastor Matthews' daughters got herself good and pregnant outside of wedlock. This spelled certain doom for a young woman when it came to finding a potential spouse, but, more importantly, it was a sin against God. Isaiah Mathews was a man of the Lord, and the fact that one of his daughters had gotten pregnant infuriated him. He placed the blame on the girl's mother, convinced that the same wickedness that had once plagued his wife now consumed his daughter, and was lying dormant in all of his girls.

"They found a note," one of the locals explained as the story was told. "The Pastor blamed himself. He said he shouldn't have been foolish enough to procreate with a sinner and a whore. He never took into consideration that the sin would be passed on to his daughters. He believed his family would be safe from sin, because they were protected by the Lord."

Isaiah Matthews thanked his wife for passing down her sinning traits to their children by stabbing her repeatedly in the stomach. He wasn't through, though. He locked his house up, went room by room, and slit each of his daughter's throats as they slept. According to the note that was found, Isaiah Matthews couldn't let sinners live who shared his wife's blood, whether they had sinned already, or were doomed to do so.

Once his entire family was dead, he piled their bodies into his pickup truck under the cover of night, and drove them to the church he presided over. He dragged each body into the church, dowsed them in gasoline, and lit them on fire. There was no explanation for this act in his note, but some people speculated that perhaps he believed that burning their bodies in the Lord's house would help with their entry into Heaven. Of course, no one knew if there was any truth to this, but it quickly became the popular theory amongst the community.

What burning those bodies did do, though, was set the entire church ablaze. That night it completely burned to the ground. At the time of Hank's visit, there had been no plans to rebuild it.

Once the bodies were burning, Isaiah Matthews returned home. There, he wrote the infamous note that explained most of his actions. In it, he also asked his peers and, more importantly, God to forgive him for the sins he had committed that night. He then took one of the pistols he owned and sinned one last time by blowing his brains out. It has been told and believed by most that a single drop of blood from the pastor's exploding head landed on a statue of the Virgin Mary he kept near his bed. The crimson droplet landed just under her eye, and looked hauntingly like she was shedding a single tear for the pastor. This was obviously nothing more than a legend that made for a haunting detail in a tragic story.

The knowledge of the demise of the man who had ruined his life did little to quell Hank Bateman's need for alcohol. Once in its grips, the bottle scarcely lets one walk away so easily. In the years that followed his visit to the town where he grew up, Hank's drinking only worsened and, along with it, his anger.

Still, through all of it, he managed to get his life in some semblance of order. He settled down in the small town of Wayne County, Pennsylvania, and got himself a job and a place to live. There, he even met the woman who would soon become Missus Emily Bateman.

"When I met your father, he was already a damaged man with a lot of anger inside of him." Emily Bateman told Joseph one September night as she tried to make her son understand why his father was the way he was.

The mother-son conversation had taken place a few nights after the only violent altercation between Joseph and his father. Sitting with his mother was difficult enough after what had happened—he couldn't even make eye contact with her—but hearing her try to justify the man's actions was sickening.

"Still," she would continue. "He had a kindness inside him. It was just buried under so much hatred. I got to see that side of your father. The man who allowed love into his heart. He even quit drinking when we got engaged. He got shipped off to the war, though. Like a lot of young men who went overseas to fight for their country, your father came back a different man from when he left."

Emily Bateman spoke the truth about her husband. He had given up the bottle in favor of an attempt for a better life. Eight months after he and Emily said 'I do', Hank found himself being shipped off to Vietnam to help his country in the fight against communism. There, he got a bullet to the leg, which became badly infected and was nearly amputated. Luckily, doctors were able to save his life and his leg. Once he was healthy enough, Hank was granted a medical discharge and sent home. He returned to his wife in the fall of 1968. That following spring, Hank and Emily welcomed the first addition to their family: their son, Joseph William Bateman.

However, the man Emily Bateman fell in love with and married was not the man who came back from the war. He had seen and gone through things that no one should have to in their lifetime. On top of that, Hank Bateman did not respond well to fatherhood. In order to escape the constant noises of his household, not to mention the deafening sounds in his own head of people dying right before his feet in a jungle halfway across the world, Hank Bateman found refuge at a local bar. There, he was reunited with his long lost friend, the bottle. Following his fall from the wagon, Hank's life took a turn for the worse, and his family would now be along for the ride.

That was the story of Hank Bateman, and why he was the man his son had come to know.

Despite his mother's hopes to resolve the issue between father and son before it escalated and reached a dire level, Joseph found his mother's excuses for her husband's behavior pathetic. They did nothing to change Joseph's perception of the man he was supposed to call his father. He hated Hank Bateman, and it was only a matter of time before the two reached the level his mother feared they would. They might never have reached that explosive level had it not been for the accident that occurred two months following Joseph's conversation with his mother.

That would all go down in 1981, though.

In June of 1974, Joseph Bateman was only five years old, and he didn't yet fully understand the kind of man his father was. The only thing he knew at that young age was that when he heard the sounds of his father's pickup truck coming up their dirt driveway, he should be afraid.

On the nights Hank Bateman managed to get home—he was infamous for spending nights in the drunk tank or on bar floors—he'd come crashing through the front door. Sometimes he'd knock into something, and send it flying to the floor. Other times, he'd just send himself crashing into a wall. No matter what, he was always angry and cursing through his drunken slurs. On occasion, he'd stumble into the kitchen, and raid the fridge of what little food the Batemans had while treating himself to another beer. Most of the time, however, he went right upstairs to the bedroom, where his wife would always be waiting for him.

As he grew up and became more aware of what was happening in his home, Joseph couldn't believe his mother just sat there and waited for his father. She was fully aware of what was in store for her, yet she still sat in their bedroom, waiting. Later on in life, as he reflected on his past, Joseph realized the reason his mother waited was because she knew it would be so much worse for her if she didn't.

Joseph's room was adjacent to his parents'. At age five, he would have to lie there in the darkness of his room, and listen to the two loud thumps of his father's boots hitting the floor as he fumbled to remove them. This was followed by a few moments of silence. When he was old enough to grasp what was happening in his parents' bedroom, Joseph considered these moments the calm before the storm.

What Hank Bateman was doing was stripping down so he could rape his wife.

Magnified by the silence that had just come before it, what came next was the deafening sound of the headboard of his parents' bed rhythmically thumping against the wall. For some children, this sound might send them wandering into their parents' bedroom to investigate, thus creating an awkward moment parents pray their children forget. For

Joseph, the sound coming from his parents' bedroom sent fear throughout his entire body.

Through the thin wall that separated the two rooms, he could hear the grunts and moans coming from his father. This would never last long. The sounds of that headboard against the wall would quicken, and Hank Bateman would let out one last moan as he reached climax.

Emily Bateman never made a single sound.

If Joseph and his mother were lucky, what followed would be the sounds of his father's loud drunken snores. More times than not, though, Hank wasn't through with his wife once he was done raping her.

If sleep didn't take him, anger did. The man who had lived with anger his entire life, chose to embrace it as an adult, instead of trying to control it. Emily Bateman served as the lightning rod to her husband's wrath. Joseph would hear his father start to curse. At first, it was low and barely audible, but as his anger grew, Hank Bateman would end up yelling at the top of his lungs. Though saturated by a night's worth of heavy drinking, the hatred in his words was always clear. *Dumb Cunt* and *Worthless Bitch* were some of Hank Bateman's favorite names to call his wife.

It wasn't the verbal abuse that was the most damaging to Emily Bateman, though.

It was the physical.

Emily Bateman may have been able to remain silent during her evening rapings, but this was not the case whenever her husband decided to beat her mercilessly. Her painful cries could be heard throughout the entire house whenever Hank Bateman landed a fist or foot on various parts of her body.

Joseph couldn't bear the sounds of his mother's painful cries as she was beaten by the man she chose to marry. He loved his mother so much, and he wanted nothing more than for the sounds of her suffering to end. He knew to never to leave his room, though. If he did, he knew things would be bad for him and worse for his mother, and he didn't want to make things worse than they already were. Still, the sounds of her being kicked, punched, and slapped around were too much for a five year old Joseph Bateman to tolerate. He needed to find a distraction.

On June 22, 1974, he found it.

Joseph listened to the sounds of his mother's beating. That night Emily Bateman's thrashing had been especially brutal. There are many tragic things in this world, but a child being able to gage the level of brutality of his mother's beating nears the top of that list. Her feeble whimpers were replaced by agonizing cries as Hank Bateman's curses and fury rained down on her.

"You..."

Painful cry.

"dumb..."

Pathetic whimper.

"fucking..."

Another cry.

"CUNT!"

As an emphasis on his final word, Hank must have added more to his final blow than he had the others. Following it, Emily Bateman actually began to plead for her husband to stop. She would always cry out whenever she was hit, but never would she speak during her nightly beatings. Joseph knew a beating was especially bad when his mother actually begged for it to end.

Emily Bateman's pleas fell on deaf ears.

Unable to bear the sounds of his mother's suffering, Joseph decided he would run away. In his childish mind, it was the only logical thing to do. There was evil inside his home, and he needed to get away from it. He got out of bed, walked over to the window, and slid it open. He crawled through the window and onto the roof. His plan was to crawl to the edge, leap down to the ground below, and run away to safety, wherever that was.

Anywhere has to be safer than here, he thought as he quickly formulated his plan.

However, his plans were thwarted when he got to the edge of the roof, and realized he was too afraid to jump down to the ground. Too afraid to go forward and too afraid to head back, Joseph just sat on his roof.

That was when he noticed the Moon.

He had always been aware of the Earth's satellite up in the night sky. He thought it was so pretty with its different phases, and his mother had even attempted to explain it to him once or twice. On that night, however, it served a whole new purpose to Joseph.

On that night, the Moon became a distraction.

He stared up at that bright object in the night sky, and imagined it as something else entirely. From that night forward, Joseph Bateman would see the Moon not as the Earth's sole satellite, but as a cosmic-sized jellybean. Each night, as he was defenseless against what was happening to his mom, he'd sneak out his window and onto his roof, where he'd stare up at the night sky. He'd then allow himself to be taken somewhere else. It was a place where there was no hatred or pain. He didn't feel useless and scared there. On those nights atop his roof when he was a small child, Joseph Bateman escaped his reality, and entered the distraction of his imagination.

Each night, he'd envision what flavor the Moon would be. It could be whatever flavor anyone wanted it to be, because the Moon was magical, and magic was boundless. As the Moon went through its usual phases, and slowly disappeared each night, Joseph imagined a giant space worm up in the heavens taking a bite out of that delicious celestial treat. When the Moon was new and couldn't be seen in the night sky it was because the space worm had finally finished its snack. That was okay, though. Soon, the Moon would reappear in the sky, and it wouldn't be long before the friendly creature floating up in space got its moon-sized jellybean back.

Throughout that summer, Joseph used the Moon and his imagination as a much needed distraction from what he felt useless to stop. When winter arrived and the cold became unbearable, he would wrap a blanket around his body, and sit as close to the window as he could. From there, he'd watch the Moon be devoured by creatures only he could see. It was how he managed to stay sane and survive his early life. Creatures from outer space, and a very sugary sweet Moon.

May 10, 1976
Joseph's Birthday

"Haaaaappy Biiiiiirthdaayyy, my sweet Joey Beans," Emily Bateman sang on the evening of her son's seventh birthday. "Happy Biiiiiiithdayyy to youuuu…"

Joseph Bateman leaned over the table, and blew out the single candle that stood atop the cake his mother spent the afternoon crafting. It was a pathetic looking confection—lopsided, dry, and thinly iced—but that didn't matter. The amount of times any sort of food other than the essentials were present in the Bateman household were few and far between, so it really didn't matter to anyone how aesthetically pleasing their evening dessert was. Plus, Joseph loved his mama; therefore he loved his cake.

After cake, Emily Bateman put on some of her favorite Elvis Presley records. She, her birthday boy, and her youngest daughter, Liz, danced around the living room to some of the king of rock 'n roll's biggest hits. Once everybody in the whole cell block was through dancing to the jailhouse rock, Joseph and his little sister were brought up to their rooms and tucked into bed. There, Joseph was told by his mother to have sweet dreams. However, he knew there'd be no such thing. Despite feeling like he had a home for a rare few hours that night, Joseph knew that Hank Bateman would eventually return. He'd be his usual mixture of drunk and angry, and once he stepped foot through the door, the Bateman household would revert back to its usual hell.

"Mama…" Joseph said as Emily Bateman was exiting his bedroom. "You can throw out the rest of the cake. I won't mind."

"Why would I do that, Joey Beans?" She asked. She walked back over to the bed, where she took a seat, and started to rub her son's little feet. "Was it not yummy?"

"Oh, no!" Joseph argued. "It was super delicious." He paused momentarily so he could concoct what he believed would be substantial reasoning for his mother to toss away the leftover cake. "It's just too many sweets gives you cavities! The dentist is very expensive, mama."

"Well that's very thoughtful of you, but I think you and your sister will be alright if you have yourselves a little bit more cake tomorrow night."

It wasn't him or his sister who Joseph was worried about.

"Are you sure?"

Yes. I'm sure, silly," Emily assured her son. She got up, and leaned over to kiss her son's forehead. "Now get some sleep."

It would be a while before Joseph heeded his mother's advice to get some sleep. Instead, he lay there in the dark, and considered things no seven year old should ever have to think about. Like, if his mom, as she sat there assuring him there was no need to throw away the extra birthday cake, was fearful of the same things he was. There were risks of not cleaning up the scene thoroughly and disposing of all the evidence, and Emily Bateman knew what was in store for her if the cake was discovered. Still, she insisted they keep it, so that her two children could enjoy dessert two nights in a row.

The night dragged on and, as it did, Joseph heard no sounds of tires rolling over dirt. He waited, anticipating the inevitable, but the sound of Hank Bateman's pickup truck never came. He let out a sigh of relief, and allowed himself to begin to relax, like he did every time his father was too drunk to make it home.

Joseph finally drifted off and, as he slept, he dreamt of a monster slowly crawling up his dirt driveway. It wasn't one of the kind monsters he imagined floating around outer space. Instead, this monster was ugly, foul, and angry. He snarled and growled as he dug his dirty long claws into the ground, and pulled himself towards Joseph's home. He wasn't interested in celestial goodies to munch on. He was coming for Joseph's family, and he was coming to cause them pain and suffering.

Joseph woke from his nightmare abruptly. Outside his window, he heard the monster he feared slowly crawling up his driveway. Only this monster was behind the wheel of a busted up pickup truck, and he was drunk off alcohol and a lifetime of endless rage.

Hank Bateman had returned home, after all.

Hank came crashing through the front door, as per usual, and Joseph could hear him drunkenly sauntering around the living room. Joseph prayed and pleaded with God to steer his father away from the kitchen. If the man went straight upstairs, it would be bad, but if Hank Bateman stopped in the kitchen and went in the fridge, it would be far worse for Joseph's mother.

Joseph lay in his bed. He was frozen with fear, and could barely get the breath he needed to live into his lungs. An unbearable anxiety was growing within him as he waited to hear his father's footsteps either ascending the stairs, or making their way across the kitchen for another beer from the refrigerator. When he finally heard the sound of his father stumbling into the kitchen table, the dense ball of anxiety that had been growing by the second finally exploded and consumed him.

He heard the sounds of the glass jars and bottles on the refrigerator door clanging together as his father opened the fridge. They emanated throughout the house like church bells in a small town. They rang a warning to the residence of the Bateman home to beware of the hell that was about to be unleashed upon them. There was nothing but terrifying silence, at first. Then Hank spoke, and Joseph knew his father had found the leftover cake.

"What the fuck is this?" Hank Bateman asked the empty downstairs living area. His words were painted with slurs from a night's worth of booze.

Joseph heard his parents' bedroom door creak as it eased open. He knew his mother was waiting in the doorway to be summoned. In a few moments, she'd have to go downstairs to face her husband's fury, but not before he called for her. If she went down there before Hank Bateman was ready for her, he'd somehow find a way for her inevitable fate to be worse than it was already destined to be.

"What the fuck is this?!" was heard again from down the stairs. "Get the fuck down here, you useless cunt!"

And like she had done every time before and would do every instance that followed, Emily Bateman obeyed her husband's commands.

"Explain this to me, bitch," Hank demanded once his wife reached the bottom of the stairs.

"It's a cake, Hank," Emily started to explain.

"I know what it is. I'm not a useless idiot, like you. Why is it here?"

"It's Joey's birthday cake. It's your son's birthday…"

The fact that it was his firstborn's birthday meant nothing to Hank Bateman. In his eyes, spending his earnings on frivolous things, such as cake and presents for any kind of special occasion, only meant you were taking money away from the few things in life he truly cared about, and those were his vices.

"You think I got any fucking cake when it was my birthday?" Hank asked his wife. "I was lucky enough to not get an ass-whipping from my stepfather on my birthday. That was his present to me, and I didn't always get that. So tell me, why are you spending my fucking hard earned money on this shit?"

"I thought it would be nice..."

"What's nice is that I don't whip the boy's ass every night."

"I know, Hank, but I thought it would be nice if the kid had something sweet... just this once"

"I'm sure you want some too, then."

Joseph then heard his mother let out a gasp that was a mixture of both shock and agony. This was followed by the sound of the cake's serving dish hitting the ground and shattering.

"Have some fucking cake, you dumb whore! Here... EAT IT!!"

Emily Bateman attempted to cry out, but her moans were distorted and muffled. Joseph knew this was because his father was attempting to shove the leftover cake down his mother's throat.

"Choke on it, for all I care," Hank Bateman shouted.

Next came the sound of Emily Bateman crashing into the side of the kitchen table. This was probably due to a hard slap to the side of her head that knocked her off balance. There was a groan that accompanied her collision, likely caused by her ribs meeting the edge of the table. One would never want to think it possible that the sounds of

31

domestic abuse would be so easily recognizable to a child of seven years of age. Sadly, Joseph Bateman knew them all too well.

"Get the fuck upstairs, you bitch! Or I'll just fucking drag you up to the bedroom, myself."

Joseph heard his mom crawling up the stairs, followed by his father's heavy footfalls. He'd hear his mother occasionally yelp as she ascended, which Joseph knew was his father planting his booted foot in the base of Emily's spine. He threw the blankets over his head, and tried to drown out the sounds coming from outside his door. This proved pointless, though. He heard each agonizing strike as his mother crawled on her hands and knees past his bedroom. When he heard his parents' bedroom door close, Joseph threw the blankets off, and leapt out of his bed. He was more eager than usual to get outside the house and deploy his usual methods to escape from reality.

His foot got caught in the blanket and he tripped, falling to the floor. The impact was utterly painless, but the moment he hit the ground, tears came pouring from his eyes.

This is all my fault, he told himself as he wept. *This is happening because of me.*

He was startled back to reality by the sound of a tremendous thud of his mother being slammed against the wall. Unable to listen to the suffering he had brought upon her, Joseph got to his feet and ran to his window.

The May weather was nice enough for Joseph to escape the confines of his home, and get as far away as possible from what was going on within its walls. He crawled to the edge of the roof and tried to clear his mind. As he was getting his imagination warmed up to envision various friendly creatures in the heavens, he noticed something run across his backyard. The object was faint, as the only source of light in his yard was moonlight, but he could make out clearly that it was a human being.

A small human being.

A child.

His sister.

Joseph's first instinct was to yell for Liz to come back to the house, but wisely ruled that option out. His father had never laid a finger on either of them, but if they were discovered outside of the house so late, and not to mention disrupting his nightly ritual, a beating was surely in store for both Bateman children. Joseph would have to go with Plan B, which was to go down there and get his sister.

He wasn't about to risk going through the house and getting caught by his father, so he would slide down the drain pipe that ran along the side the house, instead. He grabbed hold of the rusty pipe, threw his legs over the edge of the roof, and slowly slid to ground. The instant his feet touched earth, Joseph took off across the yard to find his sister.

The Bateman's owned a vast piece of property. Their backyard would have been the perfect place for two children to play in while growing up. Only it was far too dangerous for two rambunctious children to be running around in. Hank Bateman may have lacked many qualities that people saw as redeeming, but the one thing that could not be taken away from the man was that he was a damn good mechanic. In fact, he was the best. There wasn't an automobile problem he couldn't diagnose and then fix with ease. There wasn't an engine he couldn't take apart, piece by piece, and then successfully put back together. It always seemed like a great idea when the desire hit to buy a broken down car and fix it up. He could resell them for a profit and the work would keep him occupied.

Sadly, addictions proved more powerful than ambition, and Hank Bateman never managed to get his business venture off the ground. That didn't stop him from acquiring broken down cars, and various engine parts, though. Over the years, the Bateman's backyard resembled more of a junkyard than it did a place where a family could barbecue or play ball during the summer months.

Joseph maneuvered through the maze of cars and engine parts that had been laid to rust away on the bare dead ground. When he got far enough away from the house, and was sure to be out of the earshot of his father, he began to call for his sister by her name. Even then, he refused to raise his voice to a decibel over that of a whisper.

A wooded area lined the back property of the Bateman house. Hank had put up barbed wire around the perimeter to keep animals from coming on his property. He hadn't really taken into consideration—nor did he care—that he had two young children, who could fall into the fence, and get seriously injured. Joseph began to fear that his sister ran straight for the woods, and got herself caught up in the barbed wire.

He headed towards the fence, whispering Liz's name. At first, he got no response, which led him to believe he'd find his sister tangled up and either choking to death or bleeding. However, through the night air, he was able to pick up the faint sounds of a toddler crying. He followed the sounds of whimpers, which luckily weren't coming from the rear of the property and the barbed wire fence. Instead, they led Joseph to the skeleton of one of the broken down cars, where he found his sister tucked away inside.

"Lizzy-girl," Joseph said as he cautiously approached his sister. "What are you doing out here?"

"I'm scared, Joe-Joe," she said. "I'm scared of pa."

Joseph climbed into the hollowed-out car, and the instant he did, his sister was in his arms. She began to cry as any petrified child would. There was nothing Joseph could but to hug his baby sister and attempt to reassure her.

"He's not going to hurt you, Lizzy-girl."

"I don't want him to hurt mama anymore."

Unfortunately, that was something Joseph couldn't promise his little sister wouldn't happen.

"I just get so scared when he's hurting mama," Liz continued. "Why did he get so mad at mama for making us a cake?"

"I don't know."

It was all Joseph could say as he caressed his sister's hair in an attempt calm her. He wished he had an answer for her, but he didn't

"I'm too scared to go back inside, Joe-Joe. Can't me, you, and mama just run away? That way daddy can't hurt her."

"No, Lizzy-girl. We can't."

"Why not?"

"Because, we just can't."

It was another thing he had wondered, and it broke his heart to hear his baby sister now wondering the same thing. Hank Bateman's poison was now affecting his daughter's happiness. Joseph felt sadness building up in his throat, but he swallowed it and fought off his tears. He wanted to protect his sister, so that she didn't have to experience what he felt on a nightly basis. He may be helpless to protect his mother, but he could try to shield Liz from the ugliness their father brought home with him every night.

"I'll tell you what, though," Joseph said. "Anytime you get scared, Lizzy-girl, you quietly sneak across the hall to my room and I'll protect you."

"Do you promise?"

"I do. I promise. Anytime you're scared, you come to me, and I'll make it okay. Never try to run away again. Can you promise me that?"

"I promise." Liz hugged her big brother tightly. "I love you, Joe-Joe."

"I love you, too, Lizzy-girl."

Liz lay her head on her big brother's shoulder, and fell asleep immediately. Joseph was aware that they needed to get back inside of the house, but he also knew that Liz wouldn't be able to climb the pipe he had slid down earlier. He wasn't even sure he could. They'd have to wait so they could go in through the back door. Liz was light enough for Joseph to be able to carry, so when he felt it was safe and their father had slipped into alcohol-induced unconsciousness for the night, he would carry her inside, and place her in her bed.

While he waited for the perfect time to reenter their home, Joseph dozed off. He was jolted awake by the sounds of a loud whispering voice echoing throughout the backyard. The voice was calling for the two of them.

It was their mother.

He wasn't sure how long he had been asleep, but their father must have finished administering his beating, and decided it was time to slip into his slumber. Being that the night's abuse had been especially loud and violent, Emily Bateman must've gone to check on her children and found them missing. Instead of jumping right into a panic, she must have drawn a conclusion as to what had happened, and decided to search for them herself before having to make a phone call to law enforcement. If the cops were called and involved, she might have to provide a reason why her children would both attempt to leave their house in the middle of the night. After searching the house and realizing they weren't anywhere inside, she'd then turn her search towards the backyard.

"I'm over here, mama," Joseph called out towards his mother. He slid his sister's head gently from his lap, and stood up.

"Is your sister with you?" his mother asked as she walked towards the sound of his voice. She wasn't mad, as most parents would be had their children snuck out into the yard in the middle of the night.

"Yes. She's asleep."

Emily Bateman walked over to the car where her two children had been hiding out. She bent down to one knee, and gave her son a hug and a kiss on his cheek. There was no lecture from her. She was just happy she found the two of them safe and sound. Emily Bateman slid her sleeping daughter out from the wrecked car, and carried her back to the house with her son by her side.

When they entered the backdoor into the lighted kitchen, Joseph found himself frozen with shock. There was a broken serving plate, and pieces of his destroyed birthday cake all over the floor. That wasn't the main cause for his stunned reaction, though.

It was the sight of his mother that caused Joseph's eyes to widen in disbelief.

Emily Bateman had learned throughout the years the best ways to conceal the signs of spousal abuse from both the public and her children. Still, there were nights just like the one of Joseph Bateman's seventh birthday, where the aftermath would be impossible to cover up, even days after the fact. Joseph was now getting to see the results of his father's handiwork minutes afterwards. His mother had no time to clean herself up, and the sight of her right after a thrashing stained Joseph's memory for the remainder of his life.

Her eye, which would've been properly iced by the time the kids woke up, was swollen and red. The blood from her split lip, which would have been cleaned up, still stained her chin and nightgown. In addition to the blood, her son's birthday cake was smeared across her nightgown and in her hair from when it was forcefully shoved down her throat.

"What's the matter, Joey Beans?" his mother asked. She took a step towards her son, and that's when he noticed his mother's fresh limp.

"Nothing," Joseph responded almost too quickly. "I just want to go to bed."

Before his mother could say anymore, Joseph ran past her. He climbed the stairs, and entered his bedroom.

He slammed the door behind him, and collapsed into his bed. He thought maybe his mother would follow, and try to pry from him what was bothering him. She never came, though. Emily Bateman knew exactly what had bothered her son so much, and there were no words of comfort or reasoning that could explain her cuts and bruises.

Joseph lay there in the dark. He expected tears to come, but they didn't, and he wasn't surprised. It wasn't sadness Joseph was feeling, after all.

It was anger.

After seeing his mother that way, the fear Joseph usually felt was gone. What replaced it was a feeling of malice.

At only seven years of age, Joseph Bateman felt hatred for the first time in his life.

October 8, 1977
Shoes in the Tree

He felt the force of contact as the set of hands connected with his back. The next thing he felt was his face smacking against the ground. Joseph didn't need to look up to know who had been cruel enough to sneak up from behind him and push him down to the ground.

Joseph Bateman never got bullied by his father, but fate was kind enough to deliver him a replacement: Mark Whitmore, the fourth grader who bullied the other kids for no reason other than just being a bad apple. He was bigger than all his peers, and he knew that meant he was stronger than them as well. He singled out kids who were much smaller than him and made their lives hell until he got bored and moved on. Over the summer of 1977, he set his sights on Joseph who soon became his main target. This carried well into the new school year.

Joseph heard the other kids, who followed Whitmore around, laughing at him as he lay face down in the grass.

"Awe, shucks," Mark said. "Did poor little Masturbateman"—a clever nickname, if there ever was one—"fall down, and get hurt?"

Another burst of laughter came rolling in from the peanut gallery. It was either directed at their leader's clever-coming-from-a-fourth-grader's-brain nickname, or at his uncanny ability to point out the obvious.

"Nice shoes!" Mark said, continuing his torment.

Joseph felt his shoes being tugged at and immediately started thrashing back and forth in an attempt to fight the inevitable.

"Hold still, Masturbateman! You're not making this any easier for yourself!"

Joseph did not heed his bully's advice, and refused to hold still as his shoes were being tugged from his feet, but his resistance did him no good. Joseph felt his shoes slide off his feet and into the possession of Mark Whitmore.

"Oh, gross!" Whitmore exclaimed as he held the shoes in front of his face, pinching his nostrils shut for emphasis. "These shoes stink! Don't you know you're supposed to get new shoes at the beginning of every school year, Masturbateman? Do these even fit you?"

The truth was Joseph's shoes didn't fit him any longer. Every morning he had to fight to squeeze into them, and once they were on, his toes were all squished. It was a very uncomfortable feeling, but he'd have to put up with it until the shoes became so worn out, they split.

"They probably don't," Mark continued. "Your family can't have new stuff because your dad is a deadbeat and doesn't make enough money to afford them."

"That's not true!" Joseph shot back at Mark Whitmore's lie.

Hank Bateman made good money working as an auto mechanic. There were just things he felt were more important to spend his earnings on than his family. Joseph's mother was lucky enough to get the money she needed to pay their bills every month, and even that was a difficult task. The Batemans were constantly getting hit with late fees. They had even lost their heat during the coldest months of the winter that year, and it had taken a full two weeks, and a handful of worse-than-usual beatings from her husband, for Emily Bateman to get the money she needed for a delivery of oil.

As far as clothing went, the Bateman children would have to ride out what they currently owned until the bitter end. For two growing children, this became quite the dilemma. Shirts became too tight. Pants became too short in the legs or tight around the waist, and would often be patched up if a hole developed and got too big. Socks would get so worn down, there'd be holes in the heel and toe; completely negating their purpose. This caused the foul stench Mark Whitmore was currently smelling. Joseph's sister, from the time she was born until she was enrolled in school, wore hand-me-downs from her big brother. A little girl, who should have been done up in dresses, tutus, and all things pink, instead wore the overalls, jeans, and green and blue shirts that her brother had once worn when he was her age.

Despite every effort to avoid asking for money, Emily Bateman would find her children in need of clothing, and would ask her husband for the funds to buy replacements. She'd then quietly and patiently take her beatings until Hank Bateman felt she had been punished enough. Then and only then would he give her enough money for her to go out and buy her children—they were always *her* children and never *their* children whenever Hank Bateman referred to Joseph and Elizabeth—the bare minimum of what they needed and never a single penny more.

"Oh, that's right," Mark Whitmore continued as he stood over a shoeless Joseph Bateman. "Your daddy can't buy you new clothes, because he spends all his money on beer."

To that point, Joseph couldn't argue.

JASON PELLEGRINI

Whitmore started to tie the shoes together by the laces that had once upon a time been white, and Joseph knew exactly what this bully was up to. He tried to get up to save his shoes, but was pushed back down to the ground by Whitmore's lackeys.

"What's the matter, Masturbateman?" Whitmore asked. "You afraid if you don't have these shoes anymore that your daddy won't have the money to replace them, and you'll have to walk around barefoot or with bags on your feet?"

This got another laugh from the Mark Whitmore Fan Club. However, it wasn't the fact that he was about to lose his shoes that upset Joseph. It was the beating that awaited his mother when she had to ask her husband for money that bothered him.

"Say goodbye, Masturbateman," Mark Whitmore said, and without hesitation, he launched the pair of shoes towards the nearest tree, where they wrapped around a branch and dangled there.

There was an explosion of laughter from the group of boys that followed. Joseph wondered if they would still think what had just transpired was so hilarious had they known the consequences. There had been whispers for years about what happened in the Bateman household late at night. However, the talks had remained amongst adults and never touched the ears of children.

"The way I see it," said Mark Whitmore as he and Joseph stared up the shoes swaying back and forth from the tree branch up above, "I did you a huge favor. You can wear plastic bags on your feet now and those will still be an improvement from those nasty shoes."

There was one last burst of hilarity from the fan club at Joseph's expense. They continued the obnoxious laughter as they walked away, and left Joseph there, barefooted.

Now that there was no one around to push him back down to the ground, Joseph got to his feet. He stared up at the branch above. His shoes swayed there, out of his reach. There was no way to get them down unless he scaled the tree, and retrieved them. That was exactly what Joseph planned to do, but there was one problem with Joseph's plan. After climbing the tree and reclaiming the shoes, he would have to climb down. The inevitable descent left Joseph frozen with fear.

Ever since the night of his seventh birthday, when he had climbed down from his roof to chase after his sister, Joseph developed a paralyzing fear of heights. Had he taken the time later on in his life to clock in some minutes on a psychologist's couch, he might have learned his sudden onset case of acrophobia, along with his sudden detest for anything sweet—sadly, even jellybeans—was caused by that particularly traumatizing event. At eight years old, though, he hadn't been able to figure out the reason for his fear. All he knew was that if he climbed up that tree, he'd be unable to come down.

"Are you going to climb up there and get those?" Joseph heard a girl's voice ask as he stared up at his shoes. "Or do you think if you stare hard enough, the shoes will just jump off the branch and land on the ground?"

Joseph turned his attention away from the dangling shoes, and saw Alexandra Casings, his fellow classmate, standing next to him. He wasn't sure how long she had been standing beside him, but he could tell it had been long enough for her to figure out he was having trepidations over the idea of scaling the tree.

"I'm going to," Joseph answered, defiantly. "I don't need to rush, though."

"Yeah, yeah, yeah," and without another word, Alexandra Casings was scaling the tree.

"What are you doing?" Joseph hollered.

"What you're too scared to do," she answered as she grabbed onto branches above her and pulled herself up.

She reached the thick branch where Joseph's shoes hung, lay flat across it, and pulled herself on her stomach towards them. As he watched Alexandra Casings inch her way towards her goal, Joseph felt his heart pounding in his throat. Just the idea of being up there was giving him anxiety. He didn't even see her reach her target. The next thing he knew, the shoes thumped to the ground, and lay at his feet. Moments later, Alexandra Casings was back on the ground.

"TA-DA!" she said, her arms up in the air and a huge smile stretched across her face.

"I was just about to climb up there," Joseph argued.

"I think what you're supposed to say is 'thank you.'"

"Thank you," Joseph said obediently, and then added, "That was very nice of you, but I really was about to get them down."

"Uh-huh."

"Really, I was!"

"I bet," Alexandra Casings said, and added a playful punch to Joseph's shoulder. "You're Joseph Bateman."

"Yeah, and you're Alexandra Casings," Joseph responded matter-of-factly. He knew exactly who she was.

Many of their classmates would consider Alexandra Casings to be Joseph's female counterpart. That was because they were both, as second graders so eloquently put it...losers. They were both considered loners, and there had been whispers amongst adults regarding both children's families.

"I prefer being called Alex," Alexandra Casings informed Joseph.

"Isn't Alex a boy's name?"

"Well...your name is Joseph, and, if you ask me, that sounds a lot like Josephine, and that's a girl's name."

Joseph thought her argument was a bit of a stretch.

"Besides," Alex continued. "I'd rather be one of the boys. The girls around here are stupid!"

The truth was Alexandra Casings really would have fit in more with the boys than the girls. In addition to her ability to gracefully scale trees and shimmy across branches high up above the ground without showing an ounce of fear, her lack of desirable bust and curvy hips that the hormones of adolescence would give her in the years to follow, gave her the stature of a male. Her wardrobe choice only accentuated her tomboyish look. While the other girls in her grade dressed their best to look the part of a mature woman, like their mothers, Alex wore baggy jeans, sneakers, and her father's flannel shirts. One time, the school had called home, and informed her father that his daughter could no longer come in wearing his shirts because they were too baggy for a girl her age to wear. Alex forced her father to go to the store, and pick up similar flannel shirts in her size to match his. She always wore her naturally pin-straight brown hair in a single ponytail, and the blue eyes that should have been mesmerizing, even at her young age, somehow seemed mundane on her pale, freckled face.

In the years that followed her and Joseph's first meeting, Alexandra Casings would develop into a beautiful woman, and she'd fully embrace it in the process. At age eight, though, Alex was certainly a more fitting name to her looks and personality than Alexandra.

"So, you going to put those on," Alex asked, looking down at Joseph's shoes. "Or did I risk my life climbing that tree for nothing?"

Joseph knelt down and slid his foot in to his worn out shoe. He was hoping he'd be able to wait until Alex was gone before doing this, so she wouldn't witness him struggling to put on a shoe that clearly no longer fit him properly. His cheeks burned up with embarrassment, and he buried his face as much as he could without tipping over to avoid making eye contact. Despite the additional efforts he needed to take to put on his shoes, Alex never pointed out that he desperately needed a new pair.

"Now that you have your shoes on, you can walk me home," Alex said once Joseph was finished.

"Huh?" was all Joseph could manage to say in response.

His face shot up and he could feel the O his mouth was forming, yet he couldn't lift his jaw from its dropped position. He may have been eight, but he knew how the world worked. If a girl asked you to walk her home, she wanted to be girlfriend and boyfriend.

Oh, the joys of being young.

"I helped get your shoes out of the tree. It wouldn't be very nice of you to not walk me home after I did that for you," Alex pointed out. "Don't worry, Masturbateman...I don't want to be your girlfriend."

"Please don't call me that," Joseph asked, obviously hurt by her use of his stupid nickname.

"I'm sorry. I just wanted to see how it felt saying it. That troll, Mark Whitmore, loves calling you that. I thought maybe there was a reason. Don't worry. I hated it. It's a stupid nickname, if you ask me. No wonder why Mark likes saying it so much. He's the biggest dummy in the entire state!"

This got a laugh from Joseph. He definitely agreed with Alex's analysis of Mark Whitmore.

"So, you going to walk me home?" she asked again.

"Yeah," Joseph said. "I can do that."

That was the moment Joseph Bateman and Alexandra Casings' friendship began, just one more step on the path that would lead Joseph to death row.

June 20, 1979
Throwing Rocks

"Are you going to jump, or not?"

"Yes! I said not to rush me."

"It's only water. Quit being such a baby, Josephine."

"How many times do I have to tell you to stop calling me that?"

"I wouldn't have to call you that if you weren't such a girl about some things. Now, JUMP!"

"I will, I will."

Joseph Bateman stared down at the water below from the branch he and Alex were perched upon. It had taken Alex a good amount of time and peer pressure to finally get him up in the tree, and now she wanted him to jump?! That notion was craziness in its purest form to Joseph. He wouldn't even consider climbing the tree until Alex found a branch sturdy enough to support both of their weight. Even when she finally did, he wasn't convinced of its strength until she spent a good two minutes bouncing up and down on it.

Now, as he stared down at the small body of water Alex wanted him to jump down into, the usual fear-driven paralysis overtook him. He was trying to play it off as cool as possible in front of his best friend because he didn't want to come off as a scaredy-cat. The only thing was, he wasn't playing it cool, and he knew Alex was well aware he was a big 'ol wuss. She also had no problem calling Joseph out on his bluffs, which made things worse for him in situations like the one he was currently in. When he said he would jump into the lake from the huge tree branch that hung above it, she immediately called bullshit—her exact choice of words—which led to the scenario in which Joseph currently found himself.

"Just admit you are too afraid to jump," Alex said, trying to force a confession from Joseph.

"I'm really not. I just don't want to get my clothes wet, and the water is probably still freezing."

"You afraid of a little shrinkage?!"

"What?! NO!" Joseph wasn't even aware of shrinkage until a week earlier when Alex informed him of what happened to boys when they jumped into extremely cold bodies of water. "I just don't see the point, Alex."

"Whatever, Josephine. I'm done arguing with you."

Alex was gone the moment the words left her mouth. A second later, Joseph heard the splashing sound of her body hitting the water below. Moments after that, he heard her squealing as she came to the surface about how cold the water was.

"I told you it was going to be cold," Joseph yelled down from the tree.

"Oh, shush! It's only cold for a second. You get used to it. Come on, and jump down. Or do you not want to mess your perm up, Josephine?"

"Stop calling me that, jerk!"

"Jos-e-phine, Jos-e-phine, Jos-e-phine," Alex repeated over and over as she eloquently backstroked through the water.

If I don't jump, she's never going to let me live this down, Joseph thought.

Still, he couldn't bring himself to jump. His feet might as well have been one with the branch he stood on, because there was no way they were leaving it, not unless it was to descend the tree the exact way he came up, which was exactly what he ended up doing. It had taken him an absurd amount of time to climb down from the tree, but when his feet finally made contact with the grass below, Joseph felt his heartrate begin to regulate, and the familiar sense of anxiety begin to lift.

He made his way around the tree to meet Alex at the water. When he came around the huge bark, he saw his best friend standing at the edge of the lake. She had stripped away the water-soaked clothing from her skin, and stood there in her pink underwear with tiny red hearts. The initial thought that popped into Joseph's head, as he watched her wring out her clothes, was shock. He would have never guessed Alexandra Casings owned anything even remotely girlie.

Once she had twisted as much water from her shirt as she was going to get, she turned around to lay it across a nearby log in order for the summer sun to aid in the drying process. She was unaware of Joseph's presence, and failed to cover her chest. At ten years old, still a few years shy of puberty, Alexandra Casings had nothing to cover up. She had a flat chest with small pink nipples that didn't look much different than Joseph's own chest. Still, he was well aware of the parts of a girl he shouldn't look at, as well as the parts he shouldn't let anyone else see. So at the sight of his friend's naked chest, he ducked back behind the tree in shame. He planned on staying there, squatting behind that tree, until he was sure it was safe to come out.

As he looked back and reflected on this memory from his jail cell sixteen years later, Joseph found it humorous that he thought seeing his friend's flat chest was the end of the world. He would have far more disturbing experiences involving sex in the years that followed, and the sight of Alex's naked, pre-pubescent chest was barely a drop in the bucket.

"Hey, Josephine," he heard Alex finally call. "You still up there? Come down. I want to go home."

Joseph took this as a cue that it was safe to come out of hiding.

"I told you not to call me that!" he said as he walked out from behind the tree.

"Wow! You made it out of the tree all by yourself. I thought I was going to have to come up there and carry you out."

"Oh, shut up! I'm not that big of a wimp."

"Suuuuuure, you're not," Alex teased with a nudge of her elbow and a wink.

Normally, someone mocking Joseph or making him the focal point of a joke would upset him. Not with Alex, though. He always laughed alongside his best friend, even when the jokes were at his expense. He enjoyed their chemistry, and he knew, no matter what she teased him about, she was only kidding around, and would always have his back whenever he needed her. They were best friends, and with that title came the right to poke fun at one another without the other taking it to heart.

They left the lake, and Joseph walked Alex home. It was a routine they practiced since their first meeting, and would remain a tradition until he left Wayne County. As they made their way down Main Street, towards Alex's home, Joseph went on about how he planned on one day becoming the WWF Champion, like the great Bruno Sammartino.

"Josephine, you're a twig. You'll never be as big as any of those wrestlers!" Alex pointed out.

Joseph planned to rebut by telling Alex he could be as big as any wrestler as long as he put in the effort, but before he could make his point, Alex's hand was covering his mouth.

"Shhhhh..." she quietly said, and pulled him behind a nearby bush.

She removed her hand from Joseph's mouth, and the moment she did he started to ask her what she was doing. He was cut off once again, this time by Alex slapping him in the arm.

"Ow! What the heck was that for?" Joseph asked.

"I said to shush!" Alex fired back. She peaked her head over the bush and pointed towards something. "Over there. Don't let her see you."

Joseph slowly rose to his knees, so he could see who Alex was talking about. Walking down the street towards them was Eve Meyers.

Eve Meyers was a fellow classmate of Joseph and Alex's. She was also Alex's sworn enemy. She and Alex detested each other, and their rivalry was well known throughout the fourth grade. The feeling of hatred between the two may have been mutual by this point, but the ongoing feud had been started and was usually continued on by Alex. Alexandra Casings could be a nasty brat just like any girl her age. When it came to Eve Meyers, though, she was just plain cruel.

Alex's grudge towards her fellow classmate never made much sense to Joseph. Eve Meyers was a nice enough girl, and had never teased nor been mean to Joseph. In fact, as far as Joseph could tell, Eve Meyers had never been mean to anyone they went to school with. Yet Alex absolutely despised her, and the only reason for this, as far as Joseph could tell, was because Eve Meyers was black.

The color of Eve Meyers skin bothered Alex so much that it caused her to act out in ways Joseph couldn't believe possible. Not many of the children in their grade talked to or associated with Alex. If they did it was mainly because they were forced to in a classroom setting, but when working with her classmates, Alex was always kind and never disrespectful.

Except when it came to Eve Meyers.

At the beginning of the school year, when the two were placed together for a group activity, Alex flipped out, and made a scene in the middle of the classroom. Later that day, as they were walking home from school, Joseph asked Alex why she had gotten so upset over the fact she was paired up with Eve. Alex explained if she was in a group with Eve, she'd end up doing all of the work, because people like Eve Meyers were nothing but lazy. At first, Joseph didn't quite understand what Alex meant when she said, *people like Eve Meyers*. Whatever it was she meant, he didn't think Eve Meyers was one of the people Alex was referring to. He had been in a group with her before, and she always contributed equally. When he tried to push the subject and get Alex to elaborate, he was told to stick it where the sun don't shine, thus ending the conversation.

As far as group activities went, Missus Liddy—their 4th grade teacher—made sure Alex and Eve Meyers were never paired together again. In fact, she went so far as to make certain the two were seated on complete opposite sides of the classroom at all times to avoid any more potential outbursts. Despite efforts to keep the two apart, the girls were constantly butting heads. Alex always found a way to get in Eve's face and cause trouble.

The day prior to Joseph and Alex's afternoon at the lake, the two young girls fond themselves engaged in a physical altercation in the schoolyard. This was provoked by Alex, of course. The two ended up rolling around in front of their classmates, all because Alex relentlessly insulted Eve Meyers' choice of clothing.

"Where'd you get them?" Alex had asked right before they came to blows. "Those rags are so filthy, The Salvation Army wouldn't even take them. You probably got them out of the dumpster. You're wearing Salvation Army rejects!"

She thought this was so funny and burst into an obnoxious fit of hilarity. No one else, Joseph included, thought this was particularly funny.

Eve attempted to take the high ground, and just walk away from the altercation. Alex was unwilling to let her rival leave that easily, and planned to embarrass her in front of all the spectators. She stuck her foot out, and tripped Eve, which sent her crashing to the floor.

"Did that hurt, nigger?" Alex's asked. Her words were now venomous. "I hope it did."

Eve, now pushed to her limits, lunged at Alex. She tackled the girl who had just tripped her, and took her down to the ground. The brawl escalated, and the two started slapping, biting and pulling at each other's hair. The fight did not last long before the teachers on lunch duty stepped in to break the two up. Verbal warnings for the two to stop proved futile, and the teachers had to go as far as to physically pry the two off of each other.

Following the separation, both girls were sent to the principal's office. When they were told to apologize to each other, Alex flat out refused. Instead, she demanded she be allowed to call her father, so he could pick her up, because she needed to go home to shower the nigger off of her. Her request was granted, although not for the reasons she gave, and Alex was sent home. She wouldn't be allowed to return for the remainder of the week.

The suspension was the extent of Alex's punishment. At home, there were no repercussions for her actions. Joseph went to her house following school on the day of the incident, and the two sat on the front porch, drinking iced tea, as if nothing had happened only a few hours earlier.

"Why did you make fun of her clothes?" Joseph asked. The words reluctantly came from his mouth, because he knew Alex was prone to go on the defensive when her actions towards Eve Meyers were questioned. Joseph still forced them, because he was trying to understand his best friend.

"Because they were old and disgusting!"

Upset that his best friend was insulting another person for the clothes they wore, Joseph pointed out that his clothes were usually old and worn out.

"Those are two completely different things," Alex explained. "You wear old clothes because you have to. Your dad doesn't give your mom the money she needs to buy you new clothes. Eve Meyers' parents can't afford to buy her clothes, because they are too lazy to go out and get jobs."

When asked how she knew this about Eve's parents, her response was that all black people were lazy, and would rather mooch off the government than earn their money the hard way. Joseph didn't think this was true. Mister Hershel, who was a very well-known face in their town, was black, and owned his own store. Joseph couldn't recollect a single time he had gone into Mister Hershel's establishment with his mother, and not seen the man working behind the counter or stocking the shelves. No matter what time of day, Mister Hershel was there and working hard. He was, by example, the exact opposite of what Alex was describing. Joseph wasn't going to bring this up, though. He knew it was better to just leave it be. When it came to certain arguments, Alex refused to see the opposite side.

Later that evening, Joseph asked his mother about what Alex had said about black people being lazy. He even brought up Mister Hershel as an example of how his best friend was wrong about her presumptions.

"There's your answer, Joey Beans," Emily Bateman told her son. "Mister Hershel works very hard to keep his store running. All of his customers—myself, included—are very pleased whenever we shop there."

"So why does Alex say that all black people are lazy?"

"There are just some things you won't understand until you are older, sweetie. Mister and Missus Meyers work hard, I'm sure. I just think Alex refuses to believe it. She has her reasons for being who she is, and you're not going to be able to change that. She's the only one who can change herself, and she might not try until she is old enough to realize she's wrong. Until then, as long as her beliefs don't bother you, just concentrate on being her friend. Alex needs a friend like you. You are a very caring boy, Joey Beans."

Joseph went to sleep that night determined to remain Alex's friend. He believed that as time went on and they got older, Alex would change and abandon her hateful beliefs. In the end, it would be Joseph who changed as they matured. He'd find himself consumed by the same feelings of resentment that he had once hoped his best friend would one day rid herself of. Although it would be an intricate part in Joseph's path to Death Row, the hatred he'd develop towards black people would only increase the bond between him and Alex.

Those years were still a while off for Joseph Bateman, and as he and Alex watched Eve Meyers from behind a bush he felt no hatred for his fellow classmate, especially for the color of her skin. Alex, however, had plenty of hate for her rival, and Joseph could see the wheels in her head working as she tried to concoct something cruel to do to Eve Meyers. It took a few moments, but that lightbulb inside Alex's head went off, and Joseph knew she had her plan. She got down on her hands and knees, and started sifting through the dirt.

"What are you doing?" Joseph whispered.

"If you wait a minute, you'll find out," Alex snapped back.

She continued digging through the dirt. When she came back up, Joseph saw she had a bunch of pebbles in her hand. He didn't need an explanation. He was well aware of their purpose.

"You can't throw rocks at her, Alex," he said.

"Oh, stop," Alex responded, brushing off Joseph's concern. "They're only pebbles. Besides, I'm not going to hit her with them."

Not hitting Eve Meyers may have been Alex's initial plan, but when the first four rocks Alex sent airborne failed to get her enemy's attention, she grew frustrated, and altered her game plan.

It was time to shoot to kill.

Alex had impeccable aim. Her throwing ability was on par with any of the boys who went to their school. During the summer, when they spent entire days together and had to keep themselves entertained, she and Joseph would choose random targets—always nonliving and always nondestructive, until now—and see who could hit it from the furthest distance. Alex was undefeated against Joseph. She had the tendency to hit her desired target nine times out of ten, no matter what the distance. It was no surprise that when she aimed for Eve Meyers, she hit her target directly in the shoulder on her first attempt.

They watched Eve as she looked around for whoever had struck her with the rock. When she saw no one, she called out, and told whoever had thrown the rock to come out from their hiding spot and show themselves. Joseph suspected she already had a strong guess as to who might have been the perpetrator. Her suspicions were correct, of

56

course, and that person was currently giggling beside Joseph. The whole thing was pure entertainment for Alex. Joseph felt otherwise. He thought it was cruel and that Alex should stop, but she wouldn't, and he knew it. She was having too much fun, and had every intention of extending her joyous experience. She launched another rock into the air when Eve Meyers' back was turned to them. This time, she nailed her target right between her shoulder blades.

"Wait until I find you," Eve shouted. "I'm going to kick your ass!"

As Joseph watched Eve Meyers searching for the coward in hiding, he thought it'd be for the best if she just run away. After all, it was exactly what he would do in Eve's position. It made the most sense to him. That wasn't Eve Meyers' style, though. When it came to fight or flight, she always fought.

"Just don't sit there," Alex instructed. "Throw one, Josephine."

Joseph didn't want to do that. He had no vendetta or ill-feelings towards Eve. She was never once mean to him, nor did she hold his association with Alex against him. He knew that if he didn't join in, however, Alex would tease him relentlessly. He also feared if he didn't do what she liked, then she might find him boring. Alex was Joseph's only friend, and if she moved on and found someone who enjoyed participating in her harassment of Eve Meyers, then he'd be left alone with no friends. He wanted nothing more than to keep Alex satisfied with their friendship, so he would join in on the rock throwing. It was okay, though. He had a solution to his dilemma.

He picked up a rock, and when Eve wasn't looking in their direction, he heaved it into the air. Since he had no real intentions of hitting her, he made sure the rock landed nowhere near her. He'd repeat the process with the next rock. Joseph normally had a terrible throw, and even worse aim, so when a rock came nowhere close to hitting its target, it was no surprise to Alex.

"C'mon, Josephine," Alex said. "You weren't even close. I don't even know why I try to include you. Just find me some rocks to throw."

Despite his better judgement, Joseph obeyed. What happened next was terrible, and over the course of the next few weeks, he tried to tell himself it wasn't his fault. He knew Alex had been the one to throw the rock, even though she knew full well she shouldn't have. Still, the pangs of guilt plagued him for his role.

He reached down into the dirt, just as Alex had instructed, and picked up another rock. Only this was no small pebble. It was an actual rock. One that could do a lot of damage if thrown at someone. Without giving it second thought, Joseph made the decision to put it down. Alex had different plans, though. Before he could toss it away, she snatched it from his hands, and got into position to throw it. Joseph immediately acted, and grabbed hold of his friend's wrist before she could begin her forward motion.

"You can't hit her with that," he told Alex. "That will really hurt her."

"You're such a worry-bee, Josephine. I'm not going to actually hit her with it. I'm just going to scare her."

Joseph didn't entirely believe Alex, but before he could object any further, she wrenched free of his grip, and lobbed the rock into the air. He followed the trajectory of the rock as it sored through the air. The moment it reached its peak and started its descent, he knew it was going to make contact. It fell in what seemed like slow motion, and Joseph wanted to yell to Eve to move out of the way. The rock's slow movement was only an illusion, though, and before he could say or do anything to save Eve, it came crashing down on her head.

Eve Meyers made no sound when the rock collided with her skull. She simply collapsed to the ground, where she remained, not moving. Joseph's heart sank in his chest as he stared at the still body in the middle of the street. The blow to the head had killed her. He knew it. They killed Eve Meyers.

The moment Eve hit the ground, Alex had Joseph by the arm, and was pulling at him. She was telling him to run, and running was exactly what Joseph wanted to do. Just not in the direction Alex was pulling him. He wanted to run to Eve to see if she was still alive. He wanted to run to a nearby house and get help. He wanted to run to the hospital, and tell them there was a young girl in need of immediate medical attention.

Joseph wanted to run towards doing the right thing, because at that age doing the right thing was still part of his nature. Alex's pull was stronger, though. Just as it would be throughout his entire life. Joseph allowed himself to be pulled away by Alex, and they left Eve Meyers lying in the middle of the street without even knowing if she was alive or dead.

June 21, 1979
The Empty Desk Chair

Despite the awful things that went on at night inside his home, Joseph always attempted to feign some resemblance of happiness every morning. He did this for his mother. Somehow, the woman who spent her night being beaten and raped by her drunk husband found joy in seeing her son's smiling face when she woke him to get ready for school. Whether she knew her son was putting on an act, Joseph never knew. All he knew was that Emily Bateman loved seeing her children with smiles on their faces, and that was reason enough for Joseph to continue his charade. The morning after he and Alex had left Eve Meyers in the middle of the street unconscious—or dead!—his mood was solemn.

His mother took notice of her son's out of character funereal mood, and asked him what was bothering him, but Joseph couldn't confide in his mother what had been eating away at him. The thought of seeing the disappointment on her face as he told her his role in what had happened to Eve Meyers didn't sit well with him. Emily Bateman already had a husband who failed to live up to expectations. She didn't need to know she might have a son who'd let her

60

down, as well. Instead, Joseph answered his mother's inquiry with a lie, and told her his mood was simply due to fatigue from a night of not sleeping well.

She might have known he was lying to her, but if she did, she didn't let on. Nevertheless, he felt shame at the possibility that his mother might be aware her firstborn had something eating away at him that he couldn't tell her about.

Emily Bateman told Joseph she would allow him to stay home if he was feeling too tired. He chose to decline her offer. He needed to go to school that day. There were answers he needed for the sake of his conscious, not to mention his sanity. He had to walk into his classroom, and see if Eve would be sitting there. He had to know if she was still alive.

He prayed as he walked down the hallway of his school that morning. Each step towards his classroom seemed to last an eternity. Joseph thought no walk could last longer than the one to class that morning—he'd learn sixteen years later that he was very wrong about that. With each footstep, his anxiety grew. He wanted nothing more than to see Eve sitting at her desk, completely fine with no more than a bump on her head.

Joseph's prayers went unanswered as he walked into the classroom. He looked across the room to Eve's desk, and saw it was vacant. He held onto one last shred of hope that maybe he had just arrived before her, but when all his classmates had filed into the room, and the bell to start the day sounded, he knew Eve was not running late. She wasn't coming to school. She was not okay.

Their teacher, Missus Libby, entered the classroom, closing the door behind her. The sound the door made as it settled into its frame was as explosive as a judge's gavel hammering down, and rendering a verdict of guilty upon Joseph for the murder of Eve Meyers.

"Last night, something tragic occurred," Missus Libby told her class once she quieted them down. "Evelyn Meyers was attacked while walking home."

Attentive silence morphed into a stunned silence as the class heard the news of what had happened to Eve. Some stared at their teacher in disbelief while a few turned towards the desk that had been occupied by their fellow classmate just the day before.

"She was found unconscious and taken to the hospital," Missus Libby continued. "She has suffered from some head trauma, but her doctors expect her to make a full recovery."

She's not dead! Joseph told himself as he heard the news being delivered. *She's not dead! She's not dead! She's... NOT... DEAD!!!!*

His celebration was tainted due to the guilt he still felt for his involvement in Eve's hospitalization. She wasn't dead, though, and her doctors expected her to come out of this ordeal with no lingering or permanent damage. Knowing Eve would be fine, Joseph thought he might be able to find a way to forgive himself for what he had done.

After school, Joseph went straight to Alex's, who was still serving her suspension for the schoolyard fight earlier that week. He told her how Eve ended up being found and brought to the hospital, and that she was going to be all right. Alex's response to this exciting news was indifference. Joseph looked at the unchanged expression on his best friend's face, and couldn't believe the lack of empathy or relief.

"Aren't you glad?" Joseph asked.

"About what?"

"That we didn't kill her!"

"Quiet down," Alex snapped. She punched Joseph in the arm for being so loud. "Someone is going to hear you yapping your gums that loud."

"Jeez… Sorry," Joseph said, lowering his voice. "Well, aren't you relieved?"

Alex responded with a simple shrugged that was as uncaring as her facial expression.

"Alex, you're glad she's not dead, right?" Joseph asked. He was almost pleading with her now. He was desperate to hear her admit she was feeling any sense of alleviation after learning she had not been responsible for ending another person's life.

"I couldn't care less what happened to that nigger, Josephine."

"I get that you don't like her, but even you have to admit—"

"I don't have to admit anything!" Alex snapped, cutting Joseph off. "What happens to Eve Meyers is probably the least important thing in the entire world to me. If you want to be relieved she's not going to die, go right ahead. Just don't expect me to give a shit!"

With her piece said, Alex turned, and headed towards her house.

"Where are you going?" Joseph asked.

"Back inside. I don't feel like hanging out today."

"Why do you hate black people so much, Alex?" Joseph asked as Alex was opening the screen door to reenter her home.

She let go of the screen door, and it closed with a loud bang. She did not turn around to acknowledge Joseph. She just stood there in silence. Joseph waited at the bottom of her porch steps for his answer. He didn't expect to get it, though. At least not a real one. Time and time again, he had tried to get an answer to this question from her. Each time, he had failed. All she would give him was the same weak excuse: she had her reasons, and she was entitled to them. She'd then make sure the subject was dropped.

This time, however, Alex's answer was different.

"Because they destroyed my family, Joseph."

Her response raised more questions than it provided answers, but Alex had no intention of elaborating. Before Joseph had the opportunity to say another word, she threw the screen door open, and entered her house. Thus stopping the conversation dead in its tracks. Years would go by before Joseph asked her what she had meant, and when he finally did, Alex would finally open up, and let Joseph in.

October 18, 1979
The Man with the Eyes

Joseph sat on the ground of the small parking lot outside an ice cream parlor, and waited for Alex, who was inside getting a root beer float. Nearly four months had passed since they left Eve Meyers unconscious in the middle of the street, and the two hadn't spoken of it since the afternoon that followed the cruel harassment gone terribly wrong. As far as Alex was concerned, all matters related to throwing rocks at Eve Meyers were closed, and not to ever be discussed again.

As for Eve, she made a full recovery following her attack and finished out the school year. She never pointed the finger or blamed Alex, but Joseph could tell that she knew. It was the way she'd stare at Alex during those last few weeks of school when she thought no one else was watching her. There was a newfound hatred in her eyes. Nothing ever came of it, though. No revenge was sought out on Eve Meyers' behalf, and that summer, her family moved, thus ending the rivalry between Alexandra Casings and Eve Meyers. Joseph wasn't sure if the attack had anything to do with the Meyers family's decision to leave Wayne's County, but whatever the reasons were, he knew that the fact that the two bitter rivalries were now states apart from one another was for the best.

That fall morning, Joseph had headed to Alex's house after breakfast. The two spent the day in her backyard, playing in the leaves. This was her father's idea, who used the idea of jumping in huge mountains of fall foliage as a means to get his daughter and her best friend to do most of the raking in the yard. After they were tired out from the day's activities, the two were rewarded for the work they weren't aware they were doing with a few dollars. Alex's father, knowing his daughter's love of root beer floats, told them to head down to the ice cream parlor, and pick up something sweet for themselves.

When they got there, Joseph told Alex to pick out whatever she wanted for him. He didn't care what she chose. He wasn't going to eat it, anyway. He was still in the midst of what would be his nearly nineteen year run without sweets. Whatever Alex chose for him, Joseph would just give to her, and she knew it, too, so she was likely to conveniently choose something she liked for Joseph.

Knowing that Alex had some imperative decisions to make regarding snacks, Joseph chose to sit outside while his best friend went inside to peruse her options of ice cream flavors. That was why Joseph was sitting in the parking lot when he was approached by a man looking for directions.

"Excuse me," the man said, startling Joseph, who didn't know he was no longer alone. "By any chance would you know how to get to Harris Brothers' Auto Repair?"

The first thought to pass through Joseph's mind was how strange it was that an adult was asking a child for directions to an auto repair shop. Car repairs were probably the last thing a child needed to concern themselves with, and would hardly know where one would go to receive them. Luckily for this man in need, Joseph did know the exact location of the establishment he was inquiring about. It was a place he avoided at all costs.

It was the shop where his father worked.

Having the information this stranger wanted, Joseph decided he would help out, and point him in the direction of the repair shop. He stood, and when he turned to address the man, his attention was immediately drawn to the man's eyes. Joseph looked into them, and found himself unable to speak. Surely, this person had other features to his face, but Joseph saw none of them. All he saw were the eyes.

The eyes…

They transcended normalcy. Joseph tried to look away. He wanted to look away. He knew if he stared any longer at those eyes, he'd see deeper into them, and whatever was there was something he was too afraid to face.

The trance Joseph was caught up in was finally broken when the stranger spoke again, and repeated his original inquiry. Joseph wanted to tell him the directions as quickly as he could. He wanted to get this guy away from him as soon as possible, so he didn't have to look into those eyes any longer. He opened his mouth in an attempt to speak; articulation was suddenly a lost art.

"Is everything okay?" the man asked.

Joseph forced himself to speak, and when he finally got words past his lips, he told the man that he didn't know how to get to the establishment he was looking for. He also managed to squeeze an apology out, but that was it. He was told not to worry about it. The man thanked Joseph, and walked back to his car. It never once dawned on Joseph as he watched the man with strange eyes get into his car that he didn't bother to go inside the ice cream parlor to ask an adult for directions.

"I got you vanilla/chocolate swirl," Alex said, as she walked out of the ice cream parlor.

Alex stood next to Joseph, but he didn't acknowledge her. He just watched as the car pulled out of the parking lot, and headed down the long block. Through his physical vision, Joseph saw the car signal, and make the left turn, but all his mind could fixate on were those eyes.

It wouldn't be the last time Joseph Bateman would look into them before he died.

February 12, 1980
Alex's President's Day Report

Looking back at it all those years later, as he waited for death—42 minutes, 18 seconds, and counting—Joseph was able to appreciate the statement Alex was trying to make with her President's Day report. At eleven years of age, however, he couldn't understand why his best friend would go out of her way to do something that would obviously get her in trouble.

The report was simple enough: Choose either President George Washington or President Abraham Lincoln, and write up a report. After a small lesson on both presidents from their teacher, Joseph chose Abraham Lincoln. From freeing an entire race from the shackles of slavery to uniting a torn country, Joseph found the things Lincoln did during his presidency interesting, and desired to learn more about the man who history viewed as one of the United States' greatest leaders.

Sadly, later on in life, as he allowed influences to steer him down the wrong path and his beliefs became corrupted, Joseph Bateman's admiration for the sixteenth president of the United States would wither away, and be replaced with disgust.

Alex had also chosen Lincoln as the subject of her report. Joseph thought the two of them could research the topic of their reports together at their local library, but when he extended the invitation to Alex, she declined. When asked why, the explanation she gave Joseph was that she knew everything she needed to know about Abraham Lincoln to write her report.

Without Alex by his side as company, Joseph spent his afternoons at the library, where he would do research for his report. From Lincoln's childhood to his assassination, Joseph made sure to cover all the key moments of President Lincoln's life that helped mold and define his legacy. After days of compiling information, Joseph wrote his paper. The end product was something of which he felt extremely proud.

Alex did not share in his excitement.

They looked at each other's reports that morning before school began. Printed neatly on the front cover of Alex's report was the title: *THE TRUTH ABOUT ABRAHAM LINCOLN.* Joseph opened it, and couldn't believe what he was seeing. This had to be one of her twisted jokes. The real report was in her bag, and she had put together a dummy one to get a reaction out of him.

"Funny, Alex," he said; handing back the paper. "Now where's your actual report?"

"What are you talking about, Josephine?" she asked. "This *is* my actual report."

Joseph waited for a smile to stretch across her face, and for her to admit it was in fact a joke. Her face remained humorless, though, and Joseph realized that she was serious. What he was holding in his hands was the actual report Alex intended to hand in to their teacher at the end of third period History.

"Alex, you can't hand this in," Joseph said. He spoke in a hushed tone, and handed back the report so quickly, it was as if he realized he was holding key evidence in a murder investigation.

"Why can't I?"

"Because, you'll get in trouble!"

"For what? Telling the truth? For putting information in my report that they refuse to teach us? If I'm going to get in trouble for that, then good. I'd rather get in trouble for telling the truth than writing down every lie they want to hear, like you have."

"What are you talking about?"

"This!" Alex exclaimed, waving Joseph's report in front of his face. "You're actually proud to be handing this in?"

"Yes. Why wouldn't I be? I put a lot of work into that."

"And the end result is the same as everyone else's: the bullshit fairytale that history has taught us is the legacy of Abraham Lincoln. If anyone shouldn't be turning in their report, it's you! Not me!"

Joseph told Alex to stop being an ass, and snatched his report from her hands.

"I'm being serious, Joseph. You're going to hand that report in, even though it is full of lies. You're a mindless drone, just like everyone else. You've written, word for word, exactly what the teachers want to read. Do you know why you've done that?"

"Why?" Joseph asked.

"Because you're desperate for acceptance. You try so hard to do what others believe to be the right thing, and look where that's gotten you. Not a single person in this shithole has ever given you an ounce of respect. Not even our teachers respect you. They're just putting on a show, because it's part of their job."

"I don't believe that's true," Joseph argued.

"Of course you don't. Why would you want to face the truth? You'd have to admit you're being a phony, and that you're trying to be who everyone else thinks you should be. I hate to be the one to tell you this, Josephine, but all those people you've been trying to gain acceptance from are the same people who make fun of you every single day. They're the people who will continue to make fun of you no matter what you do to try and please them. I like you for you, but if you hand that report of lies in just to please a few teachers, I'm probably going to lose some respect for you."

With what was on her mind now spoken, Alex turned away, and headed towards her first period class. Joseph did the same, and as he sat through his first two morning classes, he thought about his best friend's little speech, especially the latter part of it.

Alex wasn't wrong when she said she was the only one there for him. While his peers constantly made fun of him, she stood by his side. She was bossy, no doubt, and thickheaded, for sure, but Joseph knew she loved him, and he loved her right back. The thought of losing her respect weighed heavily on him leading into history that morning.

As third period History ended, their teacher, Mister Mullein, instructed the class to leave their reports on his desk as they exited. Joseph stood at the back of the line, and watched his classmates drop their reports onto Mister Mullein's desk. Alex did the same, and Joseph still could not believe she was intentionally submitting work that would undoubtedly land her in trouble. As she exited the classroom, she looked over her shoulder at Joseph, and shook her head in disappointment as she saw him approaching the desk with his report in hand.

Joseph approached the desk to leave the report that only a few hours ago he had been so proud of creating, but before he could drop it on the desk, he hesitated. He looked up, and saw Mister Mullein preoccupied with erasing the chalkboard. He then looked outside the class, and saw Alex standing by the door, waiting for him. He felt himself being pulled in both directions, and, once again, Alex's pull ended up being stronger. Without leaving his report with his teacher, as instructed, Joseph walked out of the classroom with it in his hands.

Alex saw the report still in Joseph's hand as he joined her in the hallway. A smile stretched across her face, and she embraced him with a hug.

"I'm proud of you, Josephine!" she said. "I knew you were better than all those other sheep."

"Thanks," Joseph responded.

Despite knowing that what he had done was wrong, there was a sense of joy he felt as Alex hugged him. It was a feeling he knew only she could give him, and no form of acceptance from his teachers would ever be able to replace it. Still, it didn't stop the shame he felt for not leaving the report. Even then, as Alex had her arms wrapped around him, he knew his decision was made for all the wrong reasons.

"I have to go to the bathroom," Joseph said following his hug with Alex. "I'll see you at lunch."

"Do you want me to wait?"

"No. That's okay. I'm going to be a few minutes."

"Yuck! Well I'll see you later, then. I hope everything comes out okay!" she joked.

Alex walked to her next class, and Joseph headed into the bathroom. He waited there for a few minutes to be sure Alex was gone. He then headed back across the hall to Mister Mullein's classroom.

"Joseph," Mister Mullein said as Joseph entered the room. "How can I help you?"

"I just forgot to hand in my report," Joseph responded, handing his History teacher the report.

"I noticed I was short one. I was just about to go through them to see who I was missing. You saved me the hassle."

"Well I hope you enjoy it. I have to get to class."

As Joseph walked to his next class, he thought about why he had changed his mind, and handed in his report, after all. He knew Alex would accuse him of doing it because he yearned for acceptance from anywhere he could take it. That wasn't the case, though, and had zero bearing on his decision. There were other factors he needed to consider, more important ones that Alex couldn't possibly understand, because there were things that went on in Joseph's life that he tried to keep hidden from his best friend.

When the report was discovered missing, there would be a phone call made to Joseph's home to see why the assignment had failed to be handed it. He knew the odds were slim to none, but if word of that phone call reached the ears of Hank Bateman, he'd have yet another excuse to beat the crap out of his wife. After he had been the reason for his mother's thrashing on his seventh birthday, Joseph refused to ever give Hank Bateman more fuel for his fire.

He knew Alex would be displeased with him when she found out she had been deceived. The day would come when their assignment was handed back, and she would see Mister Mullein place a graded copy of Joseph's report on his desk. It wouldn't take much figuring out to realize what he had done when he excused himself to go to the bathroom that day after class. Joseph would just have to accept whatever form of punishment Alex decided to dish out for his trickery, and wait until her fury passed.

The punishment he anticipated never came, though. Alex never learned of her best friend's deceit, because the day their Presidents report was handed back, she was serving out a suspension for what she had written in hers. It was a suspension that came as little surprise to Joseph. He could barely imagine Mister Mullein's shock when he opened one of his student's reports, and saw impeccably handwritten in big bold letters across the first page:

BOOTH

ABRAHAM LINCOLN WAS NOTHING MORE THAN A NIGGER LOVER!

Followed on the next page by:

HE ALSO LET SOLDIERS SLEEP IN HIS BED, SO HE COULD SUCK THEIR COCKS!

May 31, 1981
Hank Bateman's Guest

The first time it happened, Joseph didn't think it was real. He believed he was caught up in the midst of some loathsome nightmare. It had to be the only explanation for what was happening. It was no dream, though, and what he heard coming from the opposite side of his bedroom wall wasn't a manifestation of his own fears. It was the sounds of a vile reality. It was Hank Bateman proving that there was no low to his inhumanity.

The familiar sounds of the front door crashing open echoed throughout the Bateman household. There was the usual movement from downstairs, and Hank Bateman could be heard mumbling drunken slurs to himself. Shortly after came the sound of ascending footsteps on the stairs. This was nothing new. It was all routine by now, and Joseph knew what to expect next. However, on the night of May 31, 1981, the routine was broken, and Emily Bateman spoke when her husband entered their bedroom.

"Hank, what's going on?" Joseph heard his mother say through the thin walls.

His heartrate began to quicken at the sound of his mother's voice. Speaking up and questioning Hank

Bateman while he was in his nightly state was the worst thing to do, and Emily Bateman was well aware of that. For her to do so must have meant that she was seriously concerned over what her husband might have in store for her. Joseph heard her rise from where she sat on the bed, and attempt to speak, yet again, but her words ceased midsentence, and were replaced with a painful grunt. Joseph knew this was due to a swift jab to her stomach, which had knocked the wind out of her.

"Get on the bed, and shut the fuck up," Hank Bateman yelled. "Take your fucking clothes off, too."

Emily obeyed her husband. Next came the familiar sound of their headboard hitting up against the wall. As his mother's rape progressed, Joseph started to hear a foreign sound coming from the opposite side of his wall. After years of hearing his mother being violated in the next room, Joseph became well acclimated with the various sounds his drunken father made as he neared orgasm. He was currently hearing the moans of a man nearing that point, but they did not belong to Hank Bateman.

They belonged to someone else, entirely.

This explained why Emily Bateman dared to speak up when she knew it was best not to. She must have known what was in store for her when a stranger entered her bedroom with her husband. She needed to make an attempt to preserve the single ounce of dignity she had left. Her pleas had proved futile, and now she was being forced by her husband to have sex with a complete stranger.

As the tempo of the headboard hitting the wall increased in time with the creaking of the floorboards, so did the sounds of this stranger's climax. It all ended with a long groan, which was followed by silence.

There was no exchange of words from the opposite side of Joseph's wall. There was just the faint sound of a belt being fastened, followed by the door to the master bedroom being opened and then closed. As Joseph heard the sound of descending footsteps on the stairs, he wanted to leap from his bed, and push the man who had just raped his mother down the stairs. He'd watch as he tumbled down each hard wooden step, and would hope that the landing broke this stranger's neck. He did no such thing, however. Joseph just lay there as the man who had just forced himself upon his mother left the house, and got away with what he had just done, scot-free. A few minutes later, the familiar sounds of Hank Bateman's orgasm filled the house.

After the raping and beating she was so familiar with had ended, Emily cried as she lay next to the unconscious man who tortured her every night. That man who had now allowed another man to come in and add to the torment Emily Bateman had to endure.

Joseph couldn't understand how his mother could allow it to continue. She could easily end the life of the soulless bastard who lay next to her in a drunken slumber. Yet she didn't, and each night she allowed herself to be victimized by her husband's inhumanity. Joseph wanted to grab a knife from the kitchen and hand it to her. He wanted to tell her it would be okay, and if she still couldn't be the one to do it, he would happily kill Hank Bateman on her behalf.

Unfortunately, just like the idea of springing from his bedroom and throwing a man down a flight of stairs, Joseph's desires to intervene on his mother's behalf remained fantasy.

They wouldn't for long, though.

That night wouldn't be the last time Hank Bateman brought a stranger home to have sex with his wife. That upcoming September, Joseph would finally decide he'd had enough, and would come to his mother's defense. He would finally stand up to his father, and the outcome of his attempt at heroism would cause Joseph Bateman long-lasting trauma.

July 4, 1981
A Man-to-man with Bill Casings

Hank Bateman didn't have friends—unless you counted the bottle. He just had people who hung around him when he was drunk so they could gamble with him and take his money.

On top of excessively binging nightly on alcohol, one of Hank Bateman's biggest vices was gambling. When sober, he was smart and calculating, but throughout the night, as the drinks flowed steadily, he'd get stupid. He'd make absurd bets in hands of poker that he had no right making, and when his funds ran out, he'd always demand at least one more hand to try to earn his money back. This always ended up the same way: He'd owe someone more money than he had.

It was the second time Hank Bateman brought someone home with him that Joseph learned his mother was being used as a way of clearing gambling debts. This specific stranger had been walked to the door once he was finished, and Joseph heard his father asking the man if they were even. The man, who had just had sex with another man's wife, said they were. That was until the next time they played cards together, and Hank got himself in over his head. The comment actually brought on a fit of laughter from the two, something seldom heard coming from Hank Bateman.

That was during the last week of June. It then continued on July third, and as July came to a close, the Bateman household would have nightly visitors on a semi-regularly basis. That was until Joseph finally decided enough was enough, and something needed to be done to end it.

That night wouldn't come until mid-September, though. As for the Fourth of July of that year, Joseph's plans were to watch the fireworks at the lake with Alex. They were plans he intended on canceling. Liz was over a friend's house for the night—something she did quite often, even on school nights—and Joseph didn't want his mother home to spend the holiday by herself. That was at least the excuse he was going to attempt to tell his mother. She saw right through his obvious lie, and insisted he go out and have some fun with his best friend. He tried to argue with her on the matter, but she wouldn't hear any of it.

He finally succumbed to his mother's demands, and kept his plans with Alex. Later that evening, as he walked to the Casings' house, he realized it wouldn't have mattered if he stayed home or not. Whether Hank Bateman came home that night with a guest or not, there would've been nothing Joseph could do about it. He had yet to discover he had the guts to stand up to his father. All it would end up being was another night he heard his mother being raped.

When he got to Alex's, she was waiting outside on the porch for him.

"Took you long enough," was her greeting as she sprung out of her seat and met Joseph in the middle of her front yard.

"Sorry, I lost track of time."

"Yeah, yeah. Just don't let it happen again," she jested. "So you going to jump from the tree tonight?"

Before Joseph could offer up an answer, Alex answered *no* for him in a mocking voice. They set off for their firework filled evening at the lake, but before they stepped off the property, Alex's father called from the front porch to his daughter.

"I'd like a moment to speak to Joseph," Bill Casings said.

"Dad, what are you doing?" Alex asked with a mixture of annoyance and embarrassment.

"This will only be a few moments, dear. Now go on ahead, sweetie. Joseph will catch up with you in a minute."

Joseph looked at Alex. It was obvious by the look on his face that he was nervous. What made it worse was that he could see by the expression on her face that she felt the same. Alex's father was always kind to Joseph, and made his daughter's best friend feel welcomed in his home. Never had he ever wanted to have a conversation with Joseph before. Especially just the two of them. The idea of a man-to-man with Bill Casings was scary, but Joseph had no options.

"Joseph," Bill Casings called out from the porch, no longer interested in waiting. "A moment of your time, please."

"I'll wait for you at the end of the block," Alex said in a low voice, and walked away as fast as her feet would allow. Joseph turned towards the porch and Bill Casings. He collected himself, and walked towards the Casings' house to face whatever awaited him.

"Take a seat, son," Bill Casings said.

Joseph did as told. Alex's father took the seat next to him. He said nothing to Joseph, at first. He just stared ahead at the western sky, contemplating his words.

"You and my Alexandra have been friends for a very long time, haven't you?" he finally said.

"Yes, sir," Joseph answered.

"And I'm glad you two have been able to stay friends for so long—I know my Alexandra is one hell of a firecracker, at times—but now you two are at the age where your bodies are starting to go through changes..."

Bill Casings was right about that. Joseph had started growing hair in places such as his legs, armpits and pubic region. A few stray hairs had even sprouted on his chin. Along with the hair came the infamous pubescent cracking of his voice from time to time, something Alex had never failed to pick up on, and jest about at his expense.

The more noticeable changes were with Alex, though.

Although her personality still screamed that she fit in more with the boys than the girls, her body began to take on womanly qualities. She hadn't shied away from her changes either. As her breasts began to develop and her hips became shapelier, Alex's began to wear more form-fitting clothing. She began to care more about how her hair looked, and Joseph even saw her experimenting with makeup on a few occasions.

"Well, anyway," Bill Casings finally continued after a few awkward moments. "I'm having this talk with you, because, believe it or not, I was once a boy of your age, and I went through the same exact changes as you. I'm well aware of certain urges boys get around this age."

At that moment Joseph believed he knew what the point of this conversation was. It was a father protecting his little girl.

"Oh... well, Mister Casings..." Joseph said. "I... I don't really know what to say..."

"You don't need to say anything, Joseph. This isn't about what you probably think it is."

"Then what is it about?"

Bill Casings took a moment before speaking to choose his words carefully.

"Don't get me wrong," he finally said. "You two are way too young to be doing... that. What I want to talk to you about is the kind of man you are, and the kind of man you will become. You see, two people who spend as much time together as you and Alex do tend to develop feelings that go beyond friendship. I just need to be sure my baby girl is going to be okay, should that occur."

Joseph wanted to stop Bill Casings right there, and tell him he had absolutely nothing to worry about. The idea of Joseph and Alex becoming anything more than just friends was completely preposterous—looking back, all those years later, Joseph found humor in how truly naïve he was at that age.

"Alex is my best friend, Mister Casings..." Joseph started to explain, but was cut off before he could continue.

"I know she is, Joseph, and you have been a great friend to my Alexandra. What I am trying to say is that these upcoming years are going to be some pretty imperative ones, and they will mold you, and help define who you are as a person."

He stopped again to collect his thoughts. Whatever it is he had to say to Joseph, Bill Casings had to choose his thoughts delicately before turning them into words.

"Listen, Joseph," Alex's father continued; shifting in his seat. Based off how visibly uncomfortable he had become, Joseph wondered if Bill Casings was regretting his decision to have this conversation. "The thing is... sometimes we can't help but to take after our parents. We just inherit certain qualities from them. Now, your mother is a sweetheart. Honestly, she's such a kind-hearted woman, and it would be amazing if she passed on some of her traits to you. Your father, though..."

"I'm not like him," Joseph interrupted. There was nothing more he needed to hear. Bill Casings' point was getting across loud and clear. "I am nothing like that man."

Bill Casings was silent for a few moments. He just sat in his chair and nodded. It seemed as if Joseph's response was sufficient enough for him. Perhaps he heard the hatred in Joseph's voice as he spoke of the man he was forced to recognize as his kin. Perhaps Bill Casings just wanted the conversation to be over. Whatever it was, the case was now closed.

"Well," he said, standing up, and adjusting his jeans. "I just wanted to clear the air. I did not mean to offend you, Joseph. I think you are a good kid. It's just that your dad has a certain reputation around town, and I only want what is best for my Alexandra. No hard feelings?"

"No, Mister Casings. There are no hard feelings."

The two shook hands, and Bill Casings sent Joseph on his way, telling him to enjoy the fireworks. As he made his way down the block to meet up with Alex, Joseph found himself becoming enraged. His anger wasn't directed at Bill Casings, or the fact that he had asked to speak with Joseph. What infuriated Joseph was the realization that he would forever be linked to Hank Bateman. No matter what, he could not escape the fact that he was that monster's son. That notion sickened him, and all hope of truly enjoying the night evaporated into the hot summer air.

Thirteen years later, as he waited patiently for his death, Joseph was forced to admit that he was, in fact, his father's son. By the day of his execution, the only emotion Joseph Bateman was capable of feeling was hatred. It was a quality he had no doubt he inherited from his father.

September 17, 1981
The Altercation

Every time Joseph Bateman heard his mother being raped and beaten by his father, he wanted to intervene. He envisioned countless scenarios in which he saved her. In the end, however, he never seemed to find the courage to turn fantasy into reality. The fear of his father, and the consequences for him and his mother, were like heavy chains that kept him pinned down to his bed. That would soon change, however, once Hank Bateman started soliciting his wife to complete strangers in order to clear his gambling debts. Each time he heard a stranger having sex with his mother, one of those heavy chains would break. On September 17, 1981, the final chain broke and Joseph finally acted.

He heard the usual sounds that emanated from the room next to his. At first, he tried to ignore it, but couldn't. He then got out of bed and started pacing the room. That, too, did no good. Then, as the sounds of a complete stranger nearing orgasm rang throughout the house, Joseph decided enough was enough. Without giving the consequences any further thought, he swung his door open and headed into his parents' bedroom.

Joseph turned his mind off and let the adrenaline take control. He swung the door to his parents' bedroom open with such force that it collided with the wall, and knocked a hole in the sheetrock. He hadn't noticed, though. He was too determined and fixated on one thing to be aware of anything else going on around him. It was something that would play a vital factor in the next few moments.

He made a beeline right towards the bed, and swung with all his might at the stranger in the bed with his mother. Joseph wasn't a strong person, by any means. When he and Alex play wrestled, she was able to pin him down with little effort. However, the force of this punch knocked the stranger off of his mother and headfirst into the wall, where he rolled off the bed and onto the floor.

The person raping Emily Bateman had no idea what was happening, but Hank Bateman took notice right away. Joseph had been so focused on the man whose face he had just buried his fist in that he completely forgot about his drunk father. He was staring down at the scumbag he had just decked when he felt what could have only been a bowling ball smash into his head. What it turned out to be was his father's fist.

Joseph fell forward, and smashed his head on the bedframe. He then lost the ability to remain standing, and collapsed to the floor. He saw double for a few moments, and when his vision finally adjusted itself, he was looking at the man he had just attacked frantically gathering up his clothes from the floor. Once all of his belongings were collected, the stranger took off, not even bothering to dress until he was a safe distance from the Bateman house. Joseph attempted to get up off the floor when he felt his father's boot smash into his ribs.

"Hank, stop!" Emily Bateman begged. "Please don't hurt him."

"Shut the fuck up, you dumb cunt!" Hank Bateman screamed at his wife, followed by a backhand. "I'll deal with you in a moment."

He turned his attention back to his son. He lifted Joseph off the floor and pushed him into the wall. Like the door hitting the wall when Joseph entered the room, the violent force of his skull hitting the wall disintegrated the sheetrock. He was then thrown down onto the bed, where he landed next to his naked and hysterical mother. Hank Bateman grabbed Joseph by the hair, and pulled him up so the two were face-to-face. They were now so close, Joseph could smell the booze on his father's breath.

"You want to play hero, boy? Let's see what that gets you." Hank Bateman punched his son in the stomach. Joseph instinctively went to keel over from the blow, but his father pulled him up by his hair, and straightened him out. "Or maybe you were jealous somebody was fucking your mama. You know... I bet that's it. You were always a pansy-ass mama's boy. I bet it's because you want to fuck your own mama. Well tonight's your lucky night, boy." He turned his attention back to his wife. "Get on your hands and knees, you whore."

"Hank, don't do this," Emily Bateman begged, yet again. "Please."

This was the most resistance Joseph had ever heard from his mother, and it wasn't something Hank Bateman liked very much. He grabbed a bottle of whiskey that was on the nightstand, gripped it by the neck, and smashed it against the edge of a dresser. Glass exploded everywhere, and whiskey stained the wood dresser and floor. Hank waved the sharp remanence of the bottle in his wife's face.

"Either you do it, or I'm going to end your pathetic life right here. Then I'm going to kill him."

Whether Emily Bateman thought her husband was bluffing or not, she didn't dare find out. She knew too well he was capable of anything when the booze and rage were flowing freely through his bloodstream. Joseph knew it wasn't the threat against her life that caused her to obey Hank's demands. It was the fact that he threatened to kill her son. Whether Hank Bateman knew it or not, Emily's Achilles Heel was her children, and she would do anything to prevent harm being done to them. With shame on her face, she gave into her husband's demands, and proceeded to get on her hands and knees in front of her own son.

Hank Bateman then turned his attention to his son.

"Take you clothes off," he told Joseph. "Your dreams are about to come true, boy."

When Joseph didn't move, Hank Bateman delivered a hard backhand. When he was once again ordered to remove his clothes, Joseph again defiantly refused. That's when Hank Bateman turned his attention and the broken glass bottle back to his wife.

"You either take your goddamn clothes off, or your bitch mama is going to get hers," he threatened.

He pushed the bottle against Emily Bateman's neck. When the sharp glass pressing into his mother's skin drew a trickle of blood, Joseph caved to his father's demand. Looking down at the mattress as he slid his basketball shorts and underwear off, he regretted his decision to finally take action against his father. Somehow, in some twisted manner, doing nothing was the better option, because he knew full well what came next.

He was forced to get on his knees. He tried not to look at his mother's naked body as she was exposed to him in the most degrading fashion. He could see through his peripheral that her entire body was trembling, and he could hear her sobs as she wept openly.

"Go ahead... touch her," Hank Bateman instructed. "I know you've always wanted to get your hands on her."

"Please, stop."

It had been Emily Bateman who had pleaded with her husband in an attempt to stop his madness before it escalated, and reached the point of no return. Now it was Joseph who was asking his father for it to stop.

"What was that?" Hank Bateman asked his son.

"Please... STOP!!" Joseph repeated.

Hank Bateman responded to his son's pleas with a hard closed fist to the temple of his wife. She collapsed into her pillow, where she began to cry even harder.

"Bitch! Stop that fucking crying, now!" Hank Bateman demanded.

Emily Bateman obeyed. She bit down hard on her pillow, which helped a little by reducing her wails to low muffled moans.

"Last chance, boy," Hank Bateman continued. "Take her, you little sicko. Like I'm sure you've always wanted to."

Still, Joseph remained stubborn. When he still didn't move, Hank Bateman grew impatient of his son's defiance. He grabbed his wife by the hair, and pulled her up towards him. He took the broken bottle, and held it mere centimeters from her eye. Joseph knew right then if he didn't obey, his mother would have that broken glass jammed through her eyeball, and right into her brain.

"OKAY... STOP!" Joseph yelled before his father could inflict permanent damage. "I'll listen. Please, don't hurt her."

"How heroic," Hank Bateman said, releasing his wife from his grip. "You listen from here on out, or next time, you won't be able to save her. You understand?"

Joseph did, and he knew his father wasn't bluffing. He would kill his wife, and then his son without an ounce of remorse. Joseph wouldn't allow that to happen. Refusing to look at his mother, naked and terrified, he lowered his hands slowly until he felt the warmth of her skin as his fingertips touched the small of her back.

"Don't be shy, boy," Hank Bateman said. "I know you've been thinking this moment for years. Let your hands roam." When Joseph didn't move—more due to the fact that he was now petrified rather than defiant—Hank Bateman screamed, "NOW!"

Joseph began to slide his hands up his mother's back, but that wasn't good enough for Hank Bateman.

"No," he told Joseph. "The other way. I want you to really get the full experience."

Joseph reversed the direction of his hands, and allowed them to roam down his mother's bony back until it turned into the meaty flesh of her buttocks. What happened next would haunt him for the rest of his life.

At thirteen years old, boys are just getting to know and understand their bodies. Joseph was just like any other child his age in that regard, and like any child his age, he only understood pieces of a bigger picture. To Joseph Bateman, all he knew was if a boy got an erection it meant he was turned on, or horny, as the other boys in his grade liked to refer to it as. He had no idea that sometimes the male reproductive organ could become stimulated whether or not the person wanted to engage in a sexual act. He wasn't educated yet on the body's instinctual desire to reproduce. So when he felt his penis beginning to get hard, all he could feel was shame.

Joseph knew what came next. All the boys in school talked about it at their age. He never got to that step, though. What he got was punched in the face by his father, and thrown from the bed into the wall. His legs gave out, and fell to the floor. The blood that had made his penis stiff drained from it, and turned it into a limp noodle.

"You sick little fuck," Hank Bateman screamed. He palmed his son's forehead and pushed it into the wall.

Joseph felt his brain shake inside his head as it hit the support beam in the wall. "What kind of twisted little shit gets hard at the opportunity to fuck his own mama? You're a pathetic disgrace."

Hank Bateman mounted the bed he shared with his wife. The same bed he allowed other men to in to violate her. There were no sounds of struggle. All Joseph heard were the familiar sounds of the headboard smashing into the wall and the creaking of the floorboards. He wanted to get to his feet and run out of the room. He wanted to leave that house and never return. He wanted to be rid of Hank Bateman forever. He couldn't move, though. He was too shaken up and traumatized—physically and emotionally— by everything that had just happened.

"Joseph, don't look," his mother pleaded while she was being raped. "Don't look, Joseph."

She didn't have to worry about him looking. Joseph crouched up in a naked ball against the wall and stared down at his hands. He repeated the same word, over and over, in his head.

Useless... Useless...

December 18, 1981

The Accident

Hank Bateman's Ford pickup truck drove along the snowy Pennsylvania back roads. Packed inside was the entire Bateman family. To Joseph's recollection, it was the only time his entire family—Hank, Emily, Liz, and Joseph—had ever been in a car together. They were on their way home from Liz's winter concert at school. Attending a school function was another thing the Bateman family never did together. The night of December eighteenth was apparently the exception.

Two months had passed since the altercation between father and son, and it was actually the first time Joseph had seen his father since the night he was nearly forced upon his own mother. Hank Bateman rarely came home anymore, but on the night that he did, he was alone. He decided to no longer use his wife as a means to settle his gambling debts. Either that, or word had traveled how one of the men who went back to the Bateman house at night had been attacked, and there was no longer interest amongst the scum with whom Joseph's father associated.

Not only did she no longer have to endure being raped by complete strangers, but Emily Bateman no longer felt the wrath of her own husband at night. On the rare occasions that Hank Bateman returned home, it would be at an hour far earlier than his family was accustomed to, and he would never make his way up the stairs to his bedroom, where his wife had been obediently waiting, like always. Instead, Joseph would hear his father kick his work boots off, which would soon be followed by the sounds of snores coming from the downstairs living room.

Joseph began to wonder, as the nightly chaos he had lived with his entire life suddenly ceased, if his father felt guilt for all that had happened. Every man has a breaking point, and perhaps, for Hank Bateman, that point came the night he almost forced his son to engage in sexual intercourse with his own mother.

Perhaps that was the reason Hank Bateman was there the night of Liz Bateman's winter concert. To try to make amends for the evil he brought upon his family, or as an attempt to save any small bit of humanity he might have still had within him.

Joseph never found out if his theory was true. After that night, he scarcely spoke of his father, especially with his mother, who possibly would have had the answers. Whatever the reasons were, they did not matter, in the end. Joseph had no interest in Hank Bateman's possible repentance, and there was nothing that would have changed the decision he had made on that cold December night of 1981.

The evening, Joseph came home from school to his nice clothes laid out for him. His initial thought was that someone they had known had died. Wakes and memorial services were the only time the Bateman kids ever had to wear their nice clothes. There was no service, though. Instead, Joseph was told they'd be going to see Liz sing in her grade's winter concert. When Joseph heard the word *they*, he assumed his mother had meant just the two of them. There were no appropriate combinations of adjectives that could properly put into words the shock Joseph felt when he walked down the stairs at six that evening, and saw his father sitting at the kitchen table.

Hank Bateman looked so out of place as he waited for his family to finish getting ready. He was wearing a faded pair of jeans and a wrinkled button-down. He sipped clear liquid from a glass that Joseph assumed was vodka, but ended up only being water. Joseph couldn't envision a single scenario where his mother would have been able to convince her husband to remove himself from a night of drinking. Of all the potential reasons, spending time with his family would have been at the bottom of the list of arguments that would've gotten Hank Bateman out of the bar for the night. Yet there he was, waiting to see his daughter perform in her winter concert.

Throughout the evening, Hank did not say a single word. He just sat there, silently, clapping when he was supposed to, and even stood at the end of the concert to participate in the standing ovation.

"Honey, that was an amazing concert. You sounded so wonderful," Emily Bateman told her daughter as they drove home following the junction. "We are so proud of you! Aren't we Hank?"

The low grunt that came from the driver's side of the vehicle was meant to be taken as a yes.

"Did you enjoy yourself?"

"Yeah, it was fun," Liz answered.

"Good! I'm glad."

Joseph was also happy for his sister. Growing up, she was exposed to the same wickedness in their home as he was, yet she was still able to find some semblance of happiness in her life. She had a group of friends, and always found reasons to smile, something her brother was unable to do. Joseph guessed Liz took after their mother in that way.

Joseph was thinking about his sister when the car started losing control. At first, he hadn't noticed the truck starting to slide, but then his mother's scream brought him to reality. When he became aware of what was happening, he immediately realized it was too late.

When the day started, rain was the only thing falling from the sky. However, as temperatures began to plummet, rain transitioned into freezing rain, which eventually became snow. It was the perfect mixture for an automobile disaster. The Pennsylvania back roads they drove home on were winding, and Hank Bateman must've taken one of the sharper turns too fast. The car began to skid, and because of the poor conditions of the road, the tires of the pickup could not find the needed traction to help regain control. Despite all efforts, the car continued to slide off the road.

Along with being winding, the back roads they traveled were extremely hilly. There were no barricades that separated the edge of the road from the side of one of these steep hills, and people tried to avoid the back roads at all costs whenever the weather took a turn for the worse. They knew the chances of losing control, and toppling over the side of one of the large hills.

Hank Bateman's pickup went front end first off the side of the road. It smashed into some large rocks and came to an abrupt stop. Momentum kept the rear of the pickup going, though, and gravity did the rest. The bed of the truck was thrown over the cabin, and flipped. As it hit the hardened ground upside down, Joseph's skull struck the metal roof, and he blacked out. When he came to, the truck was no longer tumbling; it had come to a stop at the bottom of the hill.

The first thing he noticed was that his head throbbed. On top of that, he was dizzy and nauseous. He'd have to worry about that later, though. He needed to get himself together the best he could so that he make sure his family was okay.

Joseph undid his safety belt, and when it was no longer latched, he fell from his seat and landed across the cold metal roof of the overturned vehicle. He decided the first thing he needed to do was get out of the wreckage. His initial plan was to climb through the front and try to escape through one of the doors. That plan was dismissed when he looked up front, and saw both his parents blocking his path to either door. He'd have to find another means of exiting the truck.

He moved around, and readjusted his body as quickly as the severe pain would allow. Once he was positioned the way he wanted, he mustered up all the strength he had, and kicked the rear window of the pickup truck.

Upon impact, nothing happened. The window remained perfectly intact.

Joseph made another attempt, and, like the prior one, was unsuccessful. Those two tries was all it took for his patience to fail him. Frustration took over, and with everything he had, he ferociously kicked the rear window. After about seven or eight kicks, the window cracked. After finally seeing some progress, he composed himself, and gave the window one last swift kick with his boot. This time, it shattered.

He reached up towards his sister's seatbelt, and after a few moments of fussing, managed to unfasten it. He guided her body safely from the seat to the roof of the flipped over truck. He gripped her under her armpits, and cautiously pulled her from the wreckage of the crash. He dragged her through the snow to what he thought was a safe distance from the crash, and laid her down on the white blanketed ground. It was then that he noticed the unnatural angle in which her neck was bent. He felt denial creeping up on him, but pushed it away. Joseph refused to lie to himself. He knew full well his little sister was dead.

He had only hoped Liz's death had been instantaneous. Not only to spare her from the pain and fear of dying, but because she didn't deserve to linger on the path between living and death where she'd be forced to remember all the horrible things she had heard and witnessed within the confines of her own home.

Joseph gently lowered his sister's head onto the ground, and made his way back to the truck. He rounded the rear, and knelt beside the passenger's side. He could see his mother through the dirty window, and could see that she was alive.

He pulled at the door handle, which proved pointless. The door was either locked or jammed from the car's tumble down the hill. He would have to break the window, and pull his mother from the wreckage to safety. His first choice of makeshift tool was a rock. Thanks to Alex, he had seen firsthand the kind of damage a rock could do, and he had no doubt it would easily shatter the window. Only when he searched the ground, there were no rocks large enough to break through the glass. Searching for plan B, he scanned the area, and noticed a large branch sticking out of the snow. He knew it wouldn't be as reliable as hitting the window with a baseball bat, but he would have to make do with it.

"Turn your head away from the window," he yelled to his mother after retrieving the branch and returning to the wreckage.

Emily Bateman gave no response. She was completely out of it, and unaware her son was attempting to rescue her. Having to ignore the risk of shattered glass cutting up his mother's skin or getting in her eye, Joseph wound up, and swung the branch full force at the passenger side window. At impact, the sound of glass shattering echoed throughout the still night air. Joseph tossed the branch aside, and crawled into the car to rescue his mother.

Despite being alive and conscious, Emily Bateman proved to be just as hard for Joseph to pull from the wreckage as his sister had been. She was too injured and shaken up to aid her son in any way. Joseph dragged her through the thickening snow over to the body of her daughter. When he laid her on the ground, she was no longer conscious, and, for a moment, Joseph thought his mother had passed on. He then noticed the faint rise and fall of her chest and relief washed over him. His mother was still alive, and he would not be left alone in this world with Hank Bateman.

Joseph turned towards the car, and saw his father. Hank Bateman's window was blown out from the fall, but he was still stuck within the wreckage of the vehicle. The two—father and son—locked eyes, and Joseph could see that his father was not only injured, but he was scared.

"Help me," Hank Bateman called out from the wreckage of his pickup truck. In response to his father's pleas, Joseph didn't move a muscle.

Let him stay there and suffer, Joseph instructed himself.

Nothing would please him more than seeing his father afraid and in agony. He only hoped Hank Bateman realized how little desire his own son had to help him in his time of need. Still, Joseph knew he had to help. Eventually, rescue would arrive, and Hank Bateman would be freed from the wreckage. Once his recovery from whatever injuries he had sustained in the crash was complete, he'd return to his regular routines, and Joseph knew once this happened, it would be his mother who suffered for this act of defiance.

He started towards the car to do what needed to be done, but after three steps, Joseph froze. Coming from the engine of the overturned vehicle he saw an orange glow. The pickup truck was on fire. His nostrils then picked up the sudden, unmistakable smell of gasoline, which could only mean one thing. The gas tank had been punctured in the crash, and it was now leaking. Hank Bateman must have smelled the gasoline also, because when he saw his son stop dead in his tracks, his face became encompassed with an unbridled fear.

"Help me," he called out. "You have to help me."

Joseph didn't have to help him, though. He didn't have to do anything. He knew what would happen if he just waited a few more minutes. He stepped backwards, away from the wreckage, so that his father could see he had lost his only hope of walking away from this accident alive. When Hank Bateman realized his own son was refusing to help him, he started to freak out.

He began to thrash back and forth in his seat in an attempt to free himself. When that proved pointless, he began to plead once again with Joseph to help him. When it became obvious his son would still not help, Hank Bateman began to apologize. Whether or not he knew exactly what he was apologizing for did not matter. The time for apologies was over.

Joseph picked his mother up and dragged her further away from the wreckage to what he thought was a safe distance. He did the same for his sister. Then he sat.

"Please...help me," Hank Bateman continued to beg. "I'm sorry... I'm sorry... Please... Just help me!"

When Joseph didn't move, Hank Bateman began to cry. He cried so hard that his words could no longer be understood. The snow seeped through Joseph's pant and soaked his leg, but he didn't feel the cold. In that moment Joseph Bateman was overwhelmed by the warming sensation of joy.

There would be no quick exit for the man who had sired him, but had never been his father. Hank Bateman would have his time to reflect and regret every terrible thing he

100

did to his family. He'd realize he was about to die, because he didn't deserve life.

Gasoline eventually met flame, and Hank Bateman was silenced by death. Joseph felt the heat of the flames from the explosion, and knew they were nothing in comparison to the flames that were in store for his father in the afterlife.

Joseph closed his eyes, and allowed the heat to tickle his numb cheeks. He knew he'd eventually have to get up and run for help—his mother was still alive and in need of medical attention—but he'd wait just a few more moments. He wanted to savior the joyous feeling of his newly found freedom.

He did what he needed to be done. Hank Bateman could no longer hurt them. His poisonous hatred was gone. Extinguished by flame and turned to ashes. Joseph opened his eyes, and watched the flames dance in the night sky.

Joseph Bateman couldn't help but smile.

December 27, 1981
Memorial Services

Elizabeth Bateman was laid to rest on the cold morning of December 27, 1981. The service was small, yet beautiful. Her closest friends, whose homes she had often stayed at to escape her own, all attended. So did some of her classmates, as well as a few of her teachers.

Alex came with her father so that she could be there for her best friend. The sight of Alexandra Casings in makeup never failed to shock Joseph, but seeing her in funeral appropriate attire—a dress, black stockings, and flats—took his shock to a whole new level. Despite the circumstances, Joseph couldn't help but notice how beautiful his best friend had become.

Joseph's mother was granted permission by the hospital to attend her only daughter's funeral. Emily Bateman had been declared stable a few days following the accident and there was no longer a danger to her health. She didn't speak a single word the entire morning. She just sat there in her wheelchair, quietly. When people approached her to give their condolences, she simply nodded in thanks.

She did not weep, either. Even as her daughter's casket was lowered into its final resting place, Emily Bateman did not shed a single tear. Joseph assumed this was due to shock. His mother had been through so much already in life that the accident had been the straw that broke the camel's back, both, figuratively and literally.

Figuratively, Emily Bateman had always been aware that there were consequences to staying in her marriage. Having to bury one of her children was probably not one she had considered. Joseph knew the death of his little sister would weigh heavily on his mother until her last breath.

Not only had the accident broken Emily Bateman's spirits, but it also broke her body. Despite being stabilized only days following a horrendous car accident, doctors quickly concluded that she would never walk again. The accident had shattered her hip, and, though the doctors could repair that injury, there was nothing they could do for her broken back.

Despite her physical and mental state on the morning of her daughter's funeral, Joseph knew his mother would pull herself far enough out of her depression to keep going. He could not understand how she did it, time and time again. Anyone else who had endured the years of abuse that she had, only to lose one of her children, not to mention the ability to walk, would have been broken to the point of being unfixable.

Not Emily Bateman, though.

She had one reason to keep on and that was her son. She would pull herself back from the brink once more for her surviving child, and she would do everything she could to make sure he'd be all right.

Sadly for Emily Bateman, her son had already been veered too far off that path, and not even she could guide him back. Everything ahead in Joseph Bateman's life— even the things disguised as blessings—were merely stepping stones on his lifelong path to Death Row.

On the final morning of his life, as he waited to ride the lightning, Joseph found himself glad his mother had not been around to witness what her son had turned into. He had become her greatest failure when he was supposed to be just the opposite. That was something he'd never want her to realize.

On the frigid winter morning of his sister's funeral, Joseph stood beside his mother's wheelchair. Alex stood beside him. They watched silently as Elizabeth Bateman's casket was lowered down into a six-foot hole where it would be covered by dirt and permanent darkness. He felt the pressure in his throat as the ball of his grief expanded. When the casket was halfway in the ground, he felt his eyes welling up. No tears fell, though.

He felt the warmth of soft fingers interlocking with his own. He looked down, and saw Alex's hand in his. He looked up at his best friend. He didn't need to cry for his best friend to know he was suffering. In that moment, Joseph's grief washed away. There was still a great sadness within him, but the threat of tears had passed. With one simple gesture, he felt safe, he felt comforted, and, most importantly, he felt loved.

Slowly, the small crowd gathering next to the lonely gravesite began to thin until it was just Joseph, his mother, and Alex.

"I'll see you later tonight?" Alex eventually asked him. "After you leave the hospital?"

"Yeah." As he spoke, Joseph did not take his eyes off the hole in the ground where his sister's casket had been. "There's just something I need to do first."

"Okay. Just come by whenever." She broke the link between their hands, and knelt down in front of Emily Bateman. "Goodbye, Missus Bateman. I'm very sorry for your loss."

Emily Bateman stared at Alex, but gave no response.

Alex left mother and son alone together to say their final goodbyes. There were no words exchanged between the two living members of the Bateman family. Nor were there tears shed. They just stood there in silence until Joseph decided it was time to leave. As he wheeled her away, his mother turned her head, and stared at her daughter's grave until it was out of sight.

Joseph returned his mother to the hospital and spent the rest of the day with her. That evening, once he made sure she was comfortable for the night, he left and headed home, briefly. There was something he needed to take care of.

From the moment he entered to when he exited, Joseph spent less than two minutes inside his house. He had no desire to be there. Since the night of the accident he had spent a total of thirty minutes inside his house, and that was to get a few changes of clothes. He spent most nights at the hospital, especially in the beginning. Other nights, he had spent on the Casings' couch. A sense of eeriness had come over Joseph as he entered the house where he had grown up. It was like entering a condemned building that hadn't been occupied for years rather than a home that was still fully furnished, and had a family living in it less than two weeks prior. It was a feeling he much desired to be rid of, and planned on making his stop a quick one. He knew exactly what he needed and where to find it.

When he was done at the house, Joseph walked until he found a deserted parking lot to conduct his business. He knelt beside a dumpster, reached into his backpack, and pulled out the contents.

A few days prior to Joseph's sister's funeral service, the cremated remains of Hank Bateman were released to his family. Planning a funeral for her daughter was taxing enough for Emily Bateman in her condition, even with the help of her son. She didn't have it in her to plan any kind of service for her late husband. That was just one reason, though. The other reason, Joseph knew, was because no one would have shown up to any service held for his late father. You needed to be respected in order for people to pay their respects, and Hank Bateman received that from no one. Unable to do so herself, Emily Bateman asked her son to take on the responsibility of disposing of his father's remains.

Now, as he sat on the side of a dumpster in the vacant parking lot, Joseph opened the canister that held the earthly remains of the man he had decided to let die rather than save. He picked up a can of beer he had just pulled from his backpack. There had only been two in the fridge back home, but two was enough. He pulled the tab and opened it, then repeated the process for the other. He held the two open beers over the canister, and poured the contents into it. Once they were emptied, Joseph moved onto the bottle of Jack Daniels he had taken from the liquor cabinet back home. He unscrewed the top, and emptied the bottle.

He watched as liquid mixed with ash. As the remains of his father floated around in a mixture of beer and liquor, Joseph realized how fitting this was for Hank Bateman. In the end, he was one with the thing he had loved the most.

Joseph screwed the lid back on the canister, and picked it up off the ground. Without a second thought, he tossed it into the dumpster, and closed the lid, thus finding Hank Bateman the perfect final resting place.

June 12, 1985
Firsts

"Have you ever kissed a girl before?"

The question had come out of nowhere. They had been sitting there—Joseph and Alex—on one of the branches that hung over the lake that Joseph had refused to jump into. They hadn't even been talking. They were just sitting there in silence, enjoying the warm breeze coming off the lake. Then, out of the blue, Alex asked him if he had ever kissed someone.

"Huh?" was Joseph's response.

"You see, Josephine, sometimes people do this thing where their lips touch. It's called kissing. There's a few different variations of it...sometimes it's done for a long time, sometimes not so long. Sometimes there's even tongue involved."

"I know what kissing is," he shot back, matter-of-factly. "Why are you asking me about it?"

"Because I'm wondering if you've ever kissed a girl before. Jeez! Just making conversation! No need to bite my head off."

He briefly debated lying to her, but realized she'd know. Chances were she already knew the answer to her question; she just wanted him to admit it.

"No, I haven't," he answered. "Have you?"

"Nah, no girls worth kissing," Alex answered, sarcastically. "Although Mindy Medford is looking like quite the hottie these days."

"You know what I meant, Alex! Have you ever kissed a boy?"

"Oh, yeah. You know me…All the boys are lining up for a smooch-a-roo. I'm just your everyday heartbreaker."

"So you haven't then," Joseph said, calling out the obvious tale she was spinning. "Glad we could establish that."

They resumed their previous position of enjoying the comfortable silence and spring breeze. It would only last for a few more moments, though.

"You want to?" Alex asked Joseph.

"Do I want to what?"

"Kiss, dummy! Everyone has to do it, eventually. We might as well get it out of the way now. Otherwise, it's going to be awkward, and we're going to be bad at it when it does happen with other people."

Joseph's cheeks and ears immediately began to burn up with embarrassment. He had no idea what to say. He had never really thought about kissing Alex before. However, now that the question was out there, he wanted to say yes.

"Okay… guess not," Alex said after a few awkward moments of silence. "Maybe I'll just find someone else then, if you're not interested."

"I am!" Joseph blurted out. "I am interested! I just don't want to suck at it."

"Oh, you're definitely going to suck at it. That's okay, though, because I'm going to suck at it, too."

"Okay, then. I guess let's do it."

Just like that it was decided. Alexandra Casings would forever be Joseph Bateman's first kiss.

"You have to do it with your eyes closed," Alex stated. "If you kiss with your eyes open, it's creepy."

As she moved closer to him for better kissing distance, a variety of emotions and thoughts ricocheted back and forth inside Joseph's head. One of them was dread. What if he was bad at it? Alex was always going to remember her first kiss, and there was a chance it was going to be terrible. He also feared this was some prank Alex had orchestrated at his expense. He'd risk all those things, though. He decided to play the odds and take the chance, because the feeling that stood out above all the others was excitement. Right then, there was nothing he wanted more than to kiss his best friend.

"Nothing longer than five seconds," Alex said. "Don't make it weird!"

Joseph tried to come up with a witty comeback, but before he could, he felt Alex's lips pressed up against his. After that, no thoughts existed. There was only Alex and her lips.

The kiss, itself, was kind of awkward. The two sat there with their hands in their laps. Both their lips had been bone dry. Joseph had seen enough movies to know most kisses didn't go like this. There was more to them, but he was too busy minding his Mississippis to think of what else he should or could be doing to make the moment more memorable. Alex ended up being the one who took the initiative to make her first kiss worth remembering.

Joseph was at four-Mississippi when her lips parted. He felt the warmth and wetness of her lips envelope his and a euphoric sensation spread through his entire body. He had never felt anything like it before, but knew he liked it. He didn't want it to end. He never wanted Alex's lips to be away from his. Then, just as soon as it had started, it was over. The final Mississippi had been counted and their lips parted.

He didn't open his eyes right away. The feeling he had experienced was slowly receding and he wanted to hold onto it for a little longer. When he finally did open his eyes, the person sitting across from him was not the same person who had been there moments before. She looked just like the Alex he had known all those years, but she was completely different now. Joseph liked the person he saw.

To be more accurate, he loved the person he was now looking at.

"Did you like it?" the new Alex asked him.

"Yeah," was all he could manage to say.

"I always knew you were a lesbian, *Josephine*!" she said just like old Alex.

Her joke made Joseph smile. The new Alex had the same quick-witted humor as the girl he had known for so long. It was like reading your favorite book, and realizing it had a chapter you had never noticed before. It doesn't change the story that you've known, but it makes you rethink the whole thing, and see it in a brand new light.

"I'd ask you if you were going to jump in, but we both know the answer is no," Alex said.

Joseph had still been fixating on his first kiss—their first kiss—but the moment had passed for Alex, and she was ready to move on. She removed her shirt, tossed it to the ground, and jumped off the tree into the water below.

Joseph did not follow. After all these years, he still couldn't find the courage to jump from that tree into the damn lake. It had become his Everest. However, on this day, his fear was not the reason he remained seated. If he had stood up, Alex would have, undoubtedly, seen the bulge that was pushing up against the crotch of his jeans.

As per their daily ritual, Joseph walked Alex home at the end of the night. Afterwards, he returned home to the two room apartment he shared with his mother.

With half her family deceased and unable to walk from the injuries she sustained in the accident, Emily Bateman felt the smartest move was to sell her house. Joseph supported the decision, fully. Only, instead of selling it, he'd much rather have set the place on fire and watch it burn to the ground.

When he returned home that night, he and his mother watched television. Neither said much, which was fine, because Joseph's mind was elsewhere. Afterwards, he got his mother ready and helped her into bed for the night. After she was comfortable and finally asleep, Joseph sat down in front of the television, and crammed in some homework before bed.

Remaining in school wasn't Joseph's choice. He felt that finding work to help support him and his mother was far more important. His mother had pleaded with him, though, so Joseph stayed in school while working part time off the books to help with bills.

Just as it had been throughout the course of the evening, Joseph found himself unable to concentrate. He had been on autopilot the entire night, because the thought of Alex's lips consumed him. He envisioned the new Alex he had seen after the kiss, and tried to imagine what she was like, and how she differed from the Alex he had once known.

When he felt as if he had done a sufficient amount of his homework, Joseph retired to his bedroom for a good night's sleep, only sleep would not come. His kiss with Alex ran on a loop and prevented the possibility of slumber. The kiss may have been awkward and only five seconds in length, but as he lay there in the darkness of his own room, Joseph let his imagination wander, and his thoughts of Alex stretched far beyond the one single kiss.

He imagined the feel of Alex's tongue as it massaged his own while they kissed deeply. He thought about the skin of her flat stomach. Joseph had seen Alex with her shirt off and in just a bra endless times, and never once did he think anything of it. Now that he was introduced to this new Alex, he wanted to feel the smoothness of her skin beneath his fingertips. He fantasized about touching her breasts. Even running his finger over her nipple. As his thoughts of Alex were fitted together to form the perfect sexual fantasy, Joseph felt his penis becoming erect, and pushing against the fabric of his boxer shorts.

By fifteen years old, most boys have the ritual act of masturbation down to a science. Joseph, however, as he slid his boxers off, was about to participate in the act for the first time in his life.

As he touched himself in the darkness of his room, he wondered if the pleasure he was feeling was anything near how it would feel to actually be with Alex...inside Alex.

As the thought of he and Alex making love for the first time entered his mind, he felt a sensation he had never known existed. His breathing increased heavily, and a moan escaped past his lips as orgasm neared. As the sounds of his pleasure filled his small, quiet room, he tried to quiet himself best as possible. His mother was in the next room. Joseph feared she might wake, and hear what he was doing.

It was that quick transition to his mother that served as the seed that in seconds blossomed into disaster.

Joseph was expelled from the comforts of his fantasy, and thrown into the memory of the most traumatizing event of his life. His best friend was no longer beneath him, staring into his eyes as they made love to each other. Replacing it was the image from almost two years ago of his mother in front of him, naked and on all fours.

With the ghastly memory invading his mind, Joseph stopped what he was doing. It was too late, though. Like it had that night he was nearly forced on his mother, his body took over, and went against Joseph's will. He felt his penis spasm in his hand, and, moments later, semen dripping down into his hand. He clinched his teeth, and tried to suppress the moan that came with his unwanted orgasm, but the sounds that escaped him filled the still night air.

When it was over, there was no euphoric sense of relief for Joseph. The only thing he was capable of feeling was shame. He had relived the worst moment of his life while experiencing his first orgasm. He didn't consider the fact that sometimes thoughts enter your mind, even if you don't want them there, or that his body was going through something it was naturally expected to do. All Joseph Bateman knew was that he was a sick and twisted boy, who relived memories involving his mother naked and bent over in front of him while orgasming.

He rolled over and wiped the semen in his hand onto the side of the bed. He'd strip the bed in the morning. Right now, all he wanted was for sleep to take him. If he was sleeping, he didn't have to face the effects of what Hank Bateman had put him through. The man may have been dead for almost two years, but the remnants from the wounds he caused were everlasting. After a few moments, sleep mercifully took Joseph.

It wouldn't be until his time in prison that he would finally masturbate again.

February 15, 1986
Special on John Wilkes Booth

The face he saw on the television looked nothing like the face of a killer. The man's hair was well kempt—parted down the side—and his face was clean shaven, sans his mustache. Killer, murderer or assassin would've hardly been the words Joseph used to describe the man whose black and white portrait appeared on Alex's television, yet he was America's most infamous killer.

They spent that cold February night on Alex's couch. Joseph sat on one end while Alex lay, sprawled out, across the entire thing. She had her legs comfortably elevated in Joseph's lap. The Alex he had met seven months before following their first kiss hadn't shown her face since the isolated event. Joseph had accepted that she likely wouldn't ever again. The new Alex was a fantasy he had concocted, and the girl he saw every day was the same Alex he had known for years.

Alex had the remote and was channel surfing when Joseph first saw the familiar face on the television. She had landed on PBS for only a brief moment before continuing on to the next channel in her quest to find something remotely interesting for them to watch.

"Hey, go back a few," Joseph said.

Alex backtracked a few channels to PBS, and there Joseph saw him full on. The man who had made his name on the stage, and defined his legacy with a single gunshot that would forever ring throughout history.

John Wilkes Booth.

The narrator's voice that came from the television informed the viewer that the man they were currently looking at was an American actor, who, following the end of the American Civil War in 1865, took it upon himself to assassinate the sixteenth president of the United States of America, Abraham Lincoln.

"You're kidding, right?" Alex asked. It was obvious she was in no way interested in Joseph's current choice of programming. "We aren't going to actually watch this crap, are we?"

"Why not?"

"Because we just learned about this whole thing in school. They teach it to us every single year at this time. Over and over again. There's nothing left to learn."

Joseph knew that wasn't true, though.

He knew the name John Wilkes Booth more than he knew the face, and he was well familiarized with the facts that everyone, educated or not, knew. He also knew other facts about the Lincoln Assassination that others probably didn't. He remembered them from the research he had done for his report six years ago. The one Alex almost convinced him to never hand in.

Most people didn't know Lincoln's assassination was only one part of a much larger conspiracy to cripple the United States government following their victory over the Confederacy in the Civil War. Vice President, Andrew Johnson, and Secretary of State, William Seward, were also targets, but were not killed. In addition, almost nobody knew four other co-conspirators were executed—

including Mary Surratt; the first and only woman to be hung by the United States government—for their part in the conspiracy. Joseph could understand people not being educated on those facts, but most people weren't even aware of what became of John Wilkes Booth following the evening he pulled the trigger of a Henry Derringer .44 at Ford's Theatre.

Joseph knew them, though, and was well educated on all of it. Even as a nine year old, doing research for a school report, he found himself fascinated by the depth of the assassination. There was so much more to it than what they were taught in school.

Now, six years after his report was handed in, Joseph stared at the face of John Wilkes Booth, and found himself once again fascinated, and realized it wasn't Lincoln who piqued his curiosity.

The report he had written had mainly focused around Abraham Lincoln. The assassination was only a small part covered in Joseph's final product. However, it was John Wilkes Booth who had made the research portion of the report so interesting. Now, as he and Alex watched the President's Day television special, Joseph's attention was devoted to Booth, and he found him wondering what force in this universe could drive a person to kill another human being. He did not need to dwell on that question for too long, though, because he already knew the answer.

It was hatred.

Booth's hatred for Abraham Lincoln was so absolute that he wanted the president dead, much like how Joseph had hated his own father so much that he wished for the same fate. When opportunity presented itself, Joseph had sat back, and let Hank Bateman burn. He had ended the man he hated. Why wouldn't Booth do the same when he saw the opportunity to do what he felt needed to be done?

Only Abraham Lincoln wasn't a drunk, who beat and raped John Wilkes Booth's mother. He didn't invite other men over to have their way with his own wife just to clear gambling debts. He sure didn't almost force John Wilkes Booth to have sex with his own mother. Hank Bateman was and had done each and every one of those things, and for them, he deserved to die. Booth's only gripe with President Lincoln was that he freed the black man from the shackles of slavery, and announced his plans to give them rights, just like any other American citizen.

Hatred is hatred, though, and for whatever reason it may exist within an individual, there comes a point where it forces us to act. Having acted on his own hatred, once before, Joseph fully understood Booth's actions, and found himself relating to the most infamous assassin in American history.

"I'm turning this off," Alex said after less than a minute of watching.

Joseph, wanting to continue watching the documentary, acted, and snatched the remote away from his friend. Alex did not take kindly to this, and would not accept defeat so easily. She shot up from her comfortable position on the couch, and leapt onto Joseph in an attempt to reclaim the television remote.

Joseph, much larger now than he once was compared to Alex, had advantages against her in both the size and strength departments. Usually, when the two wrestled, he'd let her win. However, this time, he'd use those the advantages to claim victory over the remote. He shifted his weight, and rolled on top of Alex. Once she was securely pinned beneath him, Joseph proceeded to tickle her. It would only take seconds before victory was his.

"Okay, okay, okay," she yelped, as she squirmed back and forth in an attempt to free herself from the onslaught of tickle-torture. "You win... you freaking win. We can watch the stupid documentary."

With victory his, Joseph released Alex from her torture, and reclaimed his spot on the couch. Alex, who did not accept defeat gracefully, gave Joseph a quick jab to the arm before returning to her original comfortable position.

"What are you two arguing over, now?" Bill Casings asked, entering the living room. He saw the programming currently on his television, and couldn't help but let out a laugh. "Wow, you must have given her one hell of a fight to get her to agree to watch this, Joseph."

"He fights dirty," Alex argued, bitterly.

Bill walked over to the couch while Alex sat up to make room for her father to sit. As they watched, Bill took notice of how interested in the documentary Joseph was.

"You enjoying this, Joseph?" he asked, as the narrator of the documentary educated the viewers on John Wilkes Booth's tortuous crossing of the Potomac River during his escape to Virginia.

"Yes, sir," Joseph answered. "I find it fascinating."

"It's a shame how history views him," Bill said, referring to Booth. "The man did what he felt was right, and because of it, he gets labeled as some sort of monster. It's disgusting."

Joseph wasn't sure he agreed with what Bill was saying, but he kept quiet, and let Alex's father make his point.

"It's just too bad Booth didn't get his chance to kill that nigger-lover before the war ended," Bill continued. "Maybe then all those niggers would have stayed in their rightful place in the world."

Upon hearing what he thought was a primitive form of thinking from Bill Casings, Joseph began to understand Alex a little better. He had no doubt Bill had given his daughter the information for the President's Day report that got her sent home for a week six years earlier. It even showed him a bit of insight to Alex's old feud with her childhood nemesis, Eve Meyers.

Despite what he was hearing from Bill, Joseph was fully aware of the truth about John Wilkes Booth. The man wasn't some sort of misunderstood hero of history. He was a bigot, and a killer.

"That's an interesting point, sir," Joseph said. He didn't seriously take into consideration what Bill was saying, but he also hadn't wanted to start a debate that had the potential to escalate. "I've never considered it that way."

"Well, maybe you should."

"I will."

"You're a smart kid, Joseph. It's great that you're willing to see other sides of the coin. You're going to go far in life, and I just want to say, I'd be proud to call you my son."

Bill Casings put a hand on Joseph's shoulder, and squeezed gently. In that exchange Joseph felt something wash over him that he had never felt before from any male figure in his life.

It was affection.

Hearing Bill Casings speak such kind and encouraging words to him filled a void in Joseph that was left by his own father. It was the first time in his life he felt a fatherly bond. He even began to wonder if this man who saw him as a son was right, after all. Maybe he saw something in Booth that history could not see. Maybe Bill told Joseph all of this because he knew one day Joseph would see it, too.

Reflecting back on the moment from his prison cell all those years later, Joseph assumed that was where and when his connection with John Wilkes Booth had been birthed.

It wouldn't be until the walls came crashing down that Joseph Bateman learned the true depth of his connection with John Wilkes Booth.

August 27, 1986
Bonding with Bill Casings

Joseph stepped out onto the Casings' porch not long after midnight. Earlier in the night, he and Alex had fallen asleep on the couch as they attempted to watch a movie to keep them occupied on that rainy evening. Joseph woke up a few hours later, and slipped out silently, leaving Alex asleep on the couch. The sounds of crickets filled the night air as Joseph stepped outside. The rain had stopped, and the late night air was thick with summer humidity. He didn't see Bill Casings next to him, sitting in one of the outside chairs. So when Alex's father asked his houseguest if he was heading home for the night, it gave Joseph quite the start.

"My apologies, Joseph," Bill said. "I didn't mean to startle you."

"It's okay," Joseph said. "I am heading home. I like to be there in the morning for my mom."

Bill took a deep pull of his cigarette, then crushed it out in the ashtray. He followed this with a long swig of his beer. He finished the contents of his bottle, placed it down on the table, and stood up.

"Let's go for a ride."

Bill saw Joseph about to object to his offer, and assured him that their ride would not be long. Not seeing the harm in a short car ride, Joseph agreed.

The two did not speak as they sat in the car. Bill gave no indication to where they were heading, and Joseph found himself wondering where they could be going, especially at the late hour they were out. Despite his curiosity, Joseph asked no questions, and remained silent. He trusted Bill Casings.

The two had developed a bond over the course of the past six months. Bill Casings had become the closest thing Joseph ever had to an actual father figure. The two shared laughs together. They had long conversations. That summer, Joseph was even invited to Alex and her father's annual fishing trip, and it ended up being one of the best days of his life. Joseph loved his mother, but Bill and Alex had made Joseph feel like he was part of a real family for the first time in his entire life.

"We're here," Bill said, as he slowed the car to a stop, and threw it into park. "We just have to walk a little bit."

Bill reached into the backseat and pulled out a duffle bag to take with them. Joseph couldn't help but notice the baseball bat sticking out. He did not like the sight of the bat, but he still asked no questions. He just got out of the car and followed Bill.

The two made their way down the block quietly. Joseph was stopped suddenly by Bill who pulled him behind a bush. It was enough to conceal them, yet Bill had positioned them perfectly so that they did not look suspicious to anyone who might drive by. Joseph realized then that it was the second time in his life he was hiding behind a bush with a Casings. Given the events and outcome of his first experience with Alex when they were children, an unsettling feeling arose in the pit of Joseph's stomach. He knew whatever Bill Casings had planned would not sit well on his conscience.

"Do you know who lives in that house, Joseph?" Bill asked.

Joseph looked at the house Bill was referring to. Just like every other house on the block, it did not look familiar to him. He saw the car in the driveway, though, and immediately knew the answer to Bill's question.

"Mister Hershel lives there."

Leonard Hershel was the owner of Wayne County's only General Store. Joseph had been going to Mister Hershel's store his entire life, whether with his mother before her accident, or on his own—never with Alex; he knew better than that. He and his wife were also the only black people who lived in Wayne County since Eve Meyer's family moved away years ago. Leonard Hershel was a kind man, who Joseph, and all who shopped at his store, liked. He always went out of his way to make sure you felt welcomed in his establishment, and that your experience made you want to come back. For his positive attitude and strong work ethic, there weren't many who spoke negatively of Leonard Hershel.

Now, as he looked over at the man standing next to him, holding a duffle bag with a baseball bat sticking out of it, Joseph realized there was one man he could think of who would never have anything positive to say about Leonard Hershel.

"Take this," Bill said, and passed the bat to Joseph.

Joseph failed to acknowledge Bill's request. He was putting the pieces together, and knew what happened next if he was to take the bat from Alex's father.

"Is everything okay, Joseph?" Bill asked.

No, Joseph thought. His eyes shifted to the baseball bat Bill Casings held out for him to take. *Everything is not okay. I know what you're going to ask me to do with that bat, and I don't want to.*

Mister Hershel had been a fixture in Wayne County for more years than Joseph had been alive. He was a good man, who didn't deserve to have his property vandalized, and Joseph had no desire to be the person who participated in doing so. He couldn't tell Bill that, though. The man had become like a father, and the last thing Joseph wanted was to let him down. He assumed one of the worst feelings for a son—at least the ones who had normal relationships with their fathers—was seeing disappointment in their father's eyes.

So with a reluctant heart, Joseph reached out, and accepted the baseball bat.

"Yeah," he lied. "Everything is fine."

"Good. I'm glad."

Bill reached into his duffle bag, and pulled out a large, and, from the looks of it, very heavy crowbar. He then cocked his head towards the house in a *follow-me* motion. Like an obedient soldier, Joseph did as he was told, and followed Bill into Leonard Hershel's front yard.

They crept up the driveway, quietly as possible. Bill Casings did not want to ruin his big surprise by alerting anyone of his presence. Joseph hadn't been let in on the exact details of Bill's plan, but he figured they were going to break some windows. Instead of creeping all the way up the driveway to the house, though, Bill stopped at Mister Hershel's car.

"Ready?" he mouthed to Joseph.

No, Joseph wanted to say, but he was too far in now to object.

He instead remained silent, and watched Bill raise the steel crowbar above his head. It would only remain there a moment before crashing down on the car's front windshield. The sound of exploding glass echoed through the summer night air. A smile was painted on the face of Bill Casings as he basked in his destruction. He was like a child who got everything he had asked for from Santa at Christmas.

He looked towards Joseph, who was standing with the wooden bat at his side at the rear of the car. Joseph thought he saw the slight hint of disappointment as Bill realized that Joseph had yet to use the bat on the car. Desperate for an acceptance he never received from Hank Bateman, Joseph raised the bat, without a second thought, and brought it down. Again, the sound of glass exploding rang through the night.

Regret was the immediate thing Joseph felt as he vandalized the property of a man who had done absolutely nothing to him. It wasn't a feeling he enjoyed. However, when he saw the look of pride on Bill Casings' face, Joseph forgot all about his shame. He had waited sixteen years for that look, and he loved it now that he had finally gotten it.

His eagerness to please overpowered his guilt, and he lifted the bat once more. He drove it through the driver's side window just so he could see the proud look once more on Bill's face. Somewhere in the distance a dog began to howl at the sound of shattering glass, but Joseph barely heard it. All that mattered was Bill Casings' approval.

Deciding to play catchup with the damage Joseph had already done, Bill lifted his crowbar, and shattered the driver's side headlight. He immediately followed this up with jamming the crowbar into the tire, and puncturing it. Joseph matched this by smashing both rear lights.

A light in the Hershel household came on suddenly, and the two took it as their cue to take off. Bill stabbed the rear tire, and took off running; leaving the crowbar buried in the rubber as an additional *FUCK YOU!* to Leonard Hershel.

They ran down the block, and got in Bill's car. Before Joseph knew what was going on, the tires were screaming in the dead of night, and they were speeding down the block in their escape vehicle.

"Fuck you, you dumb nigger!" Bill yelled to the man standing on his front lawn with his wife, looking at his vandalized vehicle.

When they were far enough from the crime scene, Bill Casings brought the car to a halt. He was too out of breath from the combination of running and excitement to speak. There was nothing he needed to say, though. The hand he put on Joseph's shoulder said it all.

Joseph was his son just as much as he was Joseph's father, and Bill Casings was proud of his son.

Unfortunately, as Joseph's adrenaline died down, his guilt came creeping back. Part of him couldn't believe what he had just done. Bill may be proud, but his mother would be so disappointed. She wouldn't have known the young man who had just wielded a baseball bat moments ago. That left him ashamed, and there was now no amount of pride from Bill that could alleviate that feeling. He was a man caught between two worlds. Both seemed equally right, even though he knew one was so obviously wrong.

Despite being pulled in these opposite directions, Joseph was fully aware of one thing.

He now knew where Alex got her extreme case of racism from.

October 29, 1986
Walking Home Miss Dunne

Three weeks after he tossed Hank Bateman's remains into a dumpster, Joseph went out and got his very first job. It was at a nearby laundromat. It didn't pay much, but it was the only place that would hire Joseph at his young age, plus the pay was off the books.

His mother never once told him he needed to go out and find work, nor did she ever hint at it. Joseph went out and found work on his own accord, because he wanted to help contribute to the bills in whatever little way he could. This wouldn't stop the weekly arguments between mother and son every time Emily Bateman refused whatever portion of Joseph's pay he tried to give her. Joseph would remain relentless, though, and made sure that every week his mother got what he felt was owed to her.

As it turned out, Joseph enjoyed working. He loved the feeling of getting paid in exchange for his services. Despite having a job so easy it could be done by a low functioning monkey, as Alex once put it, Joseph had quickly developed a strong work ethic.

Two nights before Halloween of 1986, Joseph worked the closing shift. He locked up a little past midnight and headed home. As he walked, he passed the bar Hank Bateman had once frequented. He wondered how much money the establishment had lost in sales after his father's untimely, yet well-deserved, passing.

He was less than a hundred yards passed the bar when he heard someone calling his name. Despite being slurred by an excessive consumption of alcohol, Joseph vaguely recognized the voice; he just couldn't place it. He turned to the person calling to him, and saw them stumbling his way. It wasn't until they were inches away from him, and stumbling into his arms for a hug, that Joseph realized it was his old second grade teacher, Miss Dunn.

"Little Joseph Bateman!" his former teacher exclaimed as she squeezed him.

She took a step back to examine the boy she had once taught so many years ago, and nearly tripped over her drunken feet. Joseph acted, and caught her before she could take the spill.

"Thanks, hon," she said. "Turns out you're not so little anymore."

Despite being older and wiser to the world since the last time he saw Miss Dunne, Joseph still felt strange seeing a person who had once served as a role model plastered from excessive alcohol consumption. The truth was there had been whispers for years about Miss Dunne amongst the students at Joseph's school, especially as they reached the middle and high school years. She had never been married and the rumor was that the now middle-aged elementary school teacher often fucked any guy willing enough to open his wallet to buy her drink. Joseph never really put much thought into these stories, but seeing Miss Dunne as drunk as she was, he wondered if perhaps there was some truth to the tales.

Looking at her swaying in place, Joseph just couldn't understand who would want to have sex with Miss Dunne.

She wasn't an attractive woman when she taught him, and time had not been kind to her since then.

"Well it was nice to see you," Miss Dunne said, and started off in the opposite direction she had come.

"Are you heading home, Miss Dunne?" Joseph asked.

"Yes, I am. Don't you worry 'bout me, though. I'll be fine."

Judging by how badly she swayed as she attempted to walk, Joseph doubted her claim. He couldn't let her walk home in the state she was in. She could fall and get hurt. Even worse, she could stumble out in front of a car and be killed.

"Let me walk you home," Joseph offered.

If he had known what was in store for him once he got to his former teacher's home, he wouldn't have offered to be her escort, no matter how drunk she was. He didn't know what was to come, though, and Joseph Bateman was still a good person at this point in his life. So as she stumbled the entire way, and rambled on about how adorable he had been when he was a little boy, Joseph walked Miss Dunne home.

She lived in a studio apartment on the side of a privately owned house. Joseph watched from the street as she stumbled up the driveway, using the house as a means of support. She fumbled with her bag as she tried to find her keys in the dark. When she finally found them, she dropped them while attempting to find the right one to match her locks. Before she had a chance to go for them and hurt herself, Joseph was up the driveway, and helping Miss Dunne get her door unlocked.

He helped her inside and sat her on the edge of her bed. Her head lolled back and forth as she tried to hold it up. Somehow, she seemed more intoxicated now than she had been when he first saw her outside of the bar.

"Do you need anything before I go?"

128

"Tylenol...medicine cabinet...and water," she managed to slur.

She pointed to the bathroom, and as Joseph made his way across the small apartment, he heard the thump of her body hitting the mattress. He assumed within the minute it took him to do as he was asked and walk back out there, Miss Dunne would pass out. He would remove her shoes, and tuck her in the best he could. Before leaving, he'd leave the Tylenol and water on her nightstand for when she woke up in the morning.

What he imagined was not what he walked out to.

The woman he had seen almost daily for about an entire year of his life was lying in bed, completely naked. Her legs were spread open, so Joseph could get a view of something he would rather have not seen. The surprising sight of his former educator in such an unflattering position left Joseph flabbergasted and at a temporary loss of words.

"I should get going," he finally managed to say.

However, Miss Dunne had other things in mind for her former student. None involved him leaving. Before he knew what was going on, she was up out of the bed, and kissing Joseph.

Even with his experience kissing Alex as his only source of comparison, Joseph knew Miss Dunne was not a good kisser. Her lips were slimy from spittle, and when she forced her tongue into his mouth, he nearly gagged on it.

He tried to push her away, but that only made her more aggressive. Joseph could have overpowered her, but, in the moment, he was so thrown off by what was happening, he didn't consider using his strength to fend off his former second grade teacher. She pulled him down to the bed with her, and on top of her naked body. She continued to kiss him, and when she wanted more, she forced Joseph's head down to her breasts. He felt her nipple brush against his lips, but he did nothing. Miss Dunne moaned in pleasure, as if he had taken it into his mouth.

Part of him hoped that if he waited it out, Miss Dunne would just pass out, and he could sneak out. Unfortunately, Miss Dunne was determined to get what she wanted, and no amount of alcohol was going to get in her way. She went for the waist band of his jeans.

"I should get going," Joseph said. He attempted to get up, but was pushed right back down onto the bed.

"Not so fast, stud," Miss Dunne said. "I still need to thank you for walking me home."

He felt her hands go to the crotch of his jeans, and start to rub. As she did, she went back to attacking Joseph's mouth with her own.

"Someone's a little nervous," she said as she groped Joseph's crotch, and didn't feel the results she was hoping for. "Never been with an older woman, huh? That's fine. I'll take care of you."

She clumsily pulled at his button until finally it came undone. She wrestled with his jeans until she was able to get them down at his knees. She then went for Joseph's underwear. Joseph was frozen with terror by what was happening, and what might happen, that he couldn't find the ability to resist her. He felt the cold room air hit his flaccid penis as his underwear traveled down his legs.

He knew his penis should have been hard by then. Even despite the awkwardness of the whole situation, and the unattractiveness of Miss Dunne, there should have been a point where his body took over. That point hadn't come, though, and he knew it wouldn't. Joseph Bateman hadn't had an erection in over a year.

Ever since the night of he and Alex's first kiss, every time he had a sexual thought, Joseph's mind would go to the moment where he was alone in his bed. He'd remember the mental image that entered his head before experiencing his first orgasm. The possibility of recalling the images of the night he was nearly forced to rape his own mother scared Joseph so much that any chance his penis had of obtaining an erection was instantly KO'd.

Joseph laid there as the woman who had once been in charge of educating him fondled his penis, and attempted to achieve something that would never come. He closed his eyes, and waited for it to just be over. Eventually, she would just give up, and let him leave. That was at least what he hoped for.

Miss Dunne was relentless, though, and as she realized heavy petting wouldn't achieve her goal, things escalated, and got worse. He felt the warmth and moisture around his penis as she took it in her mouth. The results were as expected, and when Miss Dunne failed to arouse Joseph through means of oral stimulation, she took it personally.

"What the hell?" she asked, slapping at his flaccid penis.

"I'm sorry," he tried to explain. "It's not you..."

"What are you; a pillow biter?"

"No!" Joseph exclaimed. He jumped out of the bed and struggled as he wrestled his underwear and pants back up.

"You must be a homo," Miss Dunne, a woman he remembered being so kind when she was his teacher, continued. "I'm sucking your fucking dick, and you can't even get hard? You must not like it, because you wish it was a fucking guy."

"No!" Joseph yelled again. There was now anger in his voice. He turned towards the door to leave before things could get any worse.

"Where are you going, homo?" Miss Dunne yelled. The anger in her voice matched Joseph's own. "Going to find a cock to suck?!"

"SHUT UP, BITCH!" Joseph didn't remember turning back towards the woman verbally harassing him. One moment he was inches away from the door. The next, he was right in her face. "SHUT THE FUCK UP!"

He raised his hand, and slapped Miss Dunne in the face. His second grade teacher fell to the floor. It was more dramatics and drunkenness than anything else, but that didn't stop Joseph from feeling immediate guilt for what he had done.

"Get the fuck out!" she screamed. "You're a fucking homo and a coward."

Joseph tried to apologize for his actions, and attempted to help her to her feet. She shrank back against her bed, and swatted at him like a scared animal.

"GET OUT!!" she repeated.

This time Joseph listened.

He made it to the end of the block before his legs gave way, and he collapsed on some random lawn. He couldn't believe what he had done. His anger had gotten the best of him, and he had struck a woman. He could still feel the skin of his palm throbbing from when it made contact with Miss Dunne's cheek. He hated himself more than anything in that moment. He felt tears forming in his eyes, but they never fell.

He had once swore to Bill Casings that he was nothing like his father. As it turned out, Joseph Bateman was his father's son, after all.

March 30, 1988
Emily Bateman's Gift

Emily Bateman's body was discovered at seven-thirty in the morning on December 27, 1987. It was six years to the date from when her daughter, Elizabeth, was laid to rest. A bottle of sleeping pills her son had refilled just four days earlier lay empty on the nightstand next to two small empty bottles of vodka.

Christmas had been quiet that year, but that was no different from any other Christmas since the accident. There was nothing Joseph could pinpoint that seemed out of the norm. The night of December twenty-sixth, his mother had asked him if he planned on coming home later that night, which she did every time Joseph headed out to spend time with Alex. When he returned home, he checked up on his mother, and she was in bed, seemingly asleep.

As he fell asleep that night, the house was quiet, and everything seemed perfectly normal. He was later awoken by the sound of his mother's whimpering voice. It wasn't the first time Emily Bateman had woken up in pain in the dead of night. Joseph climbed out of bed to check on his mother.

"Please," Joseph heard his mother beg as he approached her bedroom door. "Please, don't."

He burst through the door to see who was harming his mother. Once inside, Joseph was frozen dead in his tracks. What he saw was not possible. It couldn't be real. Yet there it was.

Emily Bateman was in her bed, completely naked. She was on her stomach, and unable to move due to her paralysis. In bed with her was Hank Bateman.

Joseph's late father looked just as he had when he was pulled out of the flaming wreckage of the car he drove off the road six years earlier. His skin was burned from head to toe. Parts of him were charred and still smoking. His hair was all gone; taken by flame. His lips had melted off, and one of his eyeballs had exploded out of its sockets. The only part of him not destroyed by fire was his penis. His undamaged member was ready to inflict its usual damage upon his wife.

He grabbed Emily Bateman, and propped her up so her butt was up in the air. The blackened flesh that gripped her waist peeled off of his bones, and stuck to his widow's hip. He pulled her towards him, and slid into her.

The sight of Hank Bateman—a monster back from the dead—raping the woman he had inflicted his torture upon for years infuriated Joseph. He needed to act, and put an immediate stop to his father's madness. However, when he went to make a move, Joseph found himself as paralyzed and helpless as his own mother. After remembering the last time he tried to play hero, and what had nearly happened, fear took him, and he found himself unable to intervene.

What if Hank Bateman made his son go through with it this time?

Unable to support his own weight any longer, Joseph's knees buckled, and his legs gave out. He collapsed to the floor, and watched as his mother was once again raped by the monster they thought had been vanquished years ago, and was no longer a threat to them. Emily Bateman turned her head towards her son. There was no sadness in her eyes. There was no anger, nor disappointment that her son had failed to act.

"It's okay, Joey Beans," she said to him. "It's okay."

Joseph brought his hands to his face to shield his eyes from the nightmare playing out before him. As he stared at them, a single word entered his mind, and lingered.

Useless... Useless...

Joseph opened his eyes, and was released from his nightmare. His dead father was no longer there; raping his paralyzed wife. Instead, all Joseph saw was the morning sun coming through his window.

It wasn't the first time he dreamt of his father scorched by fire and back from the dead. Each time he had a dream like this, Joseph would go check on his mother. He'd knock on the door and each time, as he opened it, he feared he would see Hank Bateman in the bed. His father would never be there, though. Joseph was protected by the laws of the real world and, in reality, the dead stayed dead.

But on December twenty-seventh, after waking from his nightmare, Joseph got up and checked on his mother, even though he knew it had only been a dream.

He didn't run to her side and desperately check for a pulse. He didn't need to call her name, repeatedly, hoping she'd suddenly answer back. Nor did he shake her body to wake her from the grips of what he prayed was deep sleep. He didn't need to do any of these things to accept what had happened. Joseph knew the moment he saw his mother lying there, peacefully, that she was gone.

Joseph sat beside his mother's bedside in the chair he sat in every night before Emily Bateman fell asleep. He took her hand in his and held it. He did not cry. He just sat there silently with her. His tears would come later on.

Six days later, on the day Emily Bateman was laid to rest, as he and Alex sat beside the fresh grave, Joseph's grief finally overtook him. One moment, the two friends were sitting silently by the graveside, and the next, Joseph was weeping in Alex's lap. Alex said nothing as Joseph collapsed into her. She just sat there, and allowed Joseph to mourn the loss of his mother.

When his grief had exhausted him, and there were no more tears to be spilled, Joseph returned home to the apartment he and his mother had lived in. Before her death, Emily Bateman had paid the rent through February of 1988. Even in her final days, she would ensure that her son would not find himself homeless after her death.

It was only a small part of Emily Bateman's final gift.

Joseph spent those last few months packing the apartment up. He held on to a few keepsakes, but he donated most of his mother's belongings to charity. He knew it was where she would want her stuff to end up.

As February came to a close, there would be no question as to where Joseph would live after leaving the apartment. Bill Casings made the decision before the subject was even considered. Joseph would be welcomed with open arms into the Casings' household and family.

Each day, he and Alex would walk to and from school. They would eat at the same table. They shared the same bathroom. At night, they'd argue over what to watch on television. Despite the close quarters, their friendship did not suffer. Alex had become his rock following Emily Bateman's passing, and on the days Joseph found himself missing his mother, he could rely on his Alex to be there to lessen his pain. For this, Joseph was eternally thankful, and their friendship was only strengthened through this new bond.

During the first week of March, Joseph was contacted by his mother's lawyer. Joseph had left no forwarding address with his old landlord, but through the school, he had finally been tracked down.

The phone call was brief. Emily Bateman's lawyer informed Joseph that he wanted to meet to discuss the details of Joseph's late mother's estate. Joseph thought the whole thing was odd. To begin with, Joseph had no idea his mother even had a lawyer. Emily Bateman told her son everything, and never once did she mention a lawyer. As it turned out, Emily Bateman had her share of secrets, and how she managed to keep them from her son, Joseph could not figure out. His mother couldn't exactly come and go as she pleased. What Joseph found stranger than his mother's secret lawyer was the nature of the meeting the lawyer was contacting him about.

Emily Bateman never had much in her life, so Joseph couldn't think of any 'details' of her estate that needed to be settled. The house was sold years ago, and the profit went towards medical bills. She had nothing in the form of savings set aside, and, as far as Joseph knew, everything she owned of importance or value was in their apartment. He would soon learn that wasn't the case, though.

Emily Bateman's best kept secret would be her greatest gift to her son.

Joseph had put off scheduling to meet with the lawyer. The part of him that refused to make the appointment was the same part of him that knew once his mother's affairs were settled there'd be nothing left of her but memories. Still, he owed it to her to see this through. Whatever it was this lawyer had for him, Emily Bateman wanted her son to have it. So on March 30, 1988, after spending way too much time obsessing over what choice of attire was the perfect median between too little and overdone, Joseph met with the lawyer to discuss Emily Bateman's last Will and Testament.

After a half hour wait, Joseph met with his mother's lawyer. He was greeted with a handshake, and gestured to take a seat. Joseph did so, and the lawyer took his own seat behind his desk.

"I apologize for the wait," the lawyer, whose name was Rothenberg. "I was trying to tie up some loose ends on another case, and lost track of time."

"It's fine," Joseph said.

"Well, I won't waste your time," Rothenberg continued. Joseph had a feeling Rothenberg really meant he didn't want to waste any more of his own time. "Your mother first came to see me not long before her accident. Over the years, she had accrued quite a lot in the form of savings. Your father was unaware of its existence. The reason your mother sought out legal counsel was to ensure all the money she had put away would go to her children in the instance of her death, and would be safe from your father."

Joseph was taken aback by this information. It was a lot to take in and process. He couldn't believe his mother had this huge secret. Even after Hank Bateman was dead, and no longer a threat to her nest egg, she kept it to herself.

More than that, what truly left Joseph speechless, not to mention saddened, was the realization that his mother had set up this secret savings because she knew that one day Hank Bateman would go too far, and would kill her. She needed to be sure her children had the means for an opportunity to escape their father once she was gone.

"How much?" Joseph asked.

The number that came from Rothenberg's mouth once again rendered Joseph unable to articulate.

"Just under two-hundred and seventy thousand dollars."

How the hell did she manage to save that much money?! Joseph asked himself. He then recalled his childhood, and was able to figure out how truly brilliant his mother was.

Hank Bateman had only given his wife the bare minimum as far as money, but because of his constant absence—not to mention, drunkenness—he had no idea what was actually needed to keep the roof over his family's head. Emily Bateman could have easily been asking for extra money each month to put aside. Throughout the years it would add up. There was also the money she made off the sale of the house. Joseph assumed all the money from that went towards her hospital and care bills, but if there was anything left over, she could have put it aside as well. Even the money Joseph handed his mother every week from his paycheck could have gone into her secret savings to eventually be returned to her son.

However she did it, she had accomplished her goal and secured her son's future.

"You still have to wait a few more months before you can touch the money," Rothenberg explained. "Your mother made sure that you couldn't access these funds until your eighteenth birthday. We should start the process of changing over the accounts to your name now. That way, when you turn eighteen, you'll have full access to your inheritance."

They had gone over a few more small details before their meeting ended. Joseph had to sign a few documents, and once all the *t*'s were crossed and *i*'s were dotted, he was the recipient of a nearly two-hundred and seventy-thousand dollar inheritance.

As he walked home, Joseph thought about his mother. He had always been aware of the sacrifices she constantly made for her family. Many times, they were ones he didn't agree with, nor fully understand. As it turned out, what he had known of his mother was only the tip of the iceberg.

Emily Bateman devoted her life to her children and securing their future. Selflessness was her true legacy. Joseph knew she would likely be remembered by others as a woman who let her drunk of a husband beat and rape her. That didn't matter, though. He knew who she was in her life, and would always remember his mother as a woman who put herself in harm's way in order to give her children a chance to escape a life they didn't deserve.

That was Emily Bateman's greatest gift.

August 23, 1988
Shelter from the Rain

Two best friends walked down the street one summer evening at dusk. The girl enjoyed a root beer float while the boy ate nothing. They didn't speak. There had been an afternoon full of conversation and laughter between the two, so the silence bothered neither of them. Massive rainclouds moved in from over the lake, and within the next few moments the two friends would find themselves caught in a sudden downpour. Neither knew it, but the entire dynamic of their relationship was about to change.

Joseph felt the first raindrop hit the back of his neck. A second followed, and hit the front of his shirt. He looked down, and saw two more smash into the fabric, followed by a third. Like tiny meteors made up of water, rain drops crashed into him. He looked over at Alex, who had tiny splash marks on her own clothing. She looked back at him, and the two friends knew they needed to get going.

They took off running, but it did not matter. Heavy rains fell from the sky and, within seconds, both were soaked. Too far from home, Joseph and Alex needed to find shelter from the rain, which currently seemed to be falling in sheets. They ran to the first establishment with an awning in sight. Joseph looked around, and when he realized where they were, he immediately wished they had ended up anywhere else.

They were standing in front of Leonard Hershel's General Store.

It was right then that the urge to urinate hit Joseph. It wasn't just a hint of the sensation, either. Despite being the one who hadn't consumed an entire beverage, Joseph was overtaken by a full blown about-to-burst need to pee.

"I'm going inside to use the bathroom," he told Alex.

The moment he spoke, he knew Alex would have something to say.

"You're going to go in there and use the same bathroom that nigger uses?" Alex asked. She made no attempted to hide the disgust in her tone.

"I'm just going in to pee."

"It doesn't matter if you sit or stand. You can catch all kinds of diseases just from standing in the same room as them!"

"I'll take my chances," Joseph said, dismissing Alex's outdated and absurdly untrue claim. "I really have to pee."

He entered the store, and headed right to the bathroom. On his way, he passed Mister Hershel, who greeted Joseph with a welcoming hello and a smile to match. Joseph gave a quick wave of his own, and hoped Alex wasn't peering inside the store to see him acknowledging Mister Hershel's existence.

The moment he was standing over the toilet bowl and in position, Joseph let the urine flow. The sense of relief had been borderline euphoric, and he was so caught up with the amazing feeling that he didn't even hear the bell above the store's door sound.

Once what seemed to be the longest piss of his life had concluded, Joseph zipped up, and washed his hands. He was in the midst of drying them when he heard the commotion out in the store. The moment he heard Alex's voice, he knew there was going to be trouble. Fearing what had already happened, and what might happen next, Joseph rushed out of the bathroom and into the store.

Joseph walked out to Mister Hershel grabbing Alex by one of her wrists. Alex was attempting to free herself while screaming racial obscenities at him. In her other hand, she held some sort of trinket, which he knew was an item being sold in the store. He also knew Alex had picked it up with no intentions, whatsoever, of paying for it. Leonard Hershel, no doubt, knew the exact same thing.

Joseph watched as the two struggled with one another, each refusing to give up. He'd have to intervene and break the scuffle up. He approached them, but neither took notice of his presence. Joseph grabbed Leonard Hershel by the arm and spun him around. The store owner turned towards Joseph and received a fist right to the cheek.

Joseph felt the force of his punch connecting with Mister Hershel's face as it resonated throughout his arm. The man, who was a half century older than Joseph, collapsed to the floor. As he looked down at a man he had seen on a semi-regular basis his entire life, Joseph immediately felt regret for his decision.

If Joseph had any intentions to apologize for what he had done, he didn't get the chance to do so. Alex had him by the arm and was pulling him towards the door. Joseph knew the authorities would be called, whether he regretted what he had done or not. He followed Alex, and left Leonard Hershel lying on the floor of his store.

The torrential rains hadn't tapered off, and pelted the two as they fled the General Store. They hadn't been running for long before Joseph spotted the chain-linked fence with a hole cut into it. He grabbed Alex's arm, and the two headed towards the fence.

They crawled through the hole and found themselves in the yard of a house that had been recently condemned. It was boarded up, except for a single basement window that had probably been kicked out by a squatter or teenager looking for a private place to drink or get high. Joseph climbed in first, and Alex followed suit. It was dark and it was damp, but it would do.

Joseph hadn't had much time to take in and assess his surroundings. One moment, he and Alex were crawling through the basement window of a boarded up house. The next, Alex was kissing him and the world around Joseph ceased to matter.

The kiss they now shared was unlike their first awkward experience. Alex's lips encompassed his, and when he felt her tongue slide into his mouth, he felt his heart pounding against his chest.

That wasn't all he felt, either.

Against his jeans, Joseph Bateman felt something he hadn't felt in years: his erect penis.

Unlike his last sexual altercation, the recollection of what had happened the last time he had been able to get an erection didn't cross his mind. The only thing his brain was able to compute was that he was kissing Alex. He was finally kissing her, and not even his demented past was going to mess that up for him.

Joseph wasn't the only one who took notice of the sudden change in his jeans. Upon feeling it brush against her, Alex's hand went from Joseph's hip to his crotch. Alex's hand found his penis, and Joseph felt he was going to experience his second orgasm right then. Luckily, by some grace of God, he was able to get himself back under control.

"You punched him in the face," Alex said, pulling away from their kiss. "You protected me. You kept me safe."

She placed her hand on his cheek and stared at him. Joseph wondered if she was seeing him differently, like he had seen her after their first kiss. He tried to speak, but she shushed him before he could get any words out. She took his hand, and placed it beneath his shirt, right on the warm skin of her stomach. This time it was Joseph who kissed Alex.

Her hands went to his jeans, and wrestled with his button. When he felt it finally pop open, Joseph took it as his cue to move forward. Both excited and petrified, he lifted Alex's shirt. She followed his lead. She broke their kiss yet again, and Joseph had to fight the urge to plead with her not to stop. She backed away from Joseph so that he could have a full view of her. She reached behind her back, unhooked her bra, and let it fall to the ground.

Her jeans and underwear went next.

"Come here," Alex instructed.

Joseph obeyed. He battled his desire to examine every inch of perfection that was Alex's naked body, and kept eye contact.

"Will you keep me safe?" she asked.

"I will."

Alex climbed on top of the workbench, and waited for Joseph. He removed his jeans and underwear, and joined her.

"Keep me safe," she pleaded with him.

"I promise…Always."

As he slid into her for the very first time, Joseph no longer remembered the regret he felt for what he had just done to Leonard Hershel.

August 24, 1988
The Source of Alex's Hatred

It lasted longer than Joseph had it expected it to. Still, despite his best efforts, he and Alex's first time together was a short-lived experience. It was also one filled with its share of awkwardness. He didn't think Alex would hold it against him, though. No one gets anything perfect on the first try, after all.

When they had finished, and their virginities were gone, like two small whispers in a booming wind, Joseph and Alex dressed. They resurfaced from the basement they had used as shelter to clear skies. The rain had stopped and the heat from summer sun beat down on their skin. Alex's fingers interlocked with Joseph's, and the two remained that way—holding hands—for the entirety of their walk home. They didn't speak. They didn't need to. They were both on the same page.

Once home, the night was as quiet as their walk. They ate dinner, and watched television on the couch until they both passed out. They were both in a temporary bubble where everything was perfect. Eventually it would burst, and they'd have to let reality back into their lives, but they chose to put that off as long as they possibly could.

Alex stirred in the middle of the night. As she attempted to head to her own bed, Joseph was woken up. He almost stayed quiet, and let her leave, just so the bubble could remain intact until the morning. He spoke, though, and as he did, the words that left his mouth served as pins that finally burst their perfect bubble.

"Why do you hate black people, Alex?"

He had asked her that very question before. The last time in 1979 on the day after Alex had pelted Eve Meyers in the head with a rock. Back then, Alex's answer was short. She told Joseph they had destroyed her family, and left it at that. Now, as she stood in the center of her dark living room, she repeated the same answer she had given nine years earlier. Joseph was prepared for Alex to leave the room, thus closing the matter abruptly, once again. However, instead of stepping forward, Alex backtracked to the couch. She sat on it, and proceeded to tell her best friend the story of how her family had been torn apart.

Growing up, Joseph Bateman's life was very different from Alexandra Casings'. While he had to hear his mother getting raped and beaten by his drunken father on an almost nightly basis, Alex got to spend those nights on the couch with her two parents.

Bill and Maureen Casings were high school sweethearts, who married the summer after they graduated. It wasn't long after their nuptials that the two became three, and their daughter was welcomed into the world. The Casings family could be seen enjoying a summer night from their front porch, taking a stroll down to the lake, or playing together at the park. To anyone who saw them, they were the picture perfect family, which was why it was a complete shock when it all fell apart.

1976, the year Joseph saw fresh cuts and bruises on his mother's face just because she wanted to bake her son a

147

cake for his birthday, saw a huge turning point in the life of Alexandra Casings. It was the year her family unit died.

Maureen Casings was a working woman. She did it to help provide for the lifestyle she and her husband wanted for their family, but she also did it because she loved it. She had a magnetic personality, and anyone who met Maureen loved to be around her. This made her the perfect door-to-door makeup saleswoman. Her loyal client base, mixed with her ability to bring in new customers, made her the top saleswoman for her company. As a reward from her bosses, she would constantly be chosen to represent her company at conventions throughout the northeast.

In 1976, the number of conventions Maureen Casings was chosen to attend increased. Her husband never once questioned a single overnight or weekend trip she made that entire summer. He had no reason to. Bill Casings, nor anyone else, would have suspected any suspicious activity from Maureen. After all, the Casings were the picture of the perfect family unit.

Well, not all pictures are as they seem.

Throughout the entire spring and summer of 1976, Maureen Casings was having an extramarital affair. That fall, she was forced to come clean about her infidelities when she found herself pregnant with the child of a man who was not her husband.

Alex, who was six at the time, was startled awake from the sound of her father's cries. She had fallen asleep in one life—a perfect one—and had woken up in another. She'd soon learn this new life was the complete opposite of the one she had known. It would be a nightmare.

She got out of her bed, and snuck into the living room to see what the commotion was. There, she saw her mother cowering in the corner of the couch. Standing over her was Bill Casings. He was screaming at his wife, although his sobs were so thick, his words were barely audible. Alex had never seen her father mad like this before. She wanted to scream for him to stop, but was too scared to say anything.

Then Alex witnessed her father strike her mother.

It was a singular blow, but Bill made it count. Desperate to protect her mother from further harm, Alex ran out of the darkness, and dove into her mother's lap. She hugged her mommy, and begged her father not to be angry anymore. Bill, realizing his daughter had just witnessed everything, backed away. He didn't apologize for what he had done. He didn't speak at all. Even his cries had ceased. He just backed away from his wife and daughter until he hit the wall behind him. He then turned and left the house. Maureen called after her husband to come back, but he didn't return.

That night Alex slept in her parents' bed, cuddled up next to her mom.

The next morning, Bill had still not returned from wherever it was he went. Alex was set up in the living room with an abundance of toys, games, and coloring books—Alex's personal favorite at six years old—to keep her busy. Maureen spent the entire morning in her bedroom, and then the entire afternoon going back and forth between her room and the front yard. By three o'clock, the babysitter was called over to watch Alex. Maureen kissed her daughter, and gave her a long hug. The hug didn't seem weird at the time, but looking back, Alex knew exactly what it meant.

Alex was told to be good for the babysitter, and she promised her mom she would. She could remember her mother lingering there for a moment. Throughout the years, Alex hoped it was hesitation that kept her mother there for that extra second. Regardless of the reason, it didn't change Maureen Casings' mind. As Alex returned to her coloring books, she heard the screen door slam shut as her mother left the house.

Alex would never see her mother again.

Bill Casings returned later that evening. After being home for not even twenty minutes, he called the babysitter back over. Alex was asleep when her father returned that night, and he was already gone by the time she woke up the following morning. For days, Alex would go without seeing either of her parents.

"He was out looking for my mom," Alex told Joseph, as they sat on the very couch she saw her father strike her mother upon. "He never told me it was what he was doing, but I figured it out when I got older. I think he wanted to forgive her."

Only Maureen Casings didn't want to be forgiven by her husband, and Bill Casings would figure that out all on his own after days of failed searches. The visitor he had nine days after his wife walked out on the family she helped build only solidified this conclusion.

One night, Bill Casings was watching television with his daughter on the couch. By then, Alex had forgiven her father for what he had done to her mommy that night they had their big fight. Truth was, she was lonely. The absence of her parents was something she had never experienced in her life. What her father had done didn't matter anymore. All that mattered to Alex was that he stayed with her at night, instead of leaving. As they watched their weekly shows, there were three hard knocks at the front door. When Bill opened the front door a fist was there to meet his face.

Alex saw her father collapse to the floor. His hands went right to his nose, which had already started to bleed and was likely broken. She ran to him, and wrapped her arms around him in an attempt to protect him from the man standing in the doorway to their house. She didn't know it

150

at the time, but the man who had struck her father was the same man who impregnated her mother. The same man who was the reason Maureen Casings walked out on her family.

He was black.

The color of his skin meant nothing to Alex at the time, but in the years to follow it would play a huge factor in molding the person Alexandra Casings would become. She, and her father, of course.

"STOP!" Alex screamed at the man in the doorway. "Leave my daddy alone!"

Luckily—for Bill Casings more than anyone else—the man who had just punched her father had no intentions of following up with additional physical damage.

"That was for hitting her," he informed Bill. "I don't have to threaten you to never do it again, because you're never going to see her again. You understand me?"

Bill remained silent. The man in the doorway didn't care if he got a response or not. He did what he came to do, and said what he needed to say. Without another word, he turned and left Bill Casings on the floor being comforted by his daughter with a busted up nose.

The divorce proceedings did not take long. Maureen was willing to give up everything for a quick and clean divorce. This included all custodial rights to her own daughter. The lawyers handled everything, and Bill and Maureen Casings did not see each other once throughout the entire process.

Alex had little understanding of what was happening. All she knew was that her family was in the process of being torn apart. It was the last thing on Earth she wanted, and she would plead with her father on a nightly basis to make her mommy come home, and live with them again. It was in these vulnerable moments where Bill Casings planted the seeds of racism in his daughter's head.

It started with Bill blaming black people for Alex's mother leaving, and never coming back. He did not single out the individual with whom his wife had an affair. Instead, he blamed the black community as a whole. According to Bill, black people were no more than a bunch of no good home wreckers. As the years went on, he would find a way to blame black people for everything that went wrong in the world, and for every ignorant thing Bill had to say, his young and impressionable daughter was there to learn from the only parental figure she had in her life.

Alex took every word her father spoke as the truth. As the years went by, the racism Bill instilled in his daughter became part of who she was. As far as she was concerned, black people were not deserving of the same air as white people breathed, and all they did was ruin society.

And that was the story of why Alexandra Casings hated black people.

Alex had concluded her story at a quarter past two in the morning. There wasn't anything left to say once she had gotten it all out. She just got up and went to bed. As for Joseph, there would be no sleep. Instead, he would lay wide awake on the couch as his mind raced.

He had known Alex's racism had come from her father. The night he and Bill destroyed Leonard Hershel's car for no other reason than the color of his skin had made that obvious. However, Joseph never really considered how deep the roots of the Casings' racism went. After hearing Alex's story, it was now fully sinking in.

Joseph refused to let the fatherly bond he had developed with Bill cloud his judgement, and it allowed him to see the man for who he really was: someone who couldn't deal with his own personal demons and took it out on the ones around him.

It was a story all too familiar to Joseph Bateman.

With the blinders off, Joseph felt hatred for Bill Casings rising up from within. It wasn't as strong as the hate he had once felt for Hank Bateman, but it was certainly cut from the same cloth.

Too angry to sleep, Joseph decided to get up and go for a walk with hopes that it would clear his head. Before leaving, he grabbed a few things. He wasn't sure if he was going to need them, or if he was going to end up being too scared, but he'd take them with him, just in case.

At first, he walked the streets aimlessly. He did this to avoid where he had planned to go. He needed time to gather up the courage. He thought if he gave himself enough time, he would be ready. He was wrong. Still, he knew what he had to do. So, as unprepared as he was, Joseph walked until, finally, he was standing in front of Leonard Hershel's house.

Even after finding his way to the residence of the man he had just assaulted the day before, Joseph found himself too petrified to step onto the property. The last time he had been there was the night he and Bill had vandalized Mister Hershel's car. That, topped with the fact he had just sucker punched the man in the face, made Joseph the last person in the world who had any right standing anywhere near Leonard Hershel's property. Yet there he was, and he couldn't leave until he did what he set out into the night to do.

He forced himself up the driveway to where Leonard Hershel's car—the same car he had vandalized years before—was parked. As he approached the vehicle, he expected Mister Hershel to spring from his home to ward off the intruder on his property. Nothing of the sort happened, and the house remained dark and quiet.

He pulled the envelope he normally kept hidden under the couch from his back pocket. Joseph opened it, and skimmed through the crisp bills the teller at the bank had

153

given him. He counted each twenty dollar bill in the envelope, and divided by five. The envelope contained four hundred and forty dollars. He closed the envelope, and temporarily returned it to his back pocket.

Next, Joseph pulled out a blank piece of paper and pen that he had taken from the kitchen table right as he was leaving the house. He leaned against the hood of the car and, with the moon as his only source of light, he composed a letter.

Mr. Hershel, he wrote. *I am sorry I punched you. I am also sorry we stole from your store. The money in this envelope covers the cost of the item stolen, as well as any other damage done.*

Whatever it was Alex had stolen—he didn't know, because she had tossed it while they were fleeing the General Store—Joseph knew it hadn't cost over four hundred dollars. He had no idea if he had broken the old man's nose, though. If he did, Mister Hershel would have medical bills that needed to be paid. If nothing was broken, Joseph considered the money he was about to leave as reimbursement for the damage he and Bill had done to Mister Hershel's car years ago. If the cost of the car damages still did not add up to the amount Joseph was leaving, the remainder would be for any emotional distress Joseph had caused Mister Hershel.

For what reason the money was being left didn't matter. The bottom line was that Leonard Hershel was going to wake up in the morning, and find four hundred and forty dollars tucked beneath the windshield wiper of his car with an unsigned apology note.

Joseph pulled the envelope of cash from his pocket. He folded the note he had written, tucked it away inside, and went to place it under the windshield wiper. He hesitated, though. Joseph wasn't completely satisfied with what he had written. Something was missing. He took a moment to collect his thoughts, and then yanked the note out of the envelope. He unfolded the paper, and added:

You will never have to worry about seeing either of us ever again.

He was referring to himself and Alex, of course. However, he did not mean that Mister Hershel would never have to see them again, because neither of them would ever again step foot in the General Store. Joseph included the last line of his note, because he planned on leaving Wayne's County forever, and he fully intended to take Alex with him.

The idea had crossed his mind while he was avoiding Leonard Hershel's home, and he battled back and forth with it. Now, however, there was no conflict within Joseph. Neither he nor Alex could stay in Wayne County. Their only option was to leave and start their lives over.

He'd just need to convince Alex.

That could wait until the morning, though. With his mind at ease, Joseph found himself exhausted. He needed to conserve what energy he had left for the walk home. He returned the note to the envelope, sealed it, and placed it underneath the windshield wiper. Without second thought, Joseph walked down Leonard Hershel's driveway, and headed home.

When he returned home, he passed out the moment his head hit the pillow. He woke late the next morning, which was good, because the next few weeks would be very busy for Joseph Bateman.

August 25, 1988

Joseph Bateman Jumps

Joseph and Alex were at the lake they had made their frequent hang out spot for the eleven years that they had been friends. They sat in the tree where they shared their first kiss together. Neither of them knew it then—although Joseph hoped—but it would be the last time the two of them would ever sit together in that spot.

Joseph hadn't talked to Alex yet about his plans and his hopes to bring her with him. He had ample opportunities the day before, but couldn't bring himself to say what needed to be said. Now, as they sat above the lake, Joseph again found himself wanting to bring his plan to light, but found, once again, the words trapped in the darkness of his throat. It didn't help matters either when the two of them started to kiss.

The kissing was nice and it was calming. When it concluded, they sat in perfect silence; watching the sun set over the lake. Alex rested her head on Joseph's shoulder, and he wrapped his arm around her. Just another layer to the perfection that was them together. He wanted so badly to say what needed to be said. He wanted them to share moments exactly like the one they were sharing right then, over and over. Only he wanted them to be away from this place that had such a negative effect on and bad memories for the both of them. Still, the words wouldn't move.

What all his trepidation boiled down to was the fact that he had to ask Alex to leave behind everything she had ever known, and she might say no. Joseph knew this was what they both needed, but Alex might not agree. She might not be ready to take the dangerous leap into uncertainty. He would have to show her that sometimes it was worth facing fear head on.

Then it dawned on him.

If he was going to ask Alex to embark on this new, scary path, he would need to finally face his own fears. He would have to come at them head on and find the courage to overcome them. If he didn't do this first, he had no right to ask anything of Alex.

So without saying a word, Joseph stood up, removed his shoes, socks, and shirt. He bent over, kissed Alex on the mouth, and did something he should have done years ago.

He finally jumped from that damn tree into the lake.

Not even a moment after he threw himself from the tree, Joseph was submerged in the lake's water.

That was it? he asked himself. *That's what I've been afraid of all these years?*

He came to the surface, and saw Alex applauding him for his long overdue accomplishment. A grin was stretched across her face and she was laughing. For the first time in their long friendship, Joseph was the one in the water, and Alex was the one left behind in the tree. That didn't last long, though. Alex removed her pants, shirt and bra, and joined Joseph in the water.

"It's about time!" Alex said the moment she came to the surface. "It only took you like ten years"

She swam into his arms, and kissed him. Her kiss broke the paralysis that froze his tongue. It shattered the barrier of lips and teeth that were holding back the words he had wanted to say for over a day now. Their lips parted, and the words poured from Joseph's mouth.

"I think we should leave this place," he said. "You and I, together. I think we should leave town, and start over fresh somewhere new."

The instant the words were out of his mouth and in the air for Alex to absorb, Joseph regretted them. After hearing what he was suggesting out loud, he saw how absurd and idiotic it was to even present. She had just told him the story of how her mother had abandoned her entire family, and here he was asking her to do the same. He waited for his suggestion to enrage her, and readied himself to watch her swim to shore and storm off.

Alex didn't swim away from him, though. She took a single moment to consider what Joseph had just said, and gave her answer.

"Okay."

"Really?" Joseph asked, thinking maybe his mind was playing tricks on him.

"I told you two nights ago that I hate black people because they destroyed my family, and that's all true, but I also hate them because they destroyed my father."

Well, a single black person destroyed both, Joseph wanted to say, *It could have easily have been a white man who your mom ran off with.*

"It's been over ten years," Alex continued. "But I still remember him. The way he was before she left. When it was the three of us. He was so happy, and full of life. He's tried to put on a front over the years, but I know it's forced. It's not natural anymore. It's like when my mom left, she took all my father's happiness with her."

She cleared her throat, and tried to play it off like she had got a bit of water in her throat. Joseph knew she was fighting off tears.

"I'm so sick of hatred, Joseph. For all these years, that's what I've had to live with. I'm not stupid. I know I am who I am because I grew up around him, and heard all the things he had to say after my mom was gone. I know I shouldn't have felt that way, but it breaks my heart to see him miserable after knowing who he once was. Not only have niggers taken my mother away from me, but they took my father away from me, as well!

"Maybe—just maybe—if I leave, and I don't have to see him every day, I can rid myself of some of this weight. I'm so sick of carrying it. It's a burden, Joseph. I'm ready not to live with it anymore."

Alex wanted the same thing Joseph had, and together they were going to find it. They swam to shore, and made love under the very tree Joseph had been petrified to jump out of for years. He had finally jumped, though. He took the risk, and was rewarded with the knowledge that there was nothing to be scared of. Now he had to take one more fearful jump. One that landed him and Alex in a new life. He was ready for this jump, though. Alex was with him to take it, and with her by his side, their happy ending seemed inevitable.

Things would not go according to plan, though, and all this life-altering decision would turn out to be was yet another stepping stone on the path to the electric chair for Joseph Bateman.

September 2, 1988
The Road to a New Beginning

Joseph's first big purchase with the money his mother had left him was a car. It wasn't anything fancy, but it would be enough to get them out of Wayne's County. Once the car was registered, inspected, insured and ready to go, Joseph paid the man who sold him the car an additional two-hundred and fifty dollars to keep it in his driveway for about a week until he was ready for it. He couldn't risk Bill Casings seeing the car and asking questions. If this was going to work, Alex's father had to have zero suspicions, whatsoever.

The decision to leave without warning was a struggle for Alex. Joseph could see it in her eyes whenever they talked about it. She was about to be the second important woman in Bill Casings' life to leave without a word, and disappear forever. It was the only option, though. Bill would not accept his daughter's decision to leave, and would do everything in his power to stop it.

So they would leave silently, and leave Bill to realize he was alone in the world.

While Joseph handled the transportation arrangements, Alex's responsibility was to discreetly pack up the things

160

they wanted to take with them to their new life. It didn't amount to much.

On the morning of September 2, 1988, after Bill had left for work, they packed up the car. Alex took a few minutes to look around the house she had spent her entire life in. The tears flowed freely from her eyes as she grieved. She walked to the kitchen table, and on it she placed a letter that she had spent days crafting. It was addressed to her father and it explained to him, to the best of her ability, why she needed to leave.

What she wrote exactly, Joseph never knew. He never asked her, and in the final minutes of his life, as his final breath rapidly approached him, he could not care less what that stupid bitch wrote to her father.

With the car packed up, and Alex's note left, there was nothing left to do but leave. Despite not having any idea where they were going, they drove in silence for a long while. Their destination did not matter. All they knew was that wherever they ended up, it would be where their new beginning was.

April 26, 1995
Joseph Bateman's Long Walk

The lights snapped on in Joseph's cell. With the small cell now lit up, he was able to look upon his masterpiece of a mess he had created throughout the night. He was proud of what he had done, but it was overshadowed by his overwhelming awareness that this was it.

This was the end.

His cell door unlocked and slid open. Standing in the doorway were two correctional officers. One he had never seen before; he must have been new. The other he knew well. His name was Conroy Nates, the C.O. Joseph saw and interacted with the most during his stint on death row. Being he was black, Nates was the C.O. Joseph gave the most shit to.

Truth was, Joseph didn't mind C.O. Conroy Nates that much. He could even say he liked the man. He had a sarcastic personality and often joked with the inmates left in his charge. He was easygoing, as long as you cooperated with him, and he wasn't a hard ass with an undeserved sense of power just because of his position. Like some of the other correctional officers Joseph had seen or interacted with.

Joseph would never admit he liked Conroy Nates. Because of the man's skin color, Joseph had to outwardly portray hatred and disrespect towards him.

C.O. Nates stepped into the cell while the other guard stood in the doorway. He looked around at the scattered jellybeans, but chose not to address the mess. Joseph could see he was annoyed by it, though.

"Please stand, inmate," Nates said, instead.

Joseph rose, and cuffs were clamped on his wrists. It was more procedural than anything else. Nates knew Joseph would give him no problems. There were some might crack as realization sank in, and attempt to physically resist the inevitable. Joseph wouldn't be one of those people, though. He had known for a long time that this moment was coming, and he was ready for it.

This was his long walk.

The atmosphere was solemn as they walked. Each of Joseph's footsteps, although probably no heavier than they had been the day before, sounded like a sledge hammer coming down on the concrete. There was no sarcasm from Conroy Nates. The corrections officer didn't speak at all. How many people had he walked to the electric chair? How many men had he escorted to their deaths? Joseph had no idea, but judging by his demeanor, whatever that number may have been, Conroy Nates never became numb to his duties.

Still, Joseph wondered if there was perhaps an ounce of satisfaction coursing through Nates' veins. It was no big secret why Joseph was on Death Row, and throughout the duration of his stay, he had shot a racial remark in Conroy Nates' direction on multiple occasions.

"You must be feeling like a pig in shit right about now," Joseph said, breaking the silence. "Death to the nigger hater, huh?"

"That's enough, inmate!"

It wasn't Nates who scolded Joseph for his language. It was the new guy. Joseph was about ready to laugh in the guy's face, but Nates saved the day by stepping between the two before things could escalate.

"That's okay, C.O.," Nates said. "Thank you, but I can handle this. May I have a moment with the inmate?"

There was a questioning look on the young man's face, but he didn't speak up. Instead, he nodded, walked away, and left Joseph alone with Conroy Nates for a one-on-one chat.

"Uh-oh," Joseph said, sarcastically "I'm in trouble."

"Oh, shut the fuck up, Bateman," Conroy Nates fired back. Joseph obeyed. "If you think you're the first ignorant white person to call me a nigger, than you're certainly the dumbest person I have ever met. I'm forty-two years old. I was eleven when segregation ended. I experienced racism, firsthand, living in the south; where being constantly called names was the least of your problems."

"I have seen racism in its ugliest form. I have met people who prayed to God for the extermination of the Negro population, and I can tell you something...you ain't one of those people."

Joseph disagreed. His past actions, including the one that landed him on death row, were certainly points he could use as a counterargument.

"What you are," Conroy Nates continued before Joseph could issue a rebuttal, "is a whole different beast, entirely. You just hate. Some crazy-ass shit must have happened in your life, and left you with a horrendous taste in your mouth, because you hate everyone, and everything. You just decide to dump all that hatred on black people. It gives you somewhere to focus all that negative shit, instead of having it all over the damn place. You are many things, Bateman, but you're not a racist. I'm sorry to burst your bubble."

Joseph could have argued with the man, but he chose not to. Instead, he considered what Nates had just said. He and Alex had left Wayne County in search of a better life, but in the years that followed, Joseph Bateman transformed into someone who barely resembled the person he once was. Who he'd turned into sounded a lot like the man Conroy Nates had just described.

"You know," Nates continued. "It's tragic that this is the case with you, Bateman. You see, racists may be ignorant, but they still have people they love. You have no one. In the end, you're truly alone. You may not regret killing that young man. Honestly, I don't blame you. I just hope you regret not being able to let go of whatever happened to you that made you this way. Maybe if you had, you wouldn't be dead at twenty-six."

Conroy Nates had been wrong about one thing. Joseph had loved something in his life. He loved Alex. He loved her so damn much that he killed for her. He had given up his right to live for her, and, in the end, all of that was a mistake. If there were any regrets to be had, it was going to be that he had sacrificed everything for that selfish bitch.

"Let's go, inmate," Nates finally said after no acknowledgement came in response to everything he had just said.

They walked to the end of the corridor, and rejoined the new guy. The three of them then made a left, and started their way down another long corridor. It may not have been any longer than twenty-five feet in length, but it might as well have been a mile. At the end was a single door. On the other side of that door was a room. There, Joseph Bateman would be prepped for his last ride.

As Joseph walked the longest yard, he continued to reflect on his life. He thought about the time he and Alex had spent together after leaving their old lives behind. He had left Wayne County so in love. It was supposed to be a new beginning, where both of them would shed the shadows of their past, and live life scar-free. Sadly, Peter Pan was the only person who could lose his shadow. Scars, no matter how long you give them, never heal.

August 26, 1991
Bar and Back Alley Altercations

Joseph's idol growing up was Bruno Sammartino, a wrestling legend, and the definition of a man. He was strong and fearless and never backed down from a challenge. His heart and brute strength were why wrestling fans, worldwide, adored him, and why he was the heavyweight champion when the calendar year started, and still the champion when it concluded.

In essence, he was everything Joseph Bateman had wished he could be.

When Joseph and Alex ended up settling down in Manhattan in the fall of 1988, they allowed themselves to make acquaintances and begin friendships with people besides each other. It was through this newfound group of friends that Joseph rediscovered WWF wrestling. On August 26, 1991, Joseph got to experience his first wrestling event live at Madison Square Garden.

Even though his childhood hero may had been long retired from the ring, Joseph had a blast at the summer event. He barely resembled the young man who had left Wayne County. In fact, over the course of the three years since leaving home, Joseph transformed into someone who was actually happy and able to have fun.

Sadly, all good things must end, and by the conclusion of the night, Joseph's happiness would be ripped out from under him. He would wake up the next morning and find himself, once again, feeling a familiar emotion he had managed to elude for three whole years.

When the wrestling event concluded, Joseph and his friends headed out to a local Manhattan bar to meet up with Alex and her girlfriends. He never drank, so Joseph always felt a bit out of place at bars. After years of experiencing what it could do, firsthand, he had very little interest in the substance that turned men into monsters.

He was also well aware that most people did not travel down the same road as Hank Bateman once drunk. He knew people liked to drink, his own girlfriend included, and bars were a common hang out in a social setting. So while everyone drank, Joseph enjoyed a water or soda while he spent time with the close-knit group of friends he and Alex had found.

The bar they chose to meet at that night was located uptown, and was called Maggie's. It was crowded from the moment they walked in, and it took nearly fifteen minutes to get a round of drinks, something that didn't bother Joseph in the slightest.

"You see...this is one of the benefits of not drinking," he joked as he and Alex watched his friends, Tim and Fred, waiting to be served.

"If I go up there now," Alex stated. "I'd be back with a drink before those two even placed their order."

"Well, no shit. You're a pretty girl. Of course you're going to take priority over everyone else."

"Well I'm going to take advantage of that, then. At this rate, those two won't be back until last call, and I want a beer now."

BOOTH

Joseph watched Alex disappear into the crowd surrounding the bar. No more than five minutes later, she emerged from the same crowd carrying a round of beer for everyone, and a water for Joseph.

As the night progressed, the crowd thinned. One group of people at the bar got up and left. This gave Joseph and his group of friends somewhere to sit. The men, being the gentlemen that they were, let the women have the seats while they stood. Unfortunately, there were only four seats and five women.

He scanned the bar for a stray empty seat, but could not find one. Next, he turned to the man sitting next to them in hopes that he would give up his seat for the lady. Given he and Alex's past track record, Joseph should have known how this was going to end the moment he turned and noticed that the man sitting next to them at the bar was black.

"Excuse me," Joseph said. "Would you mind giving up your seat for this lovely lady who has been standing all night?"

The man gave no response. He didn't even acknowledge the fact that someone was trying to talk to him. He just sat there, silently. This annoyed Joseph. He knew the man had heard him. There was no loud crowd, nor music blasting to drown out the sound of his voice. He decided he wasn't going to let this man get away with ignoring him. He tapped the young man on the shoulder, and made him acknowledge his presence.

"I asked you if you could kindly give up your chair for this lady," Joseph said once he had the man's attention.

During his first attempt to get the seat, Joseph's tone was polite. He tried to keep the same tone the second time around, but was not successful. There was an obvious hint of rudeness that accompanied his request.

"When I'm done," was the cold response Joseph got.

169

As the man turned his attention back to his drink, Joseph fought the urge to punch him in the back of the head. This man should have done the polite thing, and given up his seat at the bar for a young woman. Joseph tabled the urge, and turned around towards his friends. As a solution, Alex decided to offer up her own chair to her friend.

"Some people are just so fucking rude," Joseph said. He purposely said it loud enough for the man who refused to relinquish his seat to hear. However, if the man heard Joseph's words, he chose to ignore them.

"Don't let him bother you," Alex said. "He's just a dumb nigger who wasn't raised to be chivalrous towards women."

Even though the past three years had proven to be happier times for Joseph and Alex, there was one aspect from their former life that they were unable to rid themselves of. That was Alexandra Casings' racism. There are just some things about a person that become so embedded in them that that they can't change them. Alex's hatred towards black people was seemingly one of those things.

In fact, it had worsened since moving to New York City.

New York City wasn't the best place to move for a racist like Alex. There seemed to be as many black people in the city as there were white people. She thought maybe if she had to live in a city equally black as it was white, she would learn to coexist peacefully.

She was wrong.

Alex would constantly get herself and Joseph thrown out of establishments because she would direct an offensive remark towards a black person for seemingly no reason at all. One moment, she'd be standing there, fine as can be, and the next she'd explode because a black person was in the same room as her. Her verbal assaults were sometimes so cruel that Joseph found himself physically removing Alex from a bar or restaurant before the person she was cursing out decided to get physical.

The fact that Alex had just said to not let the man standing next to them bother Joseph was shocking. If Joseph had to bet on Alex's reaction, he would've put all his money on her provoking him to start a fight. Even if she didn't attempt to get Joseph riled up, the odds favored her saying something to instigate a confrontation. She didn't, though. Instead, she told Joseph to ignore him.

Joseph didn't want to ignore it, though. This man next to them had awoken an anger inside him, and now that it was up, it refused to go back to sleep.

Instead of heeding Alex's advice, Joseph once again tapped the man on the shoulder.

"I tried asking politely. Now I am telling you. Get up! Do the right thing, and give your chair to this woman who has been standing all night."

"I told you... when I'm done. You and your girl need to relax."

"No," Joseph said, venomously. "What you need to do is get the fuck up. Do you understand me... *nigger*?"

With a single racial slur, Joseph's goal to get the man up was obtained. He shot up out of his seat with such fury, he knocked the chair to the floor. Standing fully erect, chest puffed out, he towered over Joseph, and made him look insignificant.

"What the fuck did you just call me?" he asked.

Despite all the years of hanging around Alex and Bill Casings, this was the first time Joseph had ever used the word *nigger*, or any racial slur, for that matter. He had never felt the need to use the term before, and had his anger not blinded his sense of judgement, he probably never would have.

Instead of addressing the man now towering over him, Joseph reached down, and attempted to pick up the chair he had wanted. The man, still not willing to relinquish it, ripped it away from Joseph, and threw it back to the ground. Instead of cowering from this man's wrath and obvious size advantage, Joseph let his own rage seize complete control.

"Give the girl the chair, *nigger*," Joseph spat with as much hatred as he could muster.

Both men were locked in a stare down. This was no longer about the chair. It had gone to a whole new level, one that was about to get physical.

Just as Joseph was preparing himself to fight, the bar door opened, and a group of people entered. Like the guy Joseph was about to fight, they were all bigger than Joseph, and they were all black. They approached the bar, and immediately picked up on the tension between their friend and this stranger.

"Is something wrong?" one of them asked.

"No! Nothing's wrong!"

It was Alex who had stepped in, and spoke up in hopes of diffusing a situation that was moments away from exploding. She may have been racist, but she wasn't stupid. They were outnumbered, and Joseph's friends had no interest in fighting his battle, anyway. She was well aware that her boyfriend would be on the losing side of the fence, and needed to get him out of there.

She pulled at Joseph's arm, but he didn't budge. Like two wrestlers before the bell of a long built-up main event bout, the two just stared each other down. She tugged again—much harder this time—and Joseph finally allowed himself to be led away. He did not break his stare, though. He and his adversary bore holes into each other up until the moment Joseph had been led out of the establishment.

The moment they were outside on the sidewalk, Alex's lips were on Joseph's. He grabbed her by the small of her back, and pulled her close to him as they kissed passionately.

"That was so hot," Alex managed to say between kisses. "How you stood up to him like that. You were fearless."

"I did it for you," Joseph said, even though his statement was only half true. The truth was his anger had him by the time the two were about to come to blows, and Joseph would've fought no matter the reason.

The two managed to gain some self-control before tearing each other's clothes off and putting on a live sex show for all those who walked by. Without any discussion, they headed towards their home. There, all the adrenaline from the bar altercation would be channeled into a marathon of mind-blowing sex.

Their plans would soon be foiled though, and it all started when Alex realized she had forgotten her purse at the bar.

Joseph, being the amazing boyfriend he was, offered to run back to the bar, and retrieve Alex's purse.

"My hero," Alex said. "Hurry back, so I can thank you properly for all you've done tonight."

In case Joseph wasn't sure what Alex meant by thanking him properly, placed her hand on the crotch of his pants. She gave a soft squeeze, and all the blood in Joseph's body seemed to have headed south. Eager to retrieve the purse, and claim his well-deserved thank you, he walked back to the bar.

When Joseph got to the bar, he approached the large outside window. He peered in to where they had planned to sit, and saw Alex's bag still hanging from the seat at the bar. Before entering, he scanned the interior of the bar for the person he had nearly come to blows with. His adrenaline had settled, and Joseph didn't feel much like fighting anymore.

Lucky for him, the bar was vacant of anyone who would likely want to fight him had they seen him. He entered the bar, grabbed the purse, and was out the door in less than thirty seconds. With his objective complete, Joseph headed in the direction of home, where Alex waited to thank him.

He walked two blocks before deciding to cut through an alleyway to save some time. As he stepped out of the loud streets into the quiet alley, he heard footsteps behind him. When he turned around, Joseph saw a person following him. He knew he wasn't the only person who cut through alleyways in Manhattan, so he didn't think much of it, and continued on his way.

"Hey," the person called to Joseph. "Hold up a minute. We got to ask you something."

Joseph ignored this, and continued to walk.

"Hey!" the person behind him called again. "I said wait up."

"Nah," Joseph answered. "I'm good."

"I said slow the fuck down, white boy!"

Joseph stopped dead in his tracks, and spun around.

"What the fuck is your problem, man?"

Joseph may not have been able to recognize the voice, but he sure knew the face. The moment he realized he was standing in an empty alleyway with the man he had called a nigger and then nearly fought less than an hour earlier, he knew he wouldn't be going home to Alex that night.

Joseph hadn't been as cautious as he thought. Obviously, the man he had insulted was still at the bar or somewhere nearby. When he spotted Joseph, he decided to follow him.

And so did his group of friends.

Joseph looked past the man from the bar, and saw three of his friends approaching.

Four on one, Joseph thought to himself. *This should end well for me.*

It didn't.

Before he could open his mouth to say he didn't want any trouble, or maybe even offer up an apology, all the air was driven from Joseph by what felt like a professional baseball pitch to the stomach.

Joseph went down to one knee, and fought desperately for air. He then experienced a sudden explosion on his temple, which could have been another ninety-five mile an hour pitch, but was actually another fist. He collapsed to the pavement. The man from the bar decided to switch things up a bit, and instead of using his freakishly cement-like fist, he started to use his feet. They didn't feel any better. Instead of an all-star pitcher, this man was now an NFL kicker who needed to kick the game-winning field goal from the fifty yard line, and Joseph's ribs were the football.

"You want to call me a nigger now, white boy?" Joseph's attacker asked, as he continuously punted him in the ribs.

Joseph felt another brutal kick connect with his ribs. It was followed by another to his back. A third landed at the base of his spine. At first, he couldn't figure out how this guy was kicking him so much all over his body. Then he realized it was no longer the one guy assaulting him. His friends had joined in.

Joseph lay there, and accepted his beating. He didn't have much of a choice. If it had been one-on-one, maybe he'd make a go to defend himself. He'd even try to mount an offense, and get a shot in. It wasn't one-on-one, though, and if he tried anything, he would be shut down by the numbers game. All Joseph Bateman could do was lay there, curled up to protect himself as much as possible, and wait for it to end.

It eventually did end, and Joseph managed to push himself up onto his elbows, but that was as far as he could physically move. He looked up, and saw the man he had started with in the bar standing in front of him. His friends were standing behind him. He was going to be the one to deliver the finishing blow.

In a last act of defiance, Joseph spat at his attacker's feet. The next thing he felt was the guy's foot connecting with his temple.

After that, there was only darkness.

August 27, 1991
Joseph Bateman Focuses His Hatred

When he regained consciousness, Joseph was no longer in an alleyway, surrounded by attackers. He was now lying in a bed in a hospital room.

The first thing he was aware of was that his body felt as if it had just been in a car accident—a feeling he was already familiar with. Pain permeated throughout his entire body, but two parts of his anatomy screamed out above all the others. The first were his ribs, and the second was the left side of his face.

As the details of his attack came back to him, Joseph was able to identify the source of his pain. His rib injuries had come from five men relentlessly kicking him while he laid on the floor defenseless. The excruciating throbbing in his head had come from the man he had insulted and nearly fought in the bar. It had been the exclamation mark on Joseph's beating.

Joseph found the ability to speak, even though it hurt his head to do so. He called out and a nurse responded. She brought a doctor with her, who looked Joseph over to determine the severity of his head injury. When the doctor concluded his patient's brain was fine, a police officer—

some hard-ass detective named Hawkins, who seemed bored the entire time Joseph recalled the details of his attack; as if what he was doing wasn't worth his time— came in, and asked a few questions. Once the detective had everything he needed to fill out a report, he asked if there was anyone they could contact on Joseph's behalf. That person was Alex. She was called, and twenty minutes later, she was there by her boyfriend's side.

That was when the shit hit the fan.

Joseph had told her the details of what had happened to him after he went back to the bar to get her forgotten purse. Upon hearing who had jumped Joseph, the racist beast inside Alex was released. At that point, no one was safe.

A young black nurse had the unfortunate displeasure of walking in to check up on Joseph during the peak of Alex's tirade. She asked how Joseph was feeling, and when she reached forward to adjust him and make him more comfortable, she fell victim to Alex's wrath.

"You get the fuck away from him!"

"Ma'am, please relax," the nurse responded, remaining calm. "I'm just doing my job."

Alex did no such thing, and when the nurse reached to check the cut above Joseph's left eyebrow, Alex actually swatted the woman's hand away.

"Don't you put your filthy hands on him! You hear me, nigger?"

"You need to calm down and let me check this young man's wound. I'm sure he doesn't want to end up with an infection."

She went to examine the wound one more time. This time, when she did, Joseph pulled away from her. Looking back on it all those years later, as he walked to his execution, Joseph tried to figure out why he chose to recoil. He had no personal vendetta against the nurse. In fact, he had let her help him earlier before Alex had arrived. He was just so angry about what had happened to him that all the hatred he had managed to bottle up and store away since leaving Wayne County came pouring out.

"Don't touch me," he said. "I want to be looked at by another nurse...A *white* nurse."

Either realizing this was a battle she couldn't win, or that she just didn't want to bother with two bigots, the nurse excused herself. Two minutes later a white nurse entered the room and examined Joseph's cut.

From that moment on, Joseph Bateman had a focal point for all of his hatred.

July 27, 1992
One More Leap

Joseph Bateman woke up with a single blanket covering him, and the dew soaked grass of upstate New York beneath him. The sky was still mostly dark, but when he looked to the east, he saw a hint of dawn as the sun made its ascent towards morning. The stars, which he once imagined so long ago were jellybeans in the heavens above, were being tucked away until night came again. Next to him, Alex slept, peacefully, under her own blanket, the earth serving as her mattress, as well.

Joseph and Alex had joined a few friends—the ones bold enough to still remain associated with the couple—on a camping trip in the Catskills. It had been a fun, upbeat weekend full of nature hikes, barbecuing, campfires, beers, friends, and laughter.

On the first night there, they all hiked up to the ridge where Joseph and Alex had just spent the night. They laid there and looked up at the thousands of stars that pierced through the vast blackness of the night sky. It was one of the most peaceful things Joseph had ever laid his eyes upon. That same serene beauty was the reason Alex had given for wanting to sleep at the top of the ridge on the last night of their trip.

Joseph knew that wasn't the real reason, though. He had seen the black family setting up camp just a few sites down earlier in the day, and figured out they were the real reason Alex asked him to sleep elsewhere. He just wasn't sure if she made the suggestion so she could get away from them, or if she did it to get Joseph away.

Since his attack in a Manhattan alleyway, Joseph's hatred was constantly aimed and frequently taken out on black people. The tiniest things would set him off. All someone had to do was brush against him accidentally while moving past him in a bar, and Joseph would end up being ejected for attempting to start a fight.

At first, Alex found Joseph's new attitude sexy. They now had something they shared together, as unhealthy as it was. Anytime Joseph nearly came to blows with a black person, the two would find themselves back home and in bed together, letting the adrenaline from the experience find its release through their love making.

However, like most things, the allure eventually faded. As they found themselves being constantly kicked out of establishments and losing friends, Alex didn't find her boyfriend's newfound attitude as sexy as she once had.

That didn't stop Joseph. No matter how much Alex would plead with him to not pick fights, his anger had full control of him, and he was incapable of quelling it.

Joseph allowed Alex to sleep a bit longer on her bed of wet grass. With his own blanket wrapped around him, he took a seat at the edge of the ridge, and watched as the sky grew brighter. The tree line, which had just been covered by the black pastels of night, was now beginning to show summer's beautiful use of colors. Hundreds of years of nature were coming to life in front of Joseph's very eyes, and as he gazed upon the magnificent scene, a sense of tranquility took him. For the first time in almost a year, Joseph felt a calm inside him. His hatred had been caged, if only for a moment, and he wanted to savor it. He wanted to hold on to it for as long as he could, because he knew, at any moment, it would be gone, and that all too familiar rancor would reclaim its rightful place within him.

Above all else, Joseph wanted to share this rare feeling. He got up from his seat, and walked over to where Alex lay, still sleeping. He knelt beside her and drank in her beauty before gently shaking her.

"Put your shoes on," he said, as she began to stir.

"Why?" she asked. "Where are we going?"

"Don't ask questions. Just trust me."

Trust him, Alex did. They put their shoes on and set off.

One of his friends had told Joseph about the particular spot earlier that weekend. He and Alex took a path, which led them onto a trail that they followed for a half hour. The trail led them to a calm stream which led them to the edge of a raging waterfall.

Joseph felt the same feeling of peacefulness rush through him that he had felt earlier. He looked over at Alex, and saw she was as awestruck by the scene as he was. Seeing that serenity in her eyes made her look younger. There was life there that he hadn't seen in a long time. Alex looked happy.

"It's gorgeous," she said, as she took it all in.

Seeing Alex like this warmed Joseph's heart, but it also broke it. He knew once they left and returned to their normal life, things would go back to what they were. The two of them being miserable. It wasn't supposed to be that way. They left Wayne County in search for a better life. Instead, things worsened. Joseph knew what needed to be done, and he needed to act on his instincts before his hatred and anger returned to cloud his better judgement.

Like he had four years earlier, Joseph decided he would have to take a physical leap before he took his metaphoric one. He removed his sneakers and socks, and without even giving himself time to consider the fifty foot drop to the water below, he took off towards the ledge and leapt off it.

This really isn't so bad, Joseph thought as he descended towards the water below.

Then he realized he had enough time to process a complete thought during his fall. Before panic could sink in, Joseph hit water, and was fully encapsulated in it. Once his downward momentum stopped, he kicked towards the surface. When he came to the surface, he looked up at the ledge he had just jumped from, and saw Alex standing at the edge, peering over.

"Jump," he yelled. "It's not so bad."

He didn't need to convince Alex to make the jump. Even if there had been an inkling of doubt in her mind, she wasn't going to let it give Joseph the right to finally boast he had done something that she could not. Moments after telling her to jump, there was a splash in the water a few feet away from him.

When Alex reached the surface, Joseph took her by the wrist, and led her towards the waterfall. When they approached it, he let go of her arm, dove beneath the water and swam under the fall. He came up on the other side of it in a little cove dug into the rock. Alex followed.

Joseph took Alex in his arms and kissed her. It wasn't like the recent kisses they had shared. Ones fueled by the adrenaline of racism and hatred. This kiss was different. It was slow and passionate. They slowly removed each other's clothes, and once both were naked, they made love.

Just like every other time since that rainy day the two of them sought refuge in the basement of an abandoned house, Joseph felt like he was experiencing Alex for the very first time. His hands and lips explored her body as he

183

was inside of her, and he was left in awe at the sight of her beauty.

As the two climaxed together underneath that waterfall in Catskills, Joseph Bateman was well aware of how truly lucky he was.

Despite every bad thing that had ever happened to him, Joseph had love, and he was lucky enough to share that love with and have it reciprocated by his best friend. Some people never got to experience true love, and most never kept contact with their childhood friends once they grew up. Joseph had both those things in one person. No matter what happened to him or how bitter life made him, Joseph was going to cherish every moment, like the one they were sharing beneath that waterfall, with Alex.

Unfortunately, there wouldn't be many moments left to cherish.

"I love you."

Joseph had never said those three words out loud to Alex. They were always there, on the tip of his tongue, but tucked safely behind his teeth. He had no intentions of saying them right there and then, but the barrier that held them back finally collapsed, and they poured from his mouth.

Alex didn't say it back right away. In fact, she didn't speak at all. Just when Joseph began to worry that she wouldn't reciprocate, she kissed him. It was a short but tender kiss, and when she pulled away, she had a smile etched upon her face.

"I love you, too," she finally said, and returned her lips to Joseph's.

The two made love one last time, and when they were finished, they swam to the nearby embankment. There, they laid together, once again clothed. Neither spoke. They just enjoyed the beauty around them, and they basked in the memory of the perfect moment they had just shared.

Soon, however, Joseph's thoughts began to drift away from his bliss. He began to remember the reality that waited for them back home in New York City. As he lay there and remembered the hatred, anger, and racism that were all solid fixtures in his and Alex's lives, Joseph decided he didn't want to live in that reality anymore. He wanted to take Alex and go somewhere they could start over, and experience the exact feeling they had felt that entire morning all the time. He wanted the two of them to finally have a happy life.

"We need to leave New York." It was Joseph who was thinking it, but it was Alex who spoke the words. In that moment of fleeting perfection, she was on the exact same page as Joseph. "When we get back from this trip, we need to leave New York."

"I know," Joseph responded.

"Where are we going to go?"

"I don't know yet."

That was the extent of the conversation. It was decided, and nothing else needed to be addressed until they returned home. For the second time in their lives, Joseph Bateman and Alexandra Casings would abandon all that they had known to relocate somewhere new.

Their big move would not be the new beginning they had, once again, been hopeful for. Instead, it would serve as the final stepping stone on Joseph Bateman's lifelong path to Death Row.

Before the calendar changed from 1992 to 1993, Joseph would find himself arrested for murder.

August 2, 1992
Sic Semper Tyrannis

Joseph gritted his teeth as the needle of the gun made contact with his skin. Going in, he knew it wouldn't be pleasant but after five minutes of having a needle repeatedly puncturing his skin, he decided it was a sensation he could go his whole life without ever experiencing again.

The tattoo had been Alex's idea. She claimed it could be something for them to remember their life in New York by, but that was just an excuse. She had always wanted to get a tattoo. She had even known exactly what she was going to get, too.

Joseph, on the other hand, had no idea what to get. He had spent days contemplating what to get etched on him for the remainder of his life, and came up with nothing. Even while they were in the shop, and Alex was explaining to the artist who'd be working on her the noose draped over the Confederate flag that she'd be getting on her ribs, Joseph sat in the small lobby area, and skimmed through binders filled with various potential artwork. Nothing he saw was worthy of a permanent spot on his body.

186

He was about to give up on the binders when he turned a page, and a spark of an idea was born. There were no pictures on this page; there were just multiple copies of the alphabet—both, lower and uppercase. Each version was a different font. Joseph scanned the page for a font he knew he absolutely loved. Once he found it, all he had to do was decide what he wanted written on him.

He expected the task of choosing the words he wanted tattooed on him to be strenuous, but now that he decided what he was going to get, the saying jumped right into his head. He walked up to the counter, and told the other tattoo artist exactly what he wanted.

"I can do that," the artist said. "Where do you want it?"

Joseph decided his first (and only) tattoo would go across his chest.

The whole process took less than an hour. To Joseph, it felt a lot longer. Each time the needle came to his chest, the vibrations of the gun radiated throughout his entire body. At one point, he looked down, expecting the piece to be nearly done, and almost lost his cool when he saw that the artist was only half finished with his work.

Eventually, it ended, and Joseph jumped from the chair as if he was just released from some medieval torture device. The artist told him to take a look in the mirror so he could see the finished product. The moment he saw his tattoo, Joseph forgot all about the pain he had just endured. He absolutely loved what he saw in the mirror's reflection. He ran his finger over the lettering on his pecs as he mouthing the words the letters formed:

SIC SEMPER TYRANNIS

Sic Semper Tyrannis was the Virginia state motto. It was also what John Wilkes Booth yelled from the stage of

Ford's Theater moments after he assassinated President Abraham Lincoln.

Of all the things from Joseph's old life, the one thing he made no attempt to shed was his fascination with Lincoln's assassination, and the man who had pulled the trigger. On his days off from work, when boredom got the best of him, Joseph would find himself in one of Manhattan's massive libraries, reading up on the subject. If there was a documentary scheduled to air on television, whether Joseph had seen it before, or not, he'd be sure he was home to catch it. He was so well-versed on the topic that if he was to appear of the popular game show, *Jeopardy*, and there was a category entitled *The Lincoln Assassination*, Joseph would be able to breeze through each question in record time.

"Do you like it?" the tattoo artist asked.

"Yeah," Joseph answered. His eyes did not leave the reflection in the mirror. "I love it."

Good." The artist placed one hand on Joseph's shoulder. "It is the key to your chance for redemption."

"Huh…? What does that mean?"

Joseph took his eyes off the mirror, and turned to the artist. Their eyes met. It was the first time Joseph and this man had made eye contact throughout the entire time Joseph was in the shop. He didn't like those eyes. There was just something about them that did not sit well with him.

Yet there was also something mesmerizing about them.

It was a feeling Joseph had felt once before in his life. He couldn't remember it then, but it wasn't the first time he had gazed into those eyes. The first time was during the fall of 1979, while he was waiting outside of an ice cream parlor for Alex. The man with the strange eyes who had asked for directions was such an insignificant part of

Joseph's life that he completely forgot about it until the day of his execution.

However, nearly thirteen years after he first looked into those eyes for the first time, Joseph felt the same unsettling feeling he had experienced when he looked into them as a child. He wanted nothing more than to get out of the shop.

"This is your key to redemption," the artist went on. "In your final moment of regret—when the hatred you have within you is turned upon yourself—the key will turn, and the walls will crumble down. Then, you will be given your moment of redemption."

The words, despite being obvious ramblings of a man who was clearly insane, resonated with Joseph. He felt the need to dig his fingernails into his own skin, and claw away his new tattoo. If that didn't work, he would find a knife, and carve away the skin of his chest.

He reached for his tee-shirt, which was draped over a chair. It got snagged on the chair, and fell to the floor. He fumbled for it with shaking hands. Finally, he grabbed it, and gracelessly pulled it over his head.

"You're crazy, asshole," Joseph told the tattoo artist. "You're a fucking looney."

He made his way towards the doorway of the small room they were in with the intention of getting the hell out of the shop. Joseph's legs locked up, though, as he heard the tattoo artist speak.

"The key is with you now, and will be until your regretful fingers take hold of it, and turn it. The walls will crack and come tumbling down, and there, in the rubble, you will find your atonement."

Joseph had heard enough. Later on he'd laugh and call himself foolish for allowing the ramblings of a crazy person affect him so much. Right then, however, he was shaken to his core. He reached into his pocket, pulled out

189

a hundred dollar bill—almost double what he was told the tattoo price would be— tossed it on the floor, and left.

"Beware of him!" the tattoo artist called as Joseph walked down the small hallway of the shop towards the exit. "He will do everything in his power to prevent your redemption. Beware of *Booth*!"

Joseph burst through the establishment's door, and stepped out into the world outside. The sun was beaming down on him, yet he felt cold with the fear that had just been instilled in him.

The overwhelming urge to rid himself of the tattoo still possessed him like a fever. He could shatter the shop's glass window, and use a shard of glass to hack away at his skin. He could pry open a car battery—New York City was infested with cars for him to choose from—and pour the acid from it over his chest until it ate away at his flesh. He would gladly let it melt his skin and muscle, all the way down to his bone, if it meant getting rid of that tattoo.

The key, he thought. *It's the key, and once it is turned, the walls will come crashing down.*

Joseph had no interest in any key. He didn't want to break down any walls. He wasn't interested in any redemption that awaited him on the other side of these walls. He wanted none of it.

STOP! he screamed to himself. *Just fucking stop! Take a minute, and relax. There's no key. There's no walls. There's no moments of regret, or redemption. There's just the crazed ramblings of a first-class nutcase. So quit freaking out, and calm the fuck down.*

He sat down on the curb and waited for Alex to finish. He managed to calm himself down a bit. His thoughts slowed, and his heartrate regulated. He no longer had images of ripping his torso to shreds. Fear loosened its grip, and he felt the sun heating up his body, finally. Joseph Bateman was finally getting himself back to normal.

Except the eyes. The image of those eyes lingered. They were there for the remainder of the day, and stayed with Joseph throughout the night. They were even with him when he woke the next day, and held up residence in his mind in the days that followed. It would be weeks before Joseph could finally get the image of those eyes out of his head on a daily basis, and months before he stopped seeing them, all together.

Minutes before his last ride, however, Joseph once again thought about those eyes. He also thought about the words that had been spoken to him all those years ago. He felt no regret for what he had done, so he guessed there'd be no turning of keys, and tumbling of walls.

There would be no redemption for Joseph William Bateman.

There were still a few minutes left in his life, though, and a lot can change in a few minutes.

Especially in your last.

As for those eyes were concerned: that day, back in August of 1992, wouldn't be the last time Joseph Bateman stared into them. It would be another two and a half years after and a hundred and twenty-seven years before his first and only tattoo that Joseph would look upon those eyes yet again.

December 20, 1992

Alex's Shower

Florida police would find Joseph Bateman sitting next to the lifeless body of Montel Parsons at one in the morning on December the twenty-first. He'd have a cigarette in his mouth, and would be smoking it, like a man without a care in the world.

Like a man who had not just violently murdered another human being by his own hand.

On the evening of December nineteenth, Alex had gone out with a few friends. She took rather quickly to a few girls she waitressed with at her new job.

The transition from Manhattan to Crystal Lake, Florida had been drastic. New York City was fast-paced and loud, while their new hometown was small in population, and had an all-around tranquil feel to it. It was also located near Lake Parker, which brought back a sense of familiarity from one positive aspect of their childhood.

The biggest appeal, however, of their new hometown was that the black community was practically nonexistent.

That had been the biggest factor to figure out while deciding on a new town to settle down in. The two of them weren't dumb. They knew part of the issue with living in

New York City was because of its large black community. At the end of their tenure in the Big Apple, they were both viciously racist people. Alex had moved away from her childhood home with hopes of escaping her racist ways, and had proven she was incapable of it. Joseph had no doubt he would be the same. The two would just fuel each other's fire, and nothing would change unless they moved to a predominantly Caucasian town.

Crystal Lake was that town. There was only a single apartment complex that had black tenants, and Joseph and Alex avoided it as much as possible.

One night a few months into their tenure in Crystal Lake, Alex had called home to tell Joseph she'd be heading out with her friends when her shift ended. She scarcely stayed out late on the exhausting nights she worked, so Joseph expected her home not long after her call. Midnight, the latest.

Still, when eleven-thirty came, and Alex was not home, Joseph found himself with an unsettling feeling in the pit of his stomach. He chose to ignore it. He knew Alex, and he knew she'd be walking through the door any minute now. The feeling lingered, though, and by a quarter after midnight, Joseph's unsettling feeling had morphed into worry.

Not once since their move south had Alex stayed out past midnight. As she headed towards her mid-twenties, she had become more of a homebody. She occasionally went out with the few friends she had made, but, more times than not, she chose to spend her nights at home with Joseph.

He knew there was the possibility Alex had lost track of time, and was running late. She would have likely found a payphone, though, and called to let him know if that was the case. Despite the fact that he was edging on a freak out, Joseph remained seated on the couch. However, when a

193

quarter after twelve turned into half past the hour, which soon became one in the morning, Joseph was out the door to look for her.

He went to every bar he thought she might be at. He went to the restaurant where she worked; hoping it would still be open at the late hour and she'd be there, but knowing it would be closed. Which it was. He scoured the streets aimlessly in hopes that he would merely come upon her. They all ended up being deserted, though. Everywhere Joseph looked, Alex was not there.

Joseph also called the apartment whenever he got a chance. With each ring, his anticipation grew. He waited to hear Alex's voice on the other end, asking him where the hell he was, and saying that she was worried sick—the irony of that scenario was not lost on Joseph. Alex never answered, though. Instead, the phone just rang and rang.

He ended his search with a desperation stop at the hospital. It was the last place he wanted to find Alex, but he had run out of places to search. Like every other place he went to before it, Alex wasn't at the hospital.

Finally, after two hours of searching, and no trace of Alex, Joseph returned home.

Exhaustion hit him like a wrecking ball the moment he sat down on the couch. His plan was to wait until morning, and if Alex hadn't returned home by then, he would go to the police. Until then, he would stay awake, and wait. His plan failed, and within minutes of sitting down, Joseph was asleep. He woke a few hours later with the morning sun creeping through the apartment windows.

His immediate thought—hope—was that everything from the night before had just been a nightmare. Maybe he had fallen asleep on the couch while Alex was out, and when she came home, she didn't have the heart to wake him.

Joseph shot up from the couch, and ran to the bedroom. He threw open the door, and as he entered the room and saw the empty bed, all his hope had withered away. All that remained was painstaking reality. None of it had been a dream. Alex was missing.

He immediately went into a freak out that topped the one from the night before. He attempted to reason with himself, and think of any reason why Alex had not returned home. He hoped maybe she had gone back to one of her friend's places, and had accidentally fallen asleep. After all, she worked hard at the restaurant, and would often find herself exhausted after a long shift. Any minute now she would come through the door. She would apologize for worrying Joseph, and he would tell her it was all okay, because she's home now, and safe.

That was the part of him attempting to keep himself calm, though. In the end, it failed him. Joseph knew what the reality was. He knew the police needed to be contacted. It was the only logical next step. Yet he hesitated. If he picked up the phone and called the police, it would be admitting the severity of the situation had escalated to a level he didn't want to imagine.

He battled back and forth over the decision. Every time he reached for the phone to make the call, he'd pull away at the last moment. This process repeated until he finally decided to compromise with the two voices inside his head. He'd wait just a little longer for Alex to walk through the door, and if she didn't, he would force himself to call the police.

Joseph Bateman would eventually pick up the phone. It would not be that morning, though, and it would not be in regards to his missing girlfriend.

Later on, after it was all said and done, Joseph wondered how things might have turned out differently had he just called the police when he first got the idea. Perhaps, if he had, he could've avoided his date with the electric chair.

Joseph would learn, however, after the electricity that meant to kill him had coursed through his body that no matter what move he made that morning, he wouldn't have been able to escape his date with death the morning of April 26, 1995.

He managed to keep himself from calling the police for a few hours that morning. Each time he told himself it was time to pick up the phone, he convinced himself, one way or another, to wait a little longer. However, once eleven o'clock hit, there was nothing Joseph could tell himself that would convince him to hold off any longer. He reached for the phone, and once it was in his hand, and he was about to dial 911, the door swung open.

On the other end of it stood Alex.

Joseph saw her, standing in the doorway of their apartment, and for a moment didn't believe she was there. He had been so desperate for her to return home that he thought he was hallucinating. Reality sank in, and he knew that the person standing in front of him was no figment of his imagination. Realizing Alex was real, Joseph shot up from the couch, and went to her. He hugged her tightly, as if she might go missing again if he let go of her.

"Jesus Christ, Alex," he said, kissing the top of her head. "Where the hell have you been? I've been flipping out over here. I've been so worried."

It was then that he noticed Alex was not hugging him back. Nor was she apologizing for being the cause of his worry. She wasn't even making an attempt to try and explain where she had been. She stood there, limp, as Joseph hugged her.

"Alex...what's wrong, baby?" Joseph asked as the relief in his voice turned into concern.

He took a step back. Alex did not acknowledge him. She just stood there, and stared down at the apartment floor. He raised her chin so that their eyes could meet. Her stare was blank. It looked as if something had drained the essence from her.

He repeated his question, and again got no response. He took his hand from her chin, and her head fell forward. They stood in an awkward silence for a few moments. Alex was the first to move. As though her boyfriend wasn't just trying to talk to her, she turned away and walked, zombielike, to the bathroom. She closed the door behind her.

Joseph waited to see if she would eventually reemerge from the bathroom. When it was obvious she wouldn't, he walked over to the bathroom, and leaned his head up to the door. From the other side, he heard the shower running.

"Alex..." he said. He knocked on the door and waited. When he got no answer, he said, "Alex, I'm coming in."

The first thing Joseph noticed when he opened the door, and entered the bathroom was the wastebasket. Alex had taken the clothes she was wearing, and stuffed them into the trash. He walked over, and fished them out. It didn't take him long to notice the blood that stained the crotch of her panties.

He made his way to the shower, and cautiously opened the curtain. Alex stood under a stream of hot water. The knob that controlled the water's temperature was cranked all the way up to HOT. The fair skin of Alex's neck and back had turned red from the scolding water.

Alex seemed not to notice the torturous temperature of the water droplets rapidly pelting her skin. Her attention was fixated on scrubbing her crotch with an overly soapy washcloth. She focused on her vagina, and ran the towel over it, repeatedly. Over and over, as if whatever it was she was trying to wash off of her wouldn't come off.

"Alex…"

Joseph reached for the wash cloth, and when his hand got within inches of it, Alex flinched. It was the first real response he had seen from her since she got home.

"Baby… relax. It's me."

He reached for the cloth again, and when his hand brushed against her inner thigh, Alex let out a blood curdling scream. Her knees gave out, and she collapsed to the porcelain floor of the tub. Hysterics took her, and she groped blindly for the washcloth she had just dropped.

Joseph, fully clothed, jumped into the shower, knelt down beside Alex, and took her into his arms. At first, she resisted, and tried to push him away. Joseph wouldn't allow her to, though. Whenever she would shove him, he would pull her back, and tell her it was okay.

Before long, Alex gave up on her resistance, and sunk into Joseph's comforting arms. She stopped trying to pick up the washcloth, and just cried as she and Joseph sat under the hot water of the running shower.

Eventually, her sobs tapered off, and calmed. Joseph asked her again what had happened to her. Alex again gave no answer. She was unable to find the willpower to form words. Joseph didn't push the matter. He would remain there, seated on the shower floor, his clothing soaked and painted to his skin, all morning if need be.

It would be some time before Alex finally spoke. When she did, she spoke a single line. It was spoken no louder than a whisper, but Joseph heard her words loud and clear as they penetrated his ear and pounded in his head.

"I was raped."

December 21, 1992

The Murder

Joseph sat on his couch as Alex napped. She had insisted on showering a second time following their talk. He had suggested she go to the hospital, but she refused, as he was expecting, not to mention hoping, she would. If Alex went to the hospital, the police would have to be called. If the police got involved, then Joseph couldn't go through with what he was planning.

Which was kill the motherfucker who had raped the woman he loved.

After Alex had told him what had happened to her, Joseph helped her out of the hot shower, which he, himself, was thrilled to get out of. He stripped out of his soaked clothes, and dried himself with the towel. When he was done, he looked to Alex, and saw she had just been standing there. A pool of water that had dripped from her naked body was pooling around her on the tile floor. Joseph grabbed a fresh towel, and when he took a step towards Alex, she shrank away.

"Alex…it's me. I'm not going to hurt you," he assured her. "I just want to dry you off."

Still, Alex's defenses were clearly on high alert. It then dawned on Joseph he was still naked. He realized that the sight of a naked man, even one who had loved and protected her his entire life, might provoke fear in a rape victim. He wrapped his own towel around himself and took a step towards Alex. She remained cautious, but did not shrink away from him.

He dried her off; remaining cautious of areas of her body that might cause her to erupt into a fit of fear. When he finished, he walked her to their bedroom where Alex allowed him to dress her.

All of Alex's movements were mechanical. Everything she did was without real thought, and she only did them because Joseph guided her. She sat on the edge of the bed, stone-like, while he dressed himself in dry clothing, and once they were both dressed, Joseph led her to the couch, where she just sat in her trauma-induced trance.

"Alex…" Joseph said cautiously. "What happened?"

Alex said nothing.

"Baby, you need to tell me what happened."

But she didn't tell Joseph what happened to her. She didn't speak at all. She barely moved a muscle. She just stared, void of all emotion, at the far living room wall.

Realizing that pushing it was pointless, Joseph decided he would be patient and wait. The urge to try again to push her to open up kept arising as Joseph to waited, but he told himself no. Alex would talk when she was ready. It would be almost forty minutes before Alex spoke, and when she did, she told Joseph what had happened to her.

Alex and her coworkers could not find a place to go following their shift that held their interest. Instead, they decided to go back to one of their places for a low key night. Just as Joseph had predicted she would, Alex got tired not long after eleven o'clock, and told the girls she was going to call it an early night, and headed home.

They had been residents of Crystal Lake for not even two months, and were still learning the streets. Both Alex and Joseph knew how to get to work, the supermarket, and a select few other landmarks, but that was it. Not long after her departure for home, Alex had found herself on a street whose name she did not recognize in a part of town foreign to her. She chose not to panic. Instead, she would roam the streets until she found a landmark or street she was familiar with. After fifteen minutes of walking, she finally saw something she recognized. The apartment complex that she and Joseph made a point to avoid at all times.

Relieved that she had finally found her way, Alex walked down the block, alongside the apartment building, and turned the corner in the direction of her home. Loitering in front of the building was a group of young men. With no interest in starting any sort of confrontation, and eager to just get home, Alex crossed the street, and continued on her way.

Where you going, baby?" one of the young men called out. "Come back over here, and say hi."

The others joined in with whistles and catcalls. None of this surprised Alex. Her racism aside, a group of boys late at night, plus a young woman by herself, was a recipe for immaturity.

It wouldn't stay at immaturity, though.

It would escalate to inappropriate, and then turn into a heinous criminal act.

One of the young men in that group was Montel Parsons who, at the young age of twenty-seven, was already a career criminal, spending time in and out of prison, not to mention juvenile detention centers before he was of legal age. When Alex chose to ignore the advances of the few men across the street from her, Parsons took exception to this.

"Hey!" he called when the young woman didn't answer them. "I said come back over here. I have something for you, honey."

His friend all thought this was funny, and burst into a fit of hilarity. Alex, tired and just wanting to get home, went against her instinct to verbally put this guy into the ground, and just continued on her way. As she turned another corner, she heard the man yell one more time at her. She dismissed it in the moment, but looking back on it, she could tell his tone had changed.

"What's the matter?" he had yelled. "Privileged white girl can't lower herself to talk to a few niggers? BITCH!"

Alex ignored the rude comment, and continued on her way. Despite the crude remarks directed at her, she didn't feel like she was in any serious danger. It was just a case of a delinquent young man trying to act cool in front of his friends. It was that reason why Alex's guard was not up to sense Montel Parsons sneaking up on her. By the time he wrapped his thick arms around her neck and torso to restrain her, it was too late for her to do anything to defend herself.

She lunged forward with all she had in an attempt to free herself from her attacker. Her efforts proved futile. It felt as if someone had strapped her down to a table, and pulled the bindings as tightly as possible. Before she knew it, she was off her feet, and being carried away.

She wasn't carried far. She heard the rattling of a fence as it opened, and then again as it slammed shut. Moments later, she was thrown to the ground. She surveyed her surroundings, and saw she was in a darkened backyard of some random house.

Her first instinct was to get up, and get the hell out of there. Alex's attacker anticipated this. The nanosecond she made an attempt to escape, he was on top of her.

Her second instinct was to scream. They were in a residential area, and she had no doubt her screams would wake up every house on the block. Her attacker predicted this, as well. Alex drew her breath in, but before she could let out a cry for help, she felt the large hand of her attacker encompass the entire lower half of her face; smothering any disturbance she had hoped to project into the quiet night. She then felt his other hand on her throat; cutting off her air supply.

"If you try to scream, I will fucking murder you, bitch. Do you understand?"

Alex gave no indication that she understood. Instead, she squirmed beneath her attacker in an attempt to break free. Feeling this, her attacker shifted his weight on top of her in such a way that when she tried to move, nothing happened.

"Bitch, are you fucking stupid?" Alex's attacker asked, tightening his grip around her neck. "I will fucking kill you if you try that again. Do you understand?"

Alex nodded to indicate she, in fact, did understand. It was in that moment that the thought that she might not live to see morning entered her mind.

"You regretting being a rude bitch now?" he asked.

It was then that Alex recognized the voice of her attacker as being one of the men whom she had heard only moments ago as she hastily walked past the apartment building. It was the voice of the one who had taken offense to being ignored.

Montel Parsons.

"Privileged white girl thinks she can just ignore a person just because she thinks her skin color is better than his," Parsons said. "I'm going to fucking humble you."

His hand left her mouth, but the grip around her neck was still so tight that she wouldn't be able to get any sounds out had she attempted to scream. Montel Parson's free hand went for Alex's jeans, and despite his threats to end her, she began to thrash back and forth. Parsons was too powerful, though, and completely in control of the situation.

"What the fuck did I tell you? I ain't playing with you here. I will fucking kill you!"

Alex submitted once again, but only for the moment.

She knew full well what his intentions were, and she had no plans of getting raped. He'd have to shift his weight eventually in order to get her pants off. She'd wait for her opportunity, and make her move.

Her attacker did precisely as she had anticipated him to. Parsons shifted his weight to remove her pants, and when he did, Alex made her move.

"I rolled over onto my belly, and freed my neck from his hand," Alex told Joseph, as tears flowed freely down her cheeks. "I was out from under him, and I made a move to get up. I was on my feet, but when I went to run, he grabbed my leg and pulled. I fell right to the ground. He was on top of me before I knew it, Joseph. I tried to scream—I wanted to scream so bad for help—but nothing would come out."

As she was pinned down on her stomach by her attacker, he grabbed the waist of her pants, and pulled. Alex heard the tear of denim as her pants and underwear came down. She felt the chill of the fall air on the now exposed skin of her buttocks. She felt Parsons' weight rise off of her, but he still had her by her ripped jeans. He wrenched at Alex's pants until they were at her ankles. Then, with one last hard yank, he pulled them off completely.

The moment her jeans were no longer an issue, Montel Parson was on Alex again; preventing any hopes of escape she might have had.

"He flipped me over," Alex told Joseph. "He was so strong. He held me down with one arm. I could hear him unzipping his pants…"

That was as far as she got before the hysterics took over. Alex broke down into a fit of uncontrollable sobs. Joseph took her trembling body in his arms and held her as she cried.

Joseph would not ask for any additional details. Alex had already relived enough, and there was no need to continue the story. There was nothing more Joseph needed to hear, anyway. He knew what happened next.

The son of a bitch had raped his girlfriend.

"I hid," she said once she had calmed down enough to speak. "There was a shed in the backyard, so I crawled across the lawn after he was finished, and sat behind it. I didn't even put my pants back on. I just sat there until I found the courage to come out, and come home. I'm sorry I worried you."

Joseph couldn't believe she was apologizing to him. She had just been the victim of a sex crime, and she was the one asking for forgiveness. Joseph felt as if he should have been the one begging for forgiveness. He should have tried harder to find her. Maybe, if he had just searched a little longer, or thought of somewhere else to look, he could've found her before any harm came upon her.

Harm did come upon Alex, though, and even though there was a part of Joseph that felt a sting of responsibility for what had happened, he knew who was to really blame.

The animal who had raped her.

Now it was time for that animal to suffer the dire consequences for what he had done.

"You don't have to apologize, ever," he told Alex. The beginning stages of his plan for revenge were already being plotted. "You need to get some rest."

"I want to shower again."

So Alex showered again, and then finally slept. As she did, Joseph sat on the couch.

The first thing he needed to do was allow the severity of what he was about to do truly sink in. This wasn't a race thing. It didn't matter if the person who raped Alex was black, white, brown, or yellow. The end result was going to remain the same.

They weren't going to get to live to see morning.

Joseph had sat back through too much of his life while someone he loved fell victim to rape. He refused to do that again.

Once he was at peace with his decision, he pieced together the finer details of his plan. It didn't take long. He knew what the end result was going to be. He just needed to figure out how he was going to get his hands on the son of a bitch who forced himself onto Alex. Once he had the specifics figured out, he waited for Alex to wake.

Alex eventually woke and emerged from the bedroom. She took a seat next to Joseph on their couch. The rest had done her well. With the exception of the faint markings on her neck from where her attacker had put his hands on her, she no longer looked like someone who had been through a traumatic ordeal. Inside, however, Joseph knew was a different story.

Inside Alexandra Casings, there were wounds that would never fully heal.

"You're planning to do something...aren't you?" she asked.

"Yes."

"What do you need from me?"

Many people in Alex's position would have shut down, emotionally, or just would have tried to put the whole thing behind them and hopefully move on.

Alexandra Casings was not one of those people.

She had been violated, and now she wanted her vengeance. Joseph was going to be the one to extract it on her behalf.

Joseph told Alex what he needed. Without giving it a moment's hesitation, she agreed. Now, all that remained was to wait for nightfall.

They headed out just before midnight. Joseph expected his nerves to be shot, but they weren't. Despite his plan's transition to reality, Joseph Bateman was shockingly calm for a man who had full intentions of murdering another human being.

They hid behind a bush for over an hour when they got to the apartment building where Alex's rapist lived. She told Joseph that she had no doubt she would be able to point out the man who had raped her if she saw him. Shortly after one-thirty in the morning, she spotted him.

Even under the faint moonlight, Joseph could see the hellfire hatred consuming Alex's eyes as she stared down the man who had violated her. Luck was on their side—if luck was what you chose to call it—and the object of Joseph's brutality was completely by himself. He was also heading away from the apartment building.

"You need to go home now, Alex" Joseph said.

"No."

"Alex, this isn't an option. You need to leave. You can't be part of this."

"Too bad, Joseph. I'm coming,"

Getting into an argument with Alex wasn't part of his plan. He looked down the block, and saw Montel Parsons moving further away. If he didn't act now, Joseph's chances of losing Parsons or him moving into a more populated area increased. He had no choice but to submit to Alex. Without saying another word, he came out from behind the bush, and followed his target.

Alex followed.

He stayed far enough away from Parsons to not be noticed, but kept close enough to not lose him in the darkness. As he stalked his target, Joseph listened to the sounds coming through the night air. He needed every part of his plan to go perfectly. If someone was to hear and interrupt him, he'd be forced to abort and flee. It would mean Alex's rapist would get to live, and Joseph refused to let that happen. So he listened intently to make sure the night air was desolate.

When he was certain that the only thing filling the air were the sounds of crickets and the suspense of the moment, Joseph closed the gap between himself and Parsons. As he drew nearer, he reached into the back of his pants, and pulled out the sock he had filled with quarters. Once close enough to strike, Joseph swung the sock, and landed a vicious blow to the back of the raping bastard's head.

Upon impact, Parson's legs buckled, and he collapsed to the floor. Joseph thought the blow from the coin filled sock had killed him, which left Joseph feeling dissatisfied and cheated. The end game may have been the death of this rotten piece of garbage, but Joseph had no intentions of making it quick and sudden. He wanted to drag it out for as long as he felt necessary, and he wanted to make sure Parsons knew it would be his last night alive. Lucky for Joseph, the still body at his feet began to move. Relieved at seeing Parsons still alive, Joseph lifted him from under the armpits, and dragged the barely conscious man a block and a half to a fenced off property where a house had recently been demolished, and a new home was in the process of being built.

Joseph searched for a hole in the fence that ran along the property, but could not find one. So with all of his strength, he lifted the body off the ground, and rolled Montel Parsons over the top of the chain link fence.

208

A painful moan came from the opposite side of the fence after Parsons' body hit the ground. This excited Joseph, because the bastard was finally waking up. Soon he would be awake, and made fully aware that he was about to suffer for his actions.

Joseph hopped the fence, and landed on the other side far more gracefully than the man who had gone over before him. Alex followed soon after.

"I want you to wait in the darkness," he told her when she landed on the ground.

"Why?" she asked. "I want to see this!"

"And you will… But I have a plan, and I need you to trust me!"

Alex agreed to go along with Joseph's plan, and walked off to the darkest part of the property.

As Alex faded into the darkness, Montel Parsons came to enough to realize he was in a predicament that did not seem promising to end well for him. He made an attempt to escape, but when he tried to get up, his legs failed him, and he collapsed onto the dirt ground. He resorted to plan B, which was to army crawl towards safety.

Joseph put a quick stop to the escape with a hard boot to the small of the back. He flipped Parsons over, and was now face-to-face with Alex's rapist. He balled his hand into a fist, and punched Parsons square between the eyes.

"What the hell?" Parsons said, bringing his hands to his nose.

Joseph pulled the man's hands away from his face.

"Look at me," Joseph demanded. When Parsons refused to acquiesce to the request, Joseph punched him again. This time in the temple. "Look at me, I said."

Parsons opened his eyes.

"What's your name?" Joseph asked.

"None of you fucking business."

Not happy with the response, Joseph lifted Parsons off the ground, and slammed him back down. Thus causing Parsons' head to whip back, and smash on the unforgiving ground.

"What's your name?" Joseph asked again.

"Montel Parsons," Alex's rapist finally answered. "What's your problem?"

"You raped my girlfriend, Montel Parsons," Joseph answered. "Now I'm going to kill you."

"Whoa!" Montel Parsons exclaimed. "I didn't rape nobody."

"Don't fucking lie to me!"

Joseph again raised Montel Parsons from off the ground, only to slam him back down.

"I ain't lying," Parsons yelled. "I'm telling you; I didn't rape nobody."

"Alex…" Joseph called out.

A moment later, Alex emerged from the darkness.

Montel Parsons' eyes widened at the sight of Alex. He realized there would be no lying his way out of this. He began to thrash in an attempt to escape, but Joseph was on him, pinning him down the way Parsons had pinned Alex when she tried to escape his sexual assault.

"Look at her!" Joseph demanded. He forced Parsons to turn his head in the direction of Alex. "Take a good long look at the woman you raped. Let it sink in that because of what you did, you're going to die."

"I didn't rape her," Parsons proclaimed desperately. "She wanted it. It wasn't rape. She came on to me!"

Ignoring the claims currently coming from Montel Parsons' mouth, Joseph scanned the construction site. In the corner, he saw a pile of bricks and cinderblocks. He grabbed Parsons by his arm, and dragged him towards the pile.

"Don't you fucking lie to me, you piece of trash."

When Parson again claimed that the sex between him and Alex was consensual, Joseph grabbed one of the bricks, and raised it high above his head.

"ADMIT TO WHAT YOU DID!" he yelled.

"Oh my god," Montel Parsons yelled out into the night. He threw his hands over his face, as if they would serve as any real protection from the impact of the brick. "I did it! I did it! I raped her!"

Joseph threw the brick into the distance, knelt down, and proceeded to pound his fist into the face and head of Montel Parsons.

"Say you're fucking sorry," he said as he landed his punches. "Apologize!"

"I'm sorry!" Montel Parsons cried out. "I'm sorry!"

Joseph looked up at the pile of bricks, and allowed the evilest, most sadistic wheels in his head to turn freely. He flipped Parsons onto his stomach, gripped him by his shirt, and dragged him within inches of the bricks.

"Bite it," Joseph said. He was referring to the bricks.

"You're fucking crazy," Montel Parsons said.

Joseph responded with a kick to the ribs.

"I said BITE IT!"

When Montel Parsons still refused, Joseph bent over, gripped Alex's rapist with one hand at the base of his skull and the other around his throat, and pulled Parsons so that his mouth was touching brick. Fearing what was in store for him, Parsons still refused to open his mouth.

"Joseph," Alex called out. "Let's just leave. I want to go home."

Joseph had a feeling Alex might change her mind about killing Parsons, despite what he did to her. Maybe seeing it all unfold before her, instead of just being an idea, made her change her tune. Whatever her reasons were at the moment, Joseph had no such desire to back out of what he planned to do to Montel Parsons.

"Open your mouth," Joseph demanded.

"Joseph, please..." Alex said. She was now pleading. "Let's just go home. We really don't need to do this. We will just leave, instead. You and I... together... just like it has always been."

It was right then Joseph realized it wasn't the idea of murdering Montel Parsons that made Alex change her mind. It was the fact that if he went through with it, he and Alex would no longer be on the same path. She didn't want to lose Joseph. She wanted him to stay with her on the one they had been traveling ever since leaving New York. The one that ended with them having a happy life together.

Only that path was no longer attainable for Joseph Bateman. It never was. The path Alex had feared he would go down if he killed Montel Parsons was the path he had been on his entire life, and in that moment, Joseph saw it with clear eyes. He was no longer blinded by the promise of false hope.

"Go home, Alex," he said, not taking his eyes off the man he would kill within a matter of minutes.

"Not without you." Alex took a step forward, and then another one. She inched towards Joseph until she was close enough to touch him. Her hand went to his arm, but he pulled away. "Joseph, you don't have to do this. Please, let's go home."

"I'm not through with him"

"Joseph... please..."

"Alex... LEAVE!"

Alex shrank away from Joseph at the sound of his voice. She looked at him as if she was looking at the face of a stranger. The truth was the person standing a few feet away from her now was a stranger. He wore the face of Joseph Bateman well, but he was not the person Alex had known her entire life. He was dangerous and he was a killer.

"You promised me, Joseph," she said. "You promised to keep me safe. Please, don't do this. If you do this, you'll go somewhere I can't follow. I'll be by myself. I can't do this without you, Joseph. I need you to keep me safe."

Joseph gave no response. He wouldn't even turn to look at Alex. He kept his focus on Montel Parsons. The man who raped the woman Joseph had promised to protect, and had failed to do so.

Eventually, he heard the sound of Alex climbing over the chain link fence. She obviously couldn't watch what her boyfriend—her best friend—was about to become. When Joseph was certain Alex was gone and not coming back, he knelt down beside Montel Parsons, who was still kissing the brick, but not biting it. He spoke in a cold voice that was void of all humanity.

"I'm going to kill you, regardless of whether or not you do as I say. Only thing is, if you continue to disobey me, I'm going to make it slow, and it's going to be painful. I mean that. You are going to wish for death. Only it's going to seem like death is never going to come. So do yourself a favor, and do as I say. Now... bite... the... fucking... bricks..."

This time, accepting defeat, Montel Parsons bit the bricks.

Joseph stood up, and placed his one foot on the small of Montel Parsons' back, so that he could not scramble away. He leaned over, and, from the ground, picked up a cinder block. He lifted it over his head, and before any doubt could creep into his mind, Joseph Bateman threw the cinder block down with all of the strength he could muster.

Beneath the foot that was pinning Montel Parsons to the ground, Joseph felt the body of the man whose neck he had just pulverized buck. His legs twitched for a few moments after his body had calmed. Then there was nothing.

Only the eerie stillness of death.

The lifeless body of Montel Parsons lay at the feet of Joseph Bateman, but it was a blur in the background to him. All Joseph could focus on was his own hands. They were the hands that murdered another human being. They could have thrown the cinder block away. They could have helped him climb over the fence to leave that abandoned lot. They could have grabbed Alex as he pulled her towards him to hold her near, as he told her he couldn't go through with killing Montel Parsons, because it meant he would be away from her.

Those hands could have been used for so many things. Instead they were used to extinguish another person's life.

As Joseph Bateman stood over the body of Montel Parsons, the only word that repeated through his mind as he stared at his hands was *Useless... Useless...*

January 28, 1994
Tried & Sentenced

Thirteen months.

That's the amount of time it took for Joseph Bateman to be tried and sentenced for the murder of Montel Parsons.

Thirteen short months.

While some trials for the same murder may have taken years before even seeing the inside of a courtroom, Joseph's was sped along and done in a timely fashion. On the surface, this looked to be because of a determined District Attorney, who made it his personal mission to make an example of Joseph. Beneath the surface, however, there were factors far greater than an enthusiastic District Attorney at work that would see to it that Joseph would ride the lightning on the morning of April 26, 1995.

In the early morning hours of December 21, 1992, a phone call was made to 911. The person placing the call did so to report a recent murder. That person was Joseph Bateman.

He had left the lifeless body of Montel Parsons in the abandoned lot, and walked to the nearest payphone to make the call.

"Are you still in immediate danger, sir?" the operator asked after being told there had been a murder, and given the location of the body.

"No," was Joseph's response. "I'm not going to kill anyone else."

He said nothing else. He hung up the payphone, and headed back to the abandoned lot to wait. He was well aware of what he was doing. He had no desire to even attempt to run. The cinder block that had snapped Parsons' neck and shattered his skull also served as the straw that broke the metaphoric camel's back. There was nothing left inside Joseph. All of his hopes for a better life were now as dead as Montel Parsons.

He took a seat beside Parsons' fresh corpse, and waited. As he sat there and waited to hear the sounds of sirens coming through the morning, he noticed something in the back pocket of Parsons' jeans. With his interest piqued, Joseph reached into the pocket of the man he had just murdered, and pulled out the pack of cigarettes along with a lighter. He studied the pack for a moment, then flipped it open, and pulled out one of the pack's contents. He placed the brown filtered tip between his lips, flicked the lighter, and brought the flame to the cigarette.

Joseph had never smoked a cigarette a day in his life, and, truth be told, he had no real desire to do so. He knew, however, his days of freedom would be soon over, and he wanted to exercise his right to make one last choice, and try something new before that right was taken away from him.

He inhaled, and as smoke entered his lungs for the first time ever, Joseph burst into a violent coughing fit.

He had suffered through three quarters of the cigarette—Joseph wasn't a fan of smoking—when he saw the flashing lights of two police cruisers appear on the opposite side of the fence. He dropped the cigarette on the ground, and stomped it out. By the time the police responding to the 911 call broke through the fence with a pair of wire cutters, Joseph was already on his knees beside Montel Parsons' lifeless body with his hands behind his head and his fingers interlocked.

The following day, Joseph was arraigned. Alex had contacted and hired the best lawyer that they could afford, and even then Joseph was denied bail. He still had a very good chunk of change in his savings from his inheritance, and was considered a flight risk due to the funds he had at his disposal.

He only sat in a prison cell for a two months before his case went to trial. While some waited years to have their cases brought before a judge and jury, Joseph only had to sit and wait fifty-seven days.

This was because Joseph had become the focal point of district attorney, Alan Fortner. Fortner wanted it be known that hate crimes against the black community in a southern state, such as Florida, were taken very seriously in the eyes of the law. Joseph was to be used as the catalyst for that campaign.

Fortner also happened to know a judge who shared the same distaste for those who couldn't accept equality amongst the races—the fact that Joseph's motivations behind the murder of Montel Parsons was revenge-based, and had nothing to do with race was irrelevant; he was still to be Fortner's poster boy. Judge Vincent Shiponelli had his schedule cleared, and made hearing the Joseph Bateman case his priority.

The defense was built around the claim that Joseph had been so distraught over the rape of his girlfriend—a fact that seemed to be ignored by the prosecution as much as possible—that he had a temporary emotional break in his sanity. Joseph knew temporary insanity was a weak defense, and he was certain his lawyer knew it, as well.

Still, Joseph was paying him, so the man had to defend him.

Psychologists were brought in by the defense to evaluate Joseph to determine his mental state during the time he committed his crime. In response, the prosecution then had their own psychologist come in to interview Joseph to contradict the findings of the doctor brought in by the defense.

Proving that Joseph Bateman was in a temporary broken mental state when he smashed in Montel Parsons' skull would prove to be a difficult task.

Proving Joseph was a racist, on the other hand, was not as difficult.

Since the attack in the alleyway that summer night in New York City, Joseph had spent a few nights in prison after being arrested for starting fights. All these fights were with black people, and there had been plenty of witnesses to tell police who had been the one to instigate each fight. The prosecution entered police reports from those New York City brawls, along with one from Atlanta that occurred during the move down south, as evidence.

Then there was the testimony from Joseph's arresting officers. They both testified that Joseph seemed of sound mind when they arrived, and was quite aware of the reason why he was being taken into custody. Michael Mann, the homicide detective assigned to the Montel Parsons case, also took the stand. He described Joseph as uncaring and unsympathetic for what he had done. He also stated for the jury that during his interrogation following his arrest, Joseph seemed quite aware of what he had done. The 911 recording of the phone call Joseph had made only helped further the prosecution's point that Joseph Bateman had a history of remorseless violence against black people and that the murder of Montel Parsons should not be seen differently.

The final nail in the coffin that was the prosecution's case was when Joseph, himself, took the stand.

This hadn't been part of the prosecution's plans, but they jumped at the opportunity when it was presented to them. It was Joseph who had his lawyer make the offer. He made the decision right after learning the prosecution had planned to call upon Alex as a witness.

Joseph's lawyer had feared his client would make a scene in the courtroom if he wasn't made aware of the prosecution's plans. He would have been right. Upon hearing Alex was being called to the stand to relive the events of that morning, and everything leading up to it— namely, her rape—Joseph blew a gasket. He told his lawyer there was no way Alex was taking the stand to testify. It wasn't an option. His lawyer went on to inform him client there wasn't much of a choice. Joseph felt otherwise, and found that choice. It was taking the stand in Alex's stead.

"I cannot emphasize how poor a decision that would be," his lawyer tried to explain after.

"I don't care," Joseph's responded. "She's not taking the stand. I pay you. So you do as I say, and I say you offer them a testimony from me in exchange for Alex's."

Knowing his client long enough to know he wouldn't change his mind, or listen to any legal counsel, Joseph's lawyer presented the prosecution with the alternative. He returned the next day, and informed Joseph that his terms had been accepted. Alex was removed from the witness list, and Joseph was added.

The morning Joseph was scheduled to take the stand, his lawyer had attempted to prep him for what might be asked. Joseph paid him no attention. He already knew his fate, and had no intentions of swaying the jury's decision. He was doing this solely for Alex.

He was asked questions regarding the events that led up to the murder of Montel Parsons. He was asked about his violent past while living in Manhattan. He was asked if he would've reacted the same way had anyone else—meaning someone who wasn't black—raped Alex.

"Yes, I would have," Joseph answered when asked if he would've reacted the same had Alex's attacker not been black. "The fact that he was a dumb nigger was just a bonus."

Judge Shiponelli did not take kindly to the callous language being used in his courtroom, and issued Joseph a stern warning to not let it happen again.

Joseph would not listen.

Joseph's own lawyer crossed-examined him once the prosecution had no further questions. He made an attempt to emphasize the point that Joseph would have acted the same way had his girlfriend's rapist been white, thus proving the crime was not race driven. Everyone in the courtroom knew it was a weak argument.

"I have one last question," Joseph's lawyer said; hoping his client would answer it correctly, instead of truthfully. "Do you feel any remorse for what you did?"

"No," was Joseph's answer. "I don't have room for remorse, especially for niggers."

After the final statements had been made, the jury was sent into deliberation. They returned two hours later with their verdict.

Joseph stood, and waited to hear the verdict. It had been written on a piece of paper, which was passed from a juror to the court officer, who then handed it to the judge. Judge Shiponelli reviewed, and then asked how the jury finds Joseph Bateman on the count of murder in the first degree.

"We find the defendant...guilty."

Joseph heard some celebration behind him coming from the family and friends of Montel Parsons. He couldn't comprehend how those people could celebrate anything after knowing what Parsons had done.

The sounds of their joy became background noise as he heard the tearful sounds of mourning coming from the bench directly behind from where he sat. Joseph refused to turn around, and acknowledge Alex. He had told himself he had done right by Alex, and he would accept whatever his fate was without an ounce of regret. He knew if he saw tears streaming down her face, he'd regret everything.

Had he known then it would be the last time he'd see Alex for nearly two years, Joseph would've turned around just to see her one last time.

On January 28, 1994, seven months after he had been found guilty of murder in the first degree, Joseph once again stood before Judge Vincent Shiponelli to receive his sentencing.

Alex was not there to hear Joseph's fate.

"Son," Shiponelli said, "you have shown zero regret for what you have done, nor have you shown an ounce of sympathy. You have not given this court a single reason not to punish you to the fullest extent of the law. So I will ask you now... Do you have a shred of remorse inside you for what you did?"

Joseph looked up at the judge. He could have told everyone in the courtroom what they all wanted to hear. That he regretted killing Montel Parsons. That he wished he hadn't taken the law into his own hands that night. He could have opened his mouth, and told them all he wished he could take it all back.

It was the truth, after all. Had Joseph walked away, he and Alex would still be together.

Instead, he had spent seven months incarcerated, and hadn't heard a single word from Alex. She had seen the monster that dwelled inside of Joseph Bateman. She saw what it was capable of, and she ran from it. As badly as he didn't want to believe it, Joseph knew the truth. Alex was gone, and he was truly alone in the world.

There was nothing left for Joseph Bateman to live for.

"No..." he said to Judge Shiponelli. "I don't."

"Then you leave the court with no other choice..."

Joseph Bateman was sentenced to death. Soon he would step into the clearing at the end of the long road he had been traveling his entire life. The electric chair would signify the end his journey towards Death Row, but it would also be the first step on Joseph's new path towards redemption.

April 20, 1995
Joseph's Last Visitor

Joseph had two visitors during the week heading into his execution. The first was his lawyer, who he had requested the presence of. The other visitor, he did not expect.

The meeting with his lawyer was simple enough. Joseph still had a substantial sum of money tucked away from his inheritance, even after all his court and lawyer fees. He had refused to spend any money on appealing the death penalty ruling, which would have prolonged his stay on death row. With no appeals to slow down what he felt was the inevitable, Joseph's date of execution was scheduled for fifteen months after he had been sentenced.

With no more lawyers left to pay, and no need for the money his mother had left him, Joseph instructed his lawyer to take what was left of his inheritance, and donate it to a charity for battered women. He wanted what was left of Emily Bateman's hard earned money—money she had taken years of beatings and rapings to earn—to go to a cause that helped women who were married to men like Hank Bateman.

It was the last shred of decency Joseph had left in him being put to good use.

Within two days' time, that last thread would finally be stripped away from him after his meeting with his second visitor of the week.

Joseph was retrieved from his cell, and escorted to see his visitor. When he entered the room, it was not his lawyer, who he had expected to see, sitting there on the other side of the acrylic glass.

It was Alex.

The shock of seeing the woman he loved for the first time in nearly two years was so overwhelming, Joseph believed Alex was nothing more than a figment of his imagination. It took a few attempts for his brain to fully process that the person sitting there, waiting to speak to him, was no apparition, but actually Alex.

When it finally clicked, and Joseph was able to take in the sight of the woman he had killed and sacrificed his own life for, he couldn't believe how much Alex had changed since he had last seen her. She had cut her hair, was very nicely dressed, and was wearing more makeup than he had ever seen her put on. She looked healthier than she had back when they were living together. She was a far cry from the tomboyish girl he had met nearly eighteen years prior.

"Hello, Joseph," Alex said into the telephone she had to speak into to communicate with Joseph through the glass divider.

Joseph could see the tears already welling up in her eyes, and, even then, despite a near two year absence from his life, he wanted nothing more than to wipe those tears away from Alex's eyes.

"Hey," was all Joseph could manage to say.

"How have you been?"

"As good as can be," he responded. "You know, for a guy who's a few days away from dying."

At the mention of his upcoming execution, the tears Alex had been fighting to hold back freely streamed down her face.

"I'm sorry I didn't come earlier," Alex said. "At first I couldn't. I was too scared to face you. I was afraid of who you might be if I came."

"Who I might be? Alex... I've always been the same person."

"You were a different person that night."

"I did that for you," Joseph reminded Alex. "I did that because of what he did to you."

"I know you did, and I know you thought it was what I wanted. I even thought it was what I wanted. But it wasn't. Being there, seeing it all go down right in front of me, I wanted to leave. The both of us. I wanted the two of us to get out of there, and leave that stranger behind us."

"That stranger was the man who raped you."

"Not him, Joseph...you. The stranger I'm referring to is you."

Joseph remembered the look on Alex's face the night he killed Montel Parsons. She was someone who was seeing for the first time a side of someone she thought she had known every side of. It had scared her so much it took her twenty-two months to finally muster up the courage to see Joseph face-to-face again.

"You shouldn't have disappeared like that," was all Joseph could say.

"I know," Alex admitted. "It took me a while to get over everything. I had to see someone—a psychiatrist. Then things happened, and I didn't know how to come here and tell you."

"What things?" Joseph asked. "Tell me what?"

"I couldn't let you die without coming to see you. I owe you an explanation. I couldn't leave you wondering."

"Alex, what are you talking about?"

It was then that Joseph looked down, and saw on Alex's finger exactly what she was trying to find the courage to tell him.

"Joseph…" Alex said, taking notice of what Joseph had seen. She spoke cautiously, as if the person she had seen kill Montel Parsons would surface, and spring through the bulletproof glass. "I'm so sorry. I know you must be upset. Please… just let me explain."

Joseph was not interested in any explanation. He got the point loud and clear by the diamond engagement ring on Alex's finger. While he was sitting on death row for killing a man for what he had done to her, she was off meeting, fucking, falling in love with, and getting engaged to some other guy.

"Whore," he said in a whisper through the phone, interrupting her attempt at an explanation.

"I'm sorry, Joseph," she said. "I truly am. What was I supposed to do?"

She had a point. He was in prison, and soon he'd be dead. It wasn't like she was going to go through the remainder of her life without meeting someone new. This outcome was inevitable.

That was Joseph's logic speaking. However, his rage far outweighed his logic, and Joseph's rational train of thought was hushed in favor of his anger.

"So I go off to prison, and you spread your legs for the first dick that points in your direction?" Joseph asked.

"I wasn't like that!"

Alex again tried to explain herself, but was once again cut off.

"Let me ask you something… Did I kill that guy for no reason?"

"What are you talking about?"

"Did he actually rape you, or did you welcome him too with open legs?!"

Joseph saw the look of hurt on Alex's face, and he knew, right then, his claim was absurd. If there was an ounce of guilt for his comment, he didn't even sense it. His rage had a full grasp on him.

"Your father should count his blessings every day that you left him," Joseph continued. "Because you're just like your mother... A GODDAMN NIGGER FUCKER!"

Joseph exploded out of his chair, kicking it out from under him and into the wall.

"FUCK YOU!" he screamed through the phone, and then heaved it at the glass.

To the sound of the phone hitting the barrier between them, Alex jumped. She fell out of her chair, and crashed to the ground. She burst into tears.

"I FUCKING HATE YOU!" Joseph yelled. Without the phone, he wouldn't be as audible, but he knew Alex could still hear his words. "I HOPE YOU DIE, YOU NIGGER LOVING BITCH!"

Conroy Nates and another guard burst through the door at the sound of the outburst. They took hold of Joseph, and tried to pull him towards the room's exit. Joseph refused to comply.

"DIE, YOU BITCH," Joseph screamed as he was dragged from the room. "DO YOU HEAR ME?! FUCKING DIE! I HATE YOU!"

Just like that, in the span of a single conversation, Joseph Bateman hated Alexandra Casings just as much as he had ever loved her.

April 26, 1995
Joseph Bateman Rides the Lightning

Corrections Officer Conroy Nates and the new guard, whose name Joseph still didn't know, led him into a room. There, Conroy Nates shaved Joseph's head. It was done with such stealth and precision, and Nates did not nick Joseph's head once. Joseph wondered how many times a man needs to do this to become that good at it. How many men did Conroy Nates prep for execution? How many lives had he seen come to a sudden end throughout his tenure?

Once Joseph was prepped, he was taken through a door, and led into a short corridor with another door at the other end. Joseph knew what lay in store for him on the other side of that door. His ticket was stamped and it was time for Joseph to ride the lightning.

The walk down the short corridor seemed to take a lot longer than it should have. It was less than twenty paces in length, yet it seemed like Joseph was walking the stretch of a football field. When they finally reached the end, Conroy Nates opened the door, and escorted Joseph into the execution room.

The chair was the first thing he saw. It sat there, in the center of the room for all who entered to see. The sight of it—the means to Joseph's end—began to stir up feelings that had been suppressed up until that point. He had told himself they weren't there at all, but now that the end was staring him in the face, the feeling of regret was finally beginning to surface.

Conroy Nates gave Joseph a few moments to observe the chair before moving forward. As he felt Nates push forward, indicating it was time to commence, Joseph resisted. This wasn't something he had told himself to do. His body was just frozen.

"It's okay," Conroy Nates whispered. "It will all be over soon."

Joseph found no comfort in Nates' words, but they got his legs moving, nonetheless.

They approached the chair, and Joseph was turned around, and lower into it by both officers who had escorted him from his cell. As his arm was lowered to be strapped in, Joseph's hand began to trembling. This time, Nates gave no comforting words.

After all, what can you say to a man about to die that would truly comfort them?

The sight of his trembling hand forced all of Joseph's regrets to the surface. He could no longer lie to himself or deny the feelings he felt moments before his death.

Joseph Bateman felt regret.

He looked away from his trembling hands at the brick wall in front of him. He hoped that if he no longer saw the physical effects his fear was having on him, then his regret would go away. That was not the case. No matter where he looked, Joseph knew that within minutes he would be dead, and he regretted every decision he made in his life that led him into the deadly hold of the electric chair.

This is your key to redemption... In your final moment of regret—when the hatred you have within you is turned upon yourself—the key will turn, and the walls will come tumbling down. Then, you will be given your moment of redemption, echoed through Joseph's head as his legs were being strapped in.

Joseph remembered what the crazy tattoo artist had told him years ago after the infamous line spoken by John Wilkes Booth had been branded onto his chest. As regret filled him faster than a boat in water with a gaping in its side, Joseph found himself hoping the walls of the prison would come crumbling down. He imagined the bricks of the wall he was staring at breaking apart. He saw himself breaking the restraints that held him to the chair, and walking through the newly created hole in the wall towards freedom. There, he'd get his second chance. There, he would get his chance for redemption. He'd turn his life around, and he would somehow find vindication for all the wrongs he had committed.

He stared at the wall, and willed it to come crashing down, but no such thing happened. It stood erect, as it had for years, and as it would for decades after Joseph was long gone.

There was no chance for redemption. All there was was a man desperately hanging on to hope, and all that turned out to be was the ramblings of an insane man from the past.

As Joseph painted the ludicrous fantasy of second chances, Conroy Nates and the other officer finished strapping Joseph into the chair. His arms, legs, chest, and groin were firmly secured, which allowed for minimal movement once the electricity started to flow. Next, Conroy Nates took a dampened sponge, and placed it on top of Joseph's head. Joseph thought he felt little beads of water dripping down his head, but, truth be told, he wasn't sure if what he felt was the water from the sponge, or his own sweat.

Joseph saw Conroy Nates' hand reach up to grab the metal skullcap. Joseph squeezed his eyes shut as the cap was lowered so that the tears forming in his eyes would not fall. Soon he would be blindfolded, and once no one was able to see his face, he'd allow the tears to flow.

Once the cap was secure, Conroy Nates stepped away from Joseph, and the young guard stepped forward with the blindfold.

"Nates…" Joseph called out right as the blindfold was coming down over his eyes. "I'm sorry."

Joseph's apology was not just for how he had treated Conroy Nates over the past fifteen months. Joseph Bateman was apologizing to everyone he had ever hurt in his life with his ignorance and racist hatred.

His apology was directed to Eve Meyers for giving Alex the rock that smashed her in the head. He was apologizing to Leonard Hershel for the night he vandalized the man's car with Bill Casings, and for sucker punching him that rainy day inside his General Store. It was for the man he called a nigger for no other reason than he had refused to give up his seat at a bar.

It wasn't just an apology for all the black people Joseph had wronged throughout his life. Joseph's apology was for Alex, too.

He was regretting a lot of things he had done in his life, but the one thing he regretted the most was how he treated Alex during their last meeting together.

Alex deserved a life after Joseph. She deserved a chance to finally escape what she had been running from her entire life. All she wanted was closure so she could fully move on, and Joseph denied her that. In the few moments Joseph Bateman had left in his life, he wished he could tell Alex that it was okay. He wanted to let her know he understood.

231

Conroy Nates acknowledged Joseph's apology with a simple head nod. It was all Joseph needed to know his apology was accepted. Nates then turned his attention to the guard holding the blindfold, and gave him the signal to lower it. It came down over Joseph's eyes, and before it engulfed him in its darkness, Joseph looked down at his hands that were strapped to the chair.

"Useless..." he whispered. "Useless..."

"Joseph Bateman," Joseph heard Conroy Nates say. "In accordance with Florida State law, electricity shall pass through you until you are dead."

He said nothing else, and what followed were the longest seconds of Joseph's life. They were his last, and they were spent waiting for the lightning.

When it came, electricity was sent coursing through the body of Joseph Bateman at twelve-hundred volts. There was a fiery pain, and he felt his body jolt from top to bottom as the electricity hit him, and rampaged through his body. That was the extent of Joseph's pain, though.

The next thing he was aware of was that he was standing in darkness. Not the same kind of darkness that came from the blindfold that covered his eyes. This one was different. It was infinite. If he was to reach out in front of him, or even below him where he stood, there would be nothing else. Only the darkness.

He no longer felt the constrictions of his restraints. It was as if at one moment he had been squeezed tightly into a deflated balloon, and then suddenly that balloon was inflated; leaving room for him to move freely.

As he stretched his free arms out in front of him, Joseph spotted something in the darkness. It was faint, but in the pitch black that surrounded him, it couldn't be missed. At first, it was a single dot. Like a lone star in an infinite sky. Then it caught fire, and started to expand and spread, slowly at first, and then more rapidly. Then, more flames began to break through the black canvas.

As he watched the fire spread, Joseph noticed the flames were forming letters. It was a C that he had been able to make out first, followed by an S, which was accompanied by another S. One by one, letters appeared in the darkness until they formed a single legible sentence.

Joseph read the single line burning in the dark of what was obviously the moment between life and death. He knew the saying well. He had seen it every day etched upon his chest.

SIC SEMPER TYRANNIS

The letters burned quickly, and then bled into each other. Soon the saying was gone, and all that remained was a burning ball in the darkness.

Joseph felt a sudden rumbling begin below his feet. If there had been a floor beneath his feet, which he knew there wasn't (there was only darkness), it would've been cracking, and falling to pieces.

He tried to keep his balance as the darkness below him broke apart, and opened up to something else entirely. His efforts failed him, and he felt himself beginning to fall through the cracks. No matter where Joseph tried to step, the darkness crumbled, and widened the hole below him.

Hell, Joseph thought. *That's what this is…This is my entry to hell.*

That was the last thought to pass through Joseph's mind before everything below him collapsed beneath his feet.

What came next was falling.

He would fall backwards for a century and a half, and there would be no hell for Joseph Bateman when he finally landed.

Instead, there would be a new path for him to travel. One that would potentially lead him to his redemption.

PART 2

REDEMPTION

??/??/????

Joseph Bateman Wakes Up

He took a sudden and deep breath in the moment he regained consciousness, like a man coming back to life. Upon inhaling, he vacuumed a sizeable amount of dirt up off the floor he was laying on, which cause an immediate coughing fit.

His body wanted air...not dirt.

Dead people didn't need air, though. In fact, dead people were more synonymous with earth than they were with oxygen. So the fact that his body was fighting for the air it so desperately needed could only mean one thing.

Joseph Bateman was alive.

That wasn't right, though. Over a thousand volts of electricity had been sent vaulting through his body. No one survives that. Especially not someone who has people trained in the art of execution watching over them. They were to make sure the electricity did its job, and killed the person it was sent through. Yet here Joseph was...

Alive.

He was full of life when he was supposed to be lifeless. He was breathing, as he had done for past twenty-six years and eleven months. Inhaling and then exhaling. Taking in oxygen, then releasing carbon dioxide. Doing all the things that people who were alive and not dead did.

Not only was Joseph still breathing, but he was no longer bound to the electric chair he had been restrained to only moments before. He wasn't even sitting in it. He was now lying on a dirt covered floor.

Had something gone wrong with the execution? Were they forced, for some reason, to abort, and get Joseph out of the chair?

Joseph rolled over onto his back. He expected to see Conroy Nates, amongst others, standing over him. There was no one, though. He was by himself and, to make matters stranger, he was no longer in the execution room of the prison.

Instead, Joseph was outside and looking up at the night sky.

He rolled back onto his stomach and pushed himself up off the dirt floor, which was actually a dirt road. The muscles he used to push his weight from the ground screamed in agony as they were engaged. The bones that were used to support him felt like they were creaking as he stood. A sudden case of lightheadedness took him, and he needed to lean against a nearby brick wall until he was able to regain his bearings.

Once he was feeling better, and able to stand without support, Joseph became aware that something else didn't feel right. It wasn't a physical ailment, like dizziness or sore muscles. It was something else entirely. He had the overwhelming feeling that he did not belong in his own body. He had heard the saying about people not feeling comfortable in their own skin, but what he was currently experiencing took it to a whole new level.

Yet as he fixated on the foreign sensation taking him, there was also a faint familiarity there. It was like Joseph was revisiting somewhere he had been when he was only a child, too young to have actual memories, but still possessing the knowledge that he has been there before.

What the fuck happened to me?

He felt confident enough now in the physical shape of his body to attempt to walk. He looked down to make sure everything below him was working properly before taking that first step, and that was when Joseph realized he was wearing a suit. An extremely outdated suit, at that. Except outdated wasn't exactly the adjective one would use to describe this particular suit Joseph was suddenly wearing. Outdated might be properly used had the suit been from the 1970's or the 1960's. Joseph didn't think it was even from the twentieth century. Wherever this mystery suit came from, it was old...very old.

Seriously...What the fuck happened to me??

Had Joseph's clothes been fried off of him during the execution, and this relic suit was all they could find in the bowels of the prison basement? That didn't make sense. If that was in fact the case, they would have just gotten Joseph another one of his regulation prison outfits. They had thousands in the building. The reasons why he was now in some ancient suit made zero sense. Then again, nothing about what was currently going on made a stitch of sense to Joseph.

He tabled the thoughts inside his head momentarily, and focused all his energy on taking a step without falling on his ass. Joseph successfully lifted his foot off the ground, and took a step forward. He followed this with another, and then a third. He repeated this process, one step at a time, until he was no longer counting his steps.

He stepped out of the alleyway he had woken up in onto a main road. This road, like the one he had just woken up on, was also paved with dirt. Brick buildings lined each side of the street. Each building attached to its neighbor, creating a block-long wall of houses. The streets were filled with people. Everyone—both man and woman—was dressed in outfits as outdated as the one Joseph wore. About fifty yards from where he had emerged onto the street, Joseph spotted a horse and carriage in front of one of the buildings. A little further down, a man on horseback was making his way down the road. It was as if Joseph had woken up in a whole different century.

A young boy turned the street corner, and was yelling something in celebration as he ran past Joseph.

"Lee surrenders to Grant!" the young boy exclaimed. "The war is over!"

As the boy ran down the street, yelling the same line— *Lee surrenders to Grant! The war is over!*—Joseph's confusion was cleared away. Everything suddenly made perfect sense.

I'm dead, he told himself. *Or I'm in the process of dying. Whatever it is, I'm sitting on that electric chair, frying. This is some hallucination that occurs in that final moment between life and death.*

That was the only explanation for what was going on. As his brain and the rest of his organs failed him and shut down, it triggered some sort of hallucination of post-Civil War Washington, D.C..

This wasn't exactly surprising to Joseph. With his huge lifelong fascination with the events that occurred in the nation's capital during April of 1865, there was no shock that it would serve as the hallucination his dying brain conjured.

Yet a big part of him rejected the idea. As much as Joseph told himself it was the only explanation, he also told himself he was wrong.

He had never experienced a hallucination before, but he imagined it might feel not too differently from a dream that blurred the lines between itself and reality. Even the most real of dreams had indicators that they were nothing more than creations of our imagination, though. Joseph saw none of those indicators as he stood in the middle of an unfamiliar road in an unfamiliar time. The ground, the street, the buildings, the horses, the people; all of it seemed as real to Joseph as every other thing he had come in contact with throughout his life.

He wandered down the dirt street, taking in everything that surrounded him. No one seemed to take any notice of him, which came as a bit of a shock. Despite the threads he was sporting, he must have still stuck out. His twentieth century appearance certainly didn't match that of a man of twenty-six years old from nearly a century and a half earlier.

Joseph walked aimlessly with no real destination. He was too busy taking in the foreign world around him to pay any attention to where his feet were leading him. When he finally stopped, he was standing in front of a stable. Instead of moving on, Joseph felt compelled to enter the building. Before he could even make the conscious decision to approach the stable, his feet had already began to lead him towards the door.

The stable was dark inside. The only source of light was a single lantern hung up on the rear wall. As Joseph walked towards it, he heard rustling coming from the darkness. He walked over to one of the nearby stalls, and peered in at its current occupant. The horse inside became restless, and backed away as far as it could from Joseph. Wanting to sooth the animal, Joseph slowly extended his hand towards it in hopes it might warm up to him.

"No point in trying to sooth that one, sir," a voice said from behind him. Joseph turned, and saw that he was no longer alone. His new company, he assumed, was likely the owner of the stable or perhaps a stable boy. "That one there is anxious as anxious can be. Likely to break her halter and escape if you try to tie her up, or even leave her unattended."

That's the horse John Wilkes Booth asked Ned Spangler to watch over when he arrived at Ford's Theatre the night he shot Lincoln, Joseph told himself as he stared at the animal in the stall.

Edmund 'Ned' Spangler was a stagehand at Ford's Theatre who was charged, convicted, and hung for the part he played in the assassination of President Abraham Lincoln. The horse Joseph was now staring at was the very horse Spangler was left in charge of watching after while John Wilkes Booth put a bullet in the back of the sixteenth president's head.

It's not real, Joseph reminded himself. *It's all part of this death hallucination.*

"You know that's not true," the man said, as if reading Joseph's mind. "This is no hallucination. No point in lying to yourself, Joseph."

Joseph turned towards the stranger, who somehow knew his name.

Of course he knows your name. He's a product of your own imagination.

Yet, no matter how much he told himself that, Joseph couldn't shake the overwhelming feeling that all of this was actually real. This complete stranger was actual flesh and bone. The stable they stood in was built from wood and nails. The horse in the stall behind him had lived over a hundred years before Joseph's birth.

"How do you know my name?" Joseph asked.

"We have met before, Joseph Bateman. I am sure you remember me."

He took the lantern from the back wall, and walked towards Joseph. He lifted it so that Joseph could get a clearer look at him. The face, itself, Joseph had never seen before, but the two men had met before. He was not lying about that, and Joseph did remember him well.

It would be impossible to forget those eyes.

Every physical feature argued that this wasn't the same person Joseph had met in a New York City tattoo shop in the summer of 1992. His eyes, however, said otherwise, and their argument outweighed all others. Joseph looked into them, and they were the undeniable proof that this was, in fact, the same person who had tattooed *Sic Semper Tyrannis* on his chest.

They were as unsettling now as they were the last time Joseph looked into them. He still tried to tell himself that this was all part of his fried brain failing him, and shutting down, but he no longer truly believed that. As he stared into those eyes, Joseph knew more than ever that this was no hallucination. It was real. Somehow, all of it was real.

"What is this?" Joseph asked, backing away from the man with the eyes of someone who had once tattooed him. "Who are you?"

"This," the man said, gesturing to their surroundings. "This is a stable. If you are speaking on a grander scale, though...This is your redemption, Joseph Bateman. As for me. I am the reason you have been given a chance for redemption."

"I'm supposed to be dead."

"You are dead in some respects. In others, you are not. That body you inhabited for the past twenty-six years has been fried. It's now toast. But as you're about to find out, Joseph, part of you is still very much alive."

"Where are we?"

"I told you; a stable."

"That is not what I meant."

"I'll give you a minute to figure it out, because I think you already know. You're just in denial over it."

Washington DC…April 9, 1865…The day the Civil War ended.

Joseph couldn't bring himself to say the actual words out loud. It was too absurd, not to mention impossible. He tried going back his death hallucination theory, but that was too far gone to try and grasp onto.

"It's not possible."

"Yet here we are. In the reality of it all. Standing here, flesh, bone and blood, at the foot of your path towards redemption."

"You keep saying that, and it's doing very little to help me figure things out."

Joseph could feel his anger levels rising. This man, who he had never seen before, yet was somehow the same man he met in 1992, was creating more questions than he was providing answers.

"You don't need me to tell you where you are," the man explained. "You already know the answer to that. What you need to do is accept it."

"Why am I here?" Joseph asked

"For your redemption."

"You've said that already. Multiple times, in fact. Including the last time we met. Only then, you were somebody completely different." Joseph's anger was becoming more obvious by the rising tone in which he was speaking. "Do you care to tell me how to obtain this redemption you won't shut up about? Because I have no idea what you're talking about."

"I don't expect you to understand. No one ever does. Not at first, at least. Unfortunately, it is not for me to explain. Understanding must be found by you, and only you. One does not walk the path of redemption with their hand held. It is a path you must find and travel on your own. Once you find it, though, it will be clear."

"Okay, for starters, the way you speak pisses me off. Second, if you aren't here to tell me how to obtain this redemption, then why exactly are you here?"

"Just because I will not walk you down the path, does not mean I won't point you in the general direction that you must travel. For you to understand your redemption, you must first understand what has happened to you. I am here to give you that explanation."

"Perfect! I've only asked you repeatedly to tell me what all this is."

"This is what happens when the walls break down, Joseph."

"That does absolutely nothing to provide me with any explanation, whatsoever."

"I told you once that in your moment of true regret, the walls will crumble, and you will be given your chance for redemption. Well, for you, and everyone else in your position, that moment comes right before death takes you. Like I promised, the wall fell, and led you here."

"Washington DC," Joseph forced from his lips. "1865."

"That is correct."

"Why am I here?"

"Because this is the catalyst."

"Of what?"

"Of what led you to the electric chair."

"What led me to the electric chair was murdering a raping nigger."

"Joseph, the reason you were executed goes far deeper than you murdering the man who raped your girlfriend. It goes far, far deeper than that. What you did here, in 1865, is the reason your life, and every life you lived in between, was one of dismay and unfortunate endings."

The man pulled a mirror from his back pocket. Joseph knew it was for him to look into. He also knew he didn't want to. The reflection he saw would not be his own. He knew that much. The mirror was held out for Joseph to take, but he made no movement for it. He was too afraid of what—who—he would see staring back at him.

"Take it," the man said when Joseph didn't move. "Look into it. Then you will only start to understand."

Despite his trepidations, Joseph obeyed, and took the mirror. He somehow willed his arm to lift it to his face, and twist the reflective glass towards him. What he saw was a face he had seen plenty of times throughout his life.

And like he had suspected, that face was not his own.

April 9, 1865
Joseph's New Face

Joseph Bateman stared into a mirror at a face that should have been his own, but was not. His deep brown eyes were replaced with hazel ones. His recently shaved head was now full of dark hair, and parted down the side. His naturally olive complexion had gone pale, and on his once smoothly shaven face there was now a handlebar mustache. Every physical feature on the face in the mirror's reflection had changed from what Joseph had always known. That was because it was no longer his own face at which Joseph was looking.

It was the face of John Wilkes Booth.

Joseph went completely numb, and the mirror he held in his nonfunctioning hand fell to the ground, and shattered into pieces.

"That's not real," he told the man who handed him the mirror.

Yet it was. Joseph brought his hand to his face, and felt the long whiskers of the handlebar mustache. It wasn't his mustache, though. It wasn't his face. It was John Wilkes Booth's.

Joseph had spent his entire life intrigued and even eventually idolizing John Wilkes Booth. So much so that he went as far as to get a tattoo of the assassin's most infamous quote across his chest. However, when Joseph saw Booth's face in the mirror's reflection, there was no admiration or excitement. Instead, in the pit of Joseph's stomach, there was an overwhelming sense of dread.

What you did here, in 1865, is the reason your life, and every life you lived in between, was one of dismay and unfortunate endings.

That's what this man, who Joseph had just met, yet somehow was the same person he had met nearly three years ago and a hundred twenty-seven years later, had told him. A single event had taken place in the sixty-fifth year of the nineteenth century, and it served as the catalyst for lifetimes worth of horribleness. Based on who Joseph saw in the mirror, it wasn't hard to figure out what the event was.

Joseph had an information overload, and his legs began to fail him. He cautiously lowered himself to the floor, and took a seat while his current company took a seat across from him, and waited as Joseph tried to process.

"I know this is a lot, Joseph," the man said. "You need to listen, though. Because what I'm here to tell you will help guide you to what I can't. It will help you understand your path.

"The path to my redemption..."

"Yes."

So Joseph listened as this mystery man explained to him the why and how of what was going on.

"Every human being has a soul. When a newborn infant takes its first breath, there is a spark. From that spark, a fire ignites. That fire is a soul.

"Like humans, all souls have a beginning and an end. They are born, and eventually they grow weary and lay

250

themselves to rest. The life span of a soul is just much longer than the life span you are familiar with.

"You can think of it this way… If your soul is a traveler, then the long road it is on represents its lifespan. Your physical body is the car your soul uses to travel down the road. Like all cars, your body eventually dies. No matter how much work you put into it, eventually, you're going to need a new one.

"Sometimes, when that newborn infant I mentioned earlier takes its first breath, instead of a new soul being born, an already existing one will enter, and become the flame that burns within that child. That infant is the new car our souls need to continue on their journey when their previous car has died.

"After our soul has jumped from the old car to the newer model," the man explained, furthering his metaphor, "a wall goes up. Think of it as looking into your rearview, and not being able to see the road you have traveled thus far. This is why a person does not remember events from their past lives. A wall goes up, and we are incapable of seeing who we once were, and what lives we have once lived. Does this make sense to you, thus far?"

It did, and Joseph indicated so with a nod.

"There are a few cases, however, when these walls get cracks," the man went on. "These are your people who claim to remember events that had never occurred during their life, or talents they might just have that they've never learned before. It's their past lives seeping through the cracks. Then there are cases like yours."

"When the walls come crumbling down…"

The man nodded.

"Are you familiar with the concept of reincarnation, Joseph?" he went on to ask.

"Yeah," Joseph answered. "Isn't that when after you die, you come back in your next life as something else?"

"Correct, and the manner in which you live your life determines what you come back as in the next. That concept isn't too far off from the actual truth. The only major flaw in that concept is that we don't become trees, or anything else, for that matter. We always come back as human, regardless of the manner we have lived and conducted ourselves."

The massive cloud of confusion began to part. Joseph now began to understand why his life was less than an appealing one.

"For most people, the trip from one life to the next is smooth sailing," the man said. "They have lived normal, and happy lives, and will continue to do so in their next incarnation. However, there are those who do something so terrible, it affects and drastically alters the fate of their soul. You are one of those people, Joseph Bateman. You did something so monumentally wicked here that that you have been punished in every life you have lived since."

"I killed Lincoln..."

That line had been floating around his head ever since he saw the reflection of John Wilkes Booth in the mirror instead of his own. He tried to grasp it, but his mind wouldn't reach out far enough. Now, with all that had been explained to him, Joseph's mind was finally able to wrap itself around the truth. Like a ghost he had been trying to summon becoming corporeal.

"That is correct," the man informed Joseph. "On the fourteenth of April, 1865—five days from where we sit right now—you walked into Ford's Theatre, entered the State Box, and shot Abraham Lincoln in the back of the head."

"I know the details of the story," Joseph said. "I don't need you to give me the damn play-by-play."

As Joseph's reality was coming together and taking form, he began to see similarities between himself and

252

John Wilkes Booth. After his date with the electric chair, the two men shared the same death day, which was April the twenty-sixth. They also shared a birthday—May 10th—and died at the age of twenty-six.

One similarity that Joseph had missed his entire life was his name. He and John Wilkes Booth had the same initials, Joseph William Bateman...

Joseph **W**illiam **B**ateman...

J.W.B....

John **W**ilkes **B**ooth.

The biggest connection that Joseph missed, however, but which came to him now, was the word *useless*. Joseph knew from reading material that in his final moments before his death, John Wilkes Booth had asked to see his hands. When the soldiers that had hunted him down obliged and raised Booth's paralyzed hands to his face, Abraham Lincoln's assassin stared at his hands and muttered the word *useless...useless*. He then died. Never before, despite all the times throughout his own life he had looked down at his own hands and uttered that same word, had Joseph ever come close to connecting that link.

"Because you killed Abraham Lincoln," the man said, "every life you've lived proceeding it was unpleasant with an abrupt ending to match. That was until now, of course."

"Why are things different now?" Joseph asked.

"Things are different now, because your soul regrets what it had once done. There comes a point in everyone's life where they look back at something they did, and wish they hadn't done it. You had that moment while sitting in the electric chair, but it goes much deeper than that.

"You see, souls, in many ways, are just like humans, but on a grander scale. Like humans, a soul can regret. They, too, reach that point where they look back, and wish things had gone differently for them. Your soul reached that point when you were born, Joseph. It looked back at over a hundred years, and loathed every miserable moment. Like you wished you hadn't done the things that led you down your path, your soul wished the same.

"For some, there comes a point where they can turn things around, and find redemption. You tried that multiple times throughout your life and failed. That was because it was impossible for you to do so. Fate wouldn't allow it. Some, however, are able to find the redemption they long for. Souls can be afforded that same opportunity to make amends, to prove that they are not what they used to be."

"This is what this is, then?" Joseph asked. "My soul's chance for redemption?"

"It is. I have allowed the walls to come down, and sent you back to the catalyst."

"And you're capable of doing this, how?"

It was just another question to add to the laundry list of questions Joseph never thought he'd have to ask. This man knew everything about Joseph, but Joseph knew nothing about him. He didn't even know the man's name. All Joseph knew was that this man had the ability to send someone's essence through time, and had the ability to do the same himself.

"I'm just like you, Joseph," the man said. "I'm a soul looking for its redemption. This is part of my redemption. I lead others to theirs in hopes of finally finding mine."

"Do you have a name?"

"I did. Now I'm just called J."

"Is that short for something?"

It was, but it was obvious J had no intention of sharing that information.

"My name should have been forgotten centuries ago," was what J said instead. "History has immortalized it, though, and I am forced to know I am that person. There's no reason others should know it, as well."

"How old are you?"

254

"Well the person you are talking to now is only nineteen years old. The man you spoke to in the tattoo shop in 1992 was fifty-one. Something tells me, though, you aren't asking the age of these mortal bodies. If it is my soul you are asking about, it is a few decades short of two-thousand years old."

Joseph Bateman was no expert on the lifespans of souls, but something told him that closing in on two-thousand years was old, even by souls' standards.

It was then that Joseph understood what it was about J's eyes that made them so different. If there was any truth to the saying that the eyes are the window to the soul, then what he saw when he looked into J's eyes were nearly two millenniums of existence. This man had seen the rise and fall of empires. He had seen war and he had seen peace. He had seen life and death. As amazing a gift as that could be, Joseph knew it was also a burden.

Joseph suddenly felt himself feeling sorry for this stranger sitting across from him. He had seen the best of the world, but he had also experienced the worst of it. Joseph knew about the weight a person carried throughout their life caused by the horrible things they see. His weight was only a fraction of J's, and no one should ever have to carry that kind of weight.

What Joseph saw when he looked into the eyes of J was despair.

"I have seen souls born, and I have seen those same souls die," J told Joseph. "For almost two millennium, I have given others the chance to find their redemption in hopes of finding my own."

"What did you do?" Joseph asked.

"That is not important."

"I don't care. You know my story. I deserve to know yours."

"I betrayed a friend." Before Joseph could inquire any further, J stood. "We are finished here. I have explained to you all you need to know. The rest is for you to figure out. It is on you to find your path."

J turned and walked towards the exit of the stable. Joseph wanted to stop him. He had more questions than he did answers, but he knew, even if he asked, J would not answer. The man spoke more in riddles than anything else, and he had made it clear that Joseph was to find his own way. Everything Joseph was meant to know, J had already said.

"One last thing, Joseph," J said in the doorway. "Beware of Booth. He will try to stray you from your path. Do not let him. I'll say it once more…beware of Booth."

With that said, their meeting had concluded. J turned and walked out of the stable; leaving Joseph alone to find his path and his redemption.

April 10, 1865
Joseph Finds His Path

Joseph stepped out of the stable and back onto the streets of 1865 Washington D.C. just after midnight. He had remained in the stable for over an hour as he attempted to fully absorb all that he had learned. He couldn't, though. Even though he knew it was all real, he was unable to make any sense of what didn't.

In a past life, Joseph Bateman was John Wilkes Booth.

That concept was mind-blowing. There had always been a lifelong connection Joseph felt with the first presidential assassin in United States history. This was a whole new inconceivable level, though.

As he stood in the dirt streets of the nation's capital, Joseph considered his next move. It didn't take him long before he realized he had no idea what his next move should be. He knew he needed one, though. J had told him he was sent back to find his redemption. So if Joseph was going to do that, he needed something that resembled a plan. He decided that he first needed to figure out what had to be done to redeem himself for his soul's past bad deeds. Once he had that figured out, he'd be able to build a plan from there. To do that, Joseph needed some time to think and get his head on a little straighter than it currently was. Perhaps a night's sleep would do him well. The only problem was that Joseph had nowhere to go. He wasn't even from the century, after all.

Except that wasn't entirely true.

Mentally, he may have still been Joseph Bateman, a product of the twentieth century, but physically he was John Wilkes Booth, and Booth very much belonged in the nineteenth century. Booth had been staying at the National Hotel in the days leading up to the night he shot Lincoln. Joseph decided to head there to spend the night. Hopefully, with a good night's rest behind him, he would find a bit of clarity.

Joseph made his way through the streets to the National Hotel, which was located on the corner of 6th and Pennsylvania Avenue. As he walked, he couldn't help but think about his surroundings, which only made accepting the reality of it all that much more difficult. The people he passed would all be dead for an entire century before his own birth. The streets he walked would soon be paved, and the buildings he passed would either be abandoned, closed down or renovated before the turn of the century. None of those things had happened yet, and as Joseph explored a life that was never meant for him to see, it felt as if he was walking in another world.

When he arrived at the National Hotel, he made his way up to room 228 and entered. He sat down on the edge of the bed, and felt exhaustion start to rear its head. Despite everything going on in his mind, Joseph didn't expect any difficulty finding sleep once he lay down, but before he could lay his head down to rest, there was a knock on the door to his room.

Joseph froze at the sound of the knock. He found himself petrified at the idea of having to interact with someone from a completely different era. What if he said something wrong, or mentioned something that hadn't even been invented yet? He may have been well-versed on the subject matter of John Wilkes Booth, the Lincoln assassination and its conspiracy, but he knew very little about the time period.

When the second rapping at the door came, Joseph forced himself to his feet. He made his way to the door, and when he opened it, there was a woman standing on the opposite side.

His initial thought was Lucy Lambert Hale, Booth's fiancé at the time he shot Lincoln. Joseph had seen only a few photos of her and couldn't quite recall her face.

"Is it late?" she asked.

Joseph said it wasn't, and motioned her into the room from the darkened hallway.

Upon entering the room, Joseph examined the young lady once again. After seeing her in a better light, he began to second guess his immediate identification of her. He was fairly certain it wasn't Lucy Lambert Hale. He began to wonder who this woman could be. It was late at night, and even though he had only been with one woman his entire life, he knew what it meant when a woman came to your hotel room in the late hours after dusk.

Booth may have been romantically involved with Lucy Lambert Hale, publicly, but that did not mean he didn't enjoy the company of other women in private. After all, he was a well-known stage actor before turning historically infamous murderer. Women back then would swoon over this man just as they did over the Hollywood heartthrobs of Joseph's time.

Joseph also recalled a fact about the morning Booth had died. After President Lincoln's assassin had expired, the soldiers at the scene searched his body. Along with a journal that would become infamous for its missing pages, five photographs were found. Each was a different woman.

One was Booth's fiancé while the others were actresses. Even though he had never seen photographs of the other four women, Joseph did not doubt the possibility that he was presently in the company of one of them.

"Is something the matter?" the young lady asked.

"No," Joseph answered. "Just tired."

The young girl took a step towards him, leaned in, and kissed Joseph softly on the lips. As he kissed this beautiful woman, two thoughts passed through Joseph's head. One was that this woman had no idea she was currently kissing the man who in just a few days would become America's most wanted fugitive.

His second thought was of Alex. Guilt took Joseph as he kissed the young woman. As much as the physical body doing the kissing wasn't his own, the sensations, and all that came with it, were very much real to Joseph.

His first instinct was to pull away from the kiss, and he was about to when he realized he had nothing to feel guilty about. Alex had moved on with her life. She had kissed another man. She had loved someone else, and let him inside her—both physically and emotionally. Now free of any unwarranted guilt, Joseph pulled the beautiful woman closer to his body, and kissed her passionately. She took him by his shirt, and pulled him towards the bed.

"Sit," she said, and Joseph obeyed.

She took a few steps back, so that Joseph could get a full view of her, and undressed.

As he watched her remove her clothes, Joseph couldn't help but recognize that he was giving life to the saying about looks being deceitful. This young woman thought she was undressing for John Wilkes Booth when that was in fact not the case. If there was any guilt over this, it wasn't enough for Joseph to speak up, or put an abrupt ending to the late night rendezvous.

Once completely naked, the woman joined Joseph at the foot of the bed. She undid his pants, and pulled them down to his ankles. When they were gone and no longer an issue, she got between Joseph's legs, went down to her knees, and took him inside her mouth.

Despite being inside another man's body, Joseph felt every little sensation that came from sexual stimulation. Wanting to explore these sensations further, Joseph took the young woman, and tossed her onto the bed. She looked up at him with yearning in her eyes as she waited for him—John Wilkes Booth, actually—to take her. Despite how unbelievably gorgeous she was, Joseph knew he could not look her in the face while they did what he had intended for them to do. Instead, he flipped her over and propped her up on her hands and knees.

Joseph had always imagined nineteenth century women being prim and proper. He had never thought about what sex in the 1800's was like, but if he had, he would've imagined the only position the act of love making was done in was missionary. Yet this woman didn't miss a beat. She arched her head back and let out a moan of excitement as Joseph tugged at her hair while he took her from behind.

Within minutes, Joseph reached climax. Through the body of Booth, Joseph experienced every euphoric feeling that came with orgasm. He felt the sweat on the back of Booth's neck, his elevated heartrate pounding in his ears. It was the first time since waking up in that alley that Joseph felt in tune with the body of John Wilkes Booth.

It'd be the closest he would ever come, as he would learn soon enough that he was not alone inside that body.

The young woman, whose name Joseph still did not know, got up from the bed, and dressed. She wished Joseph a good night, and left him alone. As he laid there, Joseph's thoughts once again traveled back to Alex. Even though he had technically done nothing wrong—it wasn't even his body he used to lay with the young woman, after all—he felt guilty for the act.

Not wanting to lay there and obsess over what had just transpired and how he should be feeling about it, Joseph got out of bed. As he dressed, he then caught a glimpse of the man in the mirror. He approached it, and stared into the eyes of John Wilkes Booth.

The man he had idolized.

The man who had sent him to death row.

The man who was the real reason why he and Alex didn't end up together.

"I hate you," Joseph said to the reflection in the mirror. "I FUCKING HATE YOU!"

He grabbed a nearby stool, and he heaved it at the mirror. The glass shattered, and John Wilkes Booth disappeared from Joseph's sight. The anger and bitterness lingered, though.

Joseph made his way back to the bed, and once again sat on its edge. He stared down at his hands and thought the same thing he had thought time and time again. The very same thing John Wilkes Booth thought in the moment before death took him.

They were useless.

But they didn't have to be.

If Joseph could will Booth to pick up a stool and throw it at a mirror, he could will it to do other things as well. Or not do, to be more specific.

Things like not pull the trigger of a gun.

Right then, Joseph found his path. He knew precisely how he was going to earn his redemption.

April 11, 1865
Joseph Meets Booth

Joseph stepped out of the National Hotel and onto the streets of Washington D.C. on the morning of April the eleventh. He had somewhere important to be later that evening, but until then he was going to take in the sights, sounds, and lifestyles of the nation's capital over a century before his own birth.

He had spent the entirety of the previous day locked inside room 228 of the National Hotel. He had woken up midmorning after only a few hours of sleep. The moment his eyes opened, his brain kicked into overdrive. He now had a plan—a path—and he needed the day to absorb the monumental severity of what he planned to do. Once he was able to somewhat wrap his mind around the magnitude of it, Joseph called upon every morsel of knowledge he had on the recorded events of the next couple of days in the nation's capital, and combed out the fine detail of his grand plan.

In addition to his preparation, memories from lives Joseph had lived between John Wilkes Booth's and his own began to come to him, and solidify into memories.

There was the man who spent his entire adult life courting vulnerable women who had inherited land or money from a recently deceased relative. Using an alias, he would convince these women to add his name to the inherited property's deed, or grant him access to the bank accounts where their newly acquired fortune was held. Once done, he would sell the land, or close the account and withdraw all the money within it. By the time the woman he had conned realized what he was doing, he was long gone with their money, leaving them broke or homeless with nothing but a false name to report to the police. His conning ended, however, on April 26, 1891 when a brother of his latest victim tracked him down and put a bullet in his head.

Then there was the man who met his end on April 26, 1969 after an accidental overdose. He had spent his teens running from the law after purposely burning down his home because his parents had grounded him after finding marijuana in his possession and destroying the drug in front of his eyes. He made it all the way to the west coast, where he settled down and spent the rest of his days practicing the art of free love. He also developed a nasty heroin addiction, which would also lead to his death at the young age of twenty-six years of age.

Joseph Bateman had lived a total of four lives between John Wilkes Booth's and his own, each life as distasteful as the last, and each one ending on April twenty-sixth at the age of twenty-six. All of this because John Wilkes Booth had shot Abraham Lincoln, and condemned his soul to over a century's worth of miserable punishment.

It was all about to change, though.

Joseph had his plan now. The one that would right the colossal wrong Booth had done and change the course of his soul, not to mention, history.

It was actually a fairly simple plan that required little action. It wasn't like some movie or comic book, where the hero has to go back in time and stop the villain from going through with some dastardly act. In this story, Joseph was not only the hero, but he was the villain as well. He had complete control over the body of John Wilkes Booth, so his only job was to make it so the villain did not play his villainous role.

If John Wilkes Booth never killed Lincoln, then every life proceeding his death wouldn't be one of suffering and heartache. There would be no reason for his soul to receive punishment in their proceeding lives. Therefore, on the date April 26, 1995, Joseph Bateman would not be sitting in the electric chair.

Instead, he'd be a free man.

Joseph had fallen asleep that night just after dark. With his plan in place, and only a few things to tend to in the upcoming days to assure everything went smoothly, he was able to close his eyes and descend into twilight just moments after his head touched the pillow. In the moments right before twilight, he thought of Alex.

At the end of their road together, Alex saw Joseph as a monster. Someone who could take another life, and not feel a shred of remorse for what he had done. That was all about to change, though. Everything would be different once Joseph's plan was executed. There would be no murder, no jail, and no death row to separate them. Alex wouldn't find comfort from the world she hated in the arms of another man. She would have Joseph, and they would be together, just like it was always meant to be.

Joseph woke the following morning—April 11, 1865— feeling refreshed. He had slept peacefully throughout the entire night and most of the morning. Now that he was fully rested and clear headed, he was eager to head out and explore nineteenth century, post-Civil War Washington, D.C.

At first, Joseph just roamed the streets. Everything was so different that no matter where he decided to go, there'd be something new and almost other-worldly for him to see. The only street Joseph made sure to steer clear of was 10th Street. He had plans to eventually make his way there before the calendar turned to the fourteenth of April, but it was not yet that time.

As the afternoon transitioned into the evening, Joseph stopped his random exploration, and headed to what would be referred to in the twentieth century as The National Mall. He crossed the Washington Canal, which no longer existed during his time, and entered the park. The spot that would be a booming tourist attraction during Joseph's time was a bleak and dismal place in the days of the Civil War.

On one end, in the distance, was The Capitol Building, which was still a few years away from true completion. On the other end of the park stood what would eventually be the Washington Monument. Construction of the landmark had been halted at the start of the war, and now stood there awkwardly unfinished.

Other than those two landmarks and the Smithsonian Institute, which stood in between The Capitol Building and the Washington Monument, The National Mall was nothing more than an open field. There would many monuments that would come within the next century and a half that were noticeably missing, two of which were built to honor the man whose destiny Joseph was about to alter. They were the Lincoln Reflection Pool and the Lincoln Memorial.

Joseph walked up B Street towards the location where the reflection pool and monument honoring Abraham Lincoln would stand in the twentieth century. There was nothing there now but the Potomac River, which would be forced back so the land could be laid to build these two premiere landmarks.

Joseph wondered, as he stared off into the river, if the pool and monument would still be there in the future. He was about to drastically change the future by not killing Abraham Lincoln. Despite the impact of his presidency, which even Joseph couldn't deny was nothing short of honor-worthy, it was the assassination that immortalized Lincoln. With his tragic death wiped from the history books, would he still be honored by the nation if he passed on peacefully in his sleep, instead of a bullet in the back of his head?

Joseph had no doubt the sixteenth president would be. Ending slavery and reuniting a torn nation after leading it through its most savage war was an impressive enough résumé to earn someone an honor as prestigious as a national monument.

It was an interesting thought to consider, but the truth was that Joseph could not care less. He was on his path to redemption, which was his path to Alex. What happened to Abraham Lincoln was no real concern of his. All that mattered was making things right so he could be with Alex.

As dusk began its rapid approach, Joseph turned his attention towards Pennsylvania Avenue and the White House. An important historic event was about to go down, and he wanted to witness it.

On April eleventh of 1865, President Abraham Lincoln gave his first public address following the end of the Civil War. It would also be his last.

In attendance that night to hear the president's speech was southern sympathizer and white supremacist, John Wilkes Booth. Enraged by Lincoln's support of black suffrage, Booth would vow the speech would be the last one Lincoln ever gave. Three days later, at Ford's Theatre, Booth would hold true to his claim.

All of that was on its way to changing, though, and being in attendance for the president's speech was a necessity to Joseph's plan.

Joseph navigated through the crowd that had assembled outside the White House's north door. A large portion of the crowd consisted of freed slaves, who were eager to hear from the man who had emancipated them. Like so many others, they wanted answers to what was in store for the nation now that the war was over, and it was once again whole. Joseph wondered how incensed John Wilkes Booth must have been while attending this speech, knowing this race of men he despised so much were now free under the Constitution of the United States.

He scanned the crowd for Lewis Powell; Booth's companion during the speech. Joseph had known Powell's face from photos in articles, textbooks and documentaries, so identifying the man wouldn't be too difficult. One of Joseph's biggest fears was that someone who John Wilkes Booth had known and should recognize would approach him, and he would not have the slightest idea of whose company he was in. It was just another reason to try and remain as low key as possible. Still, he knew there would be interactions with people, and there would be some he would have to engage. Luckily, from a lifelong fascination, Joseph knew the faces of all the key players Booth had come in contact with during the days leading up to Ford's Theatre. He didn't expect any hiccups to develop in his plan if he managed to keep all his major interactions with those specific people.

Joseph spotted Powell in the distance, and made his way over to the man who would attempt to take the life of United States Secretary of State, William Seward, on the night Lincoln was shot.

"Where have you been?" Powell asked.

"I was running late," Joseph answered.

The two said no more, which was how Joseph preferred it. They waited in silence for Abraham Lincoln to appear and address the crowd. After a few minutes, the crowd erupt into cheers and applause. Joseph looked up towards the White House, and standing in the window above the north door was Abraham Lincoln.

The first thing to cross Joseph's mind upon seeing the sixteenth president of the United States of America was the fact that he was the only person born in the twentieth century to see Abraham Lincoln alive. It was a privilege that belonged only to him.

The second thing Joseph felt was pity.

Abraham Lincoln looked like a man who had gone too many nights without peaceful rest. He was the great leader, who had reunited a torn nation, but to Joseph he looked like a man defeated. The president was tall and gaunt, and it was clear the years were finally catching up with him. Not just the years of brutal war, either.

Joseph was familiar with Lincoln's life, and knew tragedy stretched into the man's past much further than his untimely ending. Death was a recurring theme throughout the life of Abraham Lincoln. His mother had died of Milk Sickness when he was very young. His sister, who had cared for him after their mother's death until a stepmother entered the picture, died during childbirth in 1828. Ann Rutledge, who historians strongly believed was Lincoln's first love, died of Typhoid fever at the young age of twenty-two.

Death followed Abraham Lincoln into his presidency. Not only was he the Commander in Chief during the Civil War—a war that cost over a million American casualties— but his son, Willie, died at the age of eleven from the same disease that had taken the president's first love.

Looking back over Lincoln's life, Joseph found more similarities between him and Lincoln than he had with

Booth. It was true he had always felt that connection to Booth through his understanding of unbridled hatred towards another human being, but Lincoln and Joseph's lives had both been full of loss. Mother, sister, lover; Joseph had known what it was like to lose those people in one form or another, and he was well familiarized with the everlasting damage it could inflict on a person's psyche.

"We meet this evening, not in sorrow, but in gladness of heart," echoed across the lawn as Abraham Lincoln began his speech.

Despite his appearance, Lincoln emanated confidence through his words. He touched vaguely on the subject of reconstruction, as many citizens of the United States did not know what was next for the nation. Lincoln tried to quell their concerns with his words the best he could.

He also, for the first time publically, stated his beliefs that all freed slaves, who were now citizens of the United States, be given the right to vote.

"It is unsatisfactory to some that the elective franchise is not given to the colored man," he said in his northern Illinois accent. "I would myself prefer that it were now conferred on the very intelligent, and on those who serve our cause as soldiers."

Like a violent wave crashing down on a calm shore, Joseph felt a sudden rush of hatred flow through his body at the sound of Lincoln's words. As fast as it came, it was gone. Like a shiver from an icy chill. One moment Joseph was feeling pity towards Lincoln, and then the next, out of nowhere, he felt absolute enmity towards him.

The feeling of malice passing through him didn't belong to him, though. Of all the emotions a single person could feel, no one was more in tune with hatred than Joseph Bateman. He had lived his entire life with it, and the hatred he felt at that exact moment in time was not his own.

After his speech concluded, the president disappeared back into the White House. The crowd outside, whether soothed by Lincoln's words or not, slowly dispersed. As Joseph and Powell walked, Powell voiced his disgust at the idea of black people being given the right to vote. John Wilkes Booth, once upon a time, had expressed the same revulsion, and swore that Abraham Lincoln would never give another public address.

This time, however, there would be no such promise. Booth simply nodded along in agreement as Lewis Powell went on. Eventually, the two would part ways, and Joseph headed back to the National Hotel.

He crawled into the bed that belonged to John Wilkes Booth, and laid his head down on his pillow. The moment he closed his eyes, he felt the presence of another in the room. Joseph shot up, and scanned the moonlit room. He expected to see J standing there; lurking in the corner. There was no one, though. Joseph was alone.

Yet the presence of another person was there. It wasn't the first time he felt it, either. Throughout the entire day, as he explored Washington D.C., Joseph kept looking over his shoulder, half expecting to find someone trailing him. Again, there was no one.

Joseph then remembered the sudden burst of hatred he felt as Lincoln discussed black suffrage during his speech earlier in the night. It was sudden and then gone, like a specter passing through him.

What if that feeling had not passed through him, but had come from within him, instead?

Beware of Booth...

That was the last thing J had said to Joseph before they parted ways a few nights back in the stable. It wasn't the first time J had issued Joseph the same warning, either. He had done so in 1992 when they met for the first time in New York City. Back then, it was just the ramblings of an insane tattoo artist. Even in the stable, it was more of riddle than anything. Now, however, as he felt the company of someone who was not there, Joseph understood what J's warning had meant. That anger Joseph had felt earlier seemed so foreign to him, because it was not his own.

It was Booth's.

J had compared the journey of one's soul to a trip down a long highway. What Joseph had done, once the walls came crashing down, was jumped from his own car, into another's vehicle, and taken control of the wheel.

So what had happened to the driver Joseph had pushed aside in order to take the wheel?

The answer was he was still in the vehicle.

Joseph had jumped inside the body of Booth, and taken control of it in order to prevent the Lincoln Assassination. That didn't mean Booth's essence hadn't left the body. Joseph had merely squeezed, unwillingly, into the body of the first presidential assassin, and pushed him aside in order to take control.

Now they were both in there, like two people squeezed into a small closet. This explained the feeling that someone was constantly lurking nearby no matter where Joseph went, and the feeling of hatred that passed through him during Lincoln's speech.

Good, Joseph thought as he sat there in the dark, *I'm glad he's here.*

John Wilkes Booth had ruined Joseph Bateman's life by killing Abraham Lincoln. Now, Joseph had his chance to rectify all that, and Booth, himself, would have a front row seat to witness it all go down. His hatred could stew and boil over all it wanted. Nothing would come of it. All Booth could do was watch as Joseph undid everything he had done.

And Joseph planned on making sure Booth was well aware of what had once happened, and what would not happen again.

April 12, 1865
A Conspiracy Never Born

Joseph stood outside of 604 H Street. Used as a place for people passing through Washington, D.C. to stay, Mary Surratt's boardinghouse, which she opened following her husband's untimely death, would earn its place in history as the location where John Wilkes Booth, along with a handful of other conspirators, launched a plan to cripple the United States government.

Tonight, Joseph was going to make sure that plan never became a reality.

Upon entering the boardinghouse, the first person Joseph recognized was David Herold. Serving as Booth's closest companion following the president's assassination, Herold had spent fourteen days preceding the infamous moment at Ford's Theatre on the run from the federal government. Unlike Booth, David Herald would live to see a trial, where he would be found guilty and be hung for his involvement in the conspiracy to assassinate Abraham Lincoln.

Also in the room was Lewis Powell, who had been with Joseph the night before at Lincoln's speech at the White House. As the three sat at a table, Powell recounted the president's speech from the night before to Herald. The two spoke of the injustice of black suffrage. Joseph chose to have Booth remain silent during the conversation. He simply nodded along and stroked Booth's mustache.

Eventually they were joined by George Atzerodt, the man appointed the task of killing the vice-president, Andrew Johnson, on the night of Lincoln's assassination. He had gotten cold feet at the last moment and spent the night drinking at a local pub.

Accompanying Atzerodt into the room was John Surratt. John Surratt was the son of Mary Surratt, who made her own history by becoming the first and only woman to be hung until dead by the federal government of the United States. Although the reason given for her execution was that her boardinghouse had been used as the nest that hatched the conspiracy that led to the president's death, some historians believe Mary Surratt was hung for no other reason than that the federal government could not track down and capture her son, who they believed to also be a co-conspirator in Lincoln's death.

As the five men sat the table and conversed, Mary Surratt did not partake in their palaver. She was, however, always nearby to hear every word exchanged during the meeting. Joseph got to witness with Booth's own two eyes the fact that Mary Surratt indeed knew of the plans that had been laid out that evening to kill key politic persons within the government.

"This is outlandish," John Surratt exclaimed. "How dare he even make the implication that niggers be given the same rights as us?"

"It is ridiculous, I agree," Joseph said; posing as John Wilkes Booth. "But what are we to do? The war is over. Lee has surrendered."

"We could try to kidnap him again," Herald suggested.

During March of 1865, Booth, along with other southern sympathizers—some sitting at that very table with him—launched a plan to kidnap Abraham Lincoln while he was en route to a play at The Soldier's House. The motivation behind this plan was that the south could use Lincoln as leverage to gain an advantage in the Civil War. However, Lincoln's plans were changed last minute, and Booth and his cohorts were never able to execute their plan.

Joseph had known that the plan to kidnap Lincoln would be brought up again at this meeting. He also knew that Booth would speak up and present an alternative plan. One that involved killing Abraham Lincoln, along with his Vice-President and Secretary of State. This time around, Joseph would see to it that Booth made no such suggestion. Instead, he would speak up, and tell those around him that all hope had died alongside the Confederacy's defeat.

"The war is over!" Joseph exclaimed. "As much as it pains me to say it, I must. The South has surrendered, and will soon rejoin the Union. The thought of niggers gaining the right to vote nauseates me, but there is nothing we can do. It is done."

Joseph looked across the table at John Surratt. Surratt was the one who would not give up so easily on the notion of defeat. Herald, Powell, and Atzerodt were all soldiers for Booth's cause. Surratt, on the other hand, was cut from the same cloth that Booth had been. He was the type to take initiative. The man had been a spy for the Confederacy during the war, and he was the one who introduced Booth to Herold and Atzerodt. If there was anyone at the table who was going to reject Booth's claims, it was Surratt.

The two stared each other down. Neither spoke. Booth could see in Surratt's eyes, the unwillingness to accept defeat. He couldn't find it within himself to admit the war was over. Still, Joseph, with just a silent stare, told John Surratt it was time to give up.

Surratt finally accepted the defeat Booth had spoken of. He let out a sigh of aggravation, threw his chair out from underneath him, and stormed out of the room. The other remained silent. Joseph was next to stand up. He simply nodded at those still seated, and left.

He stood outside Mary Surratt's boardinghouse, and watched as people in the street walked by him. He had now gone through with the main part of his plan. The one part he saw that could potentially be the hiccup in his redemption was taken care of. All that remained was for him to not kill Abraham Lincoln. After that, history would change drastically and unpredictably. That did not concern Joseph, though. All he could think about was how Lincoln's survival would ensure his date with the electric chair would be averted. Instead, he would be with Alex. They would be together, and they would be happy. All because he finally did what was right. In two days' time, when the single shot ceased to ring out through Ford's Theatre, Joseph would be reunited with his true love.

He soaked in the glory of that for a bit. He then turned his thoughts inward towards John Wilkes Booth. Booth was in there. Joseph could feel him. He had heard every word Joseph spoke inside the boarding house, and Joseph could feel Booth's animosity towards those words. The knowledge that Joseph was going against and destroying everything this man desired brought Joseph unconditional joy. John Wilkes Booth had ruined Joseph's life.

Now it was time for Joseph to pay the favor back.

April 13, 1865
Booth Tours Ford's Theatre

Joseph had fallen asleep the night of the twelfth to John Wilkes Booth rage permeating throughout his entire body. There are some who might find it difficult to sleep under such circumstances, but Joseph found the sound of Booth's fury soothing. There was not a thing in the world more pleasant than hearing the man responsible for ruining his entire life suffering.

When Joseph woke the next morning, the anger inside him had dimmed, but he could still sense Booth's presence. There was still an entire day before Joseph would witness history go down—or not go down, depending on how one looked at it. He decided to use this time to add salt to Booth's already festering wounds.

On the day he had explored the streets of 1865 Washington D.C., Joseph had made it a point to avoid 10th Street. He knew he would eventually step foot on the street, and inside the walls of Ford's Theatre; he just expected it would be the night of April fourteenth, when Abraham Lincoln entered Ford's Theatre to enjoy that night's production of *Our American Cousin* and lived to see the play's final act.

Joseph decided to change his plans, though, and take the trip to Ford's Theatre a day early to give John Wilkes Booth a full-blown guided tour, what Joseph liked to call *The Assassination that Would Not Be*.

Joseph found himself in awe as he approached the building on 10th Street. He had read about it in numerous texts, and seen countless pictures of it—both, exterior and interior. He and Alex even got to take a guided tour of the building on their way down to Florida after leaving New York City. It was not the same as seeing it now, though. Joseph was walking up to a living and breathing giant. One he had heard the legend about his entire life, but was only able to envision within the grasp of his own imagination. Now he was about to walk up to it, reach out, and feel the warmth of its flesh.

He entered Ford's Theatre and stood in the lobby.

"You walked through the front door of this building just after 10pm," Joseph told Booth. "First you went to the pub next door, where you ordered a bottle of whiskey and some water."

Joseph climbed the stairs that led to the balcony, and walked slowly from one end of the theater to the other. The whole time he gave a play-by-play of Booth's movements from the night Lincoln died.

When he saw the painted white door of Lincoln's State Box, Joseph got butterflies in his stomach. He knew in just over twenty-four hours, Lincoln would enter that box, and once the play they came to watch had concluded, he and his wife, Mary Todd Lincoln, would leave and return to the White House. Ford's Theatre would lose its spot in the history books.

Still, the knowledge of what had once happened made gooseflesh rise on his arms and the back of Joseph's neck.

"Lincoln's guard was sitting in front of the door," Joseph explained. "Somehow, you convinced him to grant you entrance to the box to have an audience with Lincoln."

Joseph opened the door and entered the State Box.

"You jammed the door with a piece of wood so that no one could enter and interrupt you. You then waited for the crowd to respond to a specific line from the play, so that their laughter would drown out any sounds of you opening this door."

Joseph opened a second door, and saw a rocking chair in front of him. It was the chair Abraham Lincoln was sitting in when he was shot.

"You stepped up to him at point blank range." As his story progressed, the hostility in Joseph's voice escalated. "You pulled out your derringer, and you shot him in the back of the head. You killed an unarmed man who didn't even know what was coming. You coward."

Joseph stepped around the rocking chair, and stood at the railing of the state box. It was bare now, but it would be dressed in presidential garb tomorrow night to honor the guest. He looked over the edge at the empty seats and the empty stage below.

"You jumped to that stage below after you put a bullet in Lincoln's head. You had immortalized yourself, and you actually believed you deserved it. You believed you had slayed a tyrant. You thought you were the hero of the south, and the Confederacy's saving grace."

Joseph turned back around, and stared down at the empty rocking chair.

"Killing Abraham Lincoln was your defining moment, and was the event that immortalized you. It was also the single event that ruined my entire life. Tomorrow night, that all changes. Tomorrow night, when that play concludes, Abraham Lincoln will still be alive and breathing. John Wilkes Booth will be nowhere near the president of the United States, and history will never know his name. I just wanted you to know that."

With that said, Joseph left the President's State Box, and exited Ford's Theatre.

He would return the next night, so he and Booth could watch as history was changed forever.

April 14, 1865
The Night at Ford's Theatre

At nine in the morning on the fourteenth of April, John Wilkes Booth met with his fiancé, Lucy Lambert Hale. The meeting was short. Afterwards, he got a hair trim before returning to the National Hotel. Not long after eleven that morning, he left the hotel, and headed to Ford's Theatre to pick up his mail. It was there he learned Abraham Lincoln would be in attendance for that night's production of *Our American Cousin*. With this new knowledge, and the fact he was so well-known and beloved at Ford's Theatre that no one would question any movements he made that night, Booth decided he now had the ideal opportunity to get close enough to the president to assassinate him.

At noon, Booth showed up at the stable on C Street, and rented the fast roam mare. He told the stable owner he'd be back around four that afternoon to pick it up, and headed back to the National Hotel.

At two that afternoon, he met with Lewis Powell at the Herndon House. There, he would lay out his instructions for Powell. Powell's role was to gain entry to Secretary of State, William Seward's home, and kill him.

Afterwards, Booth picked up the mare from Pumphrey's stable, and then met up with George Atzerodt on a side street. There, he gave Atzerodt his marching orders to kill Vice President Andrew Johnson as closely to ten-fifteen that night as possible.

Just after six that evening, he returned to Ford's Theatre, and mapped out his exact path from entry to exit. Once satisfied, Booth returned to his hotel for some rest. He then met with his co-conspirators one last time to finalize all the plans for that night. At nine o'clock, John Wilkes Booth headed to Ford's Theatre to make history.

When Booth arrived, he had a stage hand named Ned Spangler hold his mare for him. He would then head to Taltavul's Star Saloon, where he would order whiskey and water. Before leaving, one of the pub's patrons would declare that Booth would never be the actor his father was. Booth responded by informing his critic that when he left the stage, he would be the most famous man in America.

He was right.

Just after ten o'clock, Booth reentered Ford's Theatre. At ten-fifteen, he shot Abraham Lincoln in the back of the head.

Now, because of Joseph Bateman, none of those things would happen. Instead, John Wilkes Booth would sit inside room 224 of the National Hotel as the man who had taken control of his body told him each detail of the day that had once happened, and was now being erased.

As the day wound down, and the minutes ticked away to that single moment at Ford's Theatre where everything would change, Joseph found it more and more difficult wrap his mind around what was about to happen.

Abraham Lincoln was not going to die, and, because of it, history was going to be rewritten.

He had known this now for days, but now that it was about to happen, Joseph found himself unable to grasp the notion.

He also thought about Alex. Joseph had gone through time and changed history to be with her. Soon, they would be together, like it was meant to be, and he would be able to hold her, kiss her, and feel the ecstasy of being inside her. Soon, everything would finally be right.

Joseph left the National Hotel that evening, and walked the streets of Washington D.C. towards 10th Street. As he made his way to Ford's Theatre, he made sure to admire the scenery. Despite coming off a gruesome war, there was a serene feeling to nineteenth century America. Joseph had lived in a day and age where everything moved so fast that life passed you by before you realized it. It wasn't like that here, and he wouldn't have many more opportunities to take it in. As he took his peaceful evening stroll, Joseph could feel the ire of John Wilkes Booth radiating from within him. It made the walk that much more fulfilling.

He turned onto 10th Street, and made his way towards the theater. At the same time that Joseph turned onto the street, a carriage pulled up to the front of Ford's Theatre. The coachman stepped down, and opened the door. Two people get out, who Joseph realized were Major Henry Rathbone and his fiancé, Clara Harris. He had never seen photos of them, but he knew their names from texts. It was the next two people who stepped out from the carriage who he recognized perfectly.

The first was a plain looking woman who wore a simple black dress. She was first lady, Mary Todd Lincoln. The man who stepped out after her was her husband, and president of the United States.

Abraham Lincoln, his wife, and their guests entered Ford's Theatre. Joseph then followed.

"Watch," Joseph told Booth as he passed through the doors of the building. "Watch as everything you did withers away before your very eyes. Please... Let it sink in that the man you once murdered now gets to live. Swallow it. I hope it's a bitter pill, and I hope you choke on it and die."

As Joseph entered, he heard the tail end of *Hail to the Chief* being played by the orchestra to announce the arrival of the president. Like Booth had done once before, he climbed the stairs in the lobby to the balcony. However, instead of making his way across the theater to the side of the building where Lincoln's state box was located, Joseph situated himself in the theater's other state box, which was located directly across from Lincoln's. From there, Joseph could see the president perfectly as he watched that night's production. In just a few moments, Joseph would witness the course of history being altered. More importantly, though, in a few small moments, Joseph Bateman would have his redemption.

"Don't know the manners of good society, eh?" Harry Hawk, the actor on stage, said. "Well, I guess I know enough to turn you inside out, old gal - you sockdologizing old mantrap!"

The crowd burst into a fit of laughter. Even Joseph, who didn't quite get the joke, let out a snicker. His hilarity only lasted a moment, though. Joseph's attention was diverted away from the play, and was now fixated on the president. That was the line Booth had waited for before opening the door to the State Box. With the crowd's laughter at an all-time high that evening, no one in the box would hear the door opening. John Wilkes Booth was now on the opposite side of Ford's Theatre, and completely out of reach of the president.

Then Joseph noticed an additional fifth person in the state box creeping up behind Abraham Lincoln.

He couldn't make out the identity of the unannounced guest. His features were masked by the darkness of the state box. Joseph watched helplessly as the dark figure standing behind Lincoln raised his arm. Joseph couldn't see what was in his hand, but he didn't have to. He knew it was a derringer .44.

It's Booth, was Joseph's immediate thought. *That is John Wilkes Booth! I got it all wrong. I'm not him. I'm supposed to stop him! I failed!*

Joseph knew this wasn't the case, though. Booth was there with him. Joseph could feel the man's overwhelming joy pass through him at the sight of a pistol being raised to Abraham Lincoln's head.

Joseph's wanted to scream, and warn the president to watch out. Before he could articulate any such warning, a sudden loud pop echoed throughout Ford's Theatre, and Abraham Lincoln hunched over in his rocking chair.

Mary Todd Lincoln let out a scream at the realization of what had just happened to her husband. Major Rathbone flew from his seat to prevent Lincoln's attacker from escaping. Joseph knew whoever it was up there who just shot Lincoln would drop the pistol, draw a knife, and stab Major Rathbone violently in his arm; cutting the Major right down to his bone.

It was what Booth had done the night he shot Lincoln.

It was exactly what this new assassin did.

Seeing that everything was playing out verbatim from the original night John Wilkes Booth had shot Abraham Lincoln, Joseph knew what came next. After Booth fired off the single round into the back of Lincoln's head and wrestled away Rathbone, he dove from the State Box to the stage below. It would be what this second-string assassin did next, and Joseph intended on meeting him on stage when he landed.

Lincoln's attacker leapt from the State Box railing to the stage below. Joseph did the same. However, his footing became compromised as he stepped off the railing, and Joseph lost his balance. He landed awkwardly on the stage, and felt a sharp pain shoot up his leg.

Booth injured his when he landed on the stage, Joseph recalled. *That's supposed to happen to him, though*, referring to Lincoln's attacker. *He's supposed to be the one with the injured leg now!*

Joseph didn't have time to mull over the fact that he had just received a leg injury that was now supposed to be inflicted upon the man standing opposite the stage as him. He needed to stop the president's attacker and apprehend him. Joseph looked across the stage, and for the first time saw the face of the man who had shot Abraham Lincoln. At the sight of it, Joseph froze.

No...It can't be, Joseph argued. He was convinced his eyes were playing tricks on him. *You're not even supposed to be in Washington, D.C. anymore. How is this possible?*

Joseph felt a body crash into him as the attacker tried to force himself past Joseph to get to the theater's rear exit. In a last ditch effort, Joseph reached for Lincoln's attacker, but when he turned and shifted his weight, an excruciating pain shot up his newly injured leg. This caused Joseph to stumble, and he missed his opportunity to grab hold of his target. Lincoln's attacker blew past Joseph, ran from the stage, and exited the building.

Joseph refused to let his injury stop him. He had set out to stop Lincoln's assassination, and had failed to do so. He would not let Abraham Lincoln's murderer get away. He moved as fast as his limp would allow him off stage, and through the rear exit. The moment he stepped outside, Joseph crashed right into Ned Spangler. The two tumbled to the ground. Joseph pushed Spangler from him, and got to his feet. He surveyed the area around him, and saw the assassin riding away on horseback.

Lincoln's attacker was getting away.

Joseph wasn't ready to admit defeat. There was still a possibility he could apprehend the attacker. He took off on foot; trying desperately to ignore the pain in his injured leg.

He had barely made it fifty yards when Joseph felt strong sensation of being pushed forward. He had felt it before. On the morning of his execution. Only then, he was being pulled.

No, no, no, Joseph pleaded. *Not now! This can't be happening now!*

He wasn't ready to go back. Not while he still needed to hunt down and capture Lincoln's assassin.

Joseph Bateman didn't have a choice, though.

The reality around him crumbled, and he fell forward. He continued to fall for twelve long days, and when Joseph finally landed, he found himself in a time and world where his soul was no longer connected to the assassination of Abraham Lincoln.

April 24, 1995
Joseph Wakes Again

When Joseph Bateman woke up, he was once again face down. This time, instead of dirt beneath him, he awoke to the feel of soft bed sheets against his skin. That was as far as pleasantries went, though. His mouth was dry, the stale taste of bile lingered in the back of his throat, and his head pounded furiously. He felt like death—he should know; he had experienced it—and he had no idea why.

It's because you're hung over, he told himself. *You were out drinking last night.*

Except that wasn't true. Last night, Joseph was sitting in the National Hotel in Washington D.C. The year was 1865. Yet the memory of being out the night before, drinking, was there.

The door to the room he was in burst open and a man entered. A young woman followed him. He knew neither of them.

Except he did.

His name was Matt, and her name was… well Joseph didn't exactly know her name, because they had just met her the night before in the casino.

Casino...Joseph recalled, as he slowly put together the pieces of a puzzle that didn't make a lick of sense. *We are in Atlantic City. I'm currently in a hotel room. That woman is a one night stand for Matt. Matt is my friend. We came here with two other friends.*

"My bad," Matt said. "I didn't know anyone was in here. I'm sorry, Becker."

Becker?

James Becker, Joseph told himself. *My name is James Becker... James Becker.*

Joseph repeated the name over in his head. Hearing it seemed so foreign, yet, at the same time, it felt so familiar. Like it had been the name he had been carrying his entire life.

And it was.

Joseph's name was now James Becker, and he had been out the entire night drinking in Atlantic City with a group of his friends.

Matt's lady friend whispered something into Matt's ear, and moments later they were gone. Joseph lay back down, and stared at the ceiling. Just a few moments ago, he was standing in Ford's Theatre, watching the assassination of Abraham Lincoln, which shouldn't have been happening in the first place. Now, he was waking up with a killer hangover after a night out with friends.

Things were getting so confusing for Joseph, he began to wonder if his headache was from his hangover, or if it was actually being caused by the thoughts running rampant through his head. Joseph needed answers, and he knew exactly who would have them.

J.

J had had the answers to Joseph's questions before, and J would have the answers yet again. There was just one small problem. Joseph had absolutely zero idea where to find J. He didn't even know where to begin. J had shown up at random throughout Joseph's life; once outside an ice cream parlor when Joseph was a child, then in a tattoo shop in 1992, and again in a stable in 1865. Each time it was J who came to Joseph. Trying to actively seek out the man would prove futile. He wasn't someone you could track down and find. When J wanted you see you, he found you.

Until that happened—*if* that happened—Joseph was on his own.

Joseph had been lying in bed for a half hour when the hotel room door burst open yet again. Two new people entered the room. Like Matt and his lady friend, Joseph had never seen them before, but he knew exactly who they were. One's name was Will, and the other's name was Ben. They, like Matt, were friends of James Becker.

"Check out is in a half hour, Becker," Ben announced to the only room occupant still in bed. "Get up, and get your shit packed. We're going to pry Matt off that gorgeous chick from last night."

"How is it that he is always the drunkest person in the bar, yet he ends up going home with one of the hottest chicks there?" Will asked.

"Well, when you target an extremely drunk and gullible female, and tell her your lineage is Kennedy, it's not that difficult," Ben answered.

"He doesn't even spell it the same way!" Will argued as he and Ben left the hotel room.

As Joseph heard the door closing behind two of James Becker's closest friends, he felt a smile stretching across the man's face. James Becker had a lifelong history with these men. They were in Little League together. When they were twelve, their parents allowed them to camp outside a movie theater overnight so that they could see *Return of the Jedi* on opening day. They drank their first beers together, and they'd had many since. These four men—

James, Matt, Will, and Ben—were as close as brothers due to decades of friendship.

Joseph sat up and looked to the far wall. There were four suitcases. Joseph knew, immediately, which one belonged to James Becker. He got up, and began to throw clothes into the suitcase. As he did this, Joseph tried to sense James Becker inside of him, like he had with Booth when his soul inhabited Lincoln's assassin's body. That feeling of being overstuffed into a small closet was nonexistent, though. There was no one else in that body with Joseph but himself. The two were one, and James Becker was where Joseph Bateman's soul would have ended up had John Wilkes Booth never been the one to assassinate Abraham Lincoln.

Then why did he still remember Joseph Bateman's life as if it had still existed?

It was just another question that seemingly could not be answered without the knowledge of J.

As Joseph was zipping up James Becker's suitcase, Will and Ben returned to the room without Matt.

"He was… uh… busy," Ben stated. "He's going to meet us downstairs."

"You all good?" Will asked, as he picked up his suitcase.

"Yeah," Joseph said. "I'm good."

"Okay, then let's get the hell out of here," Will said.

"Hey, guys." Joseph said as the three walked down the hall towards the elevator. "I have a weird question. Who killed Abraham Lincoln?"

They both stopped and turned to Joseph. Will and Ben both had dumbfounded looks on their faces, as if they just heard the most ridiculous question ever, which it probably was. Lincoln had surely died the morning following his visit to Ford's Theatre. Regardless of the perpetrator, the assassination would have gone down as one of history's most important events, one that everyone learned about in school as they grew up.

"Are you still drunk?" Ben asked. "Wasn't your college major history?"

"Yeah, I'm just having a serious brain fart right now, and can't remember his name for the life of me."

"Congrats," Will said. "You've reached a new level of hung over. You can't recall a historic name that every one learns about throughout their entire education."

"Make fun all you want," Joseph said, playing along with the friendly banter. "Just tell me his name, because it's freaking driving me nuts."

Ben answered Joseph's question.

"John Wilkes Booth killed Abraham Lincoln."

Throughout the duration of the car ride back home to Long Island, New York, where James Becker and his friends grew up, Joseph remained silent. He tried to sleep off his hangover and exhaustion, but they were no match for the words echoing in Joseph's head.

John Wilkes Booth killed Abraham Lincoln.

He recited the line, over and over, as if practicing for a play. Each time, it was as unbelievable as the last. Booth did not kill Lincoln. Joseph knew that as fact, because he had watched the whole thing go down, firsthand.

Yet history still remembered John Wilkes Booth as the man who shot sixteenth president, Abraham Lincoln, in the back of his head, when in fact it was John Surratt who pulled the trigger of the derringer .44.

At some point either right before or immediately after Lincoln's assassination—the original one—John Surratt fled the nation's capital to avoid arrest as a conspirator in the president's death. He'd eventually find his way to Europe, where he would disappear for years. Regardless of when he fled Washington D.C., John Surratt was nowhere near Abraham Lincoln the night the sixteenth president was shot. In fact, other than maybe knowing what Booth's grave intentions were, Surratt's involvement in all that went down of the fourteenth of April 1865 was minimal.

All that had changed, however, when Joseph took it upon himself from preventing John Wilkes Booth from becoming the first ever presidential assassin. Surratt had taken over the reins, and did the deed in Booth's stead. Joseph knew this for a fact. He had stood face-to-face across the stage of Ford's Theatre from John Surratt just moments after Lincoln had been shot.

So why did history say otherwise?

Why did kids learn from their Social Studies teachers that Abraham Lincoln had been shot and killed by John Wilkes Booth?

The only person with the answers to that could only be found when he sought you out. If J didn't reappear, Joseph would never know why Booth had been given credit for a crime he did not commit.

Knowing it would be pointless to continue to fixate on something he had no answers to, Joseph attempted to open his mind up a bit, and allow other things to enter it.

He thought of Alex.

Joseph searched the memories of James Becker's life, where he hoped to find Alex, somewhere. She wasn't there, though. James Becker and Alexandra Casings had never crossed paths throughout their entire lives. Joseph had traveled down the path of redemption to be with Alex, and once he reached the clearing, she was not there.

Joseph couldn't help but feel that familiar resentment rising up from inside. It was an anger from a life that was no longer his. Yet the sensation was still as strong as it had been from a life with Hank Bateman, Bill Casings, and Montel Parsons. He had traveled through centuries and across multiple lifetimes to change history so he and Alex could be together. In the end, he was denied his happy ending, and history still remembered John Wilkes Booth as the man who killed Abraham Lincoln.

Just like his confusion over the Lincoln assassination, Joseph needed answers about Alex. There had to be a way he could still be with her. After all, the year was 1995, she was alive somewhere. He just had to find her. He knew the person who'd be able to bring them together, too.

Joseph desperately needed to find J.

James Becker got dropped off at home by his friends around midday. He went right to his room, and lay in bed. Instead of allowing James Becker to sleep off his hangover, Joseph kept him up thinking about the same two things he'd been obsessing over since leaving the Atlantic City hotel.

Abraham Lincoln and Alexandra Casings.

Joseph tried to think of ways to track down J so he could get his answers, but nothing came to him. The guy was a phantom who only became corporeal when he wanted. Joseph knew his attempts to form any kind of plan were pointless. Growing frustrations reached a tipping point, and Joseph threw the covers off of him, got out of bed, and left James Becker's house.

He had no way of finding J. So until J decided to show up—if J decided to show up—Joseph would have to try to and obtain the answers he wanted himself. If he didn't, he would surely go insane.

The matter he was going to tackle first was the Lincoln assassination. Growing up, Joseph Bateman had spent countless hours researching that exact event, so he knew where he was headed.

The public library.

After that, he'd try to track down Alex. Hopefully by then, J would show himself, but if he didn't, Joseph would need to think up an alternate plan. That would come soon enough, though. First, Joseph would figure out why history remembered John Wilkes Booth as Abraham Lincoln's assassin instead of John Surrat.

Joseph arrived at James Becker's local library, where he asked the librarian where he would find the books on the Lincoln assassination. After being led to the volumes he desired, Joseph pulled each and every one of them from the shelves, lugged them to the most secluded table in the library, and dropped them down.

Over the course of the next five hours, Joseph sat with his books, and read each and every one. The more he read, the more he was left confused. Somehow, nothing had changed. Every last detail Joseph had learned, from the plotting of the conspiracy, to the assassination, to hunt for John Wilkes Booth, was the same as it had been once before. All the work Joseph had done to assure John Wilkes Booth never went down in history as the killer of Abraham Lincoln meant nothing. There was not a single mention of John Surratt in any of the texts Joseph studied. The man who actually shot Abraham Lincoln had escaped eternal villainy, and Booth had become the scapegoat.

There was one text in particular that Joseph found himself returning to. It focused heavily on the twelve days following Lincoln's assassination. Despite falling through time from 1865 to 1995 only moments after he stepped out of Ford's Theatre, Joseph still remembered the events that followed the night Lincoln was shot. He had stayed with Booth while he fell into the life of James Becker. The explanation for that, he had no idea, but whatever the reason might be, Joseph knew the truth about the twelve days John Wilkes Booth had spent in the wilderness.

Booth may have died on the morning of April 26, 1865 outside of a burning barn in Virginia, but what had really happened and what history claimed to have happened were two very different tales.

April 14 – April 20, 1865
The Hunt for John Surratt

As part of Joseph Bateman fell into James Becker, the part of him that still remained inside John Wilkes Booth came around the front of Ford's Theatre on 10th Street. Right before he pushed forward in time, Joseph had seen John Surratt on horseback, heading down a back alley outside the theater exit that led to F Street. He couldn't continue his pursuit in his current condition. His leg was too badly injured, and there was no way he'd be able to catch up to Surratt. He scanned 10th Street, and spotted a horse secured to a pole. Joseph limped towards it as fast as he could, untethered it, and mounted the steed, not taking into consideration that the horse's owner might spot him and shoot him dead right there and then. He turned the horse towards F Street and took off.

The moment Joseph saw Surratt heading down the alley that led from the back of Ford's Theatre to F Street, he knew exactly where Surratt was going. So many events inside Ford's Theatre had remained the same with Surratt as the assailant that Joseph had no doubt the escape route of the president's assassin would be the same as John Wilkes Booth's had been.

John Surratt would escape Washington D.C. via the Navy Yard Bridge.

Joseph rode down F Street to Pennsylvania Avenue. He then turned onto 11th Street, and took it to the Navy Yard Bridge. When he reached the bridge, he was stopped by a patrolman. Just as Booth had been stopped the original time he attempted to cross the bridge not long after shooting Abraham Lincoln.

"The bridge is closed after dark," the patrolman said.

Joseph had no doubt that Surratt had been there only minutes before, and had been granted permission to cross. He considered telling the patrolman that the man he had just let over the bridge was the man who had just shot the president. He thought better of it, though. Surely the knowledge that Abraham Lincoln had been shot would arouse suspicion, and earn Joseph an arrest.

"My apologies," Joseph said, instead. "I'm not looking to cause any sort of inconvenience."

"What's your name?" the patrolman asked.

"Booth."

The patrolman took his time sizing up Booth. As the seconds ticked away, Joseph became more reckless. Each moment this guard took to decide whether or not to let him cross the bridge was another moment John Surratt was allowed to create more of a distance between himself and Joseph.

"I shouldn't be allowing you to do this," the patrolman finally said. "But you may pass."

He moved aside, and Joseph crossed the Navy Yard Bridge, exiting Washington, D.C. When he felt he was far enough out of sight of the bridge's patrolman, Joseph hastened his horse's pace.

Joseph entered Maryland and headed south. Surratt Tavern, a piece of land owned by John Surratt's mother, Mary Surratt, was his destination. It had been the first stop for John Wilkes Booth and his companion on the run, David Herald, the night he shot Lincoln. It would be the logical first place for John Surratt to head, as well. Even if things weren't going to go exactly for Surratt as they had for Booth, Surratt Tavern was a familiar place for the new presidential assassin, and would certainly be the first place he stopped on his run from the law.

Joseph traveled twelve miles, and arrived at Surratt Tavern just after midnight. He saw no horse tethered, and there was no evidence that anyone was there other than John Lloyd, the man left in charge of the tavern that night.

Joseph dismounted his horse, and an agonizing pain shot up his injured leg as it made contact with the earth below. He limped towards the door to the tavern and knocked.

John Lloyd answered the door, and asked Booth what he could do for him. Originally, Booth had Mary Surratt send word to Lloyd to have weapons and supplies ready to be picked up the night of Lincoln's assassination. Did John Surratt have his mother do the same? Joseph wasn't sure, but he was willing to bet Surratt had.

"I need a weapon," Joseph said, playing his odds. "I was told you'd have a weapon ready for me."

"They were picked up already," Lloyd said in a nervous voice.

So Surratt was here, Joseph pointed out to himself.

John Surratt had come, and collected the weapons his mother had waiting for him. He then took off into the night at some point before Joseph had arrived. Still, despite his absence at the tavern, the fact he had been there was a good sign. It meant Joseph was on the right trail. He also had an idea, given the similarities between Booth's assassination and Surratt's, where it was all going to end. Joseph just needed to reach that destination before Surratt.

"I fell behind," Joseph lied. "Are there any weapons?"

"No pistols," Lloyd informed Joseph. "There's a knife, though."

"Give it to me."

Joseph extended his hand, and John Lloyd handed him a large bowie knife. It was the same knife soldiers found on John Wilkes Booth after he had expired on the front porch of the Garrett's house when Booth was Lincoln's killer. As James Becker learned, it would remain one of the items found on Booth's body after he, once again, died on the morning of April the twenty-sixth.

Joseph left Surratt Tavern with a few supplies and a weapon. He headed south. He knew exactly what he had to do next, and where to go to get it done. It was the same exact place John Wilkes Booth had ended up that same morning once before.

The one thing that kept coming to and bothering Joseph as he rode through the night was why had it been Booth's leg that was injured by the leap from the State's Box to the stage below at Ford's Theatre, instead of John Surratt's. Everything Surratt had done mirrored Booth's actions from the night he shot Lincoln. Surratt should've been the man with the broken fibula. Not Booth. As Joseph read text and history books through the eyes of James Becker, and saw how history had been rewritten to make Booth the antagonist of the Lincoln assassination, he realized his leg had to be the one that was injured that night. Otherwise, John Wilkes Booth would have never ended up at the house of Doctor Samuel Mudd.

When John Wilkes Booth and David Herold showed up on the doorstep of Doctor Samuel Mudd's home six hours after Booth shot Abraham Lincoln, the physician was unaware of the crime the man at his home had just committed. Still, the act of tending to John Wilkes Booth's injury was enough to land the doctor a life sentence, along a small place in history, for his involvement in Booth's evasion of federal law enforcement for as long as he did.

Joseph Bateman would lead John Wilkes Booth to the doorstep of Samuel Mudd, once again, and, once again, he would seek care for his wounded leg. This time, however, it was not as the man who shot the president, but as the man pursuing the villain who did. Unfortunately, despite Booth not being the man who pulled the trigger on that infamous night in Ford's Theatre, Samuel Mudd would suffer the same fate as he had once before.

Joseph saw the doctor's house in the distance as he approached it in the early morning hours of April fifteenth. The sight of it was Joseph's salvation. With each forward step of the horse he rode, he had felt a sharp pain jettison up his leg. It had been that way since leaving the nation's capital, and grew more agonizing as the miles pressed on.

Joseph cautiously dismounted his horse, and limped towards the door. Originally, it had been David Herold who did all the talking to the doctor while John Wilkes Booth sat on his horse. There was no Herald this time around, and Joseph would have to talk to Mudd himself.

After a few minutes of knocking, a balding man with a bushy goatee, dressed in his eveningwear, appeared at the door. Joseph knew the face well from the books he read, and documentaries he had watched. It was Samuel Mudd. He immediately apologized to the doctor for disturbing him at such an inconvenient hour. He then lied, and said he had injured himself by falling from his horse. Without questioning why the man at his door was riding at such an hour, Samuel Mudd told John Wilkes Booth to come in so he could take a look at the extent of his injuries.

Joseph was lowered onto a couch. There, Samuel Mudd cut the boot from his left leg to examine the extent of the injury. This boot was crucial in the story of Samuel Mudd. It was the only piece of physical evidence that proved Abraham Lincoln's assassin had spent time at the doctor's home. As history would somehow still acknowledge, John Wilkes Booth as Abraham Lincoln's assassin, this boot would soon, once again, incriminate Samuel Mudd, and land him a prison sentence at Fort Jefferson.

After an examination, Mudd concluded that Booth had fractured his fibula. He fashioned a splint, and bandaged the injured leg. He told his patient to rest, and that he would have a crutch made for him. Joseph had no intention of taking the suggested rest. He needed to get on with his pursuit of John Surratt. Exhaustion quickly gripped him though, and once the doctor left him alone, he slipped into slumber for the night.

That following morning, Joseph was jolted from his sleep, momentarily. Through his heavy eyes, he looked out a nearby window, and saw the sun freshly risen in the eastern sky. A new day had dawned, and in that brief moment, Joseph felt a rush of sadness pass through him. Despite the beautiful scene he was looking out on, grief was the only emotion Joseph Bateman knew. Before he could process this emotion, sleep took him for a few more hours. He wasn't aware of it, but it was 7:22 on the morning of April 15, 1865.

Abraham Lincoln had finally succumbed to his wound and taken his last breath.

It was midday when Joseph was released from his sleep. The sun was high in the sky, and he had slept far too long. He needed to get on the road and continue his pursuit. Yet before he could gather up what little belongings he had on him and leave the Mudd residence, realization, not to mention hunger, hit him. He knew his destination, but he was still eleven days out from arriving there. He'd be spending days in the Zekiah Swamp, and he'd then have to cross the Potomac River, which was something that proved extremely difficult for Booth and Herold when they had crossed it, originally.

He needed a plan, and he needed supplies.

As he ate the food Samuel Mudd's wife prepared for her unexpected guest, Joseph put the pieces together that would successfully get him to his final destination. It didn't prove too difficult, as Booth and Herold were once faced with some on the same exact problems that Joseph would be faced with over the course of the next eleven days. Being so well-versed in Booth's escape to Virginia, Joseph knew who Booth had come into contact with, and who had helped him in his escape. Joseph would use those same sources to aid him.

It was late afternoon when Joseph left the comfort of Doctor Samuel Mudd's home to continue his pursuit of John Surratt. With a few additional supplies and a crutch for his leg injury, Joseph headed towards the southern borders of the property. He was almost off Mudd's land when he heard the sound of a horse approaching. Moments later, he was joined at the property's edge by Samuel Mudd.

"You idiot!" Mudd exclaimed. "What have you brought upon myself and my family?"

"What are you talking about?" Joseph asked.

This had also happened to Booth and Herold as they left Mudd's home. The doctor had gone into Bryantown during the day, and would learn the news of what had happened to Abraham Lincoln. He had figured out he was harboring the two fugitives who were being hunted by the federal government, and rushed home to get them off his property.

This, however, could not be the reason for the confrontation Joseph was currently a part of. Except he was about to learn it was.

"You killed the president!" Mudd said in a whisper, as if fearing his voice would travel to wrong ears if he spoke any louder. "You killed Abraham Lincoln, and you've been hiding here at my home."

"It's not true," Joseph argued. He couldn't believe it. Why was Booth being blamed for shooting Lincoln? "I didn't shoot him."

Mudd shushed Joseph, again fearing that their voices would travel if they spoke too loudly.

"You did! Everyone knows it. It's the only thing anyone is talking about."

Joseph tried to explain himself to Mudd, but the doctor wasn't interested in hearing his explanation. The only thing the doctor was interested in was getting Booth off his property.

"I don't want to hear it!" Mudd said; interrupting Joseph. "The less I know, the better. I just want you off my land...NOW!"

With that final exchange, Mudd rode off on his horse towards his home to check on his family. Later on, Mudd would claim that assuring the safety of his family was why he did not immediately go back to town, and inform authorities that the most wanted man in the nation had just left his house.

As Joseph made his way towards the Zekiah Swamp and his next destination, his mind desperately tried to digest and understand the news he had just received.

John Wilkes Booth was still being blamed for the assassination of Abraham Lincoln.

The more Joseph thought about it, though, the more it didn't surprise him. He had jumped to the stage from the opposite State Box to confront the man who had actually shot Lincoln. The building was filled to capacity with theater-goers that night. None of them had the slightest idea who John Surratt was, but nearly all of them would know the face of John Wilkes Booth. After all, the man was one of America's most famous stage actors. Given the frantic state of the crowd after the gunshot from the president's State Box, it was clear that the audience had assumed Booth had been the man to pull the trigger.

It all made sense. Booth was seen jumping down to the stage moments after Abraham Lincoln was shot. All it took was a few confused witnesses, and the rest would follow. Soon enough, a mistake would become a cold hard fact, and John Wilkes Booth had become, once more, the man who shot the president.

Night encompassed the land not long after Joseph's departure from the home of Samuel Mudd. It wouldn't be long before he found himself completely lost. He needed to get to Rich Hill, but in order to do so, he needed to cross the Zekiah Swamp. After nightfall, that would be an impossible task if unassisted. Joseph was familiar with the swamp's dangerous reputation, and knew, as Booth did, that he would need someone to guide him and Herold through if he wanted to see the other side. It took some time, but Joseph eventually found himself at the small house of Oswell Swann.

Oswell Swann was a black tobacco farmer. He was also the man who helped guide John Wilkes Booth and David Herold across the Zekiah Swamp safely for a fee of five dollars. For the same fee, Joseph convinced Swann to get him across the swamp by sunrise. Throughout the night, two men crossed the Zekiah Swamp in silence, and at sunrise, Joseph found himself in Rich Hill at the home of Samuel Cox.

Samuel Cox was a well-known southern sympathizer and supporter of the Confederacy. After Lincoln's assassination, Booth and Herold turned to Cox to help aid them as they attempted to get to Virginia, and what they thought would be safety. Over the next few days, Cox would have fellow Confederate sympathizer Thomas Jones bring the outlaws food, drink, newspapers and other supplies as they hid in a nearby pine thicket waiting to cross the Potomac River. It was Samuel Cox who kept those two men alive while they were on the run, and Joseph fully intended to use him in the same capacity.

Joseph assumed the role of a man on the run after committing the nation's gravest crime. In the early hours of that spring morning, he explained to Cox his need for assistance and supplies, and Cox, as he had done once before, agreed to help John Wilkes Booth cross the Potomac River.

As he did with Booth and Herold, Cox had Joseph hide out in the pine thickets. For five days before crossing the Potomac River, Joseph remained hidden while Thomas Jones brought him the supplies. He kept himself occupied during the long days by reading various newspapers Jones had delivered to him.

Joseph had read how the nation, both North and South, despised and villainized John Wilkes Booth for killing Abraham Lincoln. After reading each individual paper to himself, Joseph would read them out loud, so that Booth, who he could still feel inside the body he occupied, could hear that the nation grieved tremendously for their fallen leader.

When John Wilkes Booth was the one who pulled the trigger of the Derringer in Ford's Theatre, he thought he was carrying out well deserved justice. He saw Lincoln as a tyrant, like Julius Caesar, and like Caesar, his evil reign needed to be ended. Booth saw himself as Brutus, the man who ended Julius Caesar's reign by stabbing the tyrant to death. He believed this so much that he even went as far as to yell *Sic Semper Tyrannis* after shooting Lincoln, because it was believed that Brutus had said the exact same thing while assassinating Caesar.

While hiding in the pine thickets with David Herold, Booth would read in the newspapers, just as Joseph had, how the nation was disgusted with his action, and, as a whole, loathed him. This came as a legitimate shock to Booth, who believed he was doing the United States a favor. It was during those few days that John Wilkes Booth started writing in his infamous journal, attempting to explain his actions, and letting all those who would read the pages know he was a hero of the story, and not the antagonist.

When Joseph learned from Samuel Mudd that the nation believed it was John Wilkes Booth who was responsible for killing Lincoln, he could feel Booth inside him, bursting with glee. John Surratt had done the deed, but Booth was getting all the credit. This brought joy to the man whose body Joseph occupied.

Now that Joseph had the printed proof that Booth was hated, he made sure Booth was thrown from his high horse. He felt the happiness of John Wilkes Booth turn sour and rot into rage. He felt strong feelings of elation every time he read the print and felt Booth's fury flare up.

Despite his bliss at Booth's unhappiness, Joseph felt it was wrong John Surratt was getting away with murder. After all, the man had committed a heinous crime, and justice deserved its chance to be brought down upon him. Joseph also felt he owed it to Lincoln to out Surratt for his crime. In an attempt to bring the truth to light, he started his own journal while hiding out in the pine thickets.

The original plan was to write down everything, from how he was Joseph Bateman and his soul was linked directly to John Wilkes Booth. He would explain how Booth had once killed Lincoln, and because of it, Joseph's life was one of unfortunate circumstances. He would write about the walls collapsing and his plan for redeeming his soul. He would tell it all in great detail.

However, Joseph dismissed this plan rather quickly. Once he realized that anyone who read the journal would think they were reading the ramblings of a crazy person, and not believe a single word written on the pages, he decided to go an alternate route.

I know many of you see me as the villainous monster who shot an unarmed and unaware man in the back of the head, Joseph wrote, pretending to be Booth. *However, I am not that man. I am, in fact, the man who tried to stop the perpetrator of the crime right after he pulled the trigger. I am the very man who pursued him in the days that followed.*

Joseph wrote how John Wilkes Booth had once been part of a group of Southern sympathizers who had orchestrated a plan to kidnap Abraham Lincoln, but once the war was over, he felt there was nothing more to fight for. He told the story of the night he went to Mary Surratt's boarding house, and how he could feel the direction in which the conversation was heading. He wrote how Booth had immediately attempted to shut down any possible plans of an assassination.

Joseph explained in the pages that the reason for Booth's presence at Ford's Theatre was to make sure none of the people who had been at Surratt's boarding house a few nights earlier tried to commit a crime there was no turning back from. He described how he had been in the adjacent States Box when Lincoln was shot, and how he leapt to the stage in an attempt to stop the assassin. He told all those who would read what was written that the man who stood across the stage from him was John Surratt. As painful as it was for Joseph to clear John Wilkes Booth's name of all blame, he knew that exposing the true identity of Abraham Lincoln's assassin was the right thing to do.

After five long days of hiding out in the pine thickets and documenting his version of history, Thomas Jones finally acquired Joseph a boat. It was time to cross the Potomac River into Virginia, and continue the pursuit of John Surratt.

Joseph's knowledge of Booth's final days proved to be more beneficial than ever when it came time to cross the river.

Originally, Booth and Herold had attempted to cross at night. This was so they would have the cover of darkness to protect them from any river patrol. They pushed off shore at Dent's Meadow in Maryland, and had hopes of landing at Point Mathias, Virginia. However, during the night, they had spotted a Union gunboat patrolling the river, as they had feared, and were forced to stop rowing in order to remain undetected. Left to the elements, the tricky currents of the Potomac River drifted Booth and Herold upstream, and they landed on the shores of Blossom Point, Maryland—not even on the side of the river they wanted to end up on. After taking a short refuge at a farm inhabited by a man named John Hughes, the two outlaws made a second and final attempt to cross the river.

Joseph had zero intentions of going through any of that. While dragging the boat Thomas Jones had sold to him, Joseph traveled north up the shoreline to a point he felt the waters would not be so treacherous, and less troublesome. There, he waited for darkness before attempting to cross. The mixture of having the difficult task of navigating while rowing, and having zero experience operating a row boat, proved difficult for Joseph. Despite these factors that worked against him, as well having the fortune of not encountering any Union gunboats throughout the night, Joseph managed a successful crossing in a single night.

Joseph was now an entire day ahead of John Wilkes Booth's original schedule. He hoped he was now an entire day ahead of John Surratt.

April 21 – April 26, 1865
The Garret's Farm

It was April 23rd when John Wilkes Booth and David Herold finally touched down on the shores of Virginia. Following their arrival just upstream of Machodoc Creek, they sought out refuge from Confederate sympathizer, Elizabeth Quesenberry. They were told by Thomas Jones before crossing the Potomac that Quesenberry would help them, but when they arrived at her house, Elizabeth Quesenberry refused them, and sent them away. They then sought out assistance from Doctor Richard Stuart—an acquaintance of Samuel Mudd's. Stuart, like Quesenberry, refused to help the two men.

Angered by rejection and desperate for shelter, Booth and Herold commandeered the home of William Lucas, a freed slave. The two forced Lucas and his family to sleep outside of their own home while they rested, and ate food. On April 24th, Booth and Herold departed from the Lucas home. While on the road, they met former Confederate soldiers on their way home from the war. One of those soldiers was Private William Jett. After learning that the identity of one of the men he was speaking to was Abraham Lincoln's assassin, Jett was left star struck, and agreed to help the two outlaws. He led them to the home of Richard Garrett. The Garrett's farm would go down in history as the place where the hunt for John Wilkes Booth came to a deadly end.

It was Joseph's final destination.

With so many aspects of Lincoln's assassination staying the same with Surratt as the triggerman instead of Booth, Joseph had known from the start of his pursuit that he needed to get to the farm of Richard Garrett.

That's where it would all come to an end.

Being he had no reason to stop at the homes of Elizabeth Quesenberry or Doctor Stuart, Joseph did not aim for shores of Machodoc Creek. His goal was to simply make it across the river, and land successfully in Virginia. From there, he would find his way to the Garrett Farm. Being he was a full day ahead of John Surratt, Joseph's plan was to arrive at Richard Garrett's home unannounced, and hide out in the tobacco barn Booth and Herold had been forced to sleep in the night federal officers finally caught up with them. There, he would wait for John Surratt's arrival. Once Surratt arrived, Joseph would confront Abraham Lincoln's true killer and help bring him to justice.

Joseph's own journey to the Garrett farm did not come without its own set of difficulties. He had landed quite a few miles north from where Booth and Herold had landed on their crossing. Being that he was not from the area, or even the era, Joseph found himself unfamiliar with his surroundings.

In other words, he was lost.

As of that moment in time, John Wilkes Booth was still the most wanted man in America, despite his innocence. Joseph couldn't just walk up to a random person and ask for directions. He would risk being recognized, which would lead to detainment and arrest, thus ending his pursuit so close to its end.

Instead, Joseph would attempt to find the farm on his own. He knew he needed to keep heading south, and had to cross the Pappannock River. Once he found and made it over the river, he was certain he'd be able to find his way to the Garrett's farm. He couldn't allow himself to get too lost on his way to the Pappannock River, though. He needed to keep up his lead on John Surratt. If he absolutely needed to—as a last resort only—Joseph would ask people for help, and hope they wouldn't recognize him from newspapers and 'Wanted' signs.

Luckily for Joseph, there was no need to interact with anyone. He traveled due south as planned, and came upon the Pappannock River. He made it across the river with no issues, and continued south by southwest toward Richard Garrett's home.

On the road, Joseph met the same former Confederate soldiers that Booth and Herold had met on their journey. One of them was Private William Jett.

Jett's role in Booth's ending was a crucial one. Federal police had figured out the young man had recently been in Booth's company, and after tracking him down to an Inn, they threatened Jett with a bullet in the head. That was all it took for the young former soldier of the Confederate army to give up Booth and Herold's location.

Joseph made some small talk with the soldiers, and it wouldn't be long into the conversation before Jett realized who he was in the company of. Jett, who admired Booth for what he did, offered his help in any way. Knowing Jett would lead him right to where he wanted to be, Joseph told the young man he needed to seek refuge in order to lay low. As predicted, Jett had a place in mind. In this moment of need, it had failed to dawn on Joseph that because of this interaction, Private William Jett would know the exact location of John Wilkes Booth when federal police once again came looking to threaten answers from him.

As they traveled down the road on their way to the Garrett's, Jett asked Joseph what it was like to kill the President of the United States. Jett had asked Booth the same exact question while traveling with the assassin and his companion. Joseph gave the same answer Booth, who was physically and mentally exhausted from spending well over a week on the run, had given.

"It's nothing to brag about."

They arrived at the farm of Richard Garrett in the early morning hours of April 24th. Jett offered to accompany Joseph to the doorstep and speak to Richard Garrett. Joseph declined the offer, and told Jett he would speak to Garrett himself. Joseph had no real intention of knocking on the door of Richard Garrett. His presence on the farm was the last thing he wanted to be made known. He parted ways with Jett and company, and snuck onto the Garrett's property to find a place to hide out.

On the evening of April 25, 1865, hours before Booth's death, John Wilkes Booth and David Herold were forced to spend the night inside the Garrett's tobacco barn. On the morning he arrived on Richard Garrett's property, Joseph looked to find that very barn. His plan was to hide out until Garrett forced John Surratt to spend the night in the barn, as he had once forced Booth to do. Once Surratt was left by himself, Joseph would emerge from his hiding spot and confront him. He would attempt nonviolent tactics at first to get Surratt to agree to surrender himself in the morning. If Surratt was not so willing to do so, Joseph had no qualms about getting physical.

Joseph spotted the tobacco barn and headed towards it. He entered, and was momentarily taken by the strong feeling of awe. During Joseph's life, the Garrett's farm no longer existed. In the twentieth century, the spot where John Wilkes Booth died sat on a highway median. There was no landmark, other than a sign, for people to visit.

Joseph now stood in the place where the man he spent his life admiring, and who he now hated, had received the gunshot that ended his life. No one else from his generation could stake that claim. Like seeing Abraham Lincoln alive, it was his own. It belonged to him. He allowed himself a moment to take in his surroundings. When he was done, he searched for a place to hide.

The ten day pursuit of John Surratt had been long and it had not been easy, but waiting in the tobacco barn for the man's arrival was torture. The end was coming, and Joseph knew, firsthand, from his final hour on death row that there is no wait longer than the wait for the end.

It was nearly forty hours before the door of the barn finally swung open. Two men entered the barn. It was now night and too dark to make out the identities of the two figures clearly, but Joseph assumed one was Richard Garrett. The other had to be John Surratt.

"You can sleep in here tonight," Joseph heard Richard Garrett say. "In the morning, we'll feed you, but then you're gone. Do you understand?"

Surratt understood, and was left by himself in the barn to wait out the night and plan his next move. Joseph wondered if Surratt regretted his decision by this point, as Booth had. Granted, Booth was the one the nation saw as the monster who killed their president, but Surratt was clearly seeking sanctuary from the south, as he was still trying to find passage to Richmond, Virginia.

Joseph's first instinct was to spring from his hiding spot the moment the two were left alone, and pummel Surratt, despite his original plan to attempt to reason with him. He resisted the urge, somehow. Joseph chose to remain hidden for a bit longer. It was still early in the night, and if a commotion was heard, the Garretts might investigate. Joseph didn't want any interruptions when he confronted Surratt.

As the hour finally approached midnight, and Joseph felt they were safe from any interruption, he stepped out of his hiding spot to confront the man he had been hunting down for the past eleven days. The moment he emerged, the man he shared the barn with became aware of his presence, and whipped around to see who else was there with him. There wasn't much moonlight that shone into the barn, but there was just enough for Joseph to make out the face of the person standing a few feet from him.

It was not the face Joseph expected to see.

He had traveled eleven days in pursuit of this man to this very barn, and the man standing across from him was not the man who shot Abraham Lincoln. It was not John Surratt in the barn with Joseph that night.

It was David Herold.

As he realized who he had been chasing for nearly two weeks, Joseph cursed his stupidity. He was well aware of so many of the similarities between Booth's assassination of Abraham Lincoln and John Surratt's. Yet it never dawned on him that David Herold—the very man who accompanied Booth his entire time spent on the run—would have rendezvoused with Surratt following the assassination.

However, at some point—likely after they stopped at Surratt Tavern the night Lincoln was shot—the two went their separate ways. Reflecting back on it from within the body of James Becker, Joseph had no doubt John Surratt headed north, where he'd eventually secure passage to Europe, like he originally had done at some point around the time Booth shot Lincoln. As for David Herold, he would likely be named by one of the conspirators who stayed behind in Washington D.C. and were eventually arrested for their involvement in the attempt to cripple the government. To avoid arrest, he had no choice but to head south to Virginia, where he thought he could seek sanctuary, when he and Surratt separated.

The shock that Joseph had been chasing the wrong person south the entire time finally wore off. Only it was moments too late. Joseph came to his senses, but before he could act, Herold was on him. Joseph was pushed hard into the walls of the barn, and the air was forced out of him. The two then wrestled to the ground, and rolled back and forth in the dirt. Joseph fought valiantly to gain an upper hand, but he had been weakened by the blow he had just taken. Joseph felt a sharp pain as Herold struck him in the temple with his fist. Herold then grabbed Joseph's skull, and slammed it into the unforgiving ground.

Joseph didn't remember much after that.

When he finally came to, Joseph was bound with rope around his ankles and wrists. He tried to struggle free. David Herold took notice that his sudden companion had regained consciousness, and was attempting to wiggle out of his restraints. He stood up, walked over to Joseph, and raised the Spencer Carbine rifle he was carrying to Joseph's face.

"I suggest you stop that," he said.

Joseph, who had no intentions of getting shot in the face, obeyed.

Instead of blowing a hole in Joseph's face, Herold landed a hard kick to Joseph's gut. He then returned to where he had been sitting. He picked up a small journal off the barn floor, and started writing in it. Joseph realized it was the journal he had kept while in the pine thickets. Next to Herold were torn out pages from the journal.

The lost pages of Booth's journal, Joseph thought to himself as he stared at the loose pieces of journal paper he had written John Wilkes Booth's innocence on.

When David Herold was arrested, and Booth was killed after the conclusion of the twelve day manhunt, Booth's body had been searched by the soldiers who had tracked him down. One of the items found was the journal Booth had kept. Later on, upon further examination, it was discovered that a great number of pages had been torn out of the journal, and were missing. Although there had been multiple theories over the many years since the journal was authored about what could have been written on those pages, no one knows for sure what Booth had written. Joseph, however, did know what was on those pages. It was the truth about who shot Abraham Lincoln at Ford's Theatre.

"Very compelling read," Herold said, noticing Joseph was staring at the pile of torn out pages. "I, however, have something far more interesting to tell."

Herold's plan, as it was told to Joseph, was to rewrite the contents of Booth's journal. He would turn Booth into a man angry at the world for not seeing him as a hero who slayed the tyrant that was Abraham Lincoln. The new content of Booth's journal would become undeniable proof that the actor was in fact the man who pulled the trigger in Ford's Theatre. Once the journal was complete, Herold would untie Joseph, but not before putting a bullet in his chest. The gunshot would bring the Garrett's from the house, and into the barn. Herold would tell the Garrett's to send for police, immediately. While the police were being summoned, Herold would dispose of the bindings and the loose journal pages that incriminated John Surratt. When the evidence against his story was gone, he would tell police he discovered John Wilkes Booth hiding out in the barn. After a physical altercation, Herold managed to get his rifle, and shoot Booth in self-defense. Herold would be declared a hero by the American people as the man who killed Abraham Lincoln's assassin.

Joseph saw a few holes in Herold's plan. The biggest being what reason would he give the police and federal officers for having to hide out in the Garrett's barn? Those arrested in Washington D.C. would name Herold as a conspirator. They might protect the true identity of the shooter in the president's State Box, but they had no reason to protect Herold. Testimonies from the other conspirators coupled with being found with John Wilkes Booth—dead or alive—would likely be enough to send David Herold to the gallows. Joseph had no desire to point out this major flaw, though.

Herold put the finishing touches on the new version of Booth's journal. He got up and walked towards Joseph with it in one hand, and the Spencer Carbine in the other. He placed the journal in Booth's pocket, and raised the rifle. Before he could pull the trigger, however, there was an explosive hammering on the barn door.

"Come out now," a voice on the other side of the door demanded. "You are surrounded. It's over."

Joseph knew who was on the other side of that door. It was the 16th New York Cavalry led by Lieutenant Edward Doherty. They were the cavalry that had once threatened William Jett in giving up the location of John Wilkes Booth and David Herold. They had apparently done it once again. A member of that cavalry was Sergeant Boston Corbett. History would remember him as the man who shot John Wilkes Booth while the cavalry was attempting to convince him to surrender.

Herold whipped himself towards the door, and for a moment Joseph thought he was going to fire his rifle. However, at the last moment, he thought better of it. Joseph could see in the limited light that Herold had no idea what to do. His master plan was now up in smoke. John Wilkes Booth was alive, and even if Herold shot him dead right there, the federal officers would still find the pages on the barn floor when they entered.

"Cooperate with us, and come out of the barn," the voice from the other side of the door bellowed. "Otherwise, we will force you out."

Joseph knew exactly what Doherty meant by that threat. It was what he had done the first time he had Booth and Herold surrounded. If the 16th New York Cavalry was met with a refusal of surrender, Doherty was going to force them out by ordering the barn be set afire.

Herold, becoming desperate, cut Joseph's bindings, and pulled him to his feet. He explained to Joseph that they were now in this together, and if they didn't find a way to escape, they both would be sent to their deaths. Joseph's only response to this was a thin smile. He had no intentions of trying to escape.

"This is your last warning," Doherty yelled. "Either you come out, or we will set this barn on fire."

The threat of being burned alive was enough to convince David Herold to cooperate and surrender. However, he had no intentions of letting his companion in the barn that night do the same. He drove the butt of the Spencer Carbine rifle with his full force into the abdomen of Joseph. This, once again, drove the air from Joseph, and forced him down to the barn floor. Herold then dropped the rifle, and headed towards the barn door while announcing his surrender.

As Joseph lay on the barn's floor, trying to get the much needed air back into his body, he felt the heat of flames begin to lick at his face. The cavalry had kept to their word, and set the barn on fire. Surely Herold helped force their hand by telling the officers Booth had no intention of coming out alive. Joseph looked over at the barn walls. The wooden planks were beginning to catch fire. The removed pages of his journal that Herold had ripped out earlier sat inches away from the growing flames. Soon enough they would be ashes, and any evidence that incriminated John

Surratt would be destroyed. Joseph couldn't allow that to happen.

Despite the screaming pain in his abdomen, Joseph forced himself up to his feet. He inhaled a lungful of smoke, and erupted into a violent coughing fit that forced him down to one knee. He pushed himself, once again, back to his feet. This time he only took shallow breaths, and when he absolutely needed to. All he needed to do was grab hold the loose pages before they were destroyed, and then he'd be able to surrender. If he could just tell his side of the story, he had no doubt Doherty and his people would be able to get a confession out of Herold. He knew there was a good chance that it might not work, but he knew he had to try.

The chance to bring John Surratt to justice would never come, though.

Before Joseph could make his move to retrieve the pages, he felt a bullet hit him. He fell to the ground, and knew exactly what had happened. It was exactly what had happened to John Wilkes Booth the night he refused to surrender to the 16th New York Cavalry, who had him surrounded outside the Garrett's tobacco barn.

He was shot by Sergeant Boston Corbett.

The officers rushed inside the burning barn and dragged out the body of the man they had been hunting for twelve days. As they did, Joseph saw the first of the loose pages catch flame. Soon they'd all burn, and turn to ash.

Joseph, who was now trapped inside the paralyzed and useless body of John Wilkes Booth, was dragged away from the barn to the porch of the Garrett's home. There, Booth's body would cling to life until morning. At dawn, John Wilkes Booth—with Joseph Bateman inside him— would finally succumb to his mortal wound, and die.

Joseph thought about all that he had set out to do, from preventing Abraham Lincoln from being assassinated to apprehending John Surratt, and bringing the president's killer to justice. None of it had gone according to plan. Joseph Bateman, as he had seen time and time again throughout his own life, had failed to bring change to something he had hoped to make better.

As he lay there, the end only moments away, Joseph asked the soldiers to raise Booth's paralyzed hands to his face. They acquiesced, and lifted the hands for Joseph to look upon. They were the hands of an evil man, but Joseph tried to do some good with them. He stared at them, and as he felt the darkness closing in on him, Joseph uttered the last words John Wilkes Booth ever said.

"Useless...Useless..."

April 25, 1995

Looking For Alex

Joseph woke in James Becker's bed after falling asleep only four short hours earlier, and stared through James Becker's eyes at the white ceiling of James Becker's room. Exhaustion weighed heavily on his body, but Joseph's mind raced with thoughts, and he knew sleep was beyond him now.

After leaving the library the night before, Joseph walked aimlessly in the rain for nearly an hour. He tried to process and register everything he had just learned. Getting a firm grasp on it was difficult, though. Somehow history had rewritten itself so that it had never been rewritten at all. John Wilkes Booth had visited the exact same places, and interacted with the same people he had when he had been the one who actually killed Abraham Lincoln.

There were even places recorded having been visited by Booth that Joseph had not been on his twelve day pursuit of who he thought then was John Surratt, but was actually only David Herold. One place, in particular, that stood out was the home of Elizabeth Quesenberry. Booth and Herold had visited her home upon coming ashore after crossing the Potomac River. They sought refuge, but were turned

322

away. This wasn't something Joseph did on his journey, as he landed a few miles north of Quesenberry's home, and traveled directly to Garrett's farm. Another case in point was when a history text cited Booth and Herold staying at the home of freed slave, William Lucas. Like the visit to the Queensberry's home, it never happened. John Wilkes Booth had been placed by history in locations he had never visited. The explanation, once Joseph was able to reach it, made perfect sense.

The reason was David Herold.

Herold had survived the incident at the Garrett's farm, and was taken to Washington D.C. There, federal officers questioned, and interrogated him. It wouldn't have been hard for him to lie, and say he and Booth had been together the night Lincoln was shot to the morning it all ended for John Wilkes Booth. Herold had read the pages of the journal Joseph had written in the pine thicket, and knew precisely where Joseph had been, and who he had dealings with before crossing the Potomac River. All he had to do was take where Joseph had been before crossing the river, and combine it with places Herold had visited after making it across the Potomac. There was no way to dispute this on Joseph's behalf. John Wilkes Booth was dead, and with his death, Joseph was silenced. Herold's testimony, combined with a falsified journal, and plenty of witness accounts from people who would tell federal officers anything they wanted to hear just to avoid being named a conspirator or accomplice, turned fabrications into historical facts.

When Joseph finally returned to James Becker's car, soaked from the rain, he had only a few minor pieces of the puzzle figured out. He still had no idea as to why it had all gone down the way it did, and he knew he wasn't going to get that answer from any historical text found on the shelf of a bookcase at the local public library.

He drove to James Becker's home, and went straight to bed. James Becker's body was exhausted from his trip to Atlantic City, and ached for sleep. There would be no such thing, though. Instead, Joseph would spend the next few hours staring up into the nothingness of James Becker's darkened room. He didn't think of Booth, Abraham Lincoln, or John Surratt. He had done all he could as far as all that went, and was done fixating on it. He turned his focus to what he considered to be the more pressing matter at hand.

Finding Alex.

He had done everything he could to be with her, and, in the end, she was not a part of Joseph's new life as James Becker. That didn't mean she couldn't be, though. There was still a chance they could end up together. Joseph just had to make it happen. He just had to find her first.

Plan A was J. Joseph knew J could take him right to wherever Alex was. Just like he could fill in the missing pieces to the Lincoln Assassination puzzle. J hadn't shown his face, though, and without J, Joseph needed an alternate plan to find Alex. It didn't take him long to figure his new plan out.

Joseph would need to return home to Wayne County.

There was a chance Alex might still be living in the town she and Joseph had grown up in. Even if she didn't, Joseph could possibly get an idea of where she had gone, and work off that.

With his plan now in place, and exhaustion reaching a pivotal peak, Joseph drifted off to sleep. Four hours later, just before seven in the morning, he awoke, ready to carry out his plan. The first step was simple enough. He would get in James Becker's car, and drive three hours to Wayne County, Pennsylvania.

Joseph made his way out of the bedroom and into the kitchen. There, he ate breakfast and conversed with James

Becker's parents. A father who scarcely drank, and when he did, was no risk to anyone around him. A mother who was accustomed to being spoiled by her husband, and never had to fear being beaten and raped on a nightly basis. Two parents who loved their son, had given him a proper childhood, and imparted the knowledge that helped mold James Becker into the good man he had become.

It had taken the entire morning for Joseph to muster up the courage to return to the place he had grown up. On paper, so to speak, his plan was simple enough. Executing it was the difficult part. He may have been James Becker now, but the memories of the life Joseph Bateman had lived in Wayne County were still very real. Joseph wasn't sure he could return to the place he had once yearned to escape. He would need to overcome his fears if he was ever going to find Alex, though. As the clock struck noon, Joseph still found himself unprepared for what lay ahead, but he could wait no longer. He got behind the wheel of James Becker's car, and took the drive to Wayne County.

Three and a half hours later, thanks to traffic, Joseph found himself parked down the street from the Casings' home. He watched the house for a little bit from behind the wheel of James Becker's vehicle, and allowed memories from his past to flood him. He thought of Alex, and the friendship they had developed in that house. A friendship that would grow and blossom into love. Joseph was ready to continue their story together. He stepped out of the car, and walked up the block, towards Alex's childhood home.

He walked up the porch steps, and as he approached the screen door to knock, he noticed toys scattered about all over the porch. Joseph knew then he wasn't going to find what he had come looking for.

"Can I help you?" a voice from inside the house asked before Joseph could decide if he was going to even bother knocking.

A woman appeared behind the screen door. Joseph had never seen this woman before in his life, but he knew she was the current homeowner of the house.

"I thought someone else lived here," Joseph responded. "I'm sorry to have bothered you."

"It's no bother at all," the young woman said. "Did you know the people who lived here before?"

Technically no, Joseph thought.

The person this woman was conversing with, whose name was James Becker, had never met Alexandra or Bill Casings. He had never visited—never even heard of—Wayne County before.

The person inside James Becker, though...He knew the Casings very well.

"When I was younger," Joseph answered. "Do you, by any chance, know where they moved to? Do you have a forwarding address?"

Joseph saw the woman's expression suddenly change, and knew whatever it was she had to say next, wasn't going to be good.

"I'm so sorry to be the one to have to tell you this..." she said "But the previous owner killed himself."

Like the lights of an arena being shut off, except for a single spotlight, which now fixated on a single object in the center of the huge room, Joseph's mind went blank, except for a single thought.

Bill Casings was dead.

He committed suicide.

Joseph didn't speak—he couldn't—but the expression on his face must've relayed the shock of how hard the news hit him. The woman opened the screen door, and stepped out onto her porch.

"Maybe you should take a minute and sit." the woman offered, motioning Joseph towards her porch swing. "Let it process. I can get you something to drink."

"No," Joseph answered. "Thank you, though."

He was about to thank the woman for her time, and excuse himself, but before he could, one last important question managed to squeeze its way through the haze of shock.

"His daughter…" he said. "Do you know what happened to his daughter?"

"I'm sorry," the woman answered. "I don't."

For a split second, Joseph feared the worst. What if Alex had died from an illness or a freak accident she was involved in, and her death was the reason Bill Casings took his own life. After all, the man had already lost his wife to infidelity. The loss of his daughter would be enough to send him spiraling into a depression that he would never be able to return form.

Joseph quickly pushed away this worst case scenario notion. Had Alex's death been part of the story, the new homeowner would likely know it. Just as she knew Bill Casings had taken his own life prior to her moving in.

Alex was still alive, and she was out there somewhere. Joseph just needed to find her.

"Thank you for your time," he said, excusing himself.

"I wish I was able to be a bigger help."

"You've been a huge help. Thank you very much."

Joseph turned away from the old Casings home and returned to James Becker's car. He got in the car, and just sat there staring through the windshield at the house that was such a huge landmark in the story of his own life. He attempted to process the fact that Bill Casings was dead, but his mind couldn't get itself wrapped around it. Joseph found himself going back to the fact that something had to happen to Bill Casings to make him reach the decision that he had no choice but to end it all. Joseph needed to find out what that something was. He needed to learn details surrounding Bill Casings' demise, and he knew exactly where to go, and who to see to get them.

The woman now living in the Casings' old home may not have had the information Joseph needed, but there was one person in town Joseph knew would have what he was looking for. Someone who had lived their entire life in Wayne County, and would have heard enough pieces of the story to know what had happened to Bill Casings and his daughter.

So with no other options at his disposal, Joseph left James Becker's car behind, and walked to the general store owned by Leonard Hershel.

He was aware of the audacity of going to see Leonard Hershel and asking the man for help. The last time the two had been together, Joseph had punched the store owner in the face. That was in another life, though, and things were different now. He was no longer that person who took a swing at an unsuspecting middle-aged man. He was James Becker now, and James Becker and Leonard Hershel had never met. James Becker would be able to get the answers Joseph sought.

Joseph entered the general store. He was so high strung and nervous, that the sound of the small bell above the door, announcing the presence of a new patron, sounded more like a church bell than the quiet one that it was. He took a moment to collect himself, and once his nerves were calm, Joseph had a look around. Not much had changed since the last time he was inside the establishment in 1988.

"May I help you?" Joseph heard a voice.

It was a voice straight out of his past. Like a ghost breaking through reality from the other side. He whipped around towards the sound of the voice, and stepping out from behind the counter was Leonard Hershel.

Mister Hershel had aged drastically over the seven years since Joseph had last seen him. His hair was greyer, his cheeks drooped, and his skin now had the lines of age running through them. Still, the familiar sense of kindness that all who entered the man's store felt was still in his eyes. Seeing this man from the past Joseph Bateman had tried so hard to escape brought on a plethora of emotions.

The one that stood out amongst the rest was shame.

Even though Joseph had gone back in time, and changed the path of his eternal soul, he still felt bad for all he had done to Mister Hershel throughout his life. Even though there was now a good chance none of those things had ever happened.

"Have we met before, son?" Mister Hershel asked after the long silence reached an awkward level.

"No," Joseph finally said, resisting his initial urge to say yes, they had met. "We haven't."

"What can I do you for, then?"

Joseph pushed his emotions aside the best he could, so that he could get what he came for.

"Well, sir… I was hoping you'd be able to help me out. See…I'm looking to track down a childhood friend. I was told you were the person to come see about what might have come of them."

"I hear enough chatter amongst people in this town to consider myself well-informed. I'll be more than happy to help you, if I can. What's the name of the person you're looking to find?"

"Alexandra Casings."

"Ahhhh, I see…" Leonard Hershel said, nodding, as if he now understood why this person in front of him was there to see him. "I suppose you've already been by the Casings' old house."

"I have."

"So you've heard about Bill Casings untimely demise?"

"Yes."

"It's a shame what happened to that man."

JASON PELLEGRINI

Hearing that come from Leonard Hershel's mouth came as a bit of a shock to Joseph. He knew the history between the store owner and Alex's father, and sympathy was the last thing Joseph had expected from Mister Hershel.

"Were you two friends?" Joseph asked, wondering if things were somehow different now that he had prevented John Wilkes Booth from assassinating Abraham Lincoln.

"We were not," Mister Hershel answered, snickering at the notion of him and Bill Casings being pals. "That man was not very fond of me. He tried to make my life hell as much as he could. He went as far as to vandalize my car in the middle of the night."

"You aren't glad he's dead then?"

"Absolutely not."

"Why not? Like you said, he hated you. He made your life hell."

"Bill Casings had his demons, son. No one can deny that. We all knew him before those demons took him, though. He was once a good man. A loving husband and father. I'm not making excuses for what he had become, but he didn't deserve to go out fighting a helpless battle with a noose."

"Why did he kill himself?"

"He left no note. So it's all pure speculation. The most common belief is he did it because his daughter left."

"Alex left?"

"Yes, sir. Summer of eighty-eight, if my memory serves me well."

This news hit Joseph like a cheap shot to the gut. He had always believed that he was the reason Alex decided to leave her life behind, and try to start new. It turned out, she was going to leave Wayne County, regardless of whether or not Joseph Bateman was a part of her life.

"Nobody knows where she went?" Joseph asked.

330

"No," Mister Hershel answered. "Her father spent a year looking for her. He couldn't find her, though. Young Alex wanted to disappear, and disappear, she did."

"And when he realized he wouldn't find her, he killed himself…"

"It took him a few months before he tied that noose around his neck, but eventually the loneliness got to him. His boss found him after he hadn't shown up for work for four days straight. It was the height of the summer, and I heard the flies and maggots had already gotten to him by the time he was found hanging in his living room."

Externally, James Becker winced at the imagery of Bill Casings' body being feasted upon by insects. Internally, Joseph was feeling pity for the man. It was a feeling that came as a bit of a shock, given Joseph's loathing for the man. In the end, Joseph felt exactly as Leonard Hershel. Bill Casings may have been a racist, who poured his hatred into his daughter, but he was a human being, and he was battling personal demons, just like anyone else. He didn't deserve death.

"Does anyone know why she left?" Joseph asked.

"Everyone has their own theory. It's been a few years, so it's not really discussed anymore. I've heard stories that her daddy used to beat her, and she got sick of it. Some said he touched her…you know…in a way a father should never touch his little girl. I never believed those stories. For all his faults, Bill Casings loved his little girl. There were some who claimed that she ran off to be with an older man. I don't think that was the case, either."

"Why do you think she left?"

"Truth be told, I just think she was sick of her daddy's hate. Alexandra Casings was a real spitfire, who also had some character flaws. Ones you knew she had picked up from her daddy. You mix those two things together, and it's a recipe for disaster. Once I caught her trying to steal from my store. When I tried to stop her, she resisted me. She finally broke free, and instead of running off with what she was trying to steal, she threw it down hard on my foot. She then ran out of the store spewing every racial slur I'd ever heard—not to mention, some that I had never heard.

"I think young Alex realized what she had turned into, and decided she didn't want to be that way anymore. I think she felt she needed to be away from this place and her daddy in order to shed the bad she felt she needed to rid herself of. So she did what she felt needed to be done. She left."

Joseph remained silent. He wanted to tell Mister Hershel he was right. The man had figured out the exact reason why Alex had left. Joseph knew this, because Alex had once told him those exact reasons in another life. There was no way James Becker would know that for sure, though. So silence was all there was.

"Anyways," Leonard Hershel said after a few moments. "I know it's not exactly what you came for, but I hope it helps you a bit."

"It does," Joseph answered. "It really does."

"Are you going to look for her?"

"Yes. I am."

"I hope you find her. I hope she found her happiness."

"I do, too."

"What's your name, son?"

"James Becker."

"Well, James Becker. I'm Leonard Hershel. It's been privilege and a pleasure to meet you."

Mister Hershel then extended his hand for James Becker to shake. Joseph looked down at it. The hand of a man whose car he had aided Bill Casings in vandalizing. A man he had once punched in the face. A man whose race Joseph had tormented for years for no other reason than he was just a miserable person who couldn't deal with his own anger.

Joseph looked down at that man's extended hand, and, without giving it a moment's hesitation, extended his own hand, and shook Leonard Hershel's hand.

"The pleasure was all mine," Joseph said.

He walked towards the door, but instead of leaving, Joseph turned back to the man he had just conversed with. He watched as Leonard Hershel tidied up the shelves in his store to make it look neater. There was one last thing for Joseph to say, and he couldn't leave without it being said.

"Mister Hershel... I'm sorry. For anything you had to endure that you didn't deserve."

"Thank you, Mister Becker. That was kind of you to say."

"You are a kind man, and I'm glad to see those idiotic hateful things never brought you down."

"You can't let hate get to you, son. Because if it does, it will destroy the person you really are, and replace you with a stranger you'll hate."

I know, Joseph thought.

With everything he wanted to say finally said, Joseph turned, opened the door, and walked out into the daylight. He knew he was no closer to finding Alex than he had been five minutes earlier, but he still felt relief as he walked from the general store. A huge weight had been lifted from his shoulders. A weight he had been carrying for a very long time.

The feeling Joseph was experiencing was closure.

April 25, 1995
Manhattan

Joseph stood in the street and looked down a long dirt driveway at a house he had once known from another life.

He wanted to find the courage to walk up that driveway, knock on the door, and see who would be standing there, on the other side of it, when it opened. He wanted to know what had happened to the little boy Emily Bateman had given birth to nearly twenty-seven years ago. J had told him that when a newborn drew its first breath, it either sparked life that would become the flame of a new soul, or an already existing soul entered that child. With Joseph's soul now tied to James Becker, he wondered what type of life Emily Bateman's first born had led, and if things turned out differently for the entire Bateman family.

Despite his curiosity, Joseph could not find it in him to take the steps towards the house he had once grown up in. He didn't think he could handle seeing his mother standing there to greet him when the door opened. If Emily Bateman answered the door, it would mean she was alive, and had lived an additional seven and a half years. As much as the sight of his mother still alive and hopefully walking would bring joy to his heart, the knowledge that it was only possible because his soul was no longer linked to their family would be devastating.

Not only could Emily Bateman still be alive, she could actually be living a normal and happy life, somehow. Hank Bateman had abandoned sobriety and returned to the bottle because he couldn't handle the pressures of parenthood. Maybe one of the reasons was because Joseph had been too difficult of an infant. Maybe the baby Emily and Hank brought home this time around could have been easier. Maybe in this new life, Hank Bateman wasn't a monster. Maybe the two were a happily married couple all because Joseph's soul ended up somewhere else.

Joseph loved his mother, but if he learned she was better off without him in life, it would crush him. That's why, in the end, he decided he was better off not knowing. Instead of walking towards the house, Joseph turned away from it and walked off.

The plan was to return to the car and head back home to Long Island. However, when Joseph reached Main Street, instead of turning right and heading back to the car, he turned left. From there, he walked until he found himself standing at the lake.

The first thing Joseph noticed was the tree he and Alex spent most of their days and evenings lounging in. It was the tree Joseph jumped from when he finally conquered his fear of heights. It was where he and Alex shared their very first (awkward) kiss together.

He walked over and climbed the tree. He sat on the same branch he and Alex always sat upon, the one that hung directly over the water. He watched the western sky, and the rays of the setting sunlight reflecting of the calm waters. It was a sight like no other. One that James Becker had never seen, but Joseph had witnessed countless times. No matter how many times he saw it, Joseph was in awe of it.

As he watched the sun sink into the horizon, he felt a calm come over him. It would only be temporary, he knew, but feeling relief, even a moment's worth, was something he desperately needed.

Once the sun was gone, and the western sky ate up what remained of its light, Joseph was left in the dark. He laid back on the branch in which he was perched, and stared up at the night sky. He noticed the moon, which had already risen pretty high into the sky, and for the first time in nearly twenty years, Joseph Bateman saw the huge jellybean floating through the cosmos. Not only that, but he could see those space monsters floating around the heavens; looking to take a bite out of the sweet treat that was the moon. They were once his distraction from the hell that went on inside his home at night, but now he saw them for what they truly were, the beautiful creations of a child's mind.

He wanted to lay there forever in that single moment of serenity, but also knew he needed to move. Even though she didn't know it, Alex waited for him, and it was time to continue his search for her. Joseph stood, but instead of descending the tree the way he climbed, he decided to go with an alternate exit. He stripped his clothes away one article at a time until he was completely naked. He dropped them to the ground below, and then, without giving it a moment's hesitation, jumped from the branch to the waters below.

Due to the time of year, the water was ice cold and the shock felt like a punch to the gut. Joseph swam desperately towards the surface. By the time he reached it, his body had adapted to the water's harsh temperature, so Joseph tilted backwards and allowed himself to float. His ears sank below the water, and all the sounds of the world ceased. There was only beautiful silence. He gave himself only a few seconds of that peacefulness before forcing himself to abandon it. He then flipped onto his stomach and swam to shore. There, he dressed and left the lake.

On his way back to James Becker's car, Joseph found himself standing in a small dirt parking lot staring at a condemned building. There were no signs from when the establishment was open, and Joseph almost failed to recall what it had once been. Then it came to him. The boarded up building he was staring at had once been an ice cream parlor, the one Alex used to get her root beer floats from. It was the place Joseph was sitting in front of one fall afternoon as a child when he met J for the first time.

"Things didn't go exactly as you thought they would," Joseph heard a voice proclaim from behind him. "Did they, Joseph? Oops! I mean, James."

Joseph whipped around so fast towards the sound of the voice behind him that he almost lost his footing and fell on his ass. Standing behind him, only older now, was that person who had asked him all those years ago where the nearest auto repair shop was.

Standing in front of Joseph was J.

Joseph walked up to J, and with James Becker's hand, he reached out and grabbed J by the throat. He kicked J's leg out from beneath him and slammed him down to the ground. Joseph's old, familiar friend—anger—retuned, and he had to battle to overcome the urge to squeeze J's throat until the man could no longer breathe.

"Haven't you learned?" J asked. He took hold of James Becker's wrist, and, with ease, freed himself from the grip of the man choking him. "Violence gets you nowhere in life. John Wilkes Booth and Joseph Bateman learned that the hard way. You don't want James Becker to go down that path, too. Now do we?"

"What the hell happened?" Joseph asked as J got up to his feet.

"What do you mean? This is exactly what you wanted, Joseph. Remember? This is what would have become of your soul had John Wilkes Booth not been the man to assassinate Abraham Lincoln."

"Apparently Booth did kill Lincoln," Joseph pointed out. "At least that's how history remembers it."

"What history remembers, and what the truth is are two very different things."

"Why was Lincoln killed? He wasn't supposed to die."

"Says you," J said, being as cryptic as usual. "You don't get to decide how history is written, Joseph. You don't wield that kind of power. No one does. Thankfully."

"J," Joseph pleaded, still not any less confused than he had been since waking up in an Atlantic City hotel room inside James Becker's body. "Please tell me what the hell is going on."

J remained silent. He made it look as if he was mulling over his options, but Joseph knew better. J had already known, probably long before he even showed his face, what information he would disclose to Joseph about what had happened. The thoughtful silence was mere theatrics.

"Fine," J finally said. "I'll tell you all you want to know, but not just yet.

"When? I can't take not knowing any longer."

"I'll tell you everything on the car ride."

"Car ride? Where are we going?"

"Manhattan, Joseph," J said as he walked away from Joseph in the direction of James Becker's car. "I'm sure you've been dying to see Alex again."

The first half hour of their trip back to New York was spent in silence. Joseph had so many questions he wanted answers to, yet he couldn't think of a single one. His mind was devoted fully to the idea of being reunited with Alex.

"You'll be united with your love soon enough, Joseph," J said, breaking the long silence the two had been sharing thus far. "For now, let's concentrate on some of the other things you've wanted answers to. We still have quite a long ride ahead of us before we reach Manhattan. Let's fill it with conversation and clarity."

"Fine," Joseph said, finding enough room in his Alex-filled mind to allow another thought to pass. "Why did Lincoln die?"

"You were not sent back to save Abraham Lincoln. You were sent back to find redemption. No one said redemption meant preventing the president from dying."

"But I chose to prevent the man who was supposed to shoot Lincoln from doing so."

"Very true. And in Booth's stead, a replacement was chosen."

"Yet it was Booth who was remembered as the man who shot Abraham Lincoln."

"There's something you need to understand, Joseph," J explained. "Lincoln was destined to be shot on April 14, 1865, and John Wilkes Booth was always meant to be remembered as the man who pulled the trigger. There's not a single thing could have done to change that. You could think up a million different scenarios of how to stop it, and every time you went to execute one of them, Abraham Lincoln would end up being shot at Ford's Theatre."

"Why?" Joseph asked, unwilling to accept what J told him. "There has to be a way to change things."

"There isn't," J told Joseph. "History is a wheel that has been turning since the very beginning, and it will keep turning, no matter how many wrenches you throw into its spokes. Believe me...I know, firsthand."

So there it was. Despite Joseph's efforts to prevent the assassination of Abraham Lincoln or apprehend the man who pulled the trigger once Booth was removed from the equation, the president was going to end up being shot, and

John Wilkes Booth was going to be remembered as the man who pulled the trigger.

"It's why you stayed for those twelve days following the shooting, even though you began to fall forward into this body of James Becker," J continued to explain. "History needed you to guide Booth to the Garrett's farm. That's where it was all destined to end for him. All those things you read about that happened to Booth along the way that never actually did was just history fixing itself."

As J's words sank in, a sadness took Joseph, and he found himself mourning Abraham Lincoln's death on a level many would never be able to understand. Despite viewing the sixteenth president of the United States as a villain throughout most of his life, Joseph now knew Lincoln deserved life for all he had done and sacrificed for his country. Instead, all he could receive was death.

Joseph and J spent the remainder of the trip riding in silence. When they arrived in Manhattan, J directed Joseph to Midtown, where Joseph left James Becker's car in a parking garage. They then walked a few blocks west to Hell's Kitchen.

Joseph quickly became aware of how out of place James Becker must've looked as he walked through the streets of one of Manhattan's worst neighborhoods. He ignored eye contact with anyone he passed, but he could still feel the eyes of New York's poor as they stared him down. He didn't belong there, yet he refused to turn away. If he had to walk through every terrible part of every city in the world to see Alex, he would. He'd welcome muggings and beatings, and he'd risk his life, over and over again, if it meant being reunited with the woman he loved.

J stopped across the street from an abandoned building. Joseph didn't know why they had stopped, but whatever the reason was, it was not important to him, whatsoever. He was too close to Alex for detours. He asked J why they were stopping, but J gave no answer. He just stared across the streets at the condemned building. Joseph followed J's line of sight.

At first, Joseph had no idea what J was staring at. All he saw was the abandoned building. Then he saw the person sitting in the stoop. It was a young woman around James Becker's age. She wore not enough clothing for the still chilly April weather, and didn't have enough meat on her bones to compensate, either. Joseph had no idea why they had taken the time to stop and stare at a random homeless woman from a distance. Before he could ask J what the point of all this was, the woman raised her head, and Joseph saw her face.

The woman Joseph was now staring at was Alex.

Joseph felt sorrow rise up in his throat and threaten to explode. He tried to swallow it down, but failed. Silent tears streamed down his face as he stared at Alex from a distance. She barely resembled the woman who had gotten her life together the last time he had seen her, around this exact time while he was waiting for his day of execution on Death Row in another life. Even from across the street, Joseph could see he was looking at the broken down remains of the person he had known his entire life.

He wanted to go to her, scoop her up off that stoop, and carry her away from Hell's Kitchen. He wanted to make everything better. Sensing Joseph's desire, J grabbed him by the wrist.

"Are you sure you want to go to her?" J asked.

"What happened to her?" Joseph asked.

There was pleading in his voice. He was desperate for an answer. J gave no answer, though.

"I cannot stop you from going to her, Joseph," J said, instead. "But you need to know that if you do, answers might come to light that will ruin this new happiness you fought so hard for."

Whatever happiness J was speaking of, it was foreign to Joseph. There wasn't an ounce of joy in his body. Not after seeing Alex the way she was. Joseph stared across the street at the abandoned building, where Alex was sitting on the stoop. Without saying another word to J, he crossed the street, and walked up to Alex.

She didn't notice him at first as he approached. Joseph attempted to speak, but there were no words. He was still so overwhelmed with emotion that he wasn't sure if he was capable of articulation. She finally became aware that she was in the presence of another human being, and raised her head. The sight of her face up close nearly brought Joseph to his knees. It was as thin as her arms. A layer of dirt covered her pale as death skin, and her once beautiful eyes were void of all liveliness. The worst part, however, about seeing Alex up close were the track marks on her arms from needle usage that she obviously couldn't care less about hiding.

"Who the hell are you?" she asked.

The voice sounded like the Alexandra Casings Joseph had once known, but it was also the voice of a complete stranger.

"Alex..." was all Joseph could manage to get out. He spoke no louder than a whisper.

"Do I know you?"

YES! Joseph screamed from within himself. *You do know me, Alex. It's me...Joseph!*

He was no longer Joseph, though. He was James Becker now, and Alex would have no idea who James Becker was.

"Hey, asshole," she said. "I asked you a question. Do...I...fucking...know...you...?"

"No," Joseph finally managed to say. "You don't."

"Well, then I suggest you get the fuck out of my face."

Joseph took Alex's suggestion. As badly as he wanted to beg her to search deep within herself to find him there, he knew it was nothing more than a fool's hope. He turned away from the building and Alex, and looked across the street. J was gone. Without saying another word to Alex, Joseph left her sitting on a stoop of an abandoned building in one of Manhattan's worst neighborhoods. He had no other choice but to head back to James Becker's life.

Alone.

April 26, 1995

Joseph's Sacrifice

Instead of returning to James Becker's car following his meeting with Alex, Joseph roamed the Manhattan streets aimlessly for an hour. He eventually ended up at Penn Station on 34th Street, where he took the Long Island Railroad back to Long Island. He was in no condition to drive, and all he wanted was to just sit and be alone with his thoughts. He would return to the city in the morning for the car. Or he wouldn't. He honestly didn't give a damn.

He sat in the last car of the train, where there were the least amount of travelers. The moment he was seated, the tears began to fall. His tears turned into sobs, and before Joseph could even attempt to get a hold of himself, his grief consumed him. He did not notice the people looking at him as the cart of the train began to fill up with last moment boarders. He did not notice as the train began to move as it left Penn Station and headed towards Long Island. Joseph was unaware of anything going on in the world around him. The only thing he knew was his despair.

Eventually, his sobs tapered off, and Joseph was able to regain some semblance of composure so that he no longer looked like an insane person. He chose not to acknowledge any of the people still staring at him. He just looked out the window at the world outside.

As Joseph watched the buildings outside pass him by in a flash, he noticed through his peripheral as someone took a seat across from him. He chose to not acknowledge J's presence.

"Do you want to know why?" J asked when it became clear Joseph had no plans in engaging him in conversation.

Joseph wasn't sure how to answer that. The last time he had seen Alex was when she came to visit him in prison just a few days before his execution. Physically, she had looked better than he had ever seen before. Emotionally, despite being nervous about seeing Joseph and then upset over his reaction to the news that she was engaged, Alex also seemed to be doing better. All of that had changed, though. Alex was now worse off than ever, both physically and emotionally. She was a homeless junky. Something had happened to alter her path in life. J knew what that something was, and Joseph wanted to know, too. He also knew deep down that J was going to tell him that what happened to Alex was Joseph's fault. Joseph didn't think he could bear to the burden of hearing he was responsible for Alex's new life.

In the end, Joseph's assumption was correct.

"The woman you met was Alexandra Casings," J went on to explain. "She was the woman you grew up with and fell in love with. Except she wasn't the woman you knew, Joseph. Was she?"

Joseph did not answer J's question. He remained silent, and continued to stare out the window. He could feel the tears returning to his eyes as J spoke.

"Alex needed you in her life," J continued. "Like you, her home situation was ruining her, and, like you, Joseph, she looked to her best friend for happiness. You took that happiness away from her when you made certain John Wilkes Booth was not the man to shoot Abraham Lincoln. When that happened, your soul ended up here." J motioned to the man sitting opposite him. "In the body of James Becker. As a result, there was no Joseph Bateman for Alexandra Casings to befriend, and Alex was left alone in a world that would eventually take her and destroy her."

"He still would have been born, though," Joseph pointed out, curiosity gripping him enough to finally engage J in conversation. "My parents still would have met and gotten married. They would've had a child. Regardless of where my soul ended up, none of those facts should've changed."

"An excellent observation," J said. "Hank and Emily Bateman did have a child. Sadly, it only lived for a few minutes. You see, with your soul ending up elsewhere, it wasn't in the hospital room that May evening to enter the body of Emily Bateman's newborn son."

"What about the spark? You said when there isn't a soul nearby to enter a newborn child, there's a spark when it takes its first breath and that spark becomes their soul."

"I did say that, and it is absolutely the truth. However, not every spark is capable of igniting a flame. For whatever reason, it doesn't catch and erupt into the wildfire we call life. The result is a child dead before it gets a chance to live. That's what happened in the case of Hank and Emily Bateman. Their son, who they named Joseph, died in his mother's arms minutes after he was brought into the world.

"The death of her child sent Emily Bateman into a pit of depression, one her husband could not handle. As a result, he turned to the bottle. They eventually had a girl, who they named Elizabeth, but she was killed in an automobile accident on a snowy December day."

"I know the story," Joseph interrupted. "No need to tell it. I know how it ends."

"Fair enough," J said. "Well, as far as Alex is concerned, without anyone in her life to bring her happiness, things ended up going quite differently than they had when you were there for her. Her father's misery and racism ate away at her, and she became a very angry person with a vicious mean streak. Especially to those who did not have the same color skin as her. Eventually she wanted out, and left home. Unfortunately, her path had already been altered so much that any form of happiness was beyond her reach. She left home truly lost.

"When she arrived in Manhattan, she only had pennies in her pocket. Hungry and without a place to sleep, she looked to the wrong crowds for food and shelter. Her life deteriorated quickly. She became a user, as you saw. She used her body to get food, shelter, and even drugs. She fell deep into a dark hole, and she's been trapped in it for years now. She never got her chance to leave New York and move to Florida..."

"She never got the chance to meet the man who helped her turn everything around," Joseph said, finishing J's point. "She never got her chance to find her happiness."

"Exactly."

The two said no more to each other. The remainder of the trip was spent in silence. When the train arrived at Mineola, a few stops before Hicksville—James Becker's stop—J got up and exited the train. Joseph spent the remainder of the trip hating himself.

He had ruined Alex's life. The person he loved more than anything in the world ended up homeless and a drug addict in New York City because of his selfishness. He swore to her on the day they took each other's virginities that he would protect her. All he did was put her in harm's way.

He failed her. All because of his selfishness.

At the end of it all, Joseph was no different than Booth. The two had acted selfishly, and, as a result, others had suffered dearly.

James Becker's train pulled into the Hicksville train station not long after midnight. From there, Joseph walked a few blocks to James Becker's home, a place he was supposed to now call home. He wouldn't, though. Joseph refused to acknowledge anything given to him in this new life as his own. He deserved none of it.

He laid down in James Becker's bed upon returning to his home. Sleep came easily, and Joseph welcomed it. He just hoped, as he drifted off into twilight, that he did not wake up come morning.

However, Joseph Bateman would not be the one Death came for that night.

Joseph dreamt he was sitting in the Presidential State Box at Ford's Theatre. He sat in the rocking chair, and next to him sat Alex. On the stage below, there was an actor dressed as Abraham Lincoln, and an actress dressed as Mary Todd Lincoln. They sat in chairs, as if watching a play from the very state box Joseph and Alex sat in. From behind the two actors, a third actor crept onto the stage. He played the role of John Surratt.

"I'll get you, Lincoln," the actor said in an overdramatic voice.

Alex rolled her eyes as she watched the performance. She released a disappointed sigh, and got up to leave.

"Where are you going?" Joseph asked.

"This isn't how it's supposed to go," Alex said.

"I know, but I changed it for you."

"I know you did, and it was a good attempt. But I can't stay here with you if this is how it's going to play out."

She made a move to get up from her seat once again. Joseph placed his hand on her wrist, and pleaded with her to stay. Reluctantly, Alex remained in her seat.

The actor on the stage portraying John Surratt snuck up behind the actor playing Lincoln. As he did, he removed a prop pistol from his jacket, and held it to Lincoln's head. The loud pop of a pistol being fired echoed through Ford's Theatre. It hadn't come from the stage, though. Next to Joseph, Alex slumped forward in her seat. Standing behind her was John Wilkes Booth. In his hand was a Derringer .44.

Joseph hugged Alex and lowered her to the floor. Tears streamed from his eyes, and he began to sob. He could feel the blood pouring from the fresh bullet wound in the back of her head. He looked up at John Wilkes Booth, who stood over them.

"Why?" Joseph asked. "Why?"

Booth gave no response, though. He just walked calmly to the edge of the state box, and jumped from the ledge to the stage below.

Joseph turned his attention back to Alex, who was dying in his arms. Her eyes were open, and she was staring up at him. He could see the heartbreak in her eyes as the life quickly left her through the bullet hole in her skull.

"You were supposed to keep me safe, Joseph," she said through a dying whisper. "Why didn't you keep me safe?"

Before Joseph could answer, Alex died.

Joseph shot up in James Becker's bed. As he shook the heaviness of sleep away, the nightmare had already begun to bury itself. However, his grief remained.

What also remained was his desire to save Alex. In the dream, Booth had shot her, and, like it had been when Booth shot Lincoln, the wound was mortal. That was a dream, though. Joseph was now in reality, and Alex was still alive in reality, which meant if Alex was still alive, then Joseph still had time to save her.

He leapt out of bed, and dressed quickly in the dark. He then used the phone James Becker had in his room to call a cab. It was late in the night and the trains to Manhattan were no longer running. He'd have to take a taxi in. He went into a drawer where James Becker kept money in case of an emergency, and took a hundred dollars. Minutes later, the cab pulled up, and Joseph was sitting in it within seconds of its arrival.

As the cab traveled down the Long Island Expressway towards the Midtown Tunnel, Joseph mulled over what he could say to Alex to convince her to leave with him. Years on the street had certainly taught her not to trust anyone, so she would not respond well to a stranger's offer. Still, Joseph knew if he remained persuasive, he could convince her to come with him. Alex had been saved once before by someone in the way that Joseph had always wanted to save her. This was his opportunity to finally be the person who gave her the happiness she spent her life searching for.

He arrived in Manhattan not long before dawn. Joseph had the cab drop him off a few blocks from the building where Alex squatted. He paid the driver, and walked the rest of the way. He needed a few more minutes to get his courage up.

He entered the condemned building he and Alex had stood in front of hours earlier. The air smelled wretchedly of rotting food, unbathed human filth, and God knows what else. There was no electricity in the building, so the hallways and apartments were pitch black. To remedy this, Joseph carried a metal flashlight which he took from the home of James Becker. Not only was it meant to serve as a source of light, but as a weapon against any homeless junkie who might try and come at him.

It had taken some time for him to finally find Alex. He had to search through multiple darkened apartments before finding the one she used to sleep in. She laid belly up upon a dirty mattress which sat on the garbage infested floor. Joseph killed the beam of light coming from his flashlight, and slowly made his way towards Alex, so as not to frighten her.

He knelt beside her, and immediately knew something was not right. The smell of vomit was strong around Alex. He tried to dismiss it and attributed it to the all-around smell from the building, but the feeling of dread coming from within him was too strong.

He called her name softly, and got no response. He did this three more times, and got the exact same result. He told himself that she was in the depths of some alcohol or drug induced slumber, and calling her name wouldn't be enough to wake her from it. He nudged her, and when his fingertips made contact with her skin, he felt dampness. He brought his fingers to his nose, and could smell the strong odor of fresh vomit on them.

Joseph fumbled with the flashlight, and managed to finally switch it on. A beam of light exploded from it, and lit up the body of Alexandra Casings. She lay there on the mattress, completely naked. Her skin was the color of porcelain, and vomit stained her cheek, chin, neck, and splattered down her chest.

From the looks of it, she had been dead for a few hours.

The sight of her lifeless body caused Joseph's legs to give way, and he fell backwards onto his butt. He refused to believe what he saw. It wasn't supposed to be that way.

"You can't be dead," he said. "I'm supposed to save you. You can't be dead!"

Joseph crawled over to Alex's body, and began shaking it. He begged her to wake up, so he could save her and they could finally be together. Alex didn't wake, though. She remained as dead as she had been moments before. Forcing himself to accept defeat, Joseph scooted away from the body of the woman he had known and loved his entire life. He backed into the nearest wall and started to cry.

He heard the footfalls of another person in the hallway. That didn't stop his sobs. He heard the person enter the room, but didn't look up to acknowledge them. He did not lift his head as they walked towards him. Joseph didn't care if it was a homeless drug addict who wanted to rob him, or even kill him. He not only welcomed death, he now wished for it.

"I'm sorry, Joseph," J said. He placed his hand on Joseph's shoulder as a gesture of comfort, but Joseph felt no such comfort. "You had good intentions, but it's not meant to be."

"Why?" Joseph asked. "Why couldn't we just be together?"

"That's not a question for me to answer."

"Why not?"

"Because I do not know the answer."

J placed an arm around Joseph, and Joseph allowed himself to be helped up from the dirty floor. Together they walked towards the bed where Alex lay. Dawn had begun to break through the eastern sky, and the darkness inside the room began to lift. It was more than could be said about the darkness Joseph felt inside his heart as he stared at Alex's lifeless body.

"She didn't deserve this," Joseph said. "This wasn't supposed to be her life."

"You cannot blame yourself for this. You could not have known the consequences."

"Yet it happened because of what I did, and I still do blame myself. I should have considered the consequences of what I was doing. Instead, I was selfish. Alex's life is over before it should be, and I'm still here. I should be the one who is dead...not her."

J attempted to lead Joseph away, but Joseph refused. He just stared at Alex, who was now nothing more than a corpse. If he had the ability, Joseph would trade his life so that she could have hers back. He would go back, and change it all, so that the person he loved his entire life could end up happy.

Then it hit him.

Joseph had the ability to save Alex, after all.

"I want to go back," he said.

"Excuse me?" J asked, as if he had maybe misheard Joseph.

"I want to go back, and change what I did. I want Booth to be the one who kills Lincoln."

"What makes you think that is as simple as it sounds, Joseph?"

"I thought it was strange that I remembered everything that had happened. Everything from my life. Everything that went down after my execution. I remembered it all, even though I have this new body and new life. I shouldn't remember any of it. Yet I do, and it's because the walls are still down."

Joseph knew that if the walls that had separated his lives had gone back up, then he'd have no memory of Joseph Bateman. He'd have no recollection of John Wilkes Booth, other than what was taught to him in high school. He would just be James Becker, and he'd be living James Becker's life. It was all still there, though, which meant the walls were down, and if the walls were down, Joseph knew he could go back. He could change what he had done.

"Lincoln dies, no matter what," Joseph told J. "You said it yourself. There's nothing that can be done to change that. Alex doesn't need to die, though. If I go back and undo everything, then she gets to live. She gets a happy life."

"If Booth is the one to kill Lincoln, then your soul will suffer the consequences. You'll live your miserable life as Joseph Bateman again. What about your redemption?"

"Fuck my redemption!" Joseph shot back. "If this is what redemption is, then I don't want anything to do with it. Not at her expense. I'll live a thousand miserable lives if it meant undoing all this."

"You truly love this woman, Joseph."

"I do," Joseph responded. He stared down at Alex, and remembered her as she had once been. A beautiful woman, who just wanted to shed her flaws, and find some harmony within herself. "You said on the train that she needed me. Well I needed her just as much. I know my life didn't turn out as planned, but she let hold onto an ounce of humanity. The humanity I inherited from my mother. Even in my final moments, it was there. It was because she helped me hold onto it."

"I am proud of you, Joseph," J said. "I knew you'd find the end of your path."

"What do you mean?"

"I think you know," J said, but explained anyways. "This was never about preventing John Wilkes Booth from shooting Abraham Lincoln. Booth was always meant to kill Lincoln, Joseph. Not be framed for it, but actually be the man to pull the trigger. That wasn't your redemption. It was just a stepping stone on your path."

"This is it… This is my redemption…"

James Becker lived a happy life with joyous memories with fun friends and a loving family. He was a smart, good looking man with a bright future ahead of him, and Joseph was choosing to sacrifice it all so that Alex could live. That was the redemption his soul sought.

"I'll give you a minute with her," J said, and left the room.

Joseph walked up to the bed, and knelt beside Alex's body. He spoke from his heart, and said everything on his mind. After all, it would be the only time he would be able to say it to her.

"Hey, Alex," he said. "I'm sorry you had to go through all this. I'm sorry you had to live the life you did. I'm going to fix all that, though. I just wanted to tell you I'm sorry for what I said to you that day you came to visit me. I know you wanted closure, and I refused to give it to you. Well here it is. I want nothing more than for you to be happy. Even if that means never being together. I know now that it is impossible. That's something I need to accept, and I do. It's just hard, because the only thing I have ever wanted in my life was you. I'm grateful for every moment I got with you, whether it was good or bad. You made me a better person, and without you, I don't think I'd be the kind of person who would do what I'm about to do. You made me selfless.

"I hope you can forgive me for the things I said to you last time we talked, and I hope you find your closure. Most importantly, I hope you find your happiness. I love you, Alex. Thank you for getting my shoes out of the tree."

Joseph leaned forward, and kissed Alex's cold forehead. He got back to his feet, and waited for J to reenter the room. When J did, Joseph turned towards him.

"I'm ready," he said, and closed his eyes.

The next thing Joseph Bateman felt was a sharp pain as J drove a knife into his stomach, and twisted the blade. Joseph collapsed to the floor, and lay there in wait as his life slipped away from him. As the darkness closed in on him, he felt the nothingness beneath him crumble, and Joseph fell back to 1865.

And his redemption.

PART III

REWARDS

April 26, 2021

Wedding Day Reflection

He woke at dawn. It was earlier than he had planned, and he needed as much sleep as he could get for the long day ahead, but he knew he wouldn't be falling back asleep. He was too excited for sleep. Today was one of the biggest days of his life, after all.

Today was his wedding day.

He allowed himself a few more minutes to enjoy the comfort of his bed. Then, he swung his legs over the side and got up. He stretched his body and walked over to the window of his bedroom. He threw open the curtains and let fresh sunlight into his room. The sight of the Manhattan skyline was beautiful in the sunrise. The city he had spent his life growing up in had changed drastically, yet it was still the same place he had always known and called home. Soon he'd be leaving it, and even though he was sad about it, he was excited about the new chapters in his life that lay ahead for him and his bride-to-be.

He had met Tina in a Starbucks during his last year of grad school. He had been there all afternoon, working on a grueling semester-long paper. She, too, had arrived to do her own work. He still remembered the first time he looked up from his laptop and saw her standing at the register as she ordered. She was, by no means, dressed to impress. She wore sweatpants and a hoodie with her hair thrown up. He couldn't take his eyes off her, though. She was beautiful.

The young man at the register took the order and told her the amount due. She searched her bag for her wallet, but he could tell she had forgotten it at home or in her car. He wouldn't waste any time and risk someone stepping in to play hero where he had planned to. He got up from his seat, and walked to the register.

"I've got this," he said, reaching for his wallet.

"That's kind, but you don't have to," she argued, looking up from her purse at the kind gentleman offering to pay her bill. "I probably left my wallet in the car. I can go get it."

"I insist," and before she could argue any further, he handed the man at the register the amount owed.

"Well, that's very kind of you. Thank you very much."

"It's no problem." He intended to end the conversation there. However, at the last moment, he decided to take the risk while his small window was still open. "Would you like to join me for a little bit?" he asked.

"Well, I do have a lot of work I need to get done," she said. "But I don't see why I can't put it off for a few more minutes."

Tina took her coffee and he ordered a fresh one. They headed back to the table he had been sitting at and they sat down.

"I'm Tina, by the way," she said.

"Jimmy."

That afternoon, they talked for nearly two hours. At the end of their meeting, he asked if he could take her to dinner one night in the near future. She agreed. He gave up the table so that she could finally get her work done, and left.

That Saturday, they had dinner together. It was the first of many.

As the sun rose in the sky—the only thing that could rise higher than Manhattan's monstrous skyscrapers—Jimmy Bolton reminisced on the two years that followed his first meeting with Tina. They were the happiest two years of his life, and it had been a no-brainer when it was time to consider proposing. They had both secured steady jobs with good pay, had money in the bank, and were about to move in together. Above all else, they loved one another. He had no reason not to marry her. On the first night together in their new apartment, he proposed. She said yes, and eight months later, he stood in the very apartment he had asked her to be his wife, and stared at the morning sky.

He stretched once more to shed the tiredness that clung to his body, and headed to the shower. After his shower, he made himself an early breakfast and poured himself a cup of coffee. Tina had spent the night at her parent's house, and he had a few hours before his friends and brother would be by to pick him up to prepare for the big day. He was going to enjoy the few hours of calm before his day of hectic wedding preparations began. He sat down on the couch with his breakfast and coffee, and streamed the Robert Redford film, *The Conspirator*, a film about the trial of the charged conspirators in the Abraham Lincoln assassination.

Jimmy Bolton was a huge history buff. The focus of his undergraduate degree was history, and he now taught an American History class at a Long Island university twice a week as an adjunct professor. He had always enjoyed any historical flicks, but ones revolving around Abraham Lincoln were his favorites. The Civil War era was his favorite era of America's history to read up on. The topic he chose for his biggest undergraduate paper was Abraham Lincoln's presidency. including the events of and following the sixteenth president's assassination. He always found the topic of Lincoln's assassination compelling for some reason.

He was completely unaware of how that event, along with a few others that had occurred a hundred and thirty years afterwards, was so crucial and instrumental in his own life.

Jimmy had absolutely no memory of Joseph Bateman or John Wilkes Booth, other than what he read in history books. The man who sacrificed himself for the woman he loved twenty-six years earlier was as much a stranger to Jimmy Bolton as anyone he would pass on the street on any given day. The walls had gone back up, and he could not recollect a single event of what had come before his own birth. He would remain unaware of what was done in order to give him the life he had lived, and would continue to live, until his death.

Jimmy received a text message from his brother as the movie was coming to an end to let Jimmy know he would be there soon to pick him up. Jimmy shut off the television as the closing credits began to roll, and got dressed. The wheels of his day were now in motion.

As he waited on his brother, his thoughts transitioned from the past to the future. It was a future he very much looked forward to, one filled with love and happiness—not to mention a home and children. In less than three months, he and Tina would be leaving their Manhattan apartment to move into a Long Island home they were in the process of closing on. After that the plan was to start a family. The process of buying a home and planning a wedding was stressful, but the idea of being a homeowner and a father was a little frightening for Jimmy. Tina would be by his side throughout it all, though, and that made it not so scary. In fact, it seemed perfect.

BOOTH

Jimmy Bolton's past, his present, and his future could all be described by using a single word.

Perfect.

April 27, 2021
Wedding Reception

The couple spoke their vows and said their "I do's." They had their first kiss as husband and wife, and their first dance as a married couple, too. They danced, they ate, they drank, and they cut the cake. They did everything you'd expect to be done at a wedding. Yet this one couldn't be compared to any other, because it was their own. They were now mister and missus Jimmy Bolton, and would be until death did them part.

Midnight came and went and even though the reception was due to wind down, the party was still going strong. There was to be an after party at the hotel bar, and if things kept up the way they were, they wouldn't be returning to their wedding suite until dawn. Jimmy Bolton would likely be up for close to twenty-four hours, but he didn't care.

He was having the time of his life.

The bride and groom sat at the table specially designated for the two of them. As the DJ slowed the mood down a bit with Aerosmith's "Don't Want to Miss A Thing," Tina's father approached his daughter, and ask for an additional dance to the traditional one they had earlier.

She, of course, accepted, and took her father's hand to be led to the dance floor.

"I hope you don't mind me stealing your bride for one more song," Tina's father said.

"Of course, I don't," Jimmy said. "But I hope you don't mind if I ask my new beautiful mother-in-law for a dance."

"Be my guest."

Jimmy made his way across the room, and asked Tina's mother for a dance. She graciously accepted.

"You're a good man, Jimmy," his new mother-in-law informed him as they danced. "My Tina is very happy she found you. Your mother would be so proud to see the man you've grown up to be."

Jimmy's mother died of stomach cancer when he was in his teens. Unfortunately, even happy endings have some tragedy and tears in them.

"Thank you, Missus Hayes. That means a lot."

"Jimmy, dear, how many times must I tell you? You have to stop calling me that!" she jested.

"I'm sorry. I guess it's just out of habit now."

"We're family now. I think you can finally bring yourself to call me Alex."

"I'll try."

As they danced, Jimmy caught Tina's mother looking at his eyes. She studied them intently, as if she was looking at someone she hadn't seen in a long time, and was trying to place.

"Is everything okay, Missus Hayes—I mean Alex?"

"Yeah..." she said as she stared at Jimmy. He could tell she was mentally elsewhere as she answered him. "Your eyes..."

"What about them?"

"They remind me of someone I used to know."

She was too deep within her own thoughts to even notice the tears welling up in her eyes.

"Missus Hayes, you're crying."

She immediately pulled away, and wiped the tears from her eyes. She was clearly embarrassed by her emotions getting to her.

"I'm so sorry, Jimmy. This is your wedding day and your mother-in-law is crying."

"Its fine," he reassured her. "Do you want to talk about it?"

"The person you just briefly reminded me of is from my past. He's sort of a sensitive subject."

Tina had told Jimmy bits and piece from her mother's past. The parts she knew, at least. Tina didn't even know the whole story. Only what her mother shared with her.

Tina didn't know either of her grandparents, because her mother hadn't had contact with either of them since she was young. He knew his mother-in-law had gone through some tough spots in her life before finding Tina's father. Although he knew barely any of the details, he felt bad for Tina's mother whenever he'd hear anything related to her troubled past. Missus Hayes—Alex—was a kind-hearted, funny, and often sarcastic person. She was also an uplifting person, who was eager to help out others and put them before her. Jimmy couldn't imagine her any other way.

"He and I were very close," she continued. "But it ended very poorly. It's something I regret to this day. When he popped in my head just now, it brought back all sorts of memories and emotions. Certainly none that I should be moping over on the dance floor on my daughter's wedding day."

She tried to put on a strong face for her new son-in-law, but Jimmy could tell she was shaken up.

"I'm not going to pry," he said. "But I'm sure whoever this person from your past is, he feels just as bad about not making an amends with you as you do."

"I'm not so sure about that, Jimmy."

"I am. You've been one of the most amazing people I have ever met, Alex. Your husband loves you and your daughter thinks the world of you. You've welcomed me into your family, and you've made me feel like a son. Whatever happened between you and this person, I know, in the end, he forgave you. I'm not just saying it. I know it."

Jimmy Bolton did know it. Somehow, he knew this person, whoever he was and whatever had gone down between him and his mother-in-law so many years ago, had forgiven her. It wasn't just comforting words he was spoke to an upset woman. It was truth. He just hoped she believed it as much as he did.

"Thank you, Jimmy," Alex said. "That was very kind of you to say. I really hope it is true."

Jimmy could tell he had made his mother-in-law feel better for the moment, but there was still doubt in her eyes. He wondered if that doubt would remain with her until her last days.

It would.

It would stay with Alexandra Hayes—once Alexandra Casings—until her final moments of life.

"Darling, are you okay?" Jimmy's father-in-law asked his wife as the song concluded.

"Mom...what's wrong?" Tina asked.

"Oh, it's nothing," Alex told her daughter. "You know your mother, dear. I have a glass or two of wine, and my emotions get the best of me. I just feel terrible that your new husband had to witness it."

"It's no biggie," Jimmy said, going along with Alex's story. "You still hold your alcohol better than your daughter."

"Funny guy," Tina said. "Come on, mom. Let's go to the bathroom and get your makeup fixed up."

Tina and her mother headed to the bathroom, and Jimmy took his seat at the bride and groom table. He was poking his cake with a fork when he felt the presence of someone standing over him. He looked up, and standing in front of him was an elderly man.

At first glance, Jimmy had no idea who this person was. However, like his mother-in-law moments before, when he looked into his eyes, a foreign sense of familiarity washed over him. Jimmy couldn't place the man, though. He had never seen him before in his life.

"Hello, Jimmy," the man said.

"Hey," Jimmy responded, trying not to make it obvious he had no idea who he was talking to. "So glad you could come. Are you a relative on Tina's side?"

"No, Jimmy. You and I have actually met on a handful of occasions. Don't worry, though. I don't expect you to remember. It was over a lifetime ago."

What Jimmy took as exaggeration was actually quite literal. The two had met over a lifetime ago, before Jimmy Bolton was ever born. Jimmy was unaware of this, of course. He also had no idea that he owed more to the man than anyone he would ever meet in his life.

"I just stopped by to tell you that I'm so proud of you," the stranger said. "You've become quite the man."

"Well thank you very much," Jimmy said. "That really means a lot. Would you like to stick around for a bit? The reception is almost over, but I'm sure I can get you a piece of cake or perhaps a drink."

"Oh, that's okay. I really must get going. I just wanted to see you on your wedding day. There are some who aren't fortunate enough to live past the age of twenty-six. Now you're married and have your whole life ahead of you!"

Jimmy again thanked the man for his kind words, and the man once again congratulated him on his wedding. The old man then turned to leave. As Jimmy watched him go, he thought about the old man's eyes. There was something unique about them. He couldn't quite place it, but he had seen something in them.

He'd finally realize what it was he saw in those eyes fifty-four years later when he looked into them one last time.

June 11, 2055
Alex's Closure

Alexandra Hayes lived an extremely healthy life. She always went for her yearly physical, and always left the doctor's office with a clean bill of health. Sadly, bodies will break down no matter how healthy we try to keep them. For Alexandra Hayes, that came in her eighty-sixth year.

She was constantly in and out of hospitals, and back and forth between home and doctors. It wore on her greatly, both mentally and physically, and she became exhausted, which just made it easier for her to get sicker. Finally, on the fourth day of June, when yet another sickness sent Alex to the hospital for yet another visit, she decided enough was enough. She had an infection that the doctors wanted to treat aggressively. Still in sound enough mind to make her own decisions, Alex told her children she didn't want to be treated.

At first, instinctively, her children argued their mother's decision. As she had throughout her life, Alex remained stubborn, and convinced the ones who loved her that it was her life, and ultimately her decision. With their mother's

372

mind made up, Alex's children told her doctors to just make her as comfortable as possible.

Alex was fortunate enough to see her grandchildren and even great grandchildren one last time before her condition took a turn for the worse. She had always joked about loving grandparenthood more than parenthood, because it was all the fun and none of the responsibilities. As a result, Alex became the favorite grandparent amongst all of her grandkids. Her own children along with their spouses stayed by her hospital bedside once her condition took a downward turn. There they remained, and waited until it was over.

The end came for Alexandra Hayes in the early morning hours of June 11th. The nurse had woken her children, who were asleep in the hospital waiting room, and informed them that it was only a matter of time before their mother passed. They filed into Alex's room, stood around her bed, and waited for their mother's suffering to end.

She opened her eyes one last time, and scanned the room. She looked from child to child. When her eyes landed on Jimmy, they stopped and remained there, fixated. The infection should have made her delirious, yet she seemed perfectly fine in that moment as she studied him. Then her dying eyes widened and tears filled them. They streamed down her face and she tried to speak. She managed to get out a whisper, but all that escaped through her thin lips was barely audible. Whatever she was saying, it was obvious she was directing it right at Jimmy.

"What is she saying?" one of her children asked.

Jimmy, who was the closest to the head of the bed, leaned in and tried to hear what his dying mother-in-law was attempting to say.

"Joseph…" he barely heard her say. "Joseph."

Jimmy pulled away, and saw Alex had a peaceful smile on her face as she continued to utter a name that meant absolutely nothing to Jimmy. She was still muttering the name as she slipped into unconsciousness.

Moments later, Alex took her last breath.

"What was she saying?" Tina asked her husband, who was the only one to hear Alex's last word.

"She was saying Joseph," Jimmy answered. "Does that name mean anything to any of you?"

It didn't. None of them knew a Joseph, nor knew if their parents had known a man by that name. In the days that followed her death, they tried to figure out the significance of the name their mother uttered in her final moments. Their father had passed away a few years earlier, so they couldn't ask him for answers regarding this mystery name. No one who came to her service or funeral went by that name. All they could do was agree that it was just the ramblings of a dying woman and let it go. Eventually, the matter was dropped and forgotten.

Jimmy didn't believe that, though. He knew there was meaning to the name. He would never know that in her final moments, Alex looked into the eyes of the man she had always known as Jimmy Bolton, and saw Joseph Bateman. He would never know that in the final moments of her life, Alex found the closure she had been searching for her entire life, because everything had worked out for the man she thought had gone to his grave hating her. He accepted the fact that he'd never know the meaning of the name his mother-in-law spoke on her death bed, but that didn't matter to him. All that matter to him is that she died happy with a smile on her face.

January 12, 2075
The Walls Come Down

Jimmy Bolton had a similar conversation with his wife that her mother had with her own children almost twenty years earlier. He didn't need machines and medicine to keep him alive, because he was ready to die. He sensed the end nearing, and didn't want the ordeal to be drawn out. He sat her down one day and told her that if he got really sick, he didn't want to linger.

Five months after their conversation, Tina honored his request.

Like his mother-in-law, it had been an infection. They had started treatment, but Jimmy's condition took a turn for the worse, and Tina told the doctors to just make her husband as comfortable as they could.

Jimmy didn't want his wife, children, and grandkids all standing around him as he died. There was no need for their last memory of him to be his slow descent into death's embrace. They visited him in the hospital when they could, and Tina spent her days at the hospital by her husband's side. She wanted to spend the nights with him as well, but he refused and insisted she spend them at home in the comfort of the bed they shared for nearly fifty-four years.

On the day before his death, Jimmy had been coherent enough to be aware of his surroundings and enjoy the people who sat by his bedside as the infection made its way through his body. He saw his two sons and daughter that day. A few of his grandchildren, some nearly grown up, had come to visit as well. Tina, his amazing wife, sat by his bedside, and the married couple shared laughs and enjoyed conversation, much like they had all those years ago in a Manhattan Starbucks. He was with his family, and he was happy. That's all anyone could ask for in their final days…to reflect and see nothing but happiness.

Jimmy Bolton woke in the middle of the night alone in a hospital room lit only by moonlight. He had drifted off while he and Tina were watching an old movie together. She had left at some point after he had fallen asleep.

With the exception of monitors and the other machines hooked up to Jimmy, the room was silent. He could hear the branches of the tree near the window brushing against the pane. It was quite peaceful.

He scanned his darkened hospital room and noticed he was in fact not alone. On the windowsill, he saw another person. The man stood, and stepped into moonlit portion of the room. Even with the full moon entering his room, the man's facial features were barely visible.

Except one.

"Hello, J…" he said, recognizing the eyes he had seen only a few times, but could never forget.

J was no longer the old man who had once tattooed Joseph Bateman. That body had died, and was long rotted in the ground. J's soul now inhabited a new body.

"Hello, Joseph," J said.

Jimmy Bolton, who just hours ago wouldn't have known who this stranger was, nor would have known who Joseph Bateman was, knew everything. The walls had come down, and he remembered all of it. He recalled the life

Joseph Bateman had lived, and he knew what Joseph Bateman had done after his execution. He knew his link to John Wilkes Booth, and he remembered the sacrifice Joseph Bateman had made to save the woman he loved. Jimmy knew that it was because of Joseph Bateman and his sacrifice that he wouldn't have had the extraordinarily amazing life he had lived.

"She was happy," he said in a voice he knew was one of a dying man's. "She got to be happy."

"She did," J answered.

"I was happy. I got to be happy."

"You did."

"Thank you."

"You're welcome, Joseph."

"I hope you get your redemption. I hope you get to be happy, too, J."

"So do I... so do I."

"Can you sit with me until the end?"

That's what J did.

The two sat until the man in the bed drifted off to sleep. He would never wake up from that sleep, and his soul would go to wherever it is souls go when they pass on from their long lives. Before his eyes closed for the final time, he looked at the man sitting next to him, a man who had done so much for him, yet he didn't even know his real name. He looked into J's eyes one last time, and finally understood what he saw every time he looked into those eyes. It was the single thing Joseph Bateman had been too blinded to see growing up, but was always there with him, by his side.

Hope.

"In the end, it's not the years in your life that count. It's the life in your years."
-Abraham Lincoln

THE REPLACEMENT

After a violent altercation with an infamous New York City drug lord, Patrick Sullivan believed his career in law enforcement was over. Yet, not even a year after his resignation, he finds himself back on the job. This time, a detective in the homicide unit.

While battling the ghosts of his past, Patrick and his new partner, veteran detective Jonathan Hawkins, find themselves chasing a killer who is constantly one step ahead of them.

As the body count increases and no substantial leads are discovered, tension between the two cops threatens to boil over. They attempt to coexist as they hunt down a sadistic serial killer who does more than just take his victims' lives.

PRAISE FOR
JASON PELLEGRINI & THE REPLACEMENT

PRAISE FOR
JASON PELLEGRINI & THE REPLACEMENT
(CONT.)

"The Replacement is a wild ride! Dark, twisted and slightly disturbing. Just the way I like my stories."

-Lisa – Goodreads.com

"Aesthetically, if I was solely rating this novel on the originality of The Long Island Surgeons gory methods, motives, and principles, more stars need to be added to this rating system."

-Maurizio – Goodreads.com

"Character development and foreshadowing is on par with Stephen King."

-Vin – Goodreads.com

"[The Replacement] is everything a book should be!"
-Etnik – Goodreads.com

"I absolutely LOVED this book!! It was 'un-put-down-able' edge of seat reading!!"

-Bethany – Goodreads.com

"A real page turner with a twist that kept me gripped to the very end."

-Rita – Goodreads.com

"Plot twists, romance, corruption, intrigue, carnage, the workings of interpersonal relationships, empathy. This book had it all!"

-Kim – Goodreads.com

Whether you loved, liked, or hated this novel, please, voice your opinion of it!
Leave a review of BOOTH *on any of the following websites:*

Amazon.com
Barnesandnoble.com
Goodreads.com

Become a fan of, Like, or Follow Jason Pellegrini on these social media platforms:

Facebook
https://www.facebook.com/jasonpellegrinibooks

Twitter
@JPellegrini1983

Instagram
@jasonpellegrinibooks

Goodreads
https://www.goodreads.com/JPellegrini

And remember, word of mouth is still the most powerful form of promotion in the world.
If you liked this novel, let people know and suggest it to your family and friends!

For more information on Jason Pellegrini and his works, visit:
www.jasonpellegrinibooks.com